To Tracey
my rock, my lo

Michael Jaden aka Paul.
xxx

A COLLISION OF WORLDS 2012

An Unparalleled Quest for Power

By Michael Jaden

Bloomington, IN  Milton Keynes, UK

AuthorHouse™
1663 Liberty Drive, Suite 200
Bloomington, IN 47403
www.authorhouse.com
Phone: 1-800-839-8640

AuthorHouse™ *UK Ltd.*
500 Avebury Boulevard
Central Milton Keynes, MK9 2BE
www.authorhouse.co.uk
Phone: 08001974150

This book is a work of fiction. People, events, and situations are the product of the authors imagination. Any resemblance to actual persons, living or dead, or historical events, is purely coincidental.

© 2006 Michael Jaden. All rights reserved.

No part of this book may be reproduced, stored in a retrieval system, or transmitted by any means without the written permission of the author.

First published by AuthorHouse 8/22/2006

ISBN: 1-4259-5515-0 (sc)

Printed in the United States of America
Bloomington, Indiana

This book is printed on acid-free paper.

Dedication

This book is dedicated to all those soldiers lost and living, those brothers in arms who constantly give their lives doing a job they love.

Special Thanks

Special thanks go to my wife Tracey and my children Stephanie and Ross for their support and understanding during my long nights at the computer in writing this book.

CONTENTS

Part 1	The World Today	1
Part 2	Karim Khan	11
Part 3	A Meeting of Minds	18
Part 4	Dragon's Breath	31
Part 5	Lights Out	40
Part 6	Divide and Conquer	57
Part 7	March from the East	65
Part 8	Diego Garcia	71
Part 9	Old Wounds Reopened	88
Part 10	U-Turn	109
Part 11	Escalation	122
Part 12	A Clash of Titans	127
Part 13	The Gateway to Asia	145
Part 14	A Battle Lost	182
Part 15	End of an Era	207
Part 16	War of Wars	222
Part 17	Crossing the Line	238
Part 18	The Forgotten Vikings	258

Part 19	Betrayal and Retribution..........................271
Part 20	Attrition and the Red Swarm...................288
Part 21	New Lines Drawn.................................297
Part 22	The New World and a Struggle for Freedom....302

War is an ugly thing, but not the ugliest of things. The decayed and degraded state of moral and patriotic feeling which thinks that nothing is worth war is much worse. The person who has nothing for which he is willing to fight, nothing which is more important than his own personal safety, is a miserable creature and has no chance of being free unless made and kept so by the exertions of better men than himself.

John Stuart Mill
English economist & philosopher (1806 - 1873)

PART 1.

THE WORLD TODAY
(2002-2012)

TODAY is January 24, 2012 and the war against terror, which began post-9/11 after the attack on the World Trade Centre, continues. Since its occurrence, 9/11 had been the catalyst for change around the world and after the second Iraq War in 2003, the violent and costly insurgent campaign continued until March 2007 before the United States eventually withdrew its forces having suffered 4, 256 troops Killed in Action (KIA) and many tens of thousands more wounded. Iraq's tenuous grasp on democracy was a brief liaison and by mid 2007 it had suffered its very own violent civil war. This resulted in the Shiite dominated security forces taking control of most of the country (less Kurdistan in the North), which finally put an end to militant Sunni ambitions. It was inevitable that atrocities would be committed on both sides but the conflict was swift and bloody, with relatively fewer casualties than most had thought possible. With Iranian backing the Shiite Muslims were able to exert their influence over the Sunni Arabs and become the dominant power but more worrying to the West, they became an ally of Iran.

The withdrawal from Iraq by US troops in March 2007 was most likely predicated by two catastrophic incidents that took place in late October and December 2006, with the first incident now a prominent driving force in the events taking place today, in 2012. This incident refers to the US/Israeli military attack on the Iranian nuclear and chemical warfare/Weapons of Mass Destruction (WMD) facilities, including the nuclear reactor complexes in Esfahan, Bushehr and, the uranium enrichment plant at Natanz. Esfahan, in addition to its nuclear prowess was also one of Iran's major chemical weapons facilities and along with the primary chemical production facility located at Damghan had continued to upgrade and expand its chemical warfare production infrastructure and munitions. Other sites targeted included Parchin and Qazvin. A uranium mill situated 35km north of Ardakan city was also included in the targeting process as this facility was capable of producing an annual output of 50-metric tons of uranium from its annual capacity of 120,000 metric tons of ore. The conflict between Israel and the Lebanon in 2006 had raised tension in the Middle East with accusations against Iran and Syria that they provided Hezbollah with the advanced weaponry that was fired into Israel. It was soon after this crisis that Israel informed America that they were seriously considering bombing the Iranian nuclear program.

The targeting of these facilities by US and Israeli aircraft was deemed clinically successful and succeeded in destroying large quantities of Iran's chemical and biological arsenal including blister, blood agents, choking agents and nerve agents. The bombing achieved an 80 percent destruction of Iran's nuclear and chemical sites but the attacks resulted in more than 6,600 localized fatalities, with many suffering agonizing deaths as clouds of choking agent and blister concoctions wove their deathly trail many miles downwind of the bombed sites before dissipation by the elements. A fact unknown to the West was that the Iranian nuclear programmes were far more advanced than US intelligence analysts had thought possible and a nuclear meltdown on a scale similar to Chernobyl was triggered by the bombing at Esfahan. The radioactive cloud spewed forth from this location for weeks before the site was eventually brought under control. This death cloud, carried by the wind, swept east across Iran and on into Afghanistan and China leaving an estimated 135,000 people suffering agonizing death or lasting contamination effects in its wake. It was a legacy that would continue for generations and even NATO troops… including US, UK, Dutch, Danish, Ukrainian and Italians serving in Afghanistan were affected by the resultant contamination.

In humanitarian terms the attack was a catastrophe. The human cost (primarily to Muslims) resulted in a violent chain reaction throughout the Muslim World, with violent anti-US/Israeli and anti-western demonstrations continuing unabated into 2007. These demonstrations eventually resulted in changes of governments in Egypt, Pakistan and Jordan by August 2007. If Iran's leaders had known that by pushing the West, Israel and the United States would eventually attack them, then they must have coldly calculated what the consequences of such an attack would be. If that was the case, then their plan had worked to perfection as Muslim nations around the world grew ever closer and began to forge stronger political, religious and military ties.

Could anything have been done to prevent such devastation? The Iranians certainly played their part and must have known that the United States and Israel would never allow them to attain a nuclear capability. They would have anticipated the response and foreseen that the bombing was inevitable, especially after the statement from the Iranian Prime Minister in 2005 when he stated that Israel should be wiped from the face of the earth. They more than anyone would have known the devastation that would occur knowing the current working capability of their own facilities. If they did understand the consequences, then they must have been prepared to sacrifice thousands of their own people in order to feed the Islamic hatred of the US and Israel. Their ultimate aim would have been to create a united Islamic nation….a nation that they hoped would rise and become one….a nation that could challenge the Great Satan? If Iran did know the possible scenarios and consequences, then almost certainly, China did too.

The bombing was, as predicted, strongly defended and justified by the US and Israel with both considering it inevitable, especially after Tehran had made promises to the European Union countries of Britain, France and Germany in November 2004 to freeze its uranium enrichment processes, but then in 2005, reversed this decision by stating it was going to continue to process and produce enriched uranium. This they did before they eventually succeeded in producing it in 2006 at the Natanz facility. Even under the threat of potential UN trade sanctions, Iran, with Chinese and Russian backing had decided to renege on those promises. This resulted in Iran's nuclear chief authorising the construction of a facility to produce anhydrous hydrogen fluoride. Anhydrous hydrogen fluoride is a gas that can be used to produce highly enriched uranium with highly enriched uranium being the precursor to attaining a nuclear capability. The reality was that this and other techniques were already taking place in Iran and production in other plants meant Iran's programme was far in advance of the statements emanating from Teheran. The US and Israel, therefore, felt impelled to act as they believed the UN and Europe had taken the appeasement route for far too long.

The attack on Iran's Nuclear Facilities centered mainly on the Esfahan Nuclear Technology Center (ENTC) and the Bushehr reactor, with these considered the most technologically advanced facilities. As early as 1990, China and Iran had signed a cooperation agreement to build a 27-megawatt plutonium reactor at Esfahan and this was secretly completed in early 2004 along with a Chinese-supplied heavy-water zero-power research reactor. The building of this and the uranium hexafluoride (UF6) conversion plant, (also with Chinese assistance) continued, even after China claimed to have abandoned the project under US pressure.

In early 2000 a senior Iranian official commented that Iran was pursuing a complete fuel cycle. It was this statement that initially caused concern as a complete fuel cycle allows for the development of the two main nuclear explosive materials - separated plutonium and highly enriched uranium. Although Iran is, or was, a signatory to the Nuclear Non-Proliferation Treaty it had failed to ratify two additional protocols. These were the International Atomic Energy Agency's Programs 93 + 2, which were designed to prevent states from developing nuclear weapons covertly. China's ambassador to Iran admitted in September 1995 that China was selling uranium enrichment technology to Iran and in early 1996 China informed the International Atomic Energy Agency (IAEA) of the proposed sale of a uranium conversion facility to Iran. In October 1997 The United States and China reached agreement stating that China would halt further assistance to Iran's nuclear efforts but China only agreed to this in order to placate the West and the agreement was broken before the ink was dry.

The second catastrophic incident on the political Richter scale in 2006 occurred on the 27th December, 2 months after the bombing of Iran, when the US made the unprecedented and much-maligned unilateral decision to take military action against the Turkish army, a NATO ally, in the North of Iraq (Kurdistan). Maybe it had something to do with the removal of US personnel and the closure of the large American airbase at Incirlik Turkey after the bombing of Iran 2 months previous, or maybe, it stemmed from a belief that many in the US administration thought Turkey was only using NATO for its own agenda, having failed to back the US over Iraq in 2003 and again against Iran in 2006. Only days after the Iranian bombing, the US base in Incirlik Turkey was attacked by thousands of enraged Turkish youths with 26 US personnel killed before the Turkish army restored order using 25,000 mechanised troops. What followed at Incirlik was a standoff that lasted for 14-days before the US military forces were requested to depart Turkish soil due to massive civil unrest in the country using only their large transport aircraft. The US was asked to leave its 125 F16 fighter jets at the base and, believing its departure was a short-term measure did so, but, after the Americans departed Turkey informed them that they were holding the fighters indefinitely and that they could not see US troops being invited back onto Turkish soil for some time.

The bombing of Turkish forces in December came about after the Turkish government started massing 150,000 troops in mid November 2006 on its southern border. By December 18th they launched their offensive into Northern Iraq in order to prevent the formation of a Kurdish state. The United Nations, already reeling from the backlash of the reactor bombing in Iran once again provided weak leadership and failed to respond with any authority to the crisis leaving the American government to act alone. 9-days after the invasion, American warplanes began their campaign against the Turkish army and after 6-days of intense bombing; more than 1,600 Turkish troops lay dead or badly injured with scores of tanks, combat aircraft and artillery pieces destroyed. Although Turkey shot down 4 American jets in the 6-days of combat, it knew it could not win a war with America if it escalated. The Americans' decision in resorting to the use of massed airpower, baffled and angered many in Europe and NATO and, almost destroyed NATO as an organisation. On the morning of 3rd January 2007, the Turkish army withdrew from Kurdistan with its politicians losing face. Just over one month later, in February 2007, amid angry scenes at the NATO HQ in Brussels, Turkey withdrew its support from NATO, relinquished its membership, accused the Americans of a unilateral act of war, severed all military ties with the West, closed all NATO bases and expelled all non-Turkish troops from its lands. Turkey, with 650.000 troops, was the second largest contributor to NATO behind the United States; Turkey, angry and shamed, would look to bide its time and one day, would have its revenge…

NATO was in disarray, unsure of its direction and starting to fragment, with the US risking becoming isolated on the world stage. Its European partners/allies were beginning to question the motives and ambitions of the US administration and what it was attempting to achieve. In America there were some who questioned why the United States was contributing billions of dollars annually to NATO when its so-called European allies continually criticised its policies and actions. Events appeared to be spiraling out of control and running away from the politicians and the world was feeling somewhat uneasy but as one giant staggered and floundered, others circled, waiting for it to fall, choosing their moment when they could attack the carcass and pick it clean.

While all this was occurring, the United Nations, who many considered impotent, had to contend with population explosions in places such as Indonesia and Pakistan, while acknowledging that a lack of drinking water worldwide was leading to increased tension between nations with access to large water supplies and those without. How long before water became more precious than oil and when would the first war be fought over what many thought was a plentiful resource. The world's population was growing at a staggering rate and Indonesian was one such country who seriously considered expanding its borders. It had always looked with envy towards the north of Australia and long considered this as an alternative state and one capable of accommodating its ever-expanding population with Darwin as its capital. Darwin, a city of northern Australia with a population in the region of 50,000, is a key port in its own right and occupies a strategic location. An inlet of the Timor Sea Darwin is known as the *'Gateway to Asia,'*

The Chinese saw themselves as the only Tiger on the mountain in Asia and were determined to keep it that way. They had been working towards curbing Indian and Japanese expansion for years; in fact, it was almost a Chinese obsession. To that end, China had ensured its allies, such as, Pakistan, Burma, Iran, North Korea and more recently, Indonesia, had the military capability to ensure any offensive action by them would be effective and sustainable for a protracted period of time. China had secretly supported military action by Indonesia for years but until the events of October 2006 had never discussed it. By 2011, the plans to invade and take a portion of the Australian continent were at an advanced stage, with overwhelming manpower, massive amphibious and naval air power plus huge logistical elements in place to support such an action.

As 2011 ended and 2012 began, the United Nations was busy focusing on a different area of the world…..The Kashmir. This flashpoint region, and the worsening relationship between Pakistan and India, had simmered for the last 3-years and escalated into conflict periodically. The worst incident occurring in late 2009 when Pakistan launched a limited military action in the mountainous area in pursuit of Indian separatists who it claimed were intent on forcing the Pakistani people from the area. This resulted in India deploying its military forces, which resulted in combined casualty figures of 800 Pakistani and Indian troops killed during the 3-week escalation.

China's support to Pakistan was well documented with the US administration in the 1990s acutely aware of China's nuclear proliferation policy to Pakistan, Iran and North Korea. They had decided against imposing sanctions against China at the time because the vast Chinese market was then just becoming available to US interests. There were many critics in the US concerned over missile proliferation and, with Beijing selling missiles to Islamabad; it was increasingly evident that the US Administration was looking the other way. The former chief of the CIA's weapons counter-proliferation efforts in 1992 even commented that intelligence agencies were 'virtually certain' that such a sale had occurred. He went as far, as informing the Senate Foreign Relations Committee, that the US Administration deliberately played down evidence that Beijing sold 34 nuclear-capable M-11 missiles to Pakistan in November 1992 in their determination not to impose economic sanctions on China.

Other accusations at the time centered around the administration doctoring federal regulations in order to prevent sanctions against China for selling missiles to Pakistan and Iran. In the terms laid out in the Missile Technology Control Regime it states that almost all high-tech trade with China should have been automatically cut off by the then President but, the administration refused to accept the unanimous conclusions by the intelligence agencies that M-11 missiles were being sold to Islamabad. The decision to ignore and disregard such damming accusations was not surprising considering the billions of dollars that were at stake and, in the end it all came down to economics and expanding markets. The American government's desire to break into the Chinese market and its lack of action in curtailing Chinese proliferation and expansion was based solely on financial gain. The American way of doing business was a success story in its own right but, the decision not to reign China in would come back to haunt them in a way they could scarcely imagine.

After the bombing of the Iranian nuclear/chemical facilities and its devastating after effects, the years from 2006 to early 2008 saw fundamental political shifts in countries such as Pakistan, Indonesia, Egypt, Jordan, Saudi Arabia and some other Muslim states. These newly installed governments and those rulers who had remained in power such as the Saudi Royal Family started to express a more radical view and, became intent on formulating policies with an anti-western stance. In some ways it was inevitable after what had occurred with millions of Muslims worldwide demanding action.

Something not anticipated, was the huge anti-US reaction from those countries that America called its friends in the Middle East. Even in the less volatile countries such as Qatar, Jordan and Dubai US embassies were attacked by rampaging mobs in the same way that others were worldwide. Many were set alight and in some instances, both attackers and US Marines were killed. In Europe, US Embassies were attacked by mobs of rampaging Muslims and left wing elements, and whole US expatriate communities were unable to work abroad for fear of being attacked or killed and were eventually forced to repatriate while embassies and consulates closed, resulting in US diplomatic isolation.

European countries such as France, Germany, Belgium, Luxemburg and Spain severely criticized the USA and, along with Muslim nations, called for US troop withdrawals from the Middle East. The subsequent closure of all US bases in Qatar, Saudi Arabia, Indonesia, Egypt, Oman and Jordan and the removal of thousands of US troops from the Middle East and parts of Asia occurred under protest from the US administration and removal from these strategic bases hit the US particularly hard. In Saudi Arabia, Saudi troops surrounded the bases, in the same way that Turkish troops had done, until all US troops had departed. Although this was explained to the world by the US government as a security measure, it was evident that the US forces were indeed surrounded and, deemed unwelcome guests. It was clear to all that they were being forced to depart under embarrassing circumstances and, one year after the bombing of Iran's nuclear facilities, the United States had not a single soldier or airman stationed in the Middle East.

With a spreading hatred of the US worldwide; primarily in Muslim countries but also in some European ones, China's long awaited opportunity to plant and cultivate the seeds of revenge was now at hand. China's spin to the Muslims was for them to see that NATO and the West's power base were crumbling, in addition to becoming politically and militarily fragmented. Events had fallen into place for China and this now gave it the motivation and incentive to push ahead with its master plan to cripple the US as a world superpower, allowing China to become the dominating economic and military power in the Asian basin with access to unlimited natural resources, and oil, in Africa and the Middle East. Finally, their dream of watching two of the most powerful ideologies in the world - Democracy and Islam- destroy each other was about to become a reality.

China's quest for world economic domination coupled with aspirations to be the next world superpower was strategically aligned to seeing India's prominence in the economical and military arena destroyed. In late 2006 China and Indian had already crossed swords and flexed their respective naval muscles with both suffering small fatalities in limited naval skirmishes over fishing rights in the Straits of Malacca near the Islands of Andaman and Nicobar. The fallout from Chinese fishermen encroaching into the Indian Exclusive Economic Zone (EEZ) had simmered ever since with both blaming each other but this was not the first time these two giants had clashed. Simmering animosity still remained as a result of the Sino/Indian war in the Himalayas in October 1962, which left China in control of large tracts of land and thousands of Indian troops dead.

The events of 9/11 up to the present day had inevitably propelled the world towards a war mentality. The continuing war on terror - the devastating events in Iran and the bombing of the Turkish army - had allowed China to cultivate the hatred and manipulate aggrieved Muslim nations and their more radical elements. It began with Chinese intelligence agencies sounding out and forming alliances and allegiances with the most aggrieved nations or those willing to pick up the sword against the West. Once these surrogate forces were on board implementation of a massive clandestine rearmament could take place. Only the highest officials were approached and from these secret meetings plans were hatched in readiness for the day that would surpass all others.

So, from 2008, agreement was reached in providing secret military support and rearming to those nations willing to commit all. When it eventually arrives, the first strike of what the Chinese called Operation Dragon's Claw will shatter the foundations of the democratic world decisively and completely and, it would be unlike anything ever witnessed before.

It is now 2012 and two very different worlds, East and West, are about to collide……the impact caused by such an irreversible collision was going to be difficult to ascertain…..but its effects were probably immeasurable and almost definitely irrevocable. What was certain, was that the world was about to change forever.

PART 2

KARIM KHAN

DTG: Tuesday-January 24th.... 2012...1230 pm

Location: The United States Capital Washington DC.

Situation: President Hilary Clinton, the first ever lady President, had served in office since November 2008 and was just hours from giving her annual State of the Union Address speech to the Joint Session of Congress with its full quota of 435 members at the Chamber of the US House of Representatives...

Karim Khan, 44-years old and born in the mountainous Kashmir region of Pakistan in 1968 to a shepherd father and devout mother, had gladly accepted the call to Jihad at 16 and joined the ranks of the Afghanistan Mujihadeen in 1984 to fight the Russians. He then fought in the second Chechnya war against the Russian Army between 2000-2002 aged 32 before joining the ranks of Al Qaeda. After the West's invasion of Afghanistan in October 2001, Khan fought against NATO forces between 2003- 2008, proving once again his worth in battle to the leaders of Al Qaeda. From early 2009 to late 2010, he had been responsible for training up and coming Jihad soldiers in the remote mountainous areas of Pakistan. He and his recruits were constantly on the move but at the same time were getting to know the region, its hidden caves and its remote valleys.

He deemed his last 2-years (2010-2012) as blessed, for he had been chosen as one of a select group responsible for protecting an aging Osama Bin Laden in the desolate mountainous regions between Pakistan and Afghanistan. Karim was devout and, like many others was prepared to give his life to see the destruction of what he saw as the Great Satan - the USA/Israeli alliance.

It was hard for him to comprehend the last 9-weeks, some of which had gone painfully slow, but Karim had eventually arrived in Washington DC. Just 24hrs earlier he had been collected from the container, which had been his home for the last few weeks and placed in a hotel by 2 Chinese agents. Once inside the room he recalled the instructions given to him by his Iranian handler in China:

'Karim…. you must not be seen by anyone, therefore you will not leave the hotel for any reason…. you will wait in the room until the designated time to complete your mission…this you must swear Karim'. Karim did so without reservation.

Chinese Intelligence used the hotel, unbeknown to Karim and, the CIA, as a front. It was located between 12th and 9th street, just to the North of the 395 Southwest Freeway and a perfect distance from The White House and The Capitol Building at Capitol Hill. As briefed he had not yet removed the large silver case under the bed but he knew it was there. He was sat staring intently at the duvet trying to imagine what power would be released once the moment arrived. As he stared, his mind wandered back to the day Al Qaeda and Osama arrived on the world stage with the attack on the twin towers. Their Jihad against the US and her Western allies had raged in intensity since 9/11. After the invasions of Afghanistan and Iraq, recruitment for Jihad had swelled their numbers considerably and the suicide bomber had become a tool favored by Al Qaeda and other affiliated Islamic terrorist groups worldwide. Although he felt some contempt for the Shiite Muslim Iranians, he reflected with pride the worldwide Islamic backlash at the US/Israeli bombing of the Iranian nuclear and chemical warfare facilities in 2006, which resulted in thousands of dead and injured and estimates of tens of thousands of fatalities over the following decades. The expulsions of US forces from the Middle East and the closure of all its bases in Turkey, Qatar, Saudi Arabia, Jordan, Egypt, Oman and Indonesia had rekindled the belief that the Great Satan was on the run and at long last the Islamic nations had come together to condemn the action of the US and its puppet Israel.

Khan smiled and shook his head at the ill-conceived unilateral decision by the US to carry out 6-days of bombing on Turkish Forces over their invasion of Kurdistan in Northern Iraq, Turkey's subsequent embarrassing military retreat and how the fallout of NATO v NATO resulted in political condemnations and isolation for the US, followed by a unilateral withdraw from NATO by Turkey. Europe and the rest of the world had questioned the actions taken by the US and rightly so.... and in Karim's eyes this had weakened the Great Satan. What Karim didn't and would never know, was that these historical world events had been the catalyst and opportunity for one country to draw together mainly Muslim nations and Muslim terrorists in order to galvanise them into one powerful force so that they could unleash what they,... **The Chinese,**... had secretly codenamed DRAGON'S BREATH and DRAGON'S CLAW and, which had taken more than 15-years in its planning. Some of those brought together were motivated by an expansion of their own borders, some came looking to finally realise their lifetimes struggle, while others sought only power and revenge. The instigator of it all- China - came seeking a new world order. China had pulled them all together and soon the day of reckoning would finally arrive. In 2hrs time there would be no turning back with the world as we know it, changed forever.

Karim was one of those about to realize his lifetimes struggle and 9-weeks ago he had begun what were to be the last 63-days of his life. That day had begun as most others until Osama had called for him personally at their remote hideaway and, it was here that Karim was asked to be the one to strike the decisive blow in the war. The request had surprised him initially, but after Osama explained what was to occur, Karim felt honoured to be the one chosen for Istish-haad (heroic martyrdom). After the meeting with Osama, things moved quickly for Karim and another of Osama's trusted aides and, a previously unseen Arab, who he believed to be Iranian, took him almost immediately to the Afghanistan/Chinese border. He had not seen or spoken to his relatives, wife or child in the Kashmir Mountains for 2-years, and neither would he before he died, but they supported the path he had chosen and his death would be celebrated once they knew it was he, Karim Khan, who took the head of the Great Satan and sent them to Jahannam (the hell fire).

At the border Karim had briefly met with 2 Chinese men who spoke to the 2 Arabs escorting him. He was then led away to a vehicle with darkened windows and after a 3hr journey halted at what was a small remote dwelling.... somewhere in China and with no other buildings in sight. One of the Arabs; known as Hesam (the Iranian) remained behind and it was this man who instructed Karim over the following week on what he was to do.

'*Karim*, said Hesam, *it is you that have been chosen to fulfill all Jihadists dreams…it is you who will be the inspiration for all and you who will strike the blow that all others wish to make*'.

Karim stared into the distance and remembered Osama's words ….'*Karim*' said Osama, '*it is you that Allah has chosen to deliver fire against the Great Satan. You will be accepted into Jannah (paradise) like no other for what you do this day and you will be remembered to the end of time and I am proud to call you brother*'.

Those words had filled Karim with unspeakable joy and he had cried and thanked Osama and prayed to Allah, thanking him many times for what he was about to do.

In the small Chinese dwelling Karim then spent the next 7-days going through exactly what he was to do once he arrived in the USA. His task was fairly simple but it required him to memorize a 6-digit numeric code and a group of four 5-digit sequenced numbers, which could not be written down. Only he was to know the numbers and only he would be able to place it into the electronic keypad when he eventually met up with the package. He was given a shoe size box with a red flashing keypad on top. As soon as the first 6 numbers were tapped into the keypad it turned green and the box was opened. Inside was a subsequent box, which contained another keypad, but for this to flash green Karim had to type in the four 5-digit numbers in the correct sequence. Once this was done the task was complete and within 10-seconds the second keypad changed back to red. He then had to close the box and do it all over again and again… and again…until he no longer had the written numbers in front of him.

He had gathered from speaking to Hesam, that he was to be taken to America by some covert means and that this was to be conducted by the Chinese, but the exact details were kept from him. Karim did not like or trust the Chinese; they were infidels and non-believers and he was suspicious of Chinese involvement but if Osama had decreed it acceptable then he too would accept the outcome. Osama had used non-believers before to achieve his aims, as was the case in Afghanistan during the Russian occupation; how ironic that those same non-believers were now his sworn enemy. Maybe one day the Chinese would be too…

After a week of placing numbers in the correct sequence over and over again, Karim was driven a further 12hrs into China and then flown by a military helicopter to an unknown location. It was here that he first saw the refrigerated ship container. It appeared to be no different than those seen and used on the large container ships travelling the world but this container was different. It had been covertly adapted so that one person could live in the small space at the far end, unseen by the naked eye and, could only be located if one measured the container inside and out noting the 3-metre discrepancy. It was self-contained with a mattress, sink, a small toilet and a refrigerator. The toilet was a chemical toilet attached above the floor but with no seat. This allowed Karim to squat over the small pipe, which then ran to a sealed oblong box on the floor. The electricity and water supply were provided from an external source, which he could not determine. Two small cupboards were installed with one containing eight changes of clothing and black plastic bags for dirty clothes and rubbish. There were instructions, explaining that washing one-self could only be achieved by use of the small sink but Karim was familiar with a sparse existence from his life in the mountainous regions and the sink would mainly provide the means to bathe before prayer. There was a small exercise bike, a sit-up mat and two 15kg dumb-bells in one corner and a small LCD screen similar to what you see on Arabic airlines indicating the direction of Mecca at all times. The light for the cabin was provided by one small bulb on the roof with a box of spare bulbs provided with a very silent fan and extractor situated in the right hand corner of the room. The switch for the light was next to Karim's mattress and he would be thankful of the detail that Osama or the Chinese had gone to in order to make his stay of 8-weeks in the cramped container as comfortable as possible. Food and water or hot sugared tea (no milk) was provided daily via a small hatch during the journey on the ship. Once the ship docked the final 2-weeks surviving in the container would be maintained solely from the quantity of bottled drinking water, along with the dried and tinned food in the second cupboard. The final 2-weeks would be the most difficult and the harsh living conditions were one reason why Karim was chosen. The smell in the container would be putrid and he certainly needed all his mental strength to settle into what was a 6-week transit by container ship to America, followed by a further 2-weeks in a container depot before it was considered safe enough for him to be recovered and taken to the hotel that he now found himself in. Although sparse and cramped, the small space came complete with a small TV/DVD player with discs showing Islamic Jihad footage and propaganda, plus two final messages from Osama and, of course, the shoe-size box with the flashing red pad and a copy of Al-Kitab (The Qur'an). There were paper, pens and envelopes and instructions that any letters to his family would be taken to them after the act was completed. This was in-fact, a lie, and after Karim left the container, all trace of his being there would be incinerated.

Karim would have plenty of time to consider his actions and its effects over the following 2 months but he knew when the time came, that he would be ready to carry out what he believed to be Allah's will. Osama had chosen well, with the world completely unaware and blind to the approaching storm.

Karim, having reflected, heaved the large rectangular heavy silver suitcase from under the bed and stared at it in wonder. It was clearly a 2-man lift and an obvious reason why it was pre-positioned. He had dreamed of this moment all his life and now he felt calm but elated at the same time that he was the one chosen to commit this great act and then be allowed to stand before Allah ready to be accepted into paradise. His family no longer entered his thoughts, as this was his destiny and he felt at ease with the knowledge that thousands were about to die. What I have been chosen to do (*he thought*) will, as Osama predicted, '*be remembered for all time*' and he stared in awe at what he could only imagine to be God's wrath that was yet to be unleashed on the unsuspecting Great Satan.

In China, Karim was provided with a 6-digit code to memorize and it was this number he now entered into the flashing red-lighted keypad, situated on the top of the case. 334215 were entered onto the 0-9 numbered keypad, followed by enter and the flashing red light on the keypad changed to a continuous green followed by an audible click. The significance of the numbers was not lost on Karim and he smiled at the Chinese black sense of humour in making every 2 digits add up to six. '666... *the sign of the devil*' he murmured.... '*and the devil soon to be destroyed by hell's fire...how fitting*'. Karim's hands now rested on the case....he closed his eyes and clicked the 2 retaining locks at each end and the case popped open. His breathing had increased with excitement and he exhaled loudly as he lifted the top of the case. His eyes lit up as he saw the second keypad and he had the urge to input the sequenced numbers now but he knew he had to follow the instructions he had been given. Another reason Karim was chosen was his discipline to follow orders to the letter. The 2 Chinese agents downstairs were there as a contingency option in-case Karim backed out of the mission and left the hotel after the specified detonation time. He could not be allowed to leave the hotel alive once he had entered. They had no inkling of what he was about to do but, their orders were simple - to kill him if he left the hotel. If they had known what Karim Khan's mission was they would have been anywhere but inside the hotel lobby - in-fact, they would have left Washington altogether. As it was, they were deemed expendable and just another sacrifice in the Great Battle that was soon to begin. Khan, however, had no intention of ever leaving the room and the 2 agents need not have been sacrificed; he would follow his instructions to the letter, input the numbers at the given time and then pray.

Staring at the keypad and thinking about what he was about to do… Karim uttered *'La ilaha illallah' (there is no god except god)*…then he began to rock gently… quietly repeating the same words over and over again *'Allah Ackbar…Allah Ackbar'…Allah Ackbar'* (God is Great, God is Great, God is Great)……

PART 3

A MEETING OF MINDS

DTG: March 18th ....2008.................almost 4-years ago...

Location: Chinese People's Liberation Army Intelligence Agency Building, Beijing...45m below ground.

Situation: The first meeting of foreign intelligence representatives. These were people chosen by their Chinese equivalents to be the instruments behind China's quest for world domination. The day had finally arrived, with General Dèng Shangkun about to reveal all.

At 56 years old, General Dèng Shangkun, was head of operations in one of China's most secret intelligence unit's. Dèng had taken the post after his predecessor, General Chu, died of a heart attack in 1998. Chu and his small team had been tasked to think the unthinkable since 1995, with the ideas eventually codenamed as Dragon's Claw scenarios. After Chu's death, it had fallen on Dèng to put flesh on the bones and take the ideas forward but it wasn't until 1999 that the Chinese State Council finally made the decision to fund the possibilities. The Chinese had waited patiently for many years before the pieces started to fall into place. The call, when it came in 2007 was half expected by Dèng, with the Central Military Commission Chairman confirming that the Chinese State Council, now believed, that the indicators around the world were present and, it was time to channel the hatred into a quest for revenge and power.

 General Shangkun had thought long and hard about how he was going to present his speech to those now in attendance in the large, well-lit, ornate briefing room. World events over the last few years had allowed this meeting to occur and, the next 2-days would be crucial in convincing those present that Dragon's Claw could prevail. The General was confident this would be the case.

 It would take almost 4-years from now to ensure all was in place and those present had already agreed that any doubters and pro-western politicians in their countries would be silenced in whatever way they deemed necessary. It had taken Dèng more than 6 months to gather the audience now sat in front of him as he had to be sure that those countries chosen, had the will and the nerve to see this through. The change of governments and anti-western stance in some Arab countries after the bombing of Iran in 2006 had made the job so much easier and, the ill-advised attack on Turkish Muslim troops in the same year had convinced all those present that maybe the US is anti-Muslim. Armed with this knowledge and, the Muslim perception of the West, Dèng knew, that all those present would be receptive to what he was about to reveal.

It was vital that those with intimate knowledge of Dragon's Claw were few in number with operational secrecy imperative and, it was no coincidence that the only ones present were the remainder of Dèng's planning team, the Central Military Commission Chairman, Chairman Zhou who was the only link to the Chinese State Council and Head of State, plus, 2 intelligence representatives from each country as agreed, with only China having full knowledge of the whole plan.

Part of Dragon's Claw hidden objective centered on betrayal, with China hoping to manipulate the more radical Muslim nations into losing almost their entire military prowess. Turkey of course, who at the moment was considered neutral would retain its army, along with Indonesia, who would remain as the Pacific gateway watch-keeper. Syria and Egypt would be tasked with leaving a small standing army of 100,000 each behind, along with a substantial missile force to counter any activity by Israel.

Once the main brief was completed, separate detailed meetings with each individual nation's intelligence representatives took place. The secret sessions ensured each country had their own detailed tasks without the others knowing and this maintained an element of operational security and confidentiality. These private meetings detailed lists of key requests, any actions a country needed to take and, offers of support and planning. In returning to their own country, these plans would then be presented by their representatives to a select few in their own governments and, once this was complete, the programme of re-equipping and re-arming, the provision of resources, extensive training and detailed real time intelligence would be forthcoming; to ensure that in 4-years time all would be ready. The following countries were present:

Iran
Pakistan
North Korea
Indonesia
Egypt
Saudi Arabia
Syria

As the lights dimmed and the presentation began; Dèng leaned forward, rested his hands on the lectern and scanned the large rectangular table at which his guests were seated... he then began to speak.

'Gentlemen...friends..... Allies...welcome to Beijing. What I am about to divulge will forever change the world that we know. Today is the first day of the long march. A march that may last for years but it will be a march that will ultimately take us to victory. It will require great sacrifice, courage, secrecy and subterfuge to ensure our enemies... the United States and her allies do not know of our intentions...

Dèng continued... 'On May 7th 1999 the United States deliberately targeted and bombed the Chinese Embassy in Belgrade; this was the first attack against the Chinese people. In October 2006, along with Israeli help, they committed an act of state terrorism against our friend and ally Iran, an act that has left many thousands dead and many more dying, not just in Iran but also in Afghanistan and China. Although indirect we consider this a second attack against the Chinese nation and its people. This we cannot ignore and neither can any of you present. It is time for change...it is time to strike back and it is time for the United States of America to be forced back to the continent from whence it came. My friends... our time has finally arrived... together we have the resources and the motivation to ensure that the destruction or neutralization of the Western World takes place. We are committed as you are in this goal and the full resources of China will be brought to bear to make this so'.

'To achieve this victory...Operation Dragon's Claw has been conceived... Dragon's Claw, gentlemen, is the assault on the Western World... it is an assault that will destroy all in its path'

The next 3hrs were a series of general presentations and discussions on how this was to be achieved; with the remainder of the next 2-days a series of secret individual sessions as each country received detailed instructions from China of its role and anticipated support over the next 4-years. Questions were obviously raised about the West's airpower and its decisive war winning capability but this was smoothed over by China, who explained that all would be revealed in due course and this threat would be nullified come the glorious day.

Iran, in addition to a massive rearming programme, received specific instructions to train and equip 10 Mujihadeen Brigades (a total of 30,000 shock troops) trained in bomb making, sabotage, urban and rural guerrilla warfare and infantry tactics.

'We also request that you prepare two hundred 30-man suicide teams (6,000 men) *trained in terrorist and assault techniques designed to inflict maximum damage and disruption to Western Countries once the detailed targeting list has been finalized and briefed nearer the time'* said Dèng.

One final request was for them to use their Mujihadeen sources in order to contact Osama Bin Laden, so that Chinese Intelligence could make him an offer he could not refuse.

Syria was instructed to offer olives braches to the West on one hand as a diversion, while being massively rearmed by China and Russia via Iran on the other. It was to increase its combat troop and logistical capacity by more than double within 4-years. It would also receive advanced ballistic missile technology and technicians from China within the first year in order to improve its missiles range and targeting capability. Syria was also requested to leave a standing army of 100,000 in Syria to deter any action by Israel once the war began with support from China if required.

Saudi Arabia was also encouraged to soften its tone to the West especially after its expulsion of US troops. It was encouraged to use its old contacts in the United Kingdom so that it could once again buy hugely from the West, in particular the new Typhoon Euro Fighter, Challenger 2 Main Battle Tank and the German Leopard 2 A6 MBT. Saudi Arabia was requested to open dialogue with the US in an attempt to gain the trust of the American administration once again before asking for spare parts and ammunition for their fleet of 315 M1A1 Abrams Tanks. China stated that this was a nice to have and not a necessity and enjoyed the irony of it more than anything.

Dèng, addressing the Saudi Arabian contingent, said *'The West will not be able to resist the chance to right the wrong done by the United States in this region and will gladly oblige you in diplomatic and military hardware transactions. After all, making money and securing their own people's jobs is how capitalism survives, does it not?'*

Saudi Arabia was also instructed to significantly increase its combat and support manpower, in addition to providing sufficient funding for the training of 1,000 six-man suicide squads (6,000 men) in Bosnia, similar to the funding it provided to Arab Mujihadeen during the Balkans campaign in the 1990s. The camps were to be small and accommodate no more than 40-trainees at any one time. No details of their intentions were to be released or presented at this stage other than to say it was part of the ongoing Jihad. Explosive training, sabotage and assault tactics were, according to the Chinese, seen as crucial to their training.

Egypt, with a more radical government now in administration and with one of the largest armies in the Middle East, was asked to instigate low level relations with Israel (even after the Iranian bombing) while increasing its military capability. By using its special connections with the United Kingdom it was instructed to secure British military equipment and weaponry (secretly funded by the Chinese) for a specialized unit containing 60,000 men. The unit would consist of Corp level strength and contain 4 Divisions, each 15,000-strong, with enough organic support for the unit to be capable of independent operations. They were to look specifically at a heavy armoured Division with Challenger 2 MBT, an Infantry Fighting Division with Warrior Fighting Vehicles, a transportable Artillery Division with a Multi Launch Rocket System (MLRS) capability and AS90 Self- Propelled 155mm Guns, plus a substantial Logistical Division with a number of direct-reporting Battalions for various support tasks such as reconnaissance, communications and combat engineers. Having brought Soviet and used American equipment in the past, they were to inform Britain that they were looking at moving away from the remainder of its Soviet type weaponry and had decided to conduct a full army-wide refit over 25-years and this was the first buy. If this integration proved successful, they would continue with the next phase of the refit after 4-years. The financial incentive of billions of pounds to the UK would be too great to pass-over. The deal was to include training for senior officers on strategic and tactical command of an Armoured Division in the second and third years and, for trainers and operators at all levels to be trained at the tactical level. No high ranking Egyptian military commanders were to be made aware of what the real reason for the equipment was before June 2011- only 7 months before Dragon's Claw was to begin. With Egypt also possessing 777 M1A1 Abrams Tanks, it was suggested that by using its UK contacts, a deal with the Americans could be implemented in the same way as that proposed to the Saudis. It would be seen as the first move to re-establishing contacts and relationships in the Middle East.

The softening of attitudes by some Islamic countries was a Chinese policy designed to lull the West into believing that time would heal the wounds of the last few years. They would be falling over themselves and be eager to comply in order to rekindle lucrative Arab and Western contacts post Iran. They would not be able to resist the potential revenue that would be generated from military arms sales and, more importantly, the strategic bases that were lost may once again be open to discussion and occupied by Western forces in the Middle East. Clearly, that would never happen, as it suited China's plan perfectly now that there were no foreign troops, US embassies or large numbers of expatriates on Middle Eastern soil and, it allowed for covert rearmament and training to take place in greater secrecy.

North Korea was instructed to remain patient more than most and advised against test firing any more Taepondong-2 ballistic missiles towards Japan. The firings in 2006 had raised the tension in the region considerably and eventually resulted in UN sanctions being imposed in July 2006 on technology capable of producing weapons of mass destruction. The North Koreans had privately dismissed the sanctions at the time as irrelevant, especially as China and Russia provided all the weaponry North Korea required. Dèng was adamant that the North Koreans had to maintain a low profile by refraining from antagonizing South Korea or Japan and, for the tension to decrease in the region. This they agreed to before Dèng explained that they would be given the attack date nearer the time and, only then, would they be allowed to implement what they had been planning since the first Korean War reached stalemate in the 1950s – total all out war against the South.

'*America will be weak at this point* said Dèng…*and 35,000 US troops will be unable to fight a sustained war in the Korean Peninsula. The 4-kilometre wide Demilitarized Zone and then South Korea will crumble before you and its wealth and technology will be yours'*

In the meantime, a huge modernisation of North Korea's military would take place and, closer to the start of Dragon's Claw, a Chinese reserve of 200,000 troops, including Armoured Divisions, Mechanised Infantry and supporting infrastructure, would be made available and committed if they were needed to ensure victory. They were to continue positive overtones to South Korea and look to gain as many subsidies and concessions as possible. The more South Korea was off guard in 2012, the better.

At the meeting with the North Korean contingent Dèng made a strange request- '*Comrades…we are aware of your recent purchase of 6 Kilo-class Attack Submarines from Russia and the further 6 you have on order by 2009. You are requested to send all 12 of these… fully armed to China along with their crews in January 2011 for specialized training with the Chinese Navy. Your submarine contribution must also come attached with 120 suicide commandos.. After they arrive in China you will not hear of them again until their task is complete…they need to bring only their personal weapons. All other equipment will be supplied and the submarines and their crews returned to you after Dragon's Claw begins '*

'*And the Commandos?'* said the Korean officer in charge

'*I am afraid their fate will be sealed once ashore….'* Replied Dèng

'*I understand'* said the Korean intelligence representative…. '*And what of Japan?'*

'*You must have patience, my friend,* interjected Dèng, *Japan and Taiwan will be dealt with at a time of our choosing and only after Korea has been liberated'*

Indonesia was presented with a 4-phased operation - The simultaneous invasion of East Timor and the Australian continent, capture of the city of Darwin, annexation of East Timor, and finally, dominion over the Sultanate of Brunei and all its oil-producing facilities. The final prize would only be sanctioned after the first 3-objectives had been completed. Funded by China, via Arab money, Indonesian was requested to immediately begin expanding its army. It was also instructed to increase its maritime capability using a newly signed, but fictitious defence agreement with China, in protecting fishing and oil transit routes from what China saw as Indian and Japanese naval expansion. This would clearly be unacceptable to Australia, so China would volunteer to act as an intermediate between Indonesia and Australia in order to smooth the concerns of the Australians, stressing that it posed no threat to their sovereign territory and, it was only in the interests of coastal security and national interests, claiming the expansion was required because of the size of the Chinese and Indonesian coastline. Nearer the planned invasion date it would be broadcast that large combined naval exercises between China and Indonesia would be taking place over a 3-week period, but this would be just a cover for what was to be an invasion fleet descending on East Timor. However, the invasion force heading for Australian would move into position somewhat differently to the East Timor fleet with the detail briefed later.

Dèng explained that the plan would be to vastly overwhelm those forces on East Timor and near Darwin, with the airfields on East Timor eventually utilised for operations on to the Australian mainland. Indigenous Chinese and Russian bought Aircraft Carriers would provide their own organic air cover until protected air heads could be established. China and Indonesia's amphibious capability would be able to transport tens of thousands of soldiers, hundreds of Medium Battle Tanks (MBTs), Armoured Personnel Carriers (APCs), various pieces of artillery, huge numbers of all terrain combat vehicles, massive amounts of munitions and huge amounts of logistical supplies to complement the invasion force.

Reinforcements on East Timor would arrive soon after the first troops had taken their objectives and, within days of landing in Australia, massive combat reinforcements would begin to arrive in order to bolster the invasion force. A second wave of smaller merchant ships would also arrive in Darwin to further supplement the logistical build-up, in order to sustain an army of 158,000 men for a further 8 months.

'You are not there to conquer the whole of Australia'- said Dèng, *'you are only there to take the strategic capital Darwin and part of the Northern Territory region as agreed'. 'The Australians are a proud people and their military will respond with force and aggression to such an invasion of their*

land… but in the end…they will be defeated. As soon as they see the West is leaderless, fractured and eventually defeated…. they will have no choice other than to succumb to the annexing of part of their land…If they do not accept the outcome and we have to destroy every last presence of the entire Australian military, then so be it'.

Pakistan was last to be briefed, but for China, it was the most important one on the list. China had spent years working the Dragon's Claw scenarios and identifying the opportunistic triggers and, it was this planning that had made today possible. China's main aim was to see India castrated militarily, nullified economically and removed entirely from the mantle as a potential superpower. Pakistan was the key to this objective and must be convinced to be a willing surrogate in the demise and eventual destruction of India. China had to ensure that Pakistan was confident of China's intervention and participation. The down side for Pakistan was that Pakistan's armed forces would be, it was hoped, destroyed as a military threat in the region. China obviously had no intention of informing Pakistan that military intervention would only occur once it appeared that Pakistan was about to be defeated and, it was a betrayal that had to be kept from the Pakistani government and its people. Dragon's Claw planning called for the tension between the 2-countries to be ratcheted up nearer the date to make the invasion of India, by Pakistan, appear more feasible. In the meantime, China would continue to secretly export missile technology to Pakistan knowing that such a move would reach and infuriate the Indian government further.

Pakistan was to be encouraged to instigate a military incursion into the Kashmir in 2009, a tactic designed to inflame the situation between the 2-countries. This would allow China the opportunity to step in as a mediator initially and, appear to the world to be a peacemaker in the region. It would be short lived, however, as China, once again, looked to cultivate a climate of distrust between the 2-nations, resulting in a further increase in tension in 2010. By the time 2012 arrived, Pakistan would be given the go ahead to reignite the Kashmir problem as a precursor to war. There was room for only one Asian superpower and China had aspired to this title long before India burst onto the economic and military stage.

With war looming between the 2-countries, China planned to up the ante with India over its contested oil trade routes and fishing grounds so that the world would see the tension between these 2-countries increasing. Before the invasion by Pakistan, it was crucial to convince Pakistan that Chinese involvement would coincide almost simultaneously with their attack, give or take a week, but this was not to be the case. The Pakistani military would be informed when to launch the massive offensive and as expected, they would face a much larger and ultimately more powerful military force. Chinese planners believed that neither Pakistan nor India would dare use the nuclear option with both waiting for the other to use it first but, if they did go nuclear, China would allow it to happen.

China was working on a delay of up to 3 months before the full force of the Peoples Liberation Army (PLA) poured into India from the Kashmir and Burma, with China claiming to the world that it was helping another ally in distress. Once the war began there would be no going back for Pakistan and they would eventually be fighting for their very existence. China would make the right noises to Pakistan about why they could not attack as planned before judging the precise moment when to strike. China would then appear as saviours to the Pakistan military and, if necessary, be in a position to conduct military operations in India for 12-months or more. China was content that it could concentrate primarily on the destruction of its main Asian rival because it was not overstretched on other Dragon's Claw missions. Facilitating the Indonesian invasion of Australia with amphibious and air assets plus 2 Divisions of Assault Marines was one commitment, while the other was providing a reserve force of some 200,000 Armoured and Mechanised Infantry for the Korean Peninsula. The end state for China was to destroy the Indian military machine and its civil industries with the intention of pushing its economy back 50-years.

The Chinese mainland, with its economic infrastructure, would remain untouched and, although its manufacturing industries would initially suffer, the business community would soon find alternative markets to improve China's economic integrity. Europe, it was assessed, would be partially destroyed from its war with the Arabs, with the destruction comparable to World War 2 wherever the armies clashed. Chinese planners had assessed that The United States, leaderless and potentially isolated, would be unwilling to conduct large-scale military operations in Europe, Korea, or the Pacific at the same time. Any countries previously aligned with the United States and abandoned would have to abide by the new world order or face the consequences- Communism was going to fill the void left by Democracy and Islam and be the one remaining and lasting powerful ideology. To fight this war, China had assessed that the United States would at least have to quadruple its military machine in order to combat the forces unleashed. China's assessment was that they could not achieve this and, more importantly, they would not have the will or the backing of the American people to conduct simultaneous warfare on European, Korean and/or Australian soil at the same time. NATO had never fully recovered from the withdrawal of Turkey, the years of political infighting and, the behind closed-door accusations that the United States was somehow to blame. This had led many in the States to question their nation's commitment to an organization that seemed to be intolerant of American policies. China believed that the United States past record in liberating or aiding continents such as Europe and countries like Korea was over and, although still hugely powerful militarily, technologically and economically, the American people would never allow it to happen. The memory of the price paid for Operation Enduring Freedom in Iraq was still relatively fresh and China believed that the American people would demand that they pull back from conflict, put up the shutters and man the guard towers in fortress U.S.A; ultimately turning their back on a Europe who had appeared to turn its back on them. The Chinese believed that the most Europe could hope for was a token show of air power but no massive influx of combat troops on the ground. Europe and Korea would burn, and America would watch and ignore it…

Over the following 2-days further detailed briefings on the exact requirements were conducted and all those involved were assured that they would receive regular access to satellite intelligence, Human Intelligence (HUMINT) and Intercepted Communications Intelligence (SIGINT) on NATO, South Korean, Indian and Australian armed forces over the next 4-years.

Before departing Dèng brought them together one last time….
'before you depart I have one more thing to say to you all……before Dragon's Claw is implemented the enemy will first feel the Breath of the Dragon … I understand your desire to know exactly what is this Dragon's Breath…but I cannot divulge to you what it is until it comes to be …… for reasons of

security this must be kept from you all... but.... when the day comes you will know of what I speak, however, this I can assure you. Dragons' Breath will be merciless, *relentless and decisive... and for those countries caught in its path*..........

With his voice raised and his heart pounding Dèng paused..... pondered for a second and upon looking at the facial expectation of his audience.... realised he was on the verge of saying far too much. Gathering himself again he continued.... *'Let's just say our enemies will be rendered impotent long enough for our glorious alliance to inflict the maximum destruction we all seek...with that in mind gentlemen I bid you all farewell. We will look to reconvene in one year's time to view the progress... my assistant Colonel Wu will provide you with all the details'* With that over, Dèng bowed and left the room.

One hour after all the teams had departed, Dèng entered the lift and made his way upstairs from the underground facility to the Military Commission Chairman's large plush office on the third floor. Dèng knocked and entered without permission, such was his relationship with the Comrade Chairman and, sat down in the large black leather chair provided. Chairman Zhou was standing on the other side of the rather large, but sparsely kept exquisite teak desk next to the window, thoughtfully scanning Beijing. Still fixed on the Beijing skyline and with his hands behind his back he spoke without turning to face General Dèng.

'So General..... how do you feel it all went?'

'So much better than I could have imagined, Comrade Chairman. *The Arabs are blinded by their hatred for the Americans and the West and this hatred will undoubtedly drive them to their own destruction and by then it will be too late for them to see their error....*

The Indonesians will clearly be an able ally in the Pacific during and after the war ends and will create a buffer should the Americans decide to attempt to flex their muscles in that region.

Korea will be united as one country yet again and we will be forever rid of that capitalist thorn in our side.

India....beaten militarily, will have no choice other than to capitulate and bow to the superior might of our glorious PLA while the Pakistani military will be so weak it will no longer be a force in that part of the world... ......it will be as we have planned... the two most powerful ideologies next to communism will be destroyed or weakened to the point that they may never recover the ground they lose......their assets and natural resources will be there for the taking and our own ideology can then shape the world for the next 200 years or more...with our main ally alongside we will be rulers of Europe, Africa, the Middle East and Asia'.... Dèng paused for a moment and then asked... *'by the way Comrade Chairman... when do our main guests arrive?'*

'*They will be here first thing tomorrow after all the others have departed* said Zhou ....*I must warn you that their participation in this is not confirmed and their identity must not be divulged to the alliance....at least not yet...... at this stage we have much to discuss with them......after all General......... it is not every day one can sit down...... discuss how to conquer one's enemy and divide two thirds of the world up between you*'

'And Turkey?' said Dèng.

Zhou turned.... *'Later old friend...we will not approach Turkey until nearer the day and only after we are sure of their participation. This is something you and your department will work on over the next few years as it would be unfortunate to have Turkey resist our request*'

'Tomorrow then, Comrade Chairman'

'Tomorrow, Comrade General....Tomorrow'

PART 4

DRAGON'S BREATH
(D-DAY)

"There will be unleashed live fire, hidden death,
Horrible and frightful within the globes,
By night the city reduced to dust by the fleet,
The city afire, the enemy amenable".
Nostradamus

DTG: Tuesday- January 24th… 2012…1400 hrs

Location: The United States Capital Washington DC, ---

Situation: 30-minutes before the State of the Nation address by the President of the United States.

As the 435 members of the House of Representatives gathered for the President's speech…Karim began typing in the sequenced numbers on the second keypad. He had practiced this so many times before he could do it blindfolded now. As the last number was placed into the keypad the digital display panel on the inner box lit up and, immediately, the time of 30-00 minutes started its countdown…29-59…29-58…29-57. It mattered not to Karim that the safety device had been disabled and the device was now armed. The countdown had begun and there was no going back… the device would run its full course and, after the 30-minutes were up, Karim would stand before Allah.

Karim's attention was momentarily distracted by police sirens in the distance. He stood and walked slowly over to the small window in the room. As he gazed out of his second floor room he smiled as he glimpsed the great dome of the Capitol Hill Building in the distance. He imagined it burning and thought…*soon it will all be gone.* Turning away he remembered briefly his wife and child, pulled out his prayer mat and decided to pray.

28-22, 28-21.....Karim Khan would be one of the lucky ones this day. He would die quickly unlike thousands of others who would die from the most horrific burns and blast injuries caused by the 8-Kilo ton nuclear device he had just armed and set in motion... a device that was the equivalent of 8,000 tons of TNT.

26-10...26-09....the countdown continued unhindered. There would not just be Americans dying this day. Tens of thousands from countries around the world were destined to die including many Muslims, but the war that Karim fought did not differentiate between the innocent and guilty. In his war the ideology that he followed would justify his actions as easily as others would condemn them, 25-36, 25-35.

A short distance away in the House of Representatives, the nation's politicians were gathering to hear the speech of the President. There would only be a few absentees from the 435 members that usually took their seats on such important days. Democrats and Republicans alike mingled and small talked about families, current issues and, the up and coming weekend. It seemed like another day at the office.... or it would do for the next 20-minutes or so, 22-03, 22-02.

There had long been concerns over a bomb in a suitcase scenario, but in 1997, this was discounted, although rumours were rife that Russia had managed to construct 100 of these devices and subsequently lost 52. The rumours, however, were never proven. Apart from their size, it was believed that the material contained within them decayed within months and rendered them useless. The device under Karim's bed was one of 5-devices that had been constructed and completed 32-days ago before being delivered to their respective locations. What Karim could not and did not know was that there were another 5 Jihadists just like him waiting for their moment to release onto the world, their own Dragon's Breath, 19-48, 19-47.

Ironically, the initial design for the device had emanated from the United States in 1964 as American was the first to design a Special Atomic Demolitions Munitions (SADM). Weighing approximately 70kg and measuring something in the region of 87cm by 65cm by 67cm, the device could be carried in a large backpack. These devices were dismantled by the first President Bush in 1991 but not before Chinese intelligence had acquired the technical specifications on how to construct such a device. The Chinese had put their most accomplished scientists to work on this project and mulled over the design for years, until finally, they had managed to perfect such a weapon. The Plutonium based device, was designed using a solid sphere of fuel (Plutonium 239) in its centre. Surrounding this was a spherical explosive charge. Once the weapon had been armed and the system fired, the explosive sphere was designed to implode upon the sphere of fuel. This in turn stimulates the neutrons present, which in turn initiates the chain reaction required in reaching critical mass. As critical mass is achieved, it begins to release heat and explode. The Chinese knew that critical mass was not enough and, for the fuel to be more efficient, super critical mass had to be achieved. The device was engineered in such a way that the explosive charge caused the Plutonium to double in density and, with its nuclei packed more tightly together, the fuel would reach super critical mass before going into super critical regime. At this instant a nuclear explosion was inevitable.

China knew Al Qaeda craved the nuclear option and using such an organization as a surrogate would make it almost impossible for the US and others to strike back with a similar weapon. Who could the West blame and bomb, especially with Al Qaeda claiming this and the many other atrocities in the days to follow? In 2003, a Saudi cleric responsible for the issuing of a fatwa condoned the use of weapons of mass destruction against the infidels and, if 10 million were killed as a result of a nuclear explosion, then it would be permissible. Al Qaeda and Bin Laden were about to see their dream realised.

17-18…17-17…17-16

Elsewhere, crowds were gathering in the Washington bars and on the sidewalks on this cold January afternoon; blue skies were overhead with a winter's sun taking some of the chill away. Children laughed as they played in the parks with their mothers, fathers, brothers, sisters and grandparents. People of all creed, colour and nationality were tuning in to hear the President's broadcast to the whole country and many other parts of the world. Those with knowledge of Dragon's Claw waited for the sign that Dragon's Breath had indeed been unleashed. They had not been informed of what this would be other than they would know it when the event occurred. They had been informed that Dragon's Breath would manifest first in America and then Europe; therefore, covert terrorist forces on the European continent along with military commanders in the Middle East and Asia were poised, watching and waiting for operation Dragon's Claw to commence. It would be the signal that would spawn World War 3. In Europe it was a mild winter's evening and in Australia and Korea the start of a new day was almost dawning. It would be a day like no other.... 10-54....10-53.

China's planning had been completed to perfection and, although information had surfaced over the years of Middle Eastern countries increasing the size of their military, Western governments had decided to take no real notice of this as they were more concerned in re-establishing political and economic relations after the catastrophe suffered by Iran, Afghanistan and China. They also refused to react to Australian concerns over the naval expansion of China and Indonesia. Even when China purchased 2 Aircraft Carriers from Russia and commissioned one of its own, nothing was done, as they preferred to believe China's lame explanation that it was in reply to India's growing military expansion. The concessions to China continued unabated and were indeed generous as Western governments fawned over the Chinese in order to have access to their expanding markets. The West, always keen to rekindle relationships with the Middle East had been taken in by the softly-softly approach to them and towards Israel and, they saw this as proof that the Arab World was recovering from the events of 2006-2008.

How very wrong they would all be....7-01.....7-00....6-59....6-58

China had convinced the Arabs that attacking Europe in January would be the ideal time. There was a misconception in Europe from some circles that Arabs only lived in hot deserts and could not fight under such circumstances but Iran, Syria, Iraq and Afghanistan suffered winters sometimes as cold as those in mainland Europe. China also knew that NATO armies in Europe were just returning from their traditional leave after the Christmas and New Year festivities and for them to prepare for an offensive war on this scale would take at least 3 to 6 months or even longer. The insertion of massive disruptive terrorist forces all over Europe combined with the covert preparation and build up of the Middle East's military, would allow for a rapid thrust into the belly of NATO....4-20.....4-19.....4-18...

Dragon's Breath was only the beginning and not the only destructive power about to be unleashed on the Western World.

0-10...0-9....0-8... Karim was kneeling on the floor with his head bowed to the east as the countdown reached its climax. He was still uttering the same words as the clock ticked down to zero hour....0-3...0-2....0-1 0-0

Karim departed this world without looking up...3-seconds later the White House and The Capitol Building lay in burning ruins...One hour later on an Arabic website Al Qaeda would release a statement claiming full responsibility...

The instant the device's energy was released hot, pressurised, compressed gases with extremely high temperatures expanded in a millisecond causing thermal radiation, accompanied by a massive blast and shock wave to pulse out across the city destroying a large area. Those near the centre of the explosion were literally incinerated as the temperature reached 1,000 degrees centigrade. With the intensity of an acetylene torch, those whose skin had been touched by the wave of thermal radiation were then hit by the blast wave travelling at three hundredths of a second behind. This combination provided sufficient exposure to cause exposed flesh to flash over into steam, resulting in exposed body areas being flayed down to the bone.

The shockwave emanating from ground zero in all directions was accompanied by a very strong wind travelling at faster than the speed of sound and this hit Washington DC with overpressures of 10psi. In nuclear explosion terms an overpressure of 10psi relates to a wind of approximately 250-mph. The effects of this overpressure resulted in the violent implosion of windows and walls, creating a deadly hail of high speed missiles. In less than the blink of an eye the blast-wave had crossed The Mall, incinerating or crushing all those waiting for a glimpse of the nations leaders later in the day. It slammed head first into Smithsonian and left the National History Museum, amongst many others completely destroyed. The Capitol Hill Building was crushed by the force of the blast as it continued outwards, only diminishing as it reached the furthest boundary of China Town to the north. On or near to the Southwest Freeway everything became a missile, including people, cars and buildings. The wave of destruction continued South across Main Avenue, Water Street and Ohio Drive before crossing the Potomac River where it caused limited but substantial damage and loss of life. A few of the reinforced buildings managed to remain standing while others were collapsing like packs of cards. In all directions the heat and blast continued to feed its terrifying hunger. The waterfront to the southwest was engulfed along with the Jefferson Memorial as it radiated outwards towards Independence Avenue, The Lincoln Memorial, Union Station and as far northwest as the George Washington University. In Pennsylvania Avenue the FBI building was stripped down to bare steel and concrete with all life extinguished in an instant. The Washington Monument was obliterated and the White House, possibly the most famous building in the world and a beacon of democracy, was unrecognizable as the majestic structure that it once was.

The scene was truly apocalyptic and secondary fires were already present from fractured gas lines up to 7km from the centre of the blast. Gas pipelines, petrol stations and exploding vehicle fuel tanks would all contribute to the devastation, but the firestorm phenomenon that descended on Hiroshima after a nuclear device exploded above the city in 1945, thankfully, would not befall the people of Washington DC this day. The combustible material present in a city such as Washington DC was phenomenal so it was fortune and luck that a firestorm did not develop. A firestorm develops after fires from a massive area begin to collapse into one huge blaze; this in turn generates its own gale force wind and consumes all before it, until all combustible material is exhausted. The temperatures generated would be many hundreds of degrees and few people would have survived such a phenomenon. Cars, roads and glass would have melted and water in lakes and rivers could boil, while those in shelters underground would be cooked alive. Whether the yield of the explosion was too small, or the area too confined, no one really knew but if the firestorm had taken effect millions could have died.

What was clear was that thousands, possibly hundreds of thousands had died and the seat of government, including the opposition, was wiped out. Many more thousands had suffered 1st, 2nd and 3rd degree burns and blast injuries. Others had suffered deeper 4th and 5th degree burns with these destroying tissues, such as muscle and connective tissues. Those caught in the main blast area would have been subjected to the worst of the thermal radiation and exposed to 15 times the strength required for 3rd degree burns.

The instantaneous overpressure, like the intense heat, lasted for just seconds and then began to decrease. With the hot air produced by the explosion now rising rapidly many thousands of feet above the city, those people who had survived or were not affected now witnessed their worst nightmare… the terrifying mushroom cloud that distinguishes a nuclear detonation from any other.

Dragging dust, debris and smoke upwards, this cloud would leave its own legacy on the United States as its radioactive dust returned to earth and contaminated generations to come.

Bone marrow and lymphatic glands being the most sensitive would be most affected, with the genetic structure also affected. The long-term affects for many people would continue for years as the latent defects manifested in later years in the form of cancer. Children would be particularly at risk with these more sensitive to the effects of radiation poisoning than adults, with the unborn being the most sensitive of all.

As America and the world were plunged into deep traumatic shock, the next phase of Operation Dragon's Claw was soon to be revealed. Al Qaeda would go on to claim this also, with the West initially assuming that they were under attack solely from terrorist forces.

Nuclear Decapitation

Elsewhere, the Chinese had housed another 5 carefully chosen Al Qaeda operatives in similar lodgings with the same type of suitcase device as that detonated by Karim Khan. Their instructions were very different to what Karim Khan had been instructed to do. Where

Khan had a set time to input his sequence of numbers, the other suicide bombers watched the TV screens intently. The Chinese knew that after such a catastrophic event the governments of Europe would demand emergency recalls of their parliaments, with almost everyone present from all parties in order to express their shock, their revulsion, their outrage and their support. An event such as this would ensure it was conducted live, in front of the cameras, to their nation's and the watching world. Broadcast on national TV, this would be the signal for 4 of the 5 Al Qaeda suicide bombers to input their coded sequence of numbers into the devices to begin their somewhat faster 10-minute countdown. Before the governments of the UK, Germany, France and Spain realised what pattern was being set, it was too late. Within hours of each other, all 4-countries had suffered the same fate as that suffered by Washington DC 15 to 18hrs earlier. China could not have realised how successful Dragon's Breath would be but, less than 24hrs after wiping out the entire US administration, 4 of the most powerful countries in NATO and the European Union, were without political leadership. The devastation in London, Berlin, Paris and Madrid was similar to that found in the US capital with hundreds of thousands dead or wounded and no political infrastructure left to govern.

In some of the cities the worst of the blast radius extended out as far as 3km in all directions consuming all within its path, with secondary damage extending out to 7km. The world's nightmare scenario had just become reality and it was about to get worse.

The fifth and final device was earmarked for the political HQ of NATO in Brussels and this was detonated 3-hours after the device exploded in London. At the same time as the nuclear detonation in Brussels and 80km (50 miles) away…the small town of Casteau, north of the Belgium City of Mons, came under a massive surprise attack by 125 Mujihadeen using 5-vehicle borne explosive devices, followed by five 20-man assault teams. Their target was SHAPE….The Supreme Headquarters Allied Powers Europe…..the military HQ of NATO……… their mission………to kill as many in the building as possible. It was a particularly vicious and bloody assault and entry was achieved relatively quickly. Those found inside were executed mainly by shooting but, after Belgium troops stormed the building the next day, they found 24 people had been beheaded in a corridor on the second floor.

Throughout the continent major European cities were now burning….panic was mounting and enduring……. and the enormity of what had occurred could not be taken in. The whole world had watched in awe at the destructive power such a small nuclear device could have once unleashed on a city and millions everywhere now feared for their own safety.

One hour after the final detonation in Brussels… Al Jazzerra and Reuters simultaneously received a video tape from Al Qaeda with a statement claiming all the devices and subsequent attacks across Europe were theirs.

PART 5

LIGHTS OUT
(D+20HRS)

After seeing the detonation in London on TV the 4-vehicle convoy with its 20-men inside had left its rural hideaway and was now driving towards its target. It consisted of 2-white minivans with a lone driver in each, followed by 2-minibuses with darkened side windows at the rear. The 2-rear vehicles contained 9-men each and their last 3-years of training and expectation was about to be unleashed upon an unsuspecting enemy. Hours earlier, London had suffered its nuclear Armageddon and now it was the turn of 12,000 Mujihadeen to make their mark by implementing their well-practiced and particular brand of terror all over Europe.

The first 2-vehicles each contained 200lbs of semtex, with the 2-drivers playing no further part after they detonated their vehicle bombs on tonight's target. The following 2-vehicles contained the assault teams, each equipped with AK47 assault rifles and fifteen 30-round magazines (450 rounds of ammunition each), 6 high explosive (HE) grenades and a satchel containing a firing device attached to a 15-second burning fuse, which was attached to a flash detonator and taped to a 20lb semtex explosive charge and 4 jerry-cans of petrol. Two of the group carried Rocket Propelled Grenade (RPG) Launchers with 3 rockets each; with a further 2 terrorists carrying a 7.62mm Dragonov sniper rifle each. What the leader of this individual group had not been told, was that all over the UK and mainland Europe, hundreds of targets were now being approached by suicide squads on foot, in cars, vans, buses, house removal vehicles and cattle trucks; some groups were smaller and some similar in size to his own team and for some of the larger targets, hundreds would be involved. The massive coordinated attacks on the West's civilian and military infrastructure was about to begin.

The 4-vehicle convoy turned off the secondary B-road, the B4632 from Winchcombe, onto Bouchers Lane on the edge of town a few miles away from their intended target and then into Hales Road. They turned right onto Thirlestane Road and continued west towards their final destination. Traffic was relatively light as the first 2-vehicles passed the police station on the left and crossed the bridge on Gloucester Road. This was the reference point for the front vehicle to accelerate from the second for what was to be its final half a mile to the target. They had driven this route 3-times previously over the last 7-days and knew it intimately. The target lay on Hubble road and as with most Western countries' policy to be open; their website had even provided the location of the entrance gate, complete with map. The target - and it was just ahead - was the Government Communications Headquarters (GCHQ) in Gloucestershire, England…..

GCHQ is the British intelligence agency responsible for providing the UK government and armed forces with signals intelligence (SIGINT) as required under the guidance of the Joint Intelligence Committee in support of government policies and is the equivalent of the United States National Security Agency (NSA). Known as her Majesty's Doughnut, which is a reference to the building design, the complex is renowned as the most powerful intelligence-gathering agency in Europe. The huge structure is 70-feet tall and 600-feet in diameter and located on a massive 176-acre site in Cheltenham. It houses a sophisticated computer network, which enables the complex to conduct electronics eavesdropping on signals and communications systems worldwide. With this facility destroyed, NATO would lose one of its prime weapons against the impending Arab armies' invasion.

Extra men were being drafted in after the London bomb hours earlier and the 4 Ministry of Defence (MoD) policemen on duty at the GCHQ main gate were looking forward to their change over at 1800hrs. The older policeman had already planned his evening in advance, as it was his 17th wedding anniversary and bomb or no bomb in London; he was going to enjoy the romantic meal he had planned with his wife. One of the younger policemen by some 12-years, married with two children aged 8 and 11, would be content with a quiet night in. The remaining officers were contemplating a pint at the local pub before continuing on their way home. It was the older one of the 4 that noticed the white minivan approaching the main gate at some speed before it began to slow down. As the vehicle continued its approach to the checkpoint the older policeman with his 9mm MP5 Heckler and Koch (H&K) machine gun slung across the front of his body made his exit from the small security hut for the customary walk over to the vehicle to check the drivers' identification. The vehicle was now close enough to the checkpoint to cause the maximum damage and, with the policeman 10-feet away, the vehicle exploded.

All 4 policemen died immediately as the pressure wave generated by 200lbs of semtex slammed into the checkpoint, the main guardhouse, which housed a further 12 policemen and surrounding buildings.

The damage was extensive and out of the 12 policemen in the guardhouse only 3 survived but they were in no fit state to react. The blast wave also shattered windows on one side of the doughnut-shaped GCHQ building a few hundred metres away, while hot shrapnel pierced fuel tanks and set fire to 3 cars parked close to the main gate. As the initial carnage subsided the second vehicle made entry past the decimated checkpoint area and proceeded to accelerate towards the main building. A lone MoD policeman patrolling on foot near the main building, having witnessed what was occurring, opened fire with his H&K 9mm at the second oncoming vehicle. The driver of the vehicle was wearing lightweight ceramic, 7.62mm resistant body armour but was struck sufficiently in the neck and shoulder area for him to crash his vehicle some 50-metres short of his planned impact area. Nevertheless, the driver still managed to detonate the second 200lb car bomb at a distance that substantially damaged the front of the main building structurally and which tore the MoD policeman to pieces.

200-metres further back were the 2-minibuses, weaving their way through the debris and destruction made by the 2 huge detonations. Their route was now clear up to the main building and people were slowly beginning to appear - cut, dazed and shocked at what had just occurred. They were the first to be callously executed by the Mujihadeen teams now approaching on foot towards the main entrance carrying all their weapons; explosives and 4 jerry-cans of petrol. After placing a charge at the main entrance they retreated as far as possible and 15-seconds later the satchel charge blew a huge hole where the doors had once been. They had made entry into Europe's main intelligence gathering facility and for the next 12hrs they systematically destroyed as many computers, servers and cables as possible, murdered whoever they came across and then prepared to fight to the death. It was late into the next day before the British Army finally assaulted and retook the building by force losing 33-men in the process, before eventually declaring it completely safe 72hrs later. The remaining satchel charges and fires had done their work well and large numbers of technicians, linguists and communications experts lay dead.

The Mujihadeen soldiers, as they called themselves, rounded up a small number of hostages in the event of a military assault and then murdered them all once the assault began. Others were lucky and escaped as they heard the gunfire and explosions at the front of the building but in the main it would be impossible to determine what capability, if any, remained.

All over the UK and mainland Europe electrical sub stations and power stations were being attacked and destroyed causing massive losses of power to all the major cities. It would take months to recover such a loss. Civil communication switching facilities in the UK such as British Telecom, O2, and Orange plus others were targeted and attacked, along with, Deutsche Telekom in Germany, France Telecom in France and similar companies throughout the rest of Europe. Satellite earth stations, with their huge saucer shaped dishes, were also infiltrated, with an excessive amount of damage caused by the powerful explosives. Petro Chemical and aviation fuel storage depots were sabotaged by timed explosive devices and set ablaze. In the UK alone, 5-main supply storage depots full of petrol and aviation fuel were burning savagely out of control, with their black obnoxious clouds plunging many parts of the country into a twilight existence for weeks after. Ports and civilian airports had also been attacked and huge amounts of civil aviation assets destroyed on the tarmac, causing all flights over Europe to cease.

Military facilities suffered quite heavily, with even ammunition depots targeted and blown up in some instances.

In Hereford, England, the UK Special Forces home base was breached with 19 people killed (mainly attached personnel and MoD policemen) before order was restored. The 8 attackers, after setting 3 explosive charges were all mortally wounded in a short firefight some time later.

Close Quarter Attacks (CQA) throughout the UK and the rest of Europe on high ranking key military personnel and their families by small 2 and 4-man teams with AK47s assault rifles proved devastating. The Chief of the Defence Staff (CDS), the highest ranking military officer in the UK, was ambushed in his drive and shot dead along with his driver as they emerged from his country home immediately after the destruction of the Houses of Parliament, the City of Westminster, the Ministry of Defence Building and Downing Street.

The greatest and most lasting damage to the military occurred when Europe's main airfields were targeted by suicide teams intent on destroying as much of NATO's airpower as possible.

In the UK the Royal Air Force (RAF) were hit particularly hard:

At RAF Benson 12 of No33 Squadrons allocated 15 Puma Helicopters were destroyed and No28 Squadrons Merlin HC3 was almost completely wiped out. 19 of the 22 Merlin HC3s were incapacitated in some form or other with only 3 surviving.

RAF Brize Norton lost 3 VC10s belonging to 101 Squadron, 6 of the 8 Tri-stars from 216 Squadron and 2 of the 4 strategic C-17s from 99 Squadron were also lost.

RAF Cotishall was home to the entire fleet of Jaguar GR3A Strike Aircraft. Also present were the specialized reconnaissance version, the Jaguar GR3s and T4s. Two thirds of this fleet was destroyed.

RAF Waddington, which operates 6 sentry AEW1 AWAC Airborne Early Warning Aircraft lost 4 of the 6 with 2 others deployed outside the UK.

RAF Coningsby was still operating the Air Defence Variant of the Tornado, the Tornado F2 and the F3. It also housed the newest aircraft on its books, the Euro Fighter Typhoon. All aircraft less those on training missions that day were destroyed and a huge loss of life occurred.

Two 15-man suicide squads targeted RAF Cottesmore, as it was known to contain RAF frontline Typhoon Squadrons and a large amount of Harrier Squadrons. The destruction and killing committed by these teams was clinically achieved with no aircraft left untouched.

RAF Kinloss in Scotland contained the entire RAF Nimrod MR2 fleet of aircraft, split between 2 Squadrons. Only 2 remained in service after the attack by a 10-man suicide team.

RAF Leeming was home to 2 Tornado F3 Squadrons who formed part of the UK's Air Defence Fighter Force and were a key element of

NATO's Joint Rapid Reaction Force (JRRF) and Immediate Reaction Force (Air). The saving grace at this station was the reaction of the resident RAF Regiment (The RAF's Infantry) who were able to respond quickly and with equal force. Only a few aircraft were destroyed at this site after the RAF Regiment reacted against the intruders and neutralised them before too much damage was achieved.

RAF Leuchers also fared well, as 20 of the base's 22 hardened shelters were not breeched or opened and the Tornado F3s remained intact. The intruders did, however, kill numerous airmen and Officers of all ranks in the indiscriminate killing spree immediately afterwards. The base's security and closest army unit who responded to the incident managed to kill 15 attackers and capture one in the subsequent 7hrs of mayhem. Not known to the defending troops, was the amount of enemy present in the attack. In total there were 20 attackers, with 4 remaining at large. These remaining Jihadists would ambush a military patrol 2-days later on the camp perimeter before been killed themselves after withdrawing to a farmhouse.

RAF Lossimouth was one of the main stations targeted by the Mujihadeen as it is known as one of the foremost stations in the RAF. It is home to 3 Operational Tornado GR4 Squadrons. The Sea-King Search Air Rescue (SAR) unit is also attached to this site in addition to 2-Ground Defence Units. Sadly they were unable to prevent a large proportion of the aircraft from being damaged or destroyed. At the majority of bases targeted, the attackers used the car bomb tactic at the main gates and this succeeded in drawing resources to the incident areas. At RAF Lossimouth the numbers of attackers numbered 40.

RAF Lyneham is the major tactical transport station and operates 55 Hercules C130K and C130J Transport Aircraft from this location. Its perimeter was quickly and easily breeched and, with the close proximity of the aircraft on the pan it was relatively easy for the attackers to destroy the whole fleet of 27 that was present quickly. The subsequent battle at RAF Lyneham was particularly violent and damaging, with over 50 Mujihadeen at large on the vast base for hours. Included in the batch of destroyed aircraft was the UKs Special Forces allocation of C130K and J-Model Transport Aircraft. It was a massive loss....and one which would be hugely felt in the coming months.

RAF Marham operated 2 Squadrons of Tornado GR4s; also present were 5 Canberra PR9 Reconnaissance Aircraft. Luckily, one Squadron was airborne conducting flying tactics in Scotland as the attack began and they would be diverted to Iceland until the enormity of what had occurred was ascertained. RAF Marham lost 16 Tornados and 4 of its 5 Canberra PR9s that night.

RAF Odiham was considered high value and a key target. It contained the heavy lift element of the Joint Helicopter Command (JHC) and the Special Forces helicopters and crews who serviced the UK's Special Forces allocation. 7 and 18 Squadron with their Chinook HC2s and HC3s had 25 aircraft between them with No27 Squadron a further 12. Setting aside 9 aircraft that were deployed on training and operational tasks, all the aircraft in RAF Odiham were seriously damaged or destroyed, including those assets used by the Operational Conversion Unit (OCU). It was later assessed that more than 70 attackers had gained entry into this site and at least 3 vehicle borne bombs were used at various stages during this attack. 8 Lynx AH7 and 4 Gazelle Helicopters were also destroyed.

RAF Wittering is a fighter base and was targeted, as it was known as 'The Home of the Harrier'. 14 aircraft- a mixture of pilot-only GR7 and the 2-seater T10 aircraft were housed at this station with 16 Mujihadeen gaining entry before they destroyed or damaged all but 4 aircraft. The attackers also managed to extract from the site without engagement of any sort and would go on to commit further secondary target attacks elsewhere over the next 72hrs.

Another high value and priority target was RAF Dishforth, which was home to HQ9 Regiment- Army Air Corp. This contained a large portion of the British army's allocation of Apache Attack Helicopters and Pumas. Out of the 67 currently in use 47 were stationed at this base. The destruction of such a powerful force was a key requirement in safeguarding Islamic combat troops at a later date. China knew this and had instructed Iran that 140 Mujihadeen were to be trained to attack this facility and then remain on site to ambush and interdict any reinforcing troops. Their initial assault was conducted with speed and overwhelming force and the subsequent battle for this station lasted 4-days with the British army deploying 2 Infantry Battalions firing 81mm High Explosive Mortars in anger on British soil for the first time in its history.

The attacks had taken the UK by complete surprise and with the military overstretched they would have difficulty preventing further attacks on other UK facilities over the next 48hrs.

The 2 US Airbases in Norfolk, RAF Lakenheath and Mildenhall, were also breached and some of their F15 Strike Eagles destroyed. As had occurred at some of the other RAF bases, the ensuing fighting was intense and the surprise achieved by the assaulting forces enabled them to penetrate deeply into the majority of bases they hit. The American troops at these locations restored order within 18hrs, but at a heavy cost to human life and hardware. However, none of the tactical nuclear devices stored at these sites were damaged or compromised. The only other US Airbase to be targeted in the UK was RAF Fairford in Gloucestershire, which is designated as a forward operating base (FOB) for 6 B-52s from the 2nd Bomb Wing from Barksdale Air force Base (AFB) in the United States. The loss at this base was felt strategically, with 5 of the 6 aircraft either damaged or destroyed with only one remaining intact.

Mainland Europe suffered just as badly as the UK with assaults on bases in France, such as Landivisiau, which is the base for the Aircraft Carrier Charles-De-Gaulle and the French Navy's Squadron of nuclear capable Super-Etendard planes. Luxeuil and Istres, both homes to Mirage 2000N Aircraft, were also hit hard

N.A.S. Hyères suffered losses including Search Air Rescue (SAR) assets from the French and Allied Carrier Fleet in the Mediterranean. These assets used this base at various intervals and at the time of the attack more than 32 aircraft were on the ground. In addition to this, 14 helicopters of the French Navy - 3 WG-13 Lynx's, 3 Allouette llls, 4 AS 365F Dauphins and 4 SA-321G Super Frelon Search Air Rescue, Long-Range Helicopters were destroyed. The 40 or so attackers also caused extensive damage and loss of life to the repair zone and communications centre. Stationed at the base was a company of French Marines who reacted quickly as soon as the attack began, however, they were unable to prevent large destruction to the base and it was mid-afternoon the next day before they regained control of the station.

Across the country more than 45 military and civilian facilities were targeted including the French airbases of NAS Cherbourg, NAS Le Touquet and NAS La Rochelle with heavy losses. Targeting was similar to that seen in the UK with communications facilities, petrochemical and gas storage depots, power stations and substations high on the agenda. French aircraft loses included large numbers of its Dassault Rafale Fighter Aircraft, 43 of its 100 Airbus Military Aircraft A400M Military Transports, 19 of its 37 Eurocopter Tiger Attack Helicopters and 7 of its 34 NH90 Transport Helicopters.

The Federal Republic of Germany was heavily targeted in a similar fashion with special consideration placed on the Kaiserslautern Military Community (KMC). Situated in the German state of Rheinland-Pfalz, which borders France, Luxemburg, Belgium and other German states such as Saarland, Nordrhein-Westfalen, Hessen and Baden-Wurttenberg, KMC is the largest military community outside of the continental United States. It is a combined community consisting of Air Force and Army components with an assortment of military bases including the Air Force facilities at Ramstein Air Base. The Army alone has 8 different installations in the region. The chaos caused by 480 suicide Mujihadeen attacking 5 separate locations over the course of one night was unprecedented and, although large areas of the community remained untouched due to its size, those areas that were attacked, suffered heavily before reinforcements and a coordinated response to what was occurring could be mounted. An attack on such a high profile target had 2-main objectives. Destroy as much of the facility as possible and kill as many military personnel as they could. More than 13,000 troops were required to conduct search and destroy missions, EOD clearance and facility security in this militarised region before order was eventually restored. The battle to kill or capture the attackers would take more than 4-days and the KMC area would not be declared clear or safe for a further 2-weeks.

Ramstein Air Base; part of the KMC and home to 34,000 Americans and many more thousands of personnel from many nation's, is the home of the 86th Airlift Wing. They come under the command of the 3rd Air Force whose Headquarters is in the United Kingdom and in addition to the US contingent; there are personnel from Canada, Germany, UK, France, Belgium and Holland. The base was of particular importance to Chinese and Arab planners as it contained the Air Mobility Support Squadron and Air Mobility Support Group operating C-5 Galaxy, C-141 Starlifters, C-130 J and

K model Hercules and Boeing C-17 Globemaster heavy lift cargo aircraft. It has the largest overseas cargo port and was a prize worth risking 150-men for. By the next morning a large proportion of the valuable heavy lift aircraft lay burning on the airfield and 1,238 troops of all nationalities lay dead or wounded.

Einsiedlerhof Air Station is where the Warrior Preparation Centre resides, using state of the art computer simulation for commanders to conduct air, land and sea campaigns at anytime. It is a joint US Army of Europe (USAREUR) and US Air Forces Europe (USAFE) training facility and, is mainly staffed or operated by senior level battle commanders. These senior ranking officers were the key target objectives at this location and along with their junior staff officers present in the building, were gunned down without mercy.

Panzer Kaserne… the eastern most installation in Kaiserslautern, Germany, near Stuttgart, and home to the 21st Theatre Support Command is responsible for all forms of logistic support within the European theatre. Logistics would be crucial in the coming months and this base was targeted by a team of 40 Mujihadeen intent on setting fire to and destroying as many warehouses and logistical supplies as possible. Killing troops was a secondary task but, nevertheless, was carried out with cold clinical efficiency.

Another huge loss was sustained from the attack on a large section of the Miesau Army Depot; the largest ammunition storage area outside the United States. The resulting explosions continued for 3-days after the Mujihadeen attackers forced guards and ammunition technicians to open many of the bunkers in the facility. All were brutally killed soon after and no mercy was shown for any of the US soldiers captured that night. The Mujihadeen methods of warfare, however, would be reciprocated before the night was out by US Troops.

In the northeastern part of Italy; 20-miles North of Pordnone at the base of the Alps, lay the Aviano Air Base, home to the 16th Air Force (AF) HQ and the 31st Fighter Wing (FW) with their contingent of Lockheed Martin F-16 Fighting Falcons. The attackers were interested in 2 of the 7 areas at this site. Area E, the 16th AF HQ and Area F, the 31st FW Flight line and the 31st FW Commander's offices. There was also a munitions storage area that Chinese satellite imagery had identified and this became a prime target. The damage to this base was extensive but centered mainly on their munitions storage facility, with the F16s escaping relatively unscathed with only 5 destroyed.

The Italian Air Force Base in Grosseto, was home to the newly arrived IT002 Typhoon Euro-Fighter and, with these aircraft based there, it was hit hard. 28 of the Italian Air Forces allocation of 121 Typhoons were destroyed at just this one location. The twin engine Euro-Fighters were regarded by 4th Squadron, as one of the most valuable assets in the Italian Air Force inventory and such a loss would be incalculable in the coming months. During the attack, Italy also lost both its Boeing KC767A Advanced Aerial Refueling Tanker Aircraft.

The Euro-Fighter numbered 620 aircraft throughout Europe with 87 sold to Spain, 121 to Italy, 180 to Germany and 232 to the United Kingdom. Britain had only just taken delivery of its final aircraft after technical delays had stalled its initial introduction. This aircraft was to replace the aging Tornados but with both aircraft on the pan throughout Europe the Mujihadeen would strike a critical blow to NATOs air force capability. On this night alone; NATO would lose a third of its Typhoon force to enemy action on the ground.

In Spain the airfields at Moron in Southern Spain and Getafe in Central Spain were targeted and the EF-18A Hornets of Ala12 based at Toriejon were severely damaged and destroyed in another attack.

Within hours of the nuclear decapitations, Europe's main players were leaderless, NATO HQ had been wiped from the face of the earth, fuel reserves were burning out of control and the lights had gone out in vast areas after the attacks on countries' power facilities. Telephone communication remained intermittent and those still working went into meltdown with the amount of people attempting to access the network. Military losses were significant and catastrophic in places, with forces stretched to the limit as they sought to protect what remained. Hospitals in Washington, London, Munich, Paris, Madrid and Brussels were swamped and unable to cope with the many thousands of dead and dying. The military set up field hospitals and makeshift morgues in an attempt to treat those needing emergency care and to store some of the dead. In the days to come huge trenches would have to be dug to accommodate the dead littering the cities. Many more would be left to die as it was impossible to treat all the injured. The nuclear explosion was only the first crisis to engulf the emergency services and they now had to contend with the huge numbers being killed by conventional terrorist attacks across the whole of Europe. Italy, Spain, Holland and Belgium were also targeted conventionally but a lot less than the UK, Germany and France. The countries that escaped entirely were the Scandinavian countries as these were thought not to pose any significant threat. China could not have predicted that the soft underbelly of Western defences could be ripped open so easily. The terrorist blade had struck deep and ensured that Democracy and NATO were bleeding badly.

Whole nations were plunged into massive shock before transcending into mass hysteria, lawlessness, panic buying and looting. The military, for years woefully undermanned and overstretched, were attempting to impose some form of Marshall Law as they were unsure of what was coming next but this proved to be unworkable in many parts of the UK and the European mainland, in particular the large cities. The Police attempted to maintain some form of law and order but rioters and looters were aided by no or limited electrical power in most of the major cities. It was frighteningly chaotic as the larger NATO countries in Europe; the UK, Germany, France and Spain were all scampering around in the dark with no leadership yet materializing. With most of the UK and mainland Europe's fuel reserve in flames, pumps would be dry within 24hrs. What could be saved would have to be earmarked for the military and emergency services.

With the West being a materialistic and somewhat pampered society, many people were unable to cope without what they saw as the means to live. It was winter and people had to face it with little or no heating and, a shortage of food. The problem was further compounded by large parts of the country still without power, limited or no gas and intermittent or no communications. There was no quick way of restocking the shops adequately without the fuel to drive the many thousands of supply vehicles that a modern society requires on a daily basis, therefore, in a short space of time the fragile fabric holding Western democracy and its throwaway lifestyle together, was stripped bare, revealing a society unable to handle the hardships it was about to face. Already there were sinister undercurrents developing and society's worst traits were starting to surface. The dog eat dog and strongest survives mentality was already evident in some cities, and over the coming days would get worse as people fought and killed each other for food and essential resources; sadly, there would always be those intent on preying on the vulnerable and those less fortunate.

6hrs after the first attacks throughout Western Europe the Arab League of Nations turned off the oil supplies and impounded all Western shipping in their ports. 1hr later, Russia turned off the gas supply to Germany, France, Italy and the UK, blaming terrorist activity on the pipeline.

12hrs later, the first elements of the Islamic armies 11th Army Group from Iran (550,000 men) began moving north towards Turkey via Iran and Northern Iraq. This force alone included 2,713 Main Battle Tanks, 24,600 other Armoured Fighting Vehicles and 3,800 artillery weapons. Following up at the rear were 15,000 men from the fanatical Iranian Mujihadeen Brigades with another 15,000 of their Mujihadeen brothers already pre-positioned throughout Europe ready to strike against NATO military convoys, utilising the same ambush techniques employed in Iraq and Chechnya. These forces had been trained to conduct guerrilla tactics in NATO's rear against military convoys moving east and had been strengthened by veterans from the Chechnya and Iraqi battlefields with a simple mission to harass and destroy any NATO military targets over the next few weeks and months until their resources had been depleted. These resources had been pre-positioned by the Chinese over the last 12 months in anticipation of this type of warfare against NATO. Such actions were designed to delay the movement of troops and their equipment, which meant NATO would have to divert precious frontline combat troops to guard government buildings, military convoys, civil/military facilities and key strategic points on Main Supply Routes (MSRs), in addition to conducting counter terrorist search and destroy operations for the enemy already in their midst.

At the same time as the 11th Army Groups move north, the 460,000 men of the Islamic 6th Army Group began their move northwards from Syria, with its strategic Missile Command and its 4 missile Brigades transporting their missile inventory on giant Russian made MAZ-543 launcher vehicles. The Syrian Missile Command located in Aleppo normally controlled the 7-mobile Surface-to-Surface Missile Brigades. Each Brigade was equipped with a Battalion of FROG-7, one Battalion of SS-21 Scarab and one advanced Scud C or Scud D Battalion. Syria had built its missile force up considerably from 2002 using North Korean, Chinese and Iranian help and now possessed 320 antiquated Russian-built Frog-7 missiles with a range of 70km and a High Explosive (HE) payload of 450kg. They had approximately 450 of the more capable SS-21 Scarab missiles, which have a range of 120km and a HE payload of 480kg. The advanced Scud C, also part of their inventory, came with improved accuracy and guidance systems and a range of 650km plus a HE payload of 985kg. The Scud C, which was upgraded by using small wings found on the Surface-to-Air (SA)-2 missiles, allowed for course deviations, making it more accurate and able to strike smaller targets. The Scud D, however, was considered its most advanced missile with a range of 700km and a HE payload of 500kg. Missile command was large enough to leave behind a control element with at least 3 additional Brigades facing south towards Israel and who were ready with an overwhelming first strike capability if required.

12 months ago the Egyptian government had received a visit from Chinese officials suggesting that Egypt instigate a request to Turkey to allow their newly formed British equipped 19 Corp to train on Turkish soil in 2011. Egypt, thinking this was madness, eventually did so and was amazed when the request was officially granted. Over the next 3 months the full compliment of armour, artillery and support vehicles for 60,000 men from the 4th Army Group were shipped to Turkey as part of a special training agreement between the 2-countries. Turkey, no longer part of NATO, could go into defence agreements with whom so ever it pleased. Turkey released a statement saying it wished to participate with Egypt in light of their equipment refit and, if impressed, go into a similar agreement with the United Kingdom…but this was, of course, for Western consumption.

6 months after 19 Corp arrived in Turkey the remainder of the Islamic 4th Army Group, consisting of 290,000 men and equipments, rolled out of barracks in Egypt and began its slow move towards the sea ports of Port Said and Alexandria where transit across the Mediterranean to Turkey was to take place. Dozens of container ships had already been pre-loaded with containers full of stores, ammunition, vehicles and equipment sent to Turkey over the last 3 months. Turkey possessed an amphibious force of 66 vessels in its inventory, which were designed to

transport Turkish tanks and troops to operational areas. It was these ships that were now being utilised to transport a different army.

The remainder of the 4th Army Groups heavy armour was to be transported by these vessels aided by Ferries and cruise ships of all shapes and sizes that had been requisitioned (some by force) by the Turkish and Egyptian Ministries. Taking longer than expected, the majority of the 4th Army Group would be unable to join up with 19 Corp for at least another 2 months. After 5-weeks and with only half of the force ready, the 4th Army Group with 180,000 men began to move north with the remainder following on in another 5-weeks time. 19 Corp were the spearhead and cutting edge for the Egyptian Army but they would not head the column. They were there to take on the more advanced Western nations, as they got closer to their main objective Germany. Soon they would be joining up with elements from the Syrian 6th Army Group. The 6th and 4th armies (although still 170,000 short) consisted of more than half a million men. Both countries would also leave a substantial force behind in order to cover any actions by Israel and although they knew Israel's capability was far greater than theirs, they had been assured by the Chinese that Israel would be warned not to intervene once operation Dragon's Claw began. Egypt, with more than 800 combat aircraft, also gained permission to deploy some of its more modern aircraft such as their American-bought F-16 and French-made Mirage 2000 on to Turkish bases. In total they deployed upwards of 320 aircraft. The Egyptian Air Force or EAF- the Al Quwwat Al Jawwiya Il Misriya also possessed C130 Hercules aircraft and began using these to transport in, air force technicians and supplies for the combat aircraft that were to be deployed.

The number of men on the march from Syria, Iran and Egypt was growing daily and, would soon swell to one and a half million combatants. In addition to this, the Saudi Arabian 10th Army Group with a contingent of 415,000, would remain in a high state of alert, ready to move in 7-days time. An Iranian reserve consisting of a further 350,000 men were also ready but, in the meantime, they would form part of the strategic reserve. Iran also had a manpower pool of one and a half million militia but these would remain in Iran as home guard type personnel. Part of the Arab Nations' strategic reserve also included Syrian and Egyptian forces who would supply a further

580,000 between them. Those heading for battle and those earmarked for battle would total some 3 million plus. Turkey, courted and seduced by the Chinese over the last 2-years would at long last have its revenge on NATO by leaving the gateway to the West open and allow the Islamic Army to storm through. No Turkish troops would be employed in a combat role outside of Turkey but their facilitating role meant Arab troops would be on European soil within days.

NATO, without Turkey's contribution, had a standing army in the region of 600-800,000 frontline combat troops. Its biggest problem would be preparing and sustaining such a force in its area of operations. Transporting its troops to the right regions via roads with potential ambushes in place would prove extremely difficult and attempting to provide enough munitions from peacetime stocks, especially high tech ammunition, would also be an issue. Logistics are the one crucial factor in deciding battles and ultimately many a commander has failed to deliver by not paying attention to his logistical requirements. The Chinese/Arab Alliance had prepared for 4-years for this moment and, had ensured the supply and movement of Arab forces around the battlefield under operational conditions could be sustained. They had done their homework and provided the means to transport tanks, artillery pieces, armoured personnel carriers and huge stocks of ammunition and fuel. The daily ammunition expenditure rate was always higher than planned and the Chinese planners had taken this into account. Fuel would not be a quantity issue for the Arab Nations but it would be for NATO. With their fuel depots burning and the oil pipes turned off in the Middle East, every drop would become precious in the months ahead. NATO countries had an agreement to stock 30-days' worth of war-fighting materials but it was well known that some did not even adhere to this after the end of the Cold War. This coupled with only 45,000 American troops left on European soil after 70,000 re-deployed back to the United States in 2006/07, meant Europe could no longer rely on the US to provide the punch it once provided. Mobility and sustainability due to lack of fuel, coupled with logistical and movement constraints, were clearly going to be NATO's Achilles' Heal…

Elsewhere, the Israeli Defence Force (IDF) went on the highest alert possible and warned its Arab neighbours at the highest level of its own military capability, including its nuclear deterrent, but so far Israel had not been threatened or attacked.

Russia also went on full military alert within hours of the nuclear detonations and began to mobilise 500,000 of its newly structured professional army of 1.2million frontline troops, including 14,000 of its 28,000 Main Battle Tanks (MBTs) on its western borders. Russia's nuclear missile facilities at Tatischevo, Kozelsk, Kostroma, Teykovo, Vypolzovo, Yoshkar-Ola and Yurya also went to fully manned 24/7 status and the strategic Air Force bases in Engels and Ryazan prepared in readiness for any outside threat.

The world would initially perceive that Russia was responding to the same threat as that faced by the West. That assumption would only last until the Russian Air Force responded to NATO aircraft and, after that, it would be impossible to explain away. The West would see Russia for what it truly was - an ally of the Arab League of Nations.

For the third time in a hundred years…. war was once more coming to Europe, with those first in the firing line; Bulgaria, Romania, Hungary, Slovakia, Poland and the Czech Republic totally unaware of the impending Arab onslaught.

PART 6

DIVIDE AND CONQUER
(THE PLAN REVEALED)

DTG: Monday-March 19th …. 2008

Location: Chinese People's Liberation Army Intelligence Agency Building, Beijing…45m below ground.

Situation: With the first secret meeting in Beijing at an end, General Dèng had waited patiently for all the Muslim delegations to depart. The following day, he was again sat in the underground briefing room with Chairman Zhou waiting for the final delegation to arrive.

The 5-men expected at the meeting had been specially chosen to make this journey by President Vladislav Sidorov himself. They were some of his closest allies and friends and trusted completely. What they were about to be told though would test all their resolves to see it through.

At 10-minutes past nine Grigory Petrova- the Prime Minister of the Russian Federation, entered the room, along with Russia's Deputy President- Nikolai Demidovsky. Also present was the **Marshal of the Russian Federation of all Forces Ranks** -Vasilii Svialoslavich, the General of the Army - General Oleg Mikhailovich and finally Marshal Iaroslav Ivanova - Chief Marshal of the Air Force of Russia.

Unlike yesterday, Chairman Zhou led the opening briefings and he began by outlining how his earlier private discussions with President Sidorov had led to this eventual meeting in Beijing taking place. With the formalities over Zhou explained the plan for Dragon's Claw but for now, omitted Dragon's Breath. He was keen to observe the reaction of those present first, knowing that China was proposing World War 3.

Chinese strategists had long believed that if a war against a technologically superior foe such as the United States and NATO occurred, the enemy would probably attempt to deploy forces rapidly and then launch a massive air campaign. Conducting preemptive strikes against an enemy's most critical targets constituted the most direct means available to Chinese thinking as this had the potential to defeat him without having to defeat his entire armed forces. The key to gaining the initiative was to attack before the enemy had time to assemble his forces thus taking advantage of this window of opportunity. By going after the core of the enemy's defence and logistical supply chain with elite units; airpower, communication systems, electronic support, ammunition storage facilities, fuel reserves and VIPs, they suddenly become vulnerable and, by using a proxy force to implement the strategy, ensures China avoids a major head-on confrontation.

The briefing (interspersed with breaks) lasted for over 2hrs. Zhou reiterated the planning and preparation phase that was to take place over the next 4-years with the countries involved. He explained how the more radical Islamic countries would improve relations with the West and Israel while, in the background; they went about improving and increasing their military capability. He spelled out China's involvement in the Korean Peninsula, its aid to Indonesia and the ultimate destruction of India as an Asian superpower using Pakistan as a conduit. During this part of the briefing Zhou noticed the raised eyebrows and the sometimes-shocked glances across the table, which confirmed to him that he had their complete attention.

General Dèng then took over and, it was he, who filled in some of the gaps on the intelligence aspects, the huge tactical and logistical requirements, the training of suicide Jihadists and their subsequent insertion into the West using well proven human trafficking smuggling routes. He followed this up by detailing the perceived attacks on Western military and civilian establishments such as fuel reserves, power, oil and gas facilities, ammunition storage depots, communications facilities, ports and airfields before he again sat down.

Chairman Zhou continued…..'*Comrades…. The West is ill-prepared for such a war with some countries in NATO unable to muster even a single combat Battalion…NATO has moved away from a collective defence principle to a collective security one and, although still a powerful entity, it can be knocked off-balance enough for a strike into its exposed underbelly. As you well know they have altered their mindset and doctrine to take on the asymmetric threats that have emerged over the last 15 to 20 years and to a certain extent…so have we. Terrorism, drug trafficking, WMD, threats* to vital infrastructure and interests has seen NATO initiate a streamlined, lighter and more mobile approach to warfare. The day the US Army moved 2 heavy Divisions back to the United States in 2007, gave a clear indication, that they saw Europe as relatively safe from Russian Expansion, or, as a direct external threat. It is this assumption that will be its downfall and, which will lead to its ultimate defeat.'

'We assess the Jihadists terrorist forces could destroy up to a third of NATO air power and heavy lift capability and, with luck- much much more. NATO has grown soft on a diet of peacekeeping operations, politically correct interference in their training regimes and continually suffered from cutbacks after the collapse of the Cold War…even their own commanders know this. They are becoming unused to hardship and whine for their playstations, Internet facilities and Coke a Cola more than they want to fight'

He continued… 'I can see that you are concerned about the military capability of NATO, especially the United States, and wondering why we are telling you all this, you are also thinking what do China want from Russia?.... You are like us in that you continue to modernize your military and your tactics, especially after the Iraqi Army collapsed using dated technology and tactics from the Cold War era. You, like us, know those old ways are over and there will be no return to the old Soviet tactics for either of us. Professional, modernized and motivated armies are the way ahead.….we now have the opportunity to make this so…to retrain and to regroup our forces ready for the day when they will be needed… and by using surrogate forces to suck the life from NATO…we will finally claim the victory that we have both wanted for so long…It is a risk of course…but one we feel is worth taking'

'You obviously know India is a major buyer of Russian arms and technology comrade Zhou' said Deputy President Nikolai Demidovsky …'their demise will not be beneficial to Russian interest's comrades'

'I do know that'…said Zhou with confidence…'and believe me Deputy President, it will be immensely beneficial to you and Russia'.… there was a pause before Zhou spoke again.… 'In 2005, China purchased $2 billion worth of weapons from Russia; in 2007 we purchased almost $5 billion. By 2009-2011, in-order to re-equip our allies we will be looking at a combined annual total closer to $210-250 billion or more…paid for, of course, by Chinese finances and, in the main, Arab oil. We are your arms industries' premier customers as you know and, over the next 4-years those countries taking the fight west will be massively rearmed by China… via Russia. It is not only China's heavy industry and manufacturing that has been working to full capacity. Our defence industries have been working flat out for 6-years now and yours must do the same… Our combined defence industries have the capability to make this rearmament a reality.. By working to full capacity, billions upon billions of dollars will flow into Russia annually. You can see how this will benefit your country and I don't need to tell you comrade, that this money will make Russia stronger militarily'.

Zhou was in full flow now and continued….

'I am sure you are all thinking this is madness and why risk a war with the West. Sooner or later it would have occurred….you know this…and you also know that NATO is only strong enough to resist with American help…. but what we have available now are surrogate forces prepared to draw NATO's sting and with our help they will achieve far more than they could ever hope for alone with both our countries being the main beneficiaries. After that, my friend, the prize will have been worth waiting for. This prize is why you are here and it is one we want to share with Russia'…

'And what is this prize, Comrade Chairman?' interjected Grigory Petrova, raising his eyebrows.

Zhou stood up and walked slowly around the table before speaking… 'Two things have blighted your aspirations over the years. One is an old enemy and the other is a relatively new one. The West has thwarted your every move since 1945 and continues to out manoeuvre you. We know, as do the United States that communism is covertly on the rise again in Russian and although not openly flaunted, your government is essentially communist in nature and belief. The second… is the rise of Islam on your southern borders. Chechnya is still a thorn in your side but what we propose will ensure their struggle and their ideology will die… along with thousands of their best fighters as they find it impossible to resist the greatest jihad of them all.

Therefore, comrade Petrova…China wants to offer you two things and in return… we ask for your assistance but three times.

The first prize we offer is the demise and destruction of the two most powerful ideologies next to Communism - Western Democracy and Islamic Fundamentalism'.

'Secondly, we want to offer you dominion over the whole of Europe once NATO is defeated… The war between the two sides will go on for months, maybe years, but rest assured they will both be weakened enough for your Forces to invade Europe when it wishes.…. small issues such as Japan's claim over the Southern Kuril Islands that you now administrate and Chechnya will become irrelevant to you…

With them both destroyed our united countries will have the freedom to plunder Africa and extract its huge untapped natural resources, plus, we will have unlimited and prime access to oil from the Middle East as the Arabs look to China and Russia to protect them because they no longer have a credible military capability after their war with NATO. Our two great countries will share these resources and with the demise of Indian, then later Japan and Taiwan we will forge the greatest communist dynasty the world has ever seen. We also make the generous offer to mutually share the technology we acquire from Japan.

Our combined military forces will have the power to achieve anything we desire - we will be the ultimate superpower. Who knows… maybe in 20-years time… we may even have the capability to invade the United States itself…nothing is impossible.…. it just takes strategy, patience and the will to succeed. This can be achieved, gentlemen, and with Al Qaeda claiming Dragon's Breath…China and Russia will be exempt from any immediate blame…just long enough for our countries to conquer the lands that we should have been able to conquer years ago if not for American intervention and Western meddling.'

'You mentioned Dragon's Breath…what is this Dragon's Breath you speak of, comrade?' said Marshal Ivanova, intrigued.

Zhou motioned towards Dèng 'General I think you are best placed to explain this'…and sat down..

Dèng now stood and began to speak and as he revealed the nature of Dragon's Breath ……there were collective gasps followed by shouts of madness in Russian over the table before Grigory Petrova restored calm. With the Russian delegates quiet once more Dèng continued but noticed there was a palpable anxiety emanating from the Russian contingent.

When Dèng finished, Nikolai Demidovsky spoke first……. 'What you propose has an element of madness to it and is impossible from a technical point of view.…. and even if you possess such a capability then how do we know you will not use it to decapitate the Russian Federation at the same time'.

'I assure you my dear comrade'...Said Zhou, *'that what we propose may be thought of as madness but it is not impossible and, we most certainly have the capability. We are telling you this as we are now allies and we are no longer fighting over insignificant border areas and Islands as we have done so in the past. We would not divulge the whole plan to you if we suspected any doubt in this alliance. Only you and we know the full plan, while the others have been denied this information. It is important they know nothing of Dragon's Breath until it takes place.*

The Americans will suspect our involvement at some stage but our political line to the world will remain the same… that the Arabs invaded Europe and we, as a nation, are greatly saddened and shocked by these barbaric acts of terrorism and the huge loss of life from the effects of the nuclear detonations. The world will see it as an Arab plot to destroy the West; an act of revenge after what occurred in 2006 with China and Russia taking advantage and filling the void…. Even if they suspect our involvement, as I'm sure they will at some stage, not even America would risk Nuclear Armageddon. Explaining away Korea, however, will be more difficult… especially after the attack on Diego Garcia in the Indian Ocean and the 200,000 Chinese troops held in reserve on the border become apparent…but…. they and the rest of the world know that North Korea are our allies and we must do all we can to aid them in their hour of need…. If America declares war on China then so be it…but where apart from Korea could they fight us?

Even America, wounded and isolated, will come back to the table to purchase oil. They need it like an alcoholic craves his next drink…and when they do it will be on our terms. By then our combined strengths will not allow America to gain a foothold in Europe, the Middle East or Asia again and although it will remain a regional power it will eventually die as a global superpower…'

Deputy President Demidovsky looked intently and searchingly around the table, engaged in further conversation for a few minutes and then asked for 15-minutes alone with his delegation. Zhou and Dèng departed and 15-minutes later returned.

'Comrade Zhou,' said Demidovsky … ……*'we have considered your offer carefully and we have reached a unanimous agreement. What are the three things you require from us'*

Zhou suppressed a smile…*'The first and most important is the use of your air force to combat the threat of NATO airpower over European airspace. We know you cannot totally defeat NATO air power alone but we do know the technology gap is closing and you have almost perfected the 5th-generation S-37 stealth aircraft now that your 3rd-generation bolt-on stealth visibility reduction system works. You clearly have the numbers to interdict and degrade their capability and it is this that will ensure they do not have air superiority or air supremacy …just long enough for the Arab armies to engage their ground troops in combat. We will also need your air forces' heavy lift capability later in the war to aid in the re-supply of Arab forces as they move west'*

The bolt-on stealth visibility reduction system on the S-37 that the Chinese referred to was a response by Russia over concerns that the technology on the American stealth aircraft, the F-117A and B-2A, was disproportionately expensive when judged in terms of its cost and the aircraft's flying ability. The Russians had been working on an alternative for years to reduce radar cross sections and the bolt-on addition worked by enveloping the aircraft in a cloud of artificial plasma, which made the aircraft invisible to radar.

'*Secondly,* said Zhou, *we require you to provide us with two of your most modern Aircraft Carriers in anticipation of the invasion of the Australian continent…*

And finally…. we want you to provide training for 500 North Korean pilots in the Sukhoi MK3 model fighter, provide all the armaments and logistical support infrastructure and ensure that within 4-years they have access to 240 of these aircraft, along with 200 more upgraded Mig 29 Fulcrums'.

'*You ask a lot, Chairman Zhou, but, subject to the President's approval, we will abide by the requests. If our air force is to be used to protect the Arab invasion forces I insist that Russian liaison officers are inserted into the forward Arab elements to ensure our aircraft are not fired upon by Arab forces. The Arabs will no doubt have large Air Defence systems available and I want to ensure Russian military air controllers are present during such interdiction missions'.*

Zhou nodded…'*I would expect nothing less'*…

After 3 intense days of detailed briefings and meetings, protocols were agreed on all the issues raised, before all parties then left to inform their immediate superiors of the historic agreement reached in Beijing this day. China had one final important task to complete and that was to convince Turkey to be a facilitator for the invasion. This they would work towards but leave until later before making the approach. After the Russian delegation departed, Zhou sat down and reflected on what had just been agreed. He had no second thoughts about what had been discussed with the Russians and, although he knew in a few years time it would cost the lives of millions of people and change the world in a way never before imagined, Zhou left the office contented and, for the first night in weeks, slept soundly.

PART 7

MARCH FROM THE EAST
(D+1)

DTG: January 25th 2012

LOCATION: EDWARDS AIR FORCE BASE in the United States and unspecified locations in the Middle East and Turkey

SITUATION: The world is in shock.... but elsewhere, the unimaginable and overwhelming apocalyptic events taking place across the world are a sign for others to begin their quest for power, revenge and world domination.

For those with knowledge of Dragon's Breath, the detonation of a nuclear device in Washington DC had left them all open-mouthed, but they knew it to be the signal they had been waiting for and, by the 25th January 2012, more than 1.7 million Arabs were on the march. These were the first of a combined force from an initial 3 million troops generated by Iran, Saudi Arabia, Syria, Egypt and Iraq. Iraqi Shiite militia groups had provided a large source of manpower and these had trained extensively in Iran, ready to fight alongside their Iranian brethren. Equipped with the latest weaponry from Russia and China, their leaders were sending their forces to engage the West in a war designed to eradicate once and for all what they saw as Western interference in Arab lands, which they believed undermined Islam. For the militant Arab nations it was the start of a journey that was to end with the ultimate destruction of what they called the Great Satan. Iran would finally be avenged and Israel would be alone and vulnerable in the region with the world witnessing, at long last, the strength gained from Arab unity.

In the United States, 12 elected senators had escaped the inferno in Washington DC by being out of the city for various reasons and now 15hrs after America's worst ever atrocity, they found themselves underground at Edwards Air Force Base in California. They were the only ones left from a privileged group of people- the elected few. One thing was certain, the President and all her immediate government officials were dead, along with more than 320,000 others and God knows how many more injured. There were no past presidents alive or capable of stepping into the breech, so to speak; therefore, it would have to be decided between the remaining 12 who was to be nominated President, as there had to be order and, a response to the atrocity. The magnitude of what had occurred had not yet sunk in and the nation was in complete shock. That nation would need strong leadership today and it would have to come from the group present, for the short term at least. The alternative was a military figure but the majority of high-ranking military personnel present dismissed this. It was General William C Bracken, the Chief of Staff, who had strongly suggested that a military figure should not head up the government because there were elected politicians still alive; as he put it, *'It had to be an elected civilian official, otherwise democracy would fail the country when it needed it the most'*. The vote was simple and without recrimination with the 12 men present only having to write down who their nomination was before he with the most votes was passed as President. He with the second most votes would be Vice President. Present in the room were 7 Republicans and 5 Democrats.

Halfway across the world, and with the world's media focused entirely on the events in the United States and Europe, the Iranian 11th Army Group was already into Southern Turkey with its columns spreading out behind it for mile upon mile. Included in its inventory and controlled by the Revolutionary Guards were large numbers of its Shahab-1, Shahab-2 and Shahab-3 ballistic missiles along with their newer cousin, the Ghader missile. All have a nuclear carrying capability but these were solely fitted with conventional warheads. Produced by the Hemmat Industries Group Factory (an important branch of Iran's Aerospace Industries Group) the Shahab missiles have a range of 1,300 to 1,900km (800-1,100 miles) and the Ghader 2,500 to 3,000km (1,150-1,850 miles). Once they entered the Balkans… Paris and even the United Kingdom would be in range.

There had never been such a powerful force mustered by the Arab World. Ever since the new equipment and weaponry arrived 18 months ago the soldiers had been training hard…but for what they had not known. Fuel for the Arabs initial transit through Turkey would be provided by the Turkish authorities, with the Arabs vast logistical back up held in reserve. The logistics for this massive operation were the key to its success and the Chinese had presented the Arabs with logistical demands as early as 2009. The Chinese knew it was logistics that maintained an army in the field and as an army marches on its stomach the feeding, equipping, refueling and rearming of such a large number of men and machine was fundamental to its success. History was littered with military disasters emanating from poor logistical practices and the Chinese had learnt from past failures in maintaining huge armies. They had passed this knowledge on to the Arabs and they soon realised that this would be crucial as their lines of communication became stretched.

Across in the west of Turkey, 19 Corp was waiting for elements of the 4th Army Group to form up before moving north. The Islamic 6th Army Group of 460,000-strong had advanced well into Turkey and this force was now heading swiftly for the Bosporus Strait near Istanbul. This stretch of water connecting the Mediterranean Sea with the Black Sea separates the European part of Turkey from its Asian counterpart. The Strait is 30km long, with a maximum width of 3,700-metres at the northern entrance, and a minimum width of 750-metres between Anadoluhisarı and Rumelihisarı with the strait crossed by 3 bridges. The first bridge is 1,074-metres long and was completed in 1973. The second bridge is 1,090-metres long, sits some 5km north of the first, and was completed in 1988. The third bridge, completed in 2010 stretches across the strait out to 1,084-metres. In addition to the bridges there is a rail tunnel, which was completed in 2008 and capable of transporting vehicles and men if required. The bridges are the strategic crossings into Europe and for that reason the area was saturated with concentrated, layered and integrated land and sea Air Defence (AD) Systems with the latest additions from the Turkish, Russian and Chinese Inventory.

Although not committing ground forces across its borders, Turkey knew its actions would be construed as aiding the enemy and, was, therefore, keen to protect its strategic links. Concerned by the threat from NATO air, they were using a tactical command and control system designed to collect air threat data from various types of radars.

These radars produced a real-time air picture for assigning anti-aircraft weapons for potential targets. The system consisted of air defence command posts at Army, Corps and Brigade levels. They were spread over a vast area with the capability to interface with units using long range, medium range and short-range air defence radars. There were also vehicles serving as interfaces to link the command posts to radar sites and weapons platforms. Finally tactical communications systems provided secure voice and data-links and maintained connectivity between sensors and weapons to minimise target interception time. Turkey also possessed advanced aircraft from its NATO days and these were deployed on interdiction missions against unfriendly aircraft. More than 150 F-16 fighter aircraft were on standby to interdict any aircraft entering Turkish airspace, with a further 100 in reserve. The first Tactical Air Force, with its Headquarters at Eskisehir Air Base in Western Turkey, was responsible for coordinating the Combat Air Patrols (CAP) over the Bosporus Straits. In addition to the Turkish contingent of aircraft, 76 F-16s from the Egyptian Air Force were also using Turkish airfields and providing air cover for the Arab ground forces.

Turkey's first line of air defence against any NATO aggression was the 4th generation Russian made 9M96E -S-400 Triumph -Theater Missile Defence (TMD) System. Capable of protecting several thousand square kilometres, even in conditions of electronic countermeasure deployment by an enemy, the S-400 Triumph came with its own network of early warning sensors, command posts, fire-control radars and anti-missile missiles. The threat from ground hugging cruise missiles from any direction plus tactical and strategic aircraft, including stealth, was the main reason for the deployment of the S-400. With the system under a sophisticated command, control, and communications (C3) umbrella the upgraded target acquisition radar and control system was capable of 3-dimensional, long-range surveillance out to 600km. Equipped with 16 of the latest upgraded S-400 missiles in each launcher, Turkey, had positioned 2-batteries in the region and these had the potential to shoot down NATOs early warning aircraft (AWAC). The engagement radar was capable of guiding 12 missiles at any one time and could simultaneously engage as many as 6 different targets. Once a target was selected the data would be relayed to the most optimal missile battery to launch the attack. An S-400 can be launched every few seconds before reaching its intercept speed thus engaging targets at altitudes from between 5-30km with its high explosive fragmentation warhead. If any missile or aircraft were to penetrate this defence then the next layer in the integrated system would attempt to hinder or destroy the attacking munitions. This next layer of air defence came from the TOR-M1 Surface-to-Air Missile System.

The Turkish army had received the Russian made TOR-M1 Surface-to-Air Missile System before the S-400 Triumph with this system designed for operations at medium, low and very low altitudes against helicopters, low flying aircraft and cruise missiles. At the Bosporus Straits its primary mission was to intercept guided missiles and precision weapons. Turkey had deployed 4 Battalions' worth of TOR-M1 with each Battalion containing 5 Companies. Each Company had at their disposal 4-missile Transporter Launcher Vehicles (TLV) with each TLV equipped with 8 ready to launch missiles, associated radars, fire control systems and a battery command post. This gave the Turkish military the ability to launch 640 missiles from this one system. The TOR-M1 was an important addition to Turkey's integrated air defence capability as it was capable of operating in an intensive jamming environment from a stationary location or on the move with an ability to track up to 48 targets while engaging 2 targets simultaneously. The missile, fitted with a proximity fuse and 15kg fragmentation warhead, was capable of downing whatever NATO could throw at it. The missile system was a pilot's worst nightmare and with speeds of up to 700-metres per second at a distance of 1–12km plus 30g-force maneuverability, it was easy to understand why.

With over 1,500 man-portable SAMs spread amongst the ground troops the airspace over the Bosporus Straits was probably the most heavily defended area in the world outside of the North Korea capital Pyeongyang. This was further enhanced out to sea; with Turkey positioning some of its German designed MEKO-200 Frigates equipped with Sea Sparrow Surface-to-Air Missile (SAM) Systems.

Turkey had been carefully courted and then eventually approached by the Chinese 2-years ago and presented with the opportunity to exact revenge for the bombing of their forces in 2006. This approach culminated in an agreement between the 2-countries, which allowed for specialist Chinese units to be secretly deployed onto Turkish soil with their recently developed anti-satellite (ASAT) capability. This system incorporated advanced laser radar with the capability to track satellites in high or low orbit and, emit a jamming capability against the satellite as it passed over. China had hoped that by 2012 its new satellite network called Compass would be up and running but technical difficulties had prevented this. Compass was designed to interface with the US military M-Code, which was the Pentagon's GPS broadcast. The aim would have been to deploy these systems on the ground with the capability to jam GPS guided weapons.

In Europe the West was struggling to come to terms with what had occurred in its major cities especially with the lack of power, fuel, gas, continual communication blackouts and public disorder. They would soon have to come to terms with no more future supplies of Russian gas or Middle Eastern oil. The overwhelming and ongoing human tragedy was further compounded by most countries' inability to provide care for the thousands of nuclear casualties with medical facilities rendered almost impotent. The fallout from this, coupled with the terrorist attacks against Western military commands and civilian facilities continued to consume precious resources. The UK, Spain and France were quickly placed under administrative military law until a government could be formed. Germany had decided to go the American route and an alliance of remaining MPs was looking to form an emergency government. Little did they know that within 24 to 48hrs time, they would be looking at events rather differently, when news of an Arab army making its way through Turkey and towards Europe, reached them. The attacks on the United States, Europe and NATO would have been more than enough to contend with even for an experienced government, never mind a freshly formed one. The horrific events had shaken the world to its core, but what the world and these new governments didn't know, was that this was only the beginning of Dragon's Claw and, the events that were to unfold over the following 3-weeks would make the world shudder even more and, cause despair for millions. It would be despair from knowing that the only world they knew was about to change forever. For those in America and Europe, it already had.

PART 8

DIEGO GARCIA
(D+3)

DTG: Friday- January 27th…..2012…..2000hrs

LOCATION: The Indian Ocean

SITUATION: 6-metres under the Indian Ocean, Task Force Sung –a 12 strong submarine force is about to surface after departing their secret base more than 4-weeks ago.

25 nautical miles northwest of Diego Garcia in the Indian Ocean and over the horizon from any land based prying eyes; Captain Kim Sun Lee of the North Korean Navy pressed his eyes to the periscope lens and scanned a full 360 degrees. Captain Lee was the commander of the submarine element of Task Force Sung and one of the most decorated and experienced submariners in the North Korean Navy having conducted numerous covert insertions of North Korean agents into South Korea over the last 17-years. They had sailed over 6,000 miles for this and, although his vessel had a range of 7,500 miles in the snorkelling mode, he had received two fuel re-supplies in the dead of night from a purpose built Chinese supply vessel, which was capable of refueling four submarines at a time. From their secret base on the Chinese/Vietnamese border they had made their way down into the South China Sea, past the contested Spratly Islands and beyond Malaysia and Indonesia before entering the Java Trench, which lies south of Indonesia's capital Jakarta. Task Force Sung then turned on a heading northeast into the Indian Ocean. Submerged, Lee's vessel could reach a speed of 20 knots and most of the journey had been underwater; only surfacing at night for the planned rendezvous (RV) with the re-supply ship.

There was just a slight swell at the surface and with a quarter moon it was a perfect night for the work they were about to undertake. Lee closed the periscope and ordered his executive officer to surface. With a displacement of 3,126 tons submerged and a crew of 52, the Improved Kilo-class Type 636 Diesel-Electric Submarine came equipped with six 21-inch torpedo tubes and 18 torpedoes. The flooding ports had been removed from the fore-body in order to reduce the submarine's acoustic signature and the hull was covered with rubber anti-sonar protection tiles to reduce risk of detection. Fitted with the MGK-400EM digital sonar the vessel was able to detect other submarine and surface ship targets in sonar listening mode at a range 3-4 times greater than it can be detected itself. In periscope and surface modes the submarine's radar provided the commander with information on the underwater and air situation. Once above the water line a final visual observatory check was conducted to ascertain that there were no ships or aircraft in the vicinity before a single sonar wave boomed out from the Kilo. 5-minutes later, 11 other Kilo-class Submarines had surfaced within a radius of a few hundred meters. 8 of the 12 Kilos were carrying 15 North Korean Special Forces Suicide Commandos each and the space taken by these 15 extra men with their equipment and Medium Inflatable Boats (MIBs), meant that 4 Torpedoes from a total of 18 in each boat had to be sacrificed.

Once the Kilos were on the surface, commandos immediately appeared on deck and began hauling up 2-tightly folded 8-metre MIBs from each submarine, 2 four-stroke 30 horse power outboard engines, 12 fuel bladders per inflatable and, their allocation of weapons and explosives in purpose made black waterproof bags. The air bottles attached to the folded up inflatables were cranked open and within 6-minutes the fully inflated boats were lowered into the water. It took a further 30-minutes to fit the engines (which were lowered over the side by ropes) attach the fuel bladders, pump the fuel through the system and start the engines. The fuel bladders and waterproof equipment bags were firmly attached to the fixed D-rings in the boats so that no equipment would be lost if any boats capsized. There was a group of 15-commandos split between each pair of boats and 50-minutes after surfacing; all 16 inflatables had rendesvoused together just 200-meters from the submarines and, who had now disappeared beneath the waves.

The commandos were elated to be out of the cramped and claustrophobic tube they had called home these past few weeks. They were now in their domain and, the excitement, tinged with a slight anxiety was evident in some of their faces, with all the commandos feeling the immediate difference from a training scenario to a real live operation. The adrenalin, surging strongly through their veins would be enough to keep them awake all night. As single men, they had been specially selected, sent to China in January 2011, trained alongside the crews of the Kilo's for almost 12 months and, before dawn, their training was about to be tested. They switched on their Global Positioning System (GPS) to confirm their location, ensured their individual night vision goggles were operating correctly and then received final confirmatory battle orders from their commander, Major Han Youg San. He reiterated the importance of the task at hand, confirmed the order of march (OOM) i.e. the order in which the inflatables were to move and clarified the final assault groupings. A time check was conducted so all the commando's watches were synchronized. He finished by covering critical actions on should anything go wrong and wished all his men luck. He had spent almost a year with these men and they were like brothers to him. He trusted each and every one implicitly with his life. He knew, as did his men, that most if not all would die on this island once they went noisy but the sacrifice would be worth the glorious death they may have to face.

Major San, believed it to be a Great honour to have been chosen by their irrepressible Leader and be the ones to fire the opening shots in the Great War. Before setting off for the beach, each boat cracked an infrared light-stick and attached it to the rear of their inflatable, so those following could see it using their night vision goggles. There were no other lights used during the transit to shore with the North Korean commandos now excited at the prospect of destroying the home of the American B-52 and its more modern successor, the B-2 Stealth Bomber.

The covert amphibious insertion party set off in 2 separate groups of 8 boats, approximately 100-meters between them and, in parallel. Each group then split into 2 lines of 4 boats approximately 20-metres apart and no more than 20-metres behind each other to aid command and control during the transit. They then sped towards the Island at 8 knots per hour; with their handheld GPS guiding them to a pre-determined RV point 2-miles off shore.

Diego Garcia, part of the British Indian Ocean Territory and now leased to the United States can best be described as a V-shaped island, approximately 60km round with a maximum elevation above sea level of 7-metres. The V was the actual land part of the island with the top or northern segment part of the V the open gateway into the enclosed and sheltered lagoon. The top of the V can best be described as an almost closed area caused by small islands and reefs running from west to east. Once ships pass these obstacles, entrance into the 20km by 9km wide lagoon is achieved. A channel called Main Pass remains open on the northwestern corner of the V to allow shipping in and out. The lagoon is no more than 20-30 metres deep and has a large anchorage area within the lagoon adjacent to the airfield, which lies on the west side of the island. Although the anchorage area is dredged the route in through the open V can be difficult to navigate through the narrow channels. The route for shipping is via Main Pass, which lies between West Island near Eclipse Point on the northwestern part of the island where the main base area is situated and Spur Reef and Middle Island almost 2.5km away to the northeast. Buoys mark the entrance through Main Pass. This allows cargo vessels and naval ships into Eclipse Bay and the anchorage area. The island is home to 1,000 US and, approximately 40 UK military personnel working to support the large base, with the vast majority of 3,500 people made up of third country nationals. The base has 2 functions. Firstly, it is a strategic location for bomber command to position their long-range bombers and secondly, it is a war stock storage facility. In addition to the bomber squadrons on site the facilities include a Naval Computer and Telecommunications Station, the Maritime Pre-positioning Ship Squadron Two (MPSRON Two), which is responsible for the ships anchored in the lagoon and the pre-positioned cargo for US military services, the Military Sealift Command (MSC), and COMPSRON Two, which controls the MSC ships.

There is also an Air Force and Army support element on the island. As part of the Navy's Strategic Sealift Capability, Squadron Two (the Maritime Pre-positioning Ship Squadron) have a clear mission - to provide command and control to facilitate sea transportation of large sets of vital military equipment and supplies to a designated area of operations. The US army called these pre-positioned stocks 'pre-po' for short and the Pentagon pays millions of dollars a year to maintain these fleets. In a crisis, troops would be airlifted to an area and the equipment stored in Diego Garcia would be shipped to them, thus negating a massive sealift from the United States.

Pre-positioned in the lagoon were more than 80 cargo vessels, including the USNS Denobola- a cargo ship, which uses Diego Garcia as its homeport. Tonight, the anchored ships were considered priority-2 targets with the strategic bombers the main effort. Two aircraft in particular were top of the list and any others would be regarded as a bonus. The B-52H Stratofortress, a multi-role bomber capable of carrying a 70,000 lb payload of conventional free fall ordnance and cruise missile weapons internally and externally and, the 5 B-2 Spirit Stealth Bombers. Both have the capability to deliver conventional and nuclear munitions and, in conjunction with the B-52, the B-2 Spirit provides the US with a capability far in excess of its numbers and the location allows for short 5-6hr flights to the Middle East and Asia. The capability of the B-2 to penetrate air defences and the payload delivered by both aircraft was the main reason why this 17-square mile/44-square kilometre atoll was earmarked as a priority target.

On shore, the US inhabitants on the island were still glued to their TVs attempting to grasp the enormity of the past 48hrs in the United States and Europe. They had witnessed the destruction of Washington DC live on prime time TV and were now hungry for snippets of news. The news had earlier alluded to 12 politicians surviving the explosion before they were taken to an undisclosed facility where they had chosen a new President. The emergency Presidential vote had installed President Jacob Manfred Maxwell, a Republican senator from Florida State, as the one chosen to lead the country in its time of crisis with Senator Carl Manish from Kansas, a Democrat, receiving enough votes to be chosen as the Vice President. They had appeared on TV together and asked for calm, outlined the rescue and recovery efforts and spelled out the cost in human lives lost. They acknowledged the vote was unconstitutional in that the people had not voted for the President, but hoped that the American people would accept the reasoning behind it. The President had also spoken of a robust and measured response to the events of January 24 but what that was had yet to be determined. They had seen the statement from Al Qaeda claiming the device in America and, their subsequent video claiming the nuclear and conventional attacks all over Europe. The world in 24hrs had been literally turned on its head and it was more akin to watching a Hollywood disaster movie than real events, but this time it was real, and the enormity of it all had hit home hard. No one spoke of anything else other than the events at home and in Europe; with many, still too numb to be angry at what had occurred. The anger would come later…that is if they were still alive the next morning…

2-miles off the coast and almost due west of the airfield, the 16-inflatables roped up into 3 separate groups for their final preparation. Each commando opened his waterproof bag and removed his NIKONOV AN-94 Abakan assault rifle. This was the folding stock variety equipped with a 30-round magazine and, an effective range of 700-metres. These weapons were normally issued only to Russian Elite Forces…. that was until 2-years ago when North Korea received shipments to equip its own 120,000 strong Special Forces. A key characteristic of this weapon was the 2-round burst mode and not the 3-round burst mode that some assault rifles incorporate. It was still fitted with the standard single shot and full automatic options but the 2-round burst was different in that it was fired at a very high rate of fire and, from a distance of 100-metres the 2-rounds almost pass through the same hole. With the increased rate of fire came increased bullet velocity, which meant the projectile had the capability to defeat normal 7.62mm body armour. The weapon was fitted with a red dot laser site, which was operated by the firer on the stock of the weapon. A torch similar to a surefire was slung under the stock and fitted with a detachable infrared filter over the lens so that it could be used in conjunction with the night vision goggles for very dark recesses. Their combat assault vests were removed from the waterproof bag and this now took the place of their Special Forces life vest, which was then worn on top of the assault vest. The medium sized backpacks would be kept in their waterproof bags as these contained High Explosive and White Phosphorous Grenades and numerous explosive door charges. The teams taking the airfield also carried specially made aircraft charges with the electrical detonators attached to a 2kg charge and a 30-second digital timer. The charge came with its own 2-sided adhesive strip, which was strong enough to hang upside down and support its own weight on any surface. Once a target was acquired a commando peeled off the protective strip, attached the charge to the target, removed the small safety pin on the timer and pressed the green illuminated button on the timer. This gave the attacker seconds to vacate the area before the charge exploded.

Split between the boats was a mixture of Rocket Propelled Grenade (RPG) launchers. The RPG-7 and advanced RPG-26 and RPG-27. The RPG-7 is a re-loadable, shoulder-fired, antitank and antipersonnel rocket propelled grenade launcher that launches its High Explosive Anti Tank (HEAT) grenade a maximum of 500-metres against stationary targets with each commando carrying 2 additional grenades for the RPG-7 launchers. The RPG 26 and 27 were effective for anti tank, anti personnel and anti material missions and purpose made for operations in built up areas. With an effective range of 250-metres the RPG 26 and 27 would be ideal for the assault against the Main Base Area and the buildings near the airport.

The airfield assault teams also carried 2 RPG-7V1 fitted with infrared and passive night sights. The RPG-7V1 fired the single-stage 4.5kg 105mm thermobaric warhead, which exploded some 2-metres from a target with devastating effects and had a kill radius of 10-metres. It was particularly effective against trenches, bunkers or light armoured vehicles and would be used to good effect against aircraft in the open.

Finally, every man less the dedicated RPG-7, 26-27 and RPG-7V1 firers carried 1 x RPG-18. This was a light short-range weapon similar in design to the American 66mm Light Anti Tank Weapon (LAW) with an effective range of 200-metres. These were slung over the shoulder by the operator and when required were extended, armed and fired.

Included in the firepower arsenal was 6 Infantry Support Weapons; the Type 67- 7.62mm General Purpose Machine Gun (GPMG) complete with night vision scope. The Type 67 is a gas operated; belt-fed, air-cooled, automatic firing-only GPMG and each man carried a 250-round belt of linked ammunition for this weapon. The commandos carried no food, only one bottle of water and no centralised medical equipment. Each man carried a pharyngeal airway, a suction bottle for clearing an airway, 4 personal first field dressings, 4 compression bandages, one tourniquet, 2-litres of blood replacement fluids along with fluid giving sets, 2 packets of quik-clot powder designed to stop arterial bleeding and 2 syringes of morphine.

30-round magazines were loaded on to the weapons and the weapons then made ready with the safety applied. A safety line was attached to the butt of the rifle and a snap D-ring clipped on to the commandos assault vest in case of capsize on the final approach. This was unlikely as the sea was relatively calm and the satellite photographs supplied by Chinese intelligence showed no surf on approach to their landing point. Small waterproof lightweight radios were attached to the vests but would not be switched on until contact with the enemy. Major San was content that he and his men could have done this without radios as they had rehearsed until they knew it blindfolded but the Chinese had insisted on them. The final act was reapplying their black face cream before moving off to their landing points. The first group of 4 boats (30 men) headed north towards Simpson Point before moving northeast along the coast. At 0130hrs hours they made land some 200-metres to the North of the main base area. After making land the boats were cached and a final reconnaissance conducted by the commander of the group and the assault team commanders. One hour later they were giving confirmatory battle orders to their teams before moving to their Final Assault Position (FAP). This group's main mission was to engage and kill the enemy in the vicinity of the main base area in order to destroy as much of the facility as possible.

A group of 6 boats (45 men) with Major San moved due east to the northern most aspect of the airfield and the final group of 6 boats (45 men) southeast to the southern aspect of the runway. Their mission was to assault the airfield simultaneously in order to destroy all B-52 and B2 bombers in situ. The assault was timed for 0300hrs. They reached the shore at 0115hrs and, after clearing the beach and posting sentries, proceeded to remove all the remaining equipment needed for the operation from the waterproof bags. The heavy outboard engines were placed inside the boats and strapped down. Two commandos to each inflatable then pushed the boat out to a depth of 1.5-metres and slashed the sides with their bayonets. There was no real attempt to cache the boats properly as this was a one-way trip and this quick sinking method ensured that the boats would not be found on the shore should a strolling couple or guard walk by. By first light it would be immaterial if they were found, as the attack on Diego Garcia would have already started.

At a depth of 30-metres Capt Lee and the rest of his submarine pack were inching slowly towards the mouth of the V. Their attack was to begin at 0305hrs. Their target was the plethora of cargo ships anchored in the lagoon. The 12 submarines had the capacity to release 184 torpedoes and this was more than enough for the 83 ships at anchor. Redundancy had been planned from the beginning and Lee could afford to lose 2 submarines and still complete his mission with what remained. The submarine force came within 1km of the Main Pass channel before each vessel entered Eclipse Bay with a 6-minute gap between them. Manoeuvering slowly and with stealth they came to rest in their designated firing points less than 700-metres from their predetermined targets. Lee was the first to enter at 0030hrs and, as planned, took the most easterly slot over towards Orient Bay on the edge of the anchorage area. He came up to periscope depth and scanned the scene in front of him and felt a surge of pride that his crew and the North Korean Navy had crept right in under the enemy's nose. In his sights lay a multitude of ships crammed with billions of dollars of key equipment and munitions. It would be like shooting ducks in a barrel. Satisfied with his location, he downed periscope and gave the order for the Kilo to sink to the seabed some 35-metres below. The remaining submarines entered, took up their positions, and after periscope checks, sank slowly to the sea floor ensuring all were in position by 0200hrs. At 0250hrs they would begin their rise to periscope depth, confirm their primary targets as rehearsed and input firing data for the first torpedoes. Satellite imagery had already provided a layout of the ships at anchor and, apart from a few small additions since it was taken, the plan required no altering. The Kilo's were laid out in an L or hook shape with the submarine of Captain Lee being the eye of the hook. Captain Lee's submarine was positioned on the northeastern tip and on a line running northeast to southwest were 7 other Kilos with the remaining four curving southeast to complete the hook. The anchorage area was covered on two sides and perfect shot scenarios for all the Kilos would be achieved.

On land the 2-airfield assault groups were now in their Final Assault Positions (FAPs). They were on the fringe of the airfield with excellent views and about to cross the start-line, the imaginary line that troops cross to begin their assault. No guards were apparent other than the odd vehicle lights every now and then and in the distance they could just make out the huge wingspan of what appeared to be B-52 Bombers. Major San looked at his watch. It was 0253hrs, only 7-minutes to H hour.

At 0300hrs the airfield assault teams began the assault using a technique called a creeping startline. This is where troops advance to contact quietly, hoping to get as close to the enemy before contact is made. Once the enemy is aware of their presence the teams can go noisy. They quickly made entry through the mesh fence and began to close the distance between them and their ultimate targets. 90-men were now swarming towards the main airport facilities and aircraft areas from 2 separate directions. To the north, the main base area assault group waited precisely 3-minutes after H-Hour and at 0303hrs started pouring hundreds of 7.62 rounds from their Type 67- 7.62mm GPMG's and dozens of explosive grenades from their RPG's into the buildings and at the military vehicles present. The initial shock effect lasted for 1-minute before the 30-man team began to advance quickly and systematically to clear the area.

At 0307hrs the airfield went noisy. Two US Air Force guards on vehicle patrol, having been aware of a huge explosion in the bay, noted people moving around the northern tip of the runway and approached them with flashing lights. One of the GPMG men and 2 other commandos had lay flat facing the oncoming vehicle and as it approached they fired at the vehicle from a distance of 35-meters. The driver and passenger were killed instantly as the bullets ripped through flesh and metal without resistance. It came to a halt with one headlight still on, the engine still running and water pouring from the radiator. The explosion in the bay and the sounds of shooting in the airport had come too late for the occupants of this small island and 90 trained killers were now in the main airport area wreaking havoc.

In the lagoon, 12 Kilo-class submarines were busily inputting fire data into their TEST-71MKE TV electric homing torpedoes, which allow the operator to switch targets if required. The remainder of the torpedoes were fired from the six 533mm torpedo tubes and loaded via the automatic rapid loader. This system allowed 2 targets to be engaged simultaneously. Only 2 of the launch tubes were able to fire the active sonar homing torpedo with TV guidance and at 0306hrs the first of what was to be a total of 138 torpedoes was fired towards the USNS Denobola; less than a minute later a warhead of 205kg of explosives exploded below the water line, lifted the Denobola up out of the water and broke her back.... she sank within 2-minutes.

Within 45-minutes the entire US war stock in Diego Garcia would be lying on the ocean floor. The first shots in the new Korean War had been fired.

In the vicinity of the airfield the first charges were placed on the first B-52s at 0317hrs and exploded, resulting in the aircraft catching fire or having their wings severely damaged. By 0355hrs all the B-52s stationed at Diego Garcia had been destroyed. Small firefights were now developing around the base but surprise and overwhelming firepower from the North Korean commandos placed them in the ascendancy. By 0500hrs the base would be in their hands with 250 prisoners and more than 400 people killed including 21 North Korean commandos. The 5 special shelters built for the B-2 Stealth Bomber would also be opened and the aircraft destroyed before 0600hrs. The commandos now focused on secondary targets and ensured over the next 8hrs that all fuel supplies, communication facilities and any military buildings were destroyed beyond repair. Major San and his men were surprised how ineffective the defence of the base had been but he put this down to its inaccessibility, a false belief that no-one would ever attack this location and the boredom one must encounter living on this thin strip of land in the middle of the Indian Ocean.

At the Main Base Area the carnage was similar to that at the airfield but there had been a concerted effort to take on the attackers after the initial shock effect of the assault, however, it turned out to be a passing moment, with the majority of people running away or too terrified to approach this unknown enemy and by first light the North Korean commandos would have accumulated over 260 prisoners. The North Korean's, not without casualties themselves, lost 6 of their own during the night.

Major San and his men were only interested in the military infrastructure and the next day began to load prisoners into the small boats harboured in the lagoon. They were given water and food and informed to head to the nearest inhabited island, away from Diego Garcia and, approximately 60km away to the northwest. The commandos did not want military hostages, as all their remaining personnel would be needed for the battle ahead when American forces arrived to retake the Island.

Major San had lost a quarter of his force in taking Diego Garcia but now he and his men would build defences, set booby traps and wait for the Americans to arrive. San and his commandos were prepared to die to a man for their country and within 8 days almost all would have their wish as more than 2,000 Marines and 60 SEAL Team 6 personnel re-took the Island. Major San was killed with only 2 Koreans taken alive from the 93 that remained. The US Marines and SEALs suffered a combined total of 31 Killed in Action (KIA) and 13 wounded in the initial assault and subsequent clearance operations.

60-miles out to sea Captain Lee and his submerged Kilo-class assault force were already moving northeast from the islands at 20-knots. When night came they would surface and travel at 11-knots and look forward to being hailed as heroes on their return to their home base. Lee's mind wandered briefly and he thought of Major San and the sacrifice he and his men were making on Diego Garcia. Why couldn't they have returned to the submarines and enjoyed the welcome their heroic action deserved? Lee could not understand the death wish these men had but he admired their devotion to duty and was proud to be associated with such dedicated professional soldiers. They had worked together for almost 12 months but, it was now over and only time would tell if North Korea could win the war. What Lee and his men didn't know was that the war they had started was just a small piece of the jigsaw in a larger world conflict. They had no idea that nuclear devices had been detonated on Western soil or that Europe had been attacked by huge numbers of Mujihadeen fighters; so, as he reflected on his own part to unite Korea, he remained ignorant to the fact that a huge Arabic army was moving steadily towards Western Europe and that Australia and India were next on the list to feel the effects of Dragon's Claw.

At around the same time that Lee and San were beginning their mission in Diego Garcia thousands of North Korean Special Forces infiltrators in South Korea were launching similar actions to those conducted in Europe by Mujihadeen fighters. Over 50 US bases had been earmarked as key targets as well as power and communication facilities along with key government and military personnel. These were tactics designed to blind and throw an enemy off balance and while this was in process the largest artillery barrage since the 2nd Gulf War erupted across the demilitarised zone (DMZ) near the 38th parallel.

EDWARDS AIR FORCE BASE - California's Mojave Desert…January 27th…1200hrs…one hour before the attack on Diego Garcia and The Korean Peninsula..

In the emergency briefing rooms, the Chief of Staff of the United States Army and Chairman of the Joint Chiefs of Staff (chief military adviser to the President of the United States), General William C Bracken, had requested the newly installed President - President Maxwell - and Vice President Carl Manish to attend an emergency briefing. It had been requested by the newly installed National Security Advisor (NSA) who serves as the Chief Advisor to the President of the United States on national security issues. Ross Cochrane, the new NSA had taken over 36hrs earlier from his predecessor Norman Carmichael who died in Washington DC along with his President. Also present were the Director of the Central Intelligence Agency, David Manheim, and the FBI Director Stephanie Peters. From the Joint Chiefs of Staff were Admiral Vernon Davis, Chief of Naval Operations; General Charles S Beasley, Chief of Staff of the US Air Force and General Richard Shuster the third, Commandant of the US Marine Corps.

Maxwell came right to the point….*'what's going on Ross?'*

'Mr President. *Firstly, the rescue operation in Washington goes as well as can be expected and, as you have directed, we now have huge civil and military resources in situ aiding those injured. In addition to the rescue effort, Stephanie* (FBI Director) *informs me that the FBI are hitting all known terrorist cells and Islamic organizations all over the country in an effort to ascertain how this device came into the country and who was behind it. We are also fearful of another device but so far we have no information to confirm or deny this. We know Al Qaeda have claimed this device and those in Europe but its difficult to believe they got it here without help, however, after 650 arrests in 48hrs and numerous searches we have found nothing to suggest state help in getting this device in to the United States'.*

*'Very well Ross,…keep at it,…it's imperative that we find out if there are any more of those nukes in our country and I want this country turned upside down until we confirm it one way or another. I don't care whose human rights we tread on while this search is ongoing - we'll loosen the screw on these organizations once we know for sure. I want the CIA involved in this as well David so crunch the numbers with Stephanie after this meeting'…*David Manheim CIA Director nodded and scribbled some notes….*I'll also need a conference call set up Ross, to the Director of FEMA* (The Federal Emergency Management Agency), *to discuss his request for more resources in the next few hours…let me know when the link is ready'*

President Maxwell looked at his National Security Advisor and realised there was something more pressing than the events going on in Washington DC… *'What is it Ross…you didn't call this meeting just for Washington did you?'*

'Mr President…….' Ross Cochrane hesitated and looked around the room at the faces around him and sensed the anticipation. He was fresh to the job and it was showing slightly as world events started unfolding at pace. He composed himself and began again.. *'Mr President, I have just received unconfirmed information from Israeli intelligence that large numbers of Arabic forces began moving through Turkey towards Eastern Europe within hours of the nuclear devices exploding…and whatever is going on over there, it appears that Turkey is allowing it to happen'*

'Large numbers…what do you mean by large numbers?' said Bracken.

'The information was specific, General, and quotes an army. The CIA is attempting to verify from our own sources as we speak and we have satellite passes within the next few hours but the low cloud in the region may prevent confirmation by this means' replied Cochrane

'Jesus' said General Shuster, *'it sounds like an invasion!'*

'That's not all Mr President' said Cochrane

'Go on Ross'

'We have been receiving reports that all maritime vessels in the Middle East have been impounded and the crews arrested. This means that all crude oil from the region has stopped and we now know that Russia has halted natural gas supplies to France, Germany and Italy in response to terrorist actions in Europe'

'Have the countries involved made any statements or explained their actions?' asked Bracken

'None at all,' said Cochrane…*'in fact, we have been unable to reach any of the government officials or Ambassadors from the Arabic countries involved'*

'Mr President, …interjected General Shuster…Commandant of the US Marine Corps, its too much of a coincidence that we have a nuclear decapitation of the West's most prominent leaders…not to mention the hundreds of thousands, if not millions, who have just died… and hours later an Arabic army is reported moving through Turkey. That and the seizure of our maritime assets is reason enough to declare war on these people and bomb the shit out of these bastards now'

President Maxwell rose from the table and with both palms on the desk, looked directly at Shuster.

'With respect, General…I am as angry as you about those who now lie dead…many of them were very close personal friends of mine and I also think we have all made the same assumption on the coincidences that you speak of, especially with the coordinated conventional attacks on NATO airfields and facilities in mainland Europe. It has all the hallmarks of a precursor to invasion; however, it was probably bombing the shit out of these bastards, as you put it, that put the last 72hrs events in motion.

Why do you think we no longer have bases or Embassies in the Middle East? Why is the Islamic World so anti US when we've done more than most to supply Muslims worldwide with humanitarian aid? Why did Turkey leave NATO and why are they now looking at closer military ties with the rest of the Middle East, especially Egypt? I'll tell you why General…It's because our bombing diplomacy has backfired on us.

I was vehemently opposed to the bombings in 2006 of the Iranian nuclear facilities and the Turkish army in Kurdistan and, I am - for the moment - opposed against bombing Arabs in Turkey. We need answers, gentlemen, and we need information that's credible and workable. We need facts to base our assumptions on and we need them fast, but make no mistake; what has occurred here on our mainland will not go unchallenged and any response will be at our choosing, at our time and not based on any assumption. Correct me if I'm wrong General, but even with a large proportion of NATO airpower destroyed we still have enough to bomb any Arab army into oblivion if required'

General Shuster nodded and the President continued… *'So if we are to believe their attacks on NATO aircraft facilities have failed…their move into Europe appears flawed from the start. The biggest problem for NATO forces will be munitions stocks and fuel reserves, which I believe are already low. We'll need to get fresh ammunition supplies over there ASAP and I want diplomatic channels opened quickly to those countries in the Middle-East including Turkey to ascertain what the hell's going on'….* President Maxwell looked around the table looking for any more comments…He turned to his Vice president…*'Carl do you have anything to add?'*

'I'll look to chase the diplomatic negotiations up and get back to you… and I should have a detailed damage and loss assessment report this evening on the conventional attacks throughout Europe and the ongoing counter insurgency campaign. Initial reports are not good, Jacob, with a substantial loss of American and European lives and extensive damage to almost every major facility… civil and military. The United Kingdom is attempting to impose Marshal Law but is stretched militarily. They, along with France, Germany, Belgium and Spain are still in turmoil in much the same way as we are after Washington DC and they have to contend with an insurgency campaign as well. There are still large areas of Europe with no power, fuel or communications and with the continuing terrorist attacks, there are still no civilian aircraft flying over Europe'

'OK…thanks Carl,'… said the President… *'We'll speak later on this tonight and see if you can confirm who the new leaders of those countries who lost their governments are'…* President Maxwell turned back to his audience… *…..'Gentlemen…..let's get cracking. Admiral Davis, General Beasley and General Shuster …please remain behind with General Bracken as we need to discuss our military options - this meeting is now closed'*

Ross Cochrane exuded a small cough *'Excuse me, Mr President …there is one more thing, which may be nothing, but I think you should all know'…*

'go on…'

'The National Security Agency (NSA) is picking up unusually large amounts of encrypted military radio communications all along the DMZ in Korea'

'Ok Ross. Make sure your guys monitor this and keep me informed of any developments…but don't divert any more resources to it as the crocodile nearest the canoe is in Turkey at the minute and I want to know what those

people are up to….and get me the Russian President on the phone…I want to get his take on what he thinks may be going on '

'Yes Sir. I'll get right on it'

PART 9

OLD WOUNDS REOPENED
(D+ 4)

(THE KOREAN OFFENSIVE)

DTG: Saturday-January 28th...2012...0555hrs

LOCATION: A small US outpost overlooking the Joint Security Area (JSA) in Panmunjeom, Korea, on the Demilitarised Zone (DMZ).

SITUATION: 5-minutes before H-Hour...the coordinated attacks on Diego Garcia and South Korea are about to begin.

Sergeant Jorge Ramirez of the 1st Battalion, 506th Infantry Regiment, 2nd Infantry Division had been for his early morning training session, as he did most days, with half of his Platoon and, having finished, was stood outside drinking fresh coffee with 3 of his men before the cold forced him indoors for a hot shower and heavier clothing. It was a frosty but windless January morning and, as it often does in Korea at this time of the year, mist was hanging like a thick blanket over the valleys and low ground. Ramirez was still trying to adjust, as all his men were, to the news that their President and Commander in Chief, with almost all the elected politicians, had perished, along with thousands of other Americans at the hands of Al Qaeda. Although he knew thousands of North Korean Troops were just across the Demilitarised Zone (DMZ), Ramirez had personally grown fond of his surroundings in the 7-weeks he had been here, unlike a lot of others in Korea... and as he gazed northwards, he found the scenery peaceful, tranquil and almost beautiful. Yes...he was bored with the endless guards and duties like everyone else and training was at a premium on the line, but he managed to stay busy and he trained his men at every opportunity.

He and his men were based on high ground overlooking the small Joint Security Area (JSA) in Panmunjeom, on the western edge of the

4km DMZ between North and South. It is located 62km northwest of the South Korean capital, Seoul, on the Tongil-ro Highway and 215km south of the North Korean capital, Pyeongyang. The JSA is outside administrative control of South and North Korea; it is 800-metres across and consists of 35 personnel each from the UN and the North, with both sides operating 6 guard posts at the site. In 1953 the JSA was where the armistice negotiations took place to end the 1st Korean War. Both sides then decided to withdraw 2km from this location and nominated it as a meeting place for further talks involving political, military and economic issues.

Ramirez and his Platoon operated from 2 permanent bunker locations for 3-week stretches before moving back to camp Freedom Bridge just a few kilometres to his south. Anti-personnel radar antennae spun constantly, seeking out movement to the north. There were 35,000 American troops in South Korea with almost 15,000 of them spread along the DMZ in case the North Koreans decided it wanted to invade the South once more.

Ramirez was facing north as he swallowed the last mouthful of warm coffee. The coffee cup was still pursed against his lips when he heard the first faint rumble in the far distance. 5-seconds later the individual rumbles sounded like distant rolling thunder yet the skies were clear. Deep down Ramirez suspected what the sound was …yet his mind refused to accept what he was hearing…. it couldn't be…could it… not after all these years and now of all times? All across the 151 mile-long, 4km-wide demilitarised zone, American and mainly South Korean soldiers were listening to the same rumbling in the distance. It was constant now and had been going on for 30-seconds and still, some soldiers stood in the open and wondered if it really could be what many knew it to be. They were caught like rabbits in a car headlight and, instead of allowing their training to take over; they were refusing to believe what may be happening. Those less mesmerized started running for cover but for some it was too late. 43-seconds after the first rumble was heard, thousands of high explosive shells from the combined Kangdong Artillery Corps and 620 Artillery Corps began raining down on the DMZ and beyond - blowing defences, minefields, bunkers and men, including Ramirez and his entire Platoon, to pieces.

The Kangdong Artillery Corps was utilising 11 of its 16 artillery Brigades to slam what it called, first strike barrages of 122mm, 130mm, and 152mm artillery shells into the South Korean defensive line. In addition to this the Kangdong Corps other Brigades were firing 240mm Multiple Rocket Launchers (MRLs) from 700 of their MRL systems at targets deep into South Korea, including Seoul. 620 Corps was utilising 4 of its 6 Heavy Artillery Brigades firing 170mm Self Propelled Guns, 4 Brigades worth of 122mm, 130mm, and 152mm, plus 400 of its MRLs with their allocation of 240mm warheads, which were targeting depth targets. The combined total of 1,100 MRLs fired an astonishing salvo of some 26,000 rounds of high explosive within 44-seconds before quickly moving position due to concern over the time sensitive targeting capability of the US Forces' Precision/Rapid Counter Rocket Launcher. The MRL counter-fire system is devastatingly efficient when launched but, luckily for the Korean artillery units this morning, the difficult terrain and the fact that a sensor using infrared surveillance and target acquisition was not overhead meant that no data was being transmitted for the unit to conduct a counter battery strike. The North Koreans didn't know it at the time but with no sensor platform overhead, their artillery was operating with relative freedom. The remaining 21 North Korean artillery Brigades from a total of 43 were equipped with 120mm self-propelled guns, 152mm self-propelled mortars, 170mm Goksan guns with a range of 50km and 240mm multiple rocket launchers with a range of 45km. Within 3hrs of the first shells falling on South Korean soil, the US army bases at Camp Stanley, Colbern, K16, Ding-gu-chun, Pochun, Yijong-bu, Yon-chun, Paju and Munsan had been obliterated, with the Yongsan Garrison complex in Seoul, which contained all the command elements for forces in Korea on the receiving end of massive bombardments.

North Korean doctrine taught that deploying vast numbers of air defence systems would go some way to deterring any US air assets that would undoubtedly respond to the invasion. To combat this threat, huge numbers of SA-2 and SA-3 missiles had been deployed against low flying aircraft. The more potent SA-5, a missile designed to attack aircraft at higher altitudes and out to a range of 250km and, one that was capable of hitting targets flying over the middle of South Korea was also deployed in considerable numbers. There were thousands of shoulder launched anti-aircraft missiles deployed including some older Korean variants such as the Wha-sung, which came in 2 models; the SA-7 with a range of 5km and the SA-16 with a range of 10km. Included in the Air Defence inventory and the successor to the SAM-7, was the more advanced Russian Igla SA18. This system was regarded as one of the most sophisticated shoulder-held anti-aircraft missiles of its time due to its simplicity and in-built training system. It had a greater range, was resistant to most of the flares used to divert anti-aircraft missiles and capable of targeting any part of an aircraft, not only the heated rear section. To supplement their Air Defence, the North Koreans had tactically deployed over 25,000 anti-aircraft guns with calibres ranging from 37mm, 23mm, 57mm and 87mm. These were mainly manually operated and not subject to the Electronic Warfare (EW) capability of the US and South Korean Air Forces. To combat the EW capability each battery of guns was provided with the latest Chinese made portable GPS jamming device, which was designed to blind the American GPS guided munitions or at least prevent them from hitting their target with one hundred percent certainty. Although a large improvement on the Russian made system used in Iraq in 2002, the Chinese versions were still electronically visible when jamming and open to American targeting.

Across South Korea, North Korean Special Forces were taking their regular and irregular war doctrine to the whole of the Southern Peninsula and were wreaking havoc across the country by attacking key military and civilian facilities, not to mention taking up precious resources from the South Korean military that had to find and destroy these forces.

It was well known that North Korean weaponry was inferior to the US and South Korean inventory and that overwhelming artillery strikes and huge manpower numbers would be the main threats. To even out the technological playing field, the enormous rearmament by China had started fairly soon after the meeting in Beijing in 2008. First on the agenda were aircraft, as Korean aircraft were no match for their US counterparts, therefore, over the last 4-years, hundreds of Korean pilots had been secretly flown to Russia for training in the Russia made Sukhoi MK3 model fighter (nicknamed Flanker). This variant of Sukhoi served not only as an interceptor but was capable of firing Anti-Ship and Anti-Radiation Supersonic Kh-31A/P series and Television-Guided Kh-59 Subsonic Cruise Missiles. Its NO11M radar provided targeting for its laser and television precision-guided missiles and it was far in advance of anything used before by the North Korean Air Force and capable of detecting F-15's at the equivalent distance that it was picked up. The MK3 Flanker was able to engage 2 targets simultaneously with its Long-Range R-27ER/ET (NATO-Code: AA-10) Air-to-Air Guided Missiles and engage 4 targets with its RW-AE missiles. The Short-Range R-73M2 -NATO-Code: AA-11- "Archer" Missile was one of the most advanced weapons with its "round the corner" launch capability. In 2006 the Archer was considered the best Russian Short-Range Air-to-Air Missile with a range of 40km and, 6-years later it still packed a punch, especially against the older US aircraft. The missile is directly connected to the pilot's helmet and in addition to exceptional maneuverability, this missile allows for engagement of targets lateral to the aircraft, which cannot be engaged by missiles with a traditional system of targeting and guidance. This fire and forget weapon was designed to engage modern and future attack aircraft, bombers and helicopters in all weather conditions day or night, even in the presence of natural and deliberate jamming.

With a capability to target one ground and one air target while still searching for other threats, it represented a giant capability leap for the North Koreans and, against the F-16 Falcons, F-18s and older A10 warthogs, this was a formidable foe. The 240 Flankers supplied by Russia arrived upgraded with more powerful engines and an improved logistics system. Originally launched as a long-range fighter with outstanding agility, the Sukhoi MK3 is a truly first-class multi-role fighter aircraft similar to its counterpart the F-15 Eagle. 90 of the MK3's were available on the day of the invasion as they were secretly hidden all over North Korea and, as soon as the main attack started, the remainder of the Flankers along with the 200 Mig 29 Fulcrums were flown from where they had been pre-positioned in China, into North Korean airspace.

Another addition for the North Koreans was the 3rd generation Type 98/99 Main Battle Tank (MBT) or ZTZ-98/99 as it is sometimes referred to. This was designed to improve North Korean tank capability. The Type 98/99 was China's main MBT up to 2008 and came fitted with a 125mm smoothbore main gun. It had an automatic loader and a new advanced aiming system. Both were used to good effect and enabled the tank to fire on the move with high first-hit-first-kill capability. The tank came fitted with advanced armor and an active protection system, which was fitted on the tank for increased survivability. It came fitted with the JD-3 Integrated Laser Range Finder/Warning/Self Defence System called a dazzler. Its high-powered laser was the first of its kind to be seen on a MBT and it worked by attacking the optics systems of an enemy gunner. China had been in full war production in anticipation of Dragon's Claw for years and had supplied North Korea with 2,000 of these tanks from 2008-2011.

Chinese Intelligence, always on the look out for Western technology, had also acquired design plans in 2005 for the Canadian ERYX Short-Range, Man-Portable and Wire Guided Anti-Tank Guided Missile (ATGM). It can be shoulder or tripod launched and fitted with a Mirabel Thermal Imager or equivalent. With a range of 50-600-metres it can be targeted against MBTs, bunkers and pillboxes using tandem warheads in order to defeat almost a metre of Explosive Reactive Armour (ERA). It works when a small warhead at the front impacts initially followed by the much larger 137mm diameter 3.6kg High Explosive Anti-Tank (HEAT) warhead. By 2010 the Chinese had succeeded in copying and designing a perfect lookalike with a similar 95 percent hit rate as the original. More than 4,300 of these were produced, with 800 going to the North Korean Infantry.

In the heart of Seoul lies the Yongsan Garrison; it was an important target to the North Koreans because it contained the major command elements for the United States Forces Korea (USFK), United Nations Command, Combined Forces Command (CFC), US Eighth Army HQ, US Air Forces Korea (7th Air Force) and US Naval Forces Korea. The base, covering more than 4,750,000 square feet of real estate, was host to a multitude of soldiers, airmen, sailors and marines along with some of The Korean Augmentation to the United States Army (KATUSA) soldiers. These are South Korean soldiers, augmented into the US Army fighting force, and are there to enhance the US army's mission capability and increase the ROK (Republic of Korea) and US combined defence on the Korean peninsula. Politically it works fine... but is more of a symbolic gesture rather than a sound military one with the US fighting soldiers unhappy at having to integrate so closely. In addition to the military, there are Department of the Army Civilians along with Embassy personnel and contractors. The Yongsan Garrison complex contained every facility associated with a small city including its own emergency electrical supply. . Within minutes of the first impacts along the DMZ…massed heavy artillery from North Korea was targeting the Garrison grounds.

In addition to the Yongsan Garrison being targeted, other camps close to Seoul, such as Camps Stanley, Casey, Red Cloud and Camp Hovey to the north and K-16, Suwon and Colbern over to the south of the city were hit just as hard.

Close, but south of the Yongsan Garrison was the Osan Air Force Base (AFB) in the Songtan district of Pyeongtaek. This is home to the 51st Fighter Wing and the 7th Air Force, whose HQ is located at the base of the famous Hill 180 where US Troops conducted the first US Army Company-strength bayonet charge since World War I against communist troops holding the hill.

The base is located about 8km (5-miles) south of Osan city itself. With its contingent of 2 U2 spy planes, 12 F-16's and 10 aging A-10's it was the most forward deployed Air Base in Korea and only 45-miles or so south of the DMZ. In the last war North Korean forces twice overran this airfield.

The mission of its airmen is to execute combat operations and receive follow-on forces. Kadena Air Base in Japan, with its Squadrons of F-16 and F-18's, is earmarked as a support base for Osan in the event that conflict returned to the Korean Peninsula. Osan contains the largest Combined Air Operations Centre in the world in the Hardened Theater Air Control Centre. It operates effectively when its U2 reconnaissance/intelligence units are airborne, with these becoming the centre's eyes and ears, using its data link capabilities to provide real time images and information. This information can then be relayed to planners, policy makers and combat troops on the ground. Some of the flying missions are standard 11 to12hr flights but, due to emergency maintenance this morning, no U2 flight had taken place.

Korea had always been thought of as a single man's tour but this was dispelled on January 28 2012 when North Korea launched its surprise attack, with over 700 families living on Osan Air Force Base caught up in the bombardment. In 2008 the US and Korean administration implemented a concept agreed in 2004 by relocating 8,000 personnel from the Yongsan Garrison to Osan. Osan provides 37 dorms with over 9,700 rooms, thus giving some idea of the amount of troops this one base holds. It was also a storage area for ammunition and explosives within the Republic of Korea (ROC) and, due to complex memorandum agreements in Korea, the United States Air force (USAF) had to abide by the concept of Munitions Storage Activities Gained by Negotiations of USAF/ROKAF Memorandum, commonly known as MAGNUM.

MAGNUMs are unique to Korea and are locations where USAF munitions are stored at facilities that are owned, operated and protected by South Korean Air Force personnel. Consequently, the USAF has little or no control over the storage of their munitions and no authority to maintain the clearance zones around these areas. Korean civilians had encroached in to these explosive clearance zones for years and it was not unusual for the South Koreans to see civilians in these areas. By taking advantage of this lax attitude to civilians in these areas, North Korean Special Forces were able to get close enough and penetrate some of the MAGNUM storage facilities where they succeeded in destroying valuable stocks of munitions before they were themselves killed by US and South Korean forces. The base was now completely locked down, with 7th Air Forces Combined Air Component Command (CACC) planning, directing and conducting Combined Air Operations in the Republic of Korea (ROC) in support of US-ROK Combined Forces Command and US Forces Korea. Headquarters 7th Air Force (AF) personnel numbered in the region of 10,000 and were located at various airfields throughout the country. These were Osan AB, Kunsan AB and 5 other collective operating bases throughout the Republic.

The combat arm of the US forces in Korea was provided by the 2nd Infantry Division (2ID), and commanded by a Two-Star Major General. The Warrior Division, as they were known, were assessed as the most lethal and combat ready Division in the whole US Army. They were there to deter war…period… and had a long history in Korea. The first time in country was 1950 to 1954 during the war, followed by a return in 1965 and further tours in the 1970s. They served throughout the 1980s on the line and left the DMZ in 1991. They served throughout Korea until 2004 before deploying to Iraq during the bitter campaign against Fallujah, west of Baghdad, before relocating to Fort Carson, where they remained until 2010.

With rotation times in Korea now shorter than anywhere else (12 months), there was a concern that there was no time for large units such as the 2nd Infantry Division to integrate with each other, never mind with a large KATUSA (Korean augmentee) contingent. During the first Korean War in 1950, US units blamed a 43 percent turnover of manpower for the dismal showing in the first days of the conflict. The modern day turnover of 2ID personnel was now 125 percent annually, which is arguably worse than it was 62 years ago. Irrespective of manning issues the Division was well equipped for war with the 1st Heavy Brigade Combat team (HBCT) providing M1A1 Abrams Tank Battalions. The 2nd Battalion - 9th Infantry (2/9th) provides a cutting edge with mechanized infantry capability, utilising M2/3 Bradley Infantry Fighting Vehicles with its sister unit, recently the 1st Battalion 9th Infantry (1/9th), equipped in a similar manner. The 1/9 having returned to the United States some 7-weeks ago had been replaced or rotated around with the 1st Battalion from the 506th Infantry Regiment (1/506th) as the first part of a phased rotation of units. Also packing a punch above their weight are the combat aviation units from the Combat Aviation Brigade with their 70 AH-64D Apache Helicopters. The 1st Battalion 38th Field Artillery (FA) and the 6th Battalion 37th Field Artillery provide the heavy firepower with more Multiple-Launched Rocket Systems (MLRS) than any other Divisional Artillery (DIVARTY) unit in the army.

When the North Korea offensive began, 15,000 2ID personnel, including the 302nd Brigade Support Battalion, were standing shoulder-to-shoulder with first-echelon Korean units immediately south of the DMZ. The Division was effectively split between 14 different installations throughout the northwestern quadrant of South Korea, with a majority stationed at Camps Casey and Hovey near Tongduchun, with smaller concentrations of combat and support units in the remaining 12 camps. The furthest most forward Battalion was the 1st Battalion, 506th Infantry Regiment, commanded by Colonel Jefferson C Winters, a 2003 West Point graduate, and located just 2km from the Demilitarized Zone (DMZ) next to Freedom Bridge and the Imjin River. Slightly north of the Battalion position was the Joint

Security Area (JSA) in Panmunjeom and, to their south, the 4-lane Tongil "Grand Unification Bridge". This 4-lane highway replaced the old 'one-way' traffic span Bridge that for so long represented the only link from Panmunjeom to the capital, Seoul. It was strategic only for the fact that it left a clear route to the capital city if captured but it wasn't essential to the North Koreans' overall mission. They regarded it as just another piece of the jigsaw if it did fall into their hands intact but they had not based their plan on it.

The assault on Col Winters Battalion began at 1300hrs on the second day.... just 7-weeks after he and his men had rotated in and taken over from the 1/9th. Winters was 37-years old, married with 3 children and renowned as a hard but fair taskmaster. His biggest challenge in Korea so far was preventing his men from becoming bored. He was a disciple of the train hard, fight easy ethos and he ensured that all his leaders from Company commanders to section corporals understood and abided by this. As most soldiers do when given realistic, challenging and rewarding training, they responded to a man. Winters worked on the premise that the weakness of any modern army is poor, unimaginative trainers, over familiarity, apathy and an attitude that it will never happen to me. 1st Battalion's 750 men had trained religiously for 10-weeks before deploying to Asia and had also managed to squeeze an extra 2-weeks in country before they were posted to their present location. The Battalion had bonded extremely well and the standards they reached had given them a confidence that only comes from believing in your own ability and the man alongside you. The North Koreans approaching their position had been preparing for this day for 4-years.

Fighting had erupted all along the DMZ and 2ID and 1st Battalion had suffered immensely from the massive artillery barrages. The 38th and 6th DIVARTY were hitting back hard but the amount of incoming fire was phenomenal and had hardly diminished at all. A battle against infantry would be welcome. A large proportion of 1st Battalion's vehicles had already been damaged in the artillery duels and in between bombardments those vehicles, along with their working guns, were prepared as defensive positions where they stood. There would be no fluid-moving battlefield for the 1st Battalion and Colonel Winters was resigned to the fact that a robust defence was required in order to safeguard the bridge and the route to Seoul. The next 36hrs were expensive in relation to men lost with 1st Battalion losing 43 soldiers dead and another 37 wounded. The concern etched on the troop's faces was clear, but Winters felt confident his men would revert to their training once the fight began in earnest and, that they and the American/South Korean army and air force would halt the North Korean advance before finally defeating them. After all, it was well known that North Korea's equipment was obsolete and outdated and no match for a modern equipped military. Winters' only concern was that he had not seen any aircraft for over 6hrs.

US troops were brought up to expect aircraft overhead almost constantly; it was part of their forces' doctrine and a major factor in the way US ground troops approached and fought a war but, today seemed different. The air activity yesterday and this morning had been intense and it was difficult to determine who was who with the aerial jousting so high up. What concerned Winters was actually seeing aircraft dog-fighting. The North's aircraft were outdated and no match for the US ones - so they were led to believe - but it now appeared that the early and effective attacks by US airpower had diminished and it nagged away at him…WHY?. Winters' Forward Air Controller (FAC) had been killed in the first 6hrs of the campaign and he was still waiting for a replacement that may also be able to shed some light on the situation. Without a qualified FAC, Winters was unable to talk in accurate fire missions to any circling aircraft, if they returned that is. It was the FACs job to control and direct the pilots so that any munitions dropped in support of 1st Battalion were dropped on the enemy and not their own men. What Colonel Winters didn't know, was that the limited number of US and South Korean aircraft in Korea and Japan were being vectored to areas deemed more at risk. A worrying development for Major General Casey (2 ID Commander) was knowing that the air force were having to contend with an enemy equipped with a sophisticated aircraft that was a match for, if not better than their own. The interdiction missions by the advanced North Korean aircraft were allowing the North's less able aircraft the opportunity to strike close to the border at the American and South Korean ground units.

At 1455hrs and with the Battalion having just endured yet another artillery barrage, the 7th of the campaign, shaken but unbowed soldiers surfaced from their underground shelters and began to treat the injured and identify the dead. Those scanning their front quickly realised that with the smoke and dust clearing they could see large numbers of infantry moving cautiously towards their position from the lower ground. Suddenly - some 900-metres away - North Korean fire support teams began pouring heavy suppressive fire in to the forward positions of 1st Battalion's defensive line. Ranged against the American positions were Type 57-7.62mm Heavy Machine Guns (HMG), the 5.8mm Belt Fed Tripod Mounted QJY-88 HMG, the Type 89-12.7mm HMG with high explosive, armour piercing, incendiary rounds and the Type 56-14.5mm Quadruple Barreled Anti Aircraft Machine Gun (AAMG) capable of penetrating 32mm of armour. Although the Type 56 AAMG was an anti-aircraft weapon it was considered highly effective in the ground role against infantry and light armoured vehicles. 5km away, Chinese-made Type 55/64 and Type 86-120mm Mortars, together with Type 84-82mm Mortars were implementing their predetermined fire plans in support of the advancing North Korean troops - their high explosive cocktail being accurate, heavy and prolonged and no doubt adjusted by a Mortar Fire Controller (MFC) on the ridge from where the suppressive fire was emanating from. The advancing North Korean infantry also carried their own integral Type 90-60mm Mortar and this was now in operation firing smoke/incendiary onto the forward elements of 1st Battalion's location. As the troops advanced closer to the Americans the heavier North Korean Mortars would lift and target depth positions to the rear.

Prior to the HMG suppression and mortar fire, it was clear to Winters and his men that there were now obvious gaps made in their defences from the intense artillery bombardments. The wire and minefields to the front had been dissipated, destroyed or split open and they had to move quickly to cover these by repositioning some of the dismounted ·50 browning and 7.62 M60 Machine Guns in the sustained fire (SF) mode to locations that overlooked the gaps and beyond. The Battalions own Light Mortars, the M224-60mm and the heavier M29A1-81mm Mortars were integral to the defence of the American lines and these gaps were already pre-recorded as indirect fire targets. On average, it took 4-rounds per target to adjust onto the exact spot by the Mortar Fire Controller (MFC) as he had to be content that the High Explosive

(HE) Mortar Bombs - when required - would hit their target. The Final Defensive Fire (FDF) line had only been silently recorded and was only 50-metres in front of the furthest most forward Platoon.... and would only be used if the Battalion was about to be overrun.

Winters dispatched orders for his dug in Bradley fighting vehicles to start suppressing the North Korean Fire Support Teams on the ridge area 900-metres away.... and for the MFC to bring HE and White Phosphorous Mortar Fire down onto the approaching enemy. *'If these sons of bitches want this piece of land they will pay a hefty price for it'*, he thought...He and his men were well dug in, well armed and motivated to halt the invasion here. If Freedom Bridge fell, the road to Seoul would be opened and under Winters' command this could not be allowed to happen. He just hoped the South Korean commanders to the east were thinking the same.

General Casey, attempting to ascertain what the North's intentions were, was hunkered down at his HQ in Camp Red Cloud, in the northwestern edge of Uijongbu City. Located between Seoul and the DMZ, Camp Red Cloud was about 40km north of the capital city. He and his staff knew this was a major offensive but so far the North had resorted to the odd infantry probe and massive artillery strikes, which were sapping the morale of his men. 2ID were receiving heavy fire all along the DMZ and the US and Korean Air Force had been completely taken by surprise to see Sukhoi MK3 Flankers and Mig 29 Fulcrums in the hands of the North Koreans. What was more disturbing was that after the first 36hrs, US made aircraft were coming second best. F-22 Raptors would have had far less trouble facing these MK3's and Mig 29s but the F-15, F-18s and A-10s in particular were seriously at risk when engaged in combat with these aircraft.

Casey was concerned greatly about the events in Washington and Europe and it now appeared that the long advocated US policy of fighting 2-wars simultaneously on separate continents was about to be tested.

The United States had 35,000 men in South Korea but a lot of these were airmen, support elements and command staff. The actual combat troops came from the 2nd Infantry Division but these relied to a certain extent on US airpower, South Korean capability and huge reinforcement from the continental United States. Casey knew the latter would be difficult now, especially after the attack on Diego Garcia. There were also a large proportion of South Korean troops having to deal with the hundreds, if not thousands, of North Korean infiltrators all over the south of the country.

Back on the front line, Winters knew the first ground attack was imminent and the North Koreans didn't disappoint. The large amount of troops initially advancing towards them had been a diversion and a feint and, after screening the area with smoke, this force had melted away as the real attack came from the western side into 1st Battalions left flank. Over 1,500 troops were involved in the assault and they had been transported to their Final Assault Position (FAP) in their diesel engine, turbo charged, air cooled Chinese made Type 92 Armoured Personnel Carriers. Carrying 9 infantry soldiers in the rear, the vehicle was equipped with a 25mm Cannon with 600 rounds of ammunition. 120 of these were HE (High Explosive) and 80 were AP (Armour-Piercing). The Type 92 was also fitted with a co-axial 7.62mm, Type 59 Machine Gun with 1,000 rounds plus 8 smoke discharges and had armour protection against 12.7mm (.50mm) calibre weapons.

With these troops on the left flank a priority, the Forward Observation Officer (FOO) attached to Winters Battalion relayed the coordinates and a description of the enemy to the 2 Batteries (8 guns) of M109A6 Paladin 155-mm Mobile Howitzers 22km further south. After receiving the request one M109A6 Paladin with a range capability out to 30km launched its first HE round for ranging purposes, and after falling 300-metres to the east and 200-metres too far north, the FOO called corrections…left *300…drop 200*. The changes were implemented on the gun line and another 98lb projectile landed with a heavy crump - this time almost in the middle of the advancing troops. *'On target fire for effect'* was the call back to the gun line. What followed were 8 guns firing the maximum rate of 4 rounds a minute for 2-minutes. A mixed total of 64 white phosphorous and high explosive ground and airburst 155mm shells fell amongst earth, flesh and metal resulting in only one outcome. They followed this up with the minimum rate of fire of one round per minute for a further 2-minutes, another 16 projectiles. 80 shells had fallen in 5-minutes of mayhem amongst the North Koreans. The suppressive fire from the Koreans on the ridge had stopped and all was quiet apart from the distant rumble of battle in the distance.

Smoke from the burning phosphorous and dust from the impacts hung in the low ground and at first it was difficult to see what affect the US artillery had achieved.

1st Battalion, having witnessed 7 artillery bombardments in just less than 36hrs, knew all too well what impact the firepower produced by those 2 batteries would be. As the noise died down and the smoke cleared, the accuracy of the shelling was all too obvious. Men and machine were strewn across the battlefield…burning fiercely and in pieces. Many had simply disappeared altogether from the direct hits they received. It was a surreal scene as the battlefield became quiet. …There were no birds singing…just an eerie silence…and then the faint sound of screaming started below. At first the cries were difficult to hear and seemed way off in the distance, but then they grew louder as the shock passed and the pain manifested itself in those who had suffered the most terrible injuries. There was to be no compassion shown from the Americans to those North Korean soldiers who now lay out there dying…and why should there be…after all, the American soldiers had seen and heard similar screams this very same day, from their own, with the North Koreans no doubt celebrating the American deaths earlier. This was all out war and before the day was over… many more would scream and die the same way.

1,500 men had advanced and had been stopped in less than 5-minutes by an awesome display of modern firepower - and literally blown to pieces. 6-minutes after the last Paladin 155mm shell fell on the North Koreans, the whole position erupted once more as the massed North Korean artillery retaliated with their most sustained and destructive barrage on Winters' Battalion yet. The continuous shelling was gradually taking its toll and nothing above ground was able to live through it. Both bunkers and Bradley Fighting Vehicles alike were taking direct hits and being completely destroyed…. with those inside killed instantly. The North Koreans had learnt a harsh lesson and underestimated the fire power available to 1st Battalion….but learnt it they had. With the latest, but most intense barrage continuing into its 9th – minute, they threw more than 6,000 troops directly onto the front of Winters position. They were only 300-meters from his forward elements when the barrage lifted but it continued its murderous onslaught further south onto his depth positions. More than a 3rd of Winters' Battalion were now dead or incapacitated and with the North Korean Fire Support Teams firing once again with their HMG's, Bravo Company, the forward Company, was now fighting for its very existence. The enemy was close now - no more than 150-meters away and the Battalion had to bring all its available firepower to bear onto the assaulting troops. The massive weight of fire pouring into the advancing North Koreans from the American .50 Browning HMG's, 7.62mm M240 Medium Machine Gun's, 5.56mm MINIMI M249Squad Automatic Weapon System's (SAWS) and the 25mm M242 Bushmaster Chain Gun from some of the hulled down Bradley fighting vehicles was immense. For the American defenders it was a truly unbelievable sight, as they witnessed first hand, thousands of North Koreans somehow managing to maintain their momentum through the wall of fire. Every now and then a mortar round from the 1st Battalion Mortars final defensive fire missions would land amongst the North Korean Infantry, interspersed by explosions from anti-personnel mines that had not been destroyed by earlier artillery strikes. Even the Paladin 155mm Howitzers could not contain the assault and eventually had to be halted due to the proximity of friendly troops. Although hundreds, possibly thousands of North Koreans had died or were being killed, the amount of firepower starting to bear down on the Americans was far in excess of that going the other way. 45-minutes after the massive assault had started the forward Platoons of Bravo Company, 1st Battalion, were overwhelmed, cut-down and destroyed as a fighting unit. Some individuals, before being overrun, had managed to extract themselves back under cover of smoke to depth positions but the situation was becoming critical. The Koreans had achieved break-in and would be looking to exploit their success quickly. Some soldiers were just too scared to run and others too stubborn. For those serving in the 1st Battalion, this day was a day like no other and they had found out that combat brings out many things in a man, ranging from cowardice to extraordinary courage. On this day of all days, the latter had prevailed.

The families of those lost would never know exactly how their loved ones had died, other than they died bravely - with friends and their brothers in arms. The bond formed through combat was greater than that of family to many and it was this bond that allowed soldiers everywhere to go beyond what those at home could never know or understand. These men were not fighting for honour, freedom or country when they died; they were fighting alongside each other for themselves and their friends. Soldiers didn't join the military to die, but they did accept it could well be part of the deal one day. Thoughts of family and the deaths of their brothers in arms would not have entered their conscious mind until each assault was over and only then, if still alive, would they have allowed them back into their thoughts....

 CRUMP....CRUMP.....2 large artillery shells slammed into the ground near to the Battalion Command Post (CP). Colonel Winters and his Second in Command, Major Robert Hudson, were knocked over by the resulting pressure wave but recovered their senses quickly. Winters was receiving worrying situational updates constantly from his ground commanders of the increasing casualty rates and a decrease in 1st Battalions own firepower due to the loss of his forward Company. Winters knew the enemy was too close now for his own artillery but he was left with no other choice. With almost 4,500 Koreans still attacking his position, the decision was made for him and he informed the FOO to order a defensive fire strike onto his own Battalion location knowing it would result in US casualties and possibly his own death. Before the strike came in he sent orders to his troops to hold their ground at all costs. Minutes later the American artillery arrived with a force mirroring that of the Korean offensive - or so it seemed to those caught in its path. The blast overpressure and shrapnel travelling at vast speed killed hundreds caught in the open, with the high velocity missiles failing to differentiate between Americans and Koreans alike.

 All around.... men were trying to push their bodies further into the ground to escape what is an infantryman's nemesis. The 6-minute onslaught seemed like forever to those caught in the maelstrom and after it was over, Winters, visibly shaken by the ferocity of it all, emerged alive. The smell of cordite was hanging thickly in the air as Winters immediately scanned the ground to his front. Meanwhile, Major Hudson was on the radio asking for updates from his commanders on the situation at their locations. Winters now witnessed first hand the devastation caused by the American shelling and some positions that were there before the barrage had disappeared completely. Winters had no time to mourn their passing or even consider who they might have been as he could still make out more enemy movement to his north and west some 300 to 350-metres away. Clearly, the artillery had only succeeded in buying some time, killing only those immediately on his position and those nearby. The North Koreans appeared to have massive reserves of men available and as soon as one group was routed, another took its place.

Suppressive fire from the ridge once more poured into his lines with renewed vigour and this time the Battalion's response was far less intensive. The FOO then informed Winters that the Divisional Artillery Batteries in support of his Battalion were redeploying on General Casey's orders and were no longer available. With or without artillery support it was a war of attrition that Winters couldn't win… and he knew it…the question now crossing Winters mind was…did General Casey know it too? It was abundantly clear that the position would soon be lost and that the sensible call would be to order a tactical withdraw for his men. 2ID had already prepared secondary defensive positions on the road to Seoul and had ambushes already in place if the 1st Battalion failed to hold the North Korean advance. All that Winters had to do was make the call and his men would fall back…but whether through pride, stubbornness or judgment, Winters found he couldn't give that order while his men were holding the line, and instead, found himself asking where was the American airpower? It was an indecision that would cost the battalion dearly.

Unbeknown to Winters, the airpower he craved for had been vectored to the same area to which the artillery units were now speeding. The North Koreans, having achieved a large breakthrough further east, were hitting the line with everything they had and anything that could be spared was being diverted to prevent it. The pressure on the whole of the DMZ was suddenly intense with the North Korean forces further east far in excess of those attacking the 1st Infantry Battalion's position.

The North Koreans had succeeded in re-occupying the forward defensive positions and were now into the next line of Winters' trenches, with fierce fighting erupting on two sides using high explosive grenades and small arms. It was now savage hand-to-hand and too late to order a tactical withdraw. The Koreans had managed to flank the US position and were attempting to roll the Americans up from west to east. The battle was entering its fifth hour now and in another 30-minutes it would be dark. As the light receded, to be replaced by a blanket of darkness, the Koreans illuminated the night sky with huge parachute flares, which bathed the scene below with an eerie flickering shadowy glow. Tracer fire was now more visible and its deadly continuous trail licked across the sky as it arched over the battlefield on its way to its next victim. The unmistakable sounds of HMG fire and explosions, interspersed with the screaming and shouting of wounded and dying men continued in to the dark hours.

Just after 2100hrs, 8hrs after it all began, Colonel Winters, along with Major Hudson and his FOO, died from blast and shrapnel injuries sustained from direct hits by 2 RPG strikes - the second of the grenades exploding just inside the bunker and only yards from Colonel Winters. A whole Battalion had been lost.......... slaughtered at a cost of 3,500 enemy dead and an equivalent number wounded. 1st Battalion from the 506th Infantry Regiment would forever be consigned to the history books, with authors depicting and glorifying yet another brave stand by brave men against the odds. History informs us that these sort of military losses have occurred many times before and, as sure as day replaces night they will occur again and again in future battles and conflicts. For those families who had lost their fathers, husbands, sons, brothers and uncles on this day… the loss of their loved ones would be with them until they died too.

What the 1st Battalion didn't know was that behind those North Koreans already committed were a further 4 Divisions with 48,000 troops ready to exploit any breakthrough. The North Korean planners had estimated over 200,000 casualties to their own forces before breaking the initial US/South Korean line of defence along the DMZ. 4-days after the largest artillery bombardment ever known, North Korean forces broke through the South's defensive lines in 6 separate areas and began pouring men and equipment into South Korea; the cost to North Korea was 97,000 lives lost and 23,500 wounded. South Korean casualty figures were close to 61,000 men killed in action or captured and of the 35,000 US troops in Korea, 4,126 were assessed as having been killed or missing in action, with 847 wounded.

US airpower, was finding the going more difficult than they could have imagined having already relocated to Japan due to artillery and North Korean Special Forces targeting the airfields in South Korea. The Air Defence threat was very real and extremely potent but the biggest shock had been the introduction in large numbers of the Sukhoi MK3 Flanker and Mig 29. The American AH-64D Apache Helicopters, with their Hellfire Missiles, had inflicted substantial losses on the North's forces - but at a cost. From the 70 Apache operating on day one, a third had been lost, 9 of which, were destroyed by indirect fire whilst on the ground at their base location. At the current attrition rate they would all be destroyed within 12-days unless they were moved out of range of the North Korean guns.

The roads to Seoul and other major cities were now open and South Korean and US units had to deploy further south to set up depth defensive positions. With Diego Garcia unable to provide any support, US Pacific Command ordered Anderson Air Force Base on Guam in the Pacific Ocean to aid the ground troops by bombing North Korean units using their B-52's, AB-1B Lancers and their 2 B-2 Spirit Stealth Bombers. The raid was only partially successful as the 2 B-2 Spirits unknowingly succeeded in disrupting the deployment of 2 complete Mechanized Divisions in the central region of the DMZ by destroying the Command HQ elements from both Divisions. The B-52's and Lancers were less successful due to the activity of the new Sukhoi MK3's and the Russian brought MiG-29 Fulcrum with 1 B-52 shot down and another seriously damaged in the attack. The fighter escort accompanying the bombers had to contend with more than 48 enemy fighters during the course of the mission with 12 enemy kills confirmed at a loss of 9 of their own including the downed B52. In addition to this, the mass of Air Defence screens placed around the invading forces was proving difficult to breach and had accounted for at least 2 of the aircraft from Guam.

The ferocity of the North Korean attack and its intense duration had shocked all those who had lived through those initial days and they now needed to regroup quickly to organise a counter offensive to halt the North's advance. Any counter offensive though was based around massive manpower reinforcement from the United States, which was then supposed to be supplied by the equipment stocks at Diego Garcia. However, with the loss of the entire US reserve war stock and the worsening events in Europe, the political picture had altered dramatically with fear of the unknown clouding the decision making process. Fear that there may be another device in another American

City; fear that conflict on a massive scale was about to begin; fear that the world's oil supply had been turned off; fear that intervention would result in massive American casualties; fear that this was part of a well thought out plan designed to deliberately draw in the US military before all the cards had been played; and fear, that it was in some way, a trap, and over committing troops to those regions affected would leave America weak at home and elsewhere. With new reports coming in by the hour to the new US administration's emergency planning centre... events were beginning to run away from the President and his team.

PART 10

U-TURN
(D+7)

DTG: Tuesday -January 31st 2012

LOCATION: United States Presidential Emergency Operations Centre.... EDWARDS AIR FORCE BASE - California's Mojave Desert

SITUATION: It has been 7-days since the attacks in Washington and Europe, and events are continuing to spiral out of control....

President Maxwell was sat in the emergency centre's operations room about to receive yet another update.... he had hardly slept; such was the pace of events over the last 7-days. Maxwell was concerned that his administration was being forced to be reactive, and not proactive, to the events unfolding before them and he didn't like it one bit. He was sitting with his Chief Military Adviser, General William Bracken, and was keen to hear more of his thoughts on the situation. Due to the information they had received 48hrs ago; the President had already placed the country's nuclear forces on Defence Condition 1 (DEFCON-1) Maximum Force Readiness and broadcast it to the world as a deterrent more than a usable option. People were dying in their tens of thousands on 3 continents and decisions were needed fast but the decisions had to be right for America and the rest of the world. It was the information they'd received 2-days ago that had altered his and the administration's initial thinking.

3-days ago the increased radio traffic along the DMZ in Korea, which had been mentioned by the National Security Advisor, Ross Cochrane, had turned out to be a precursor to a North Korean invasion and the United States was now facing the double war scenario that its doctrine preached. The United States, along with the United Nations, had taken its eye off the Korean Peninsula with the horrific events in

Washington and Europe taking precedence and, it appeared that the North Koreans had well and truly taken advantage. The 2-war doctrine analysts had, in the past - ran simultaneous war scenarios against North Korea alongside smaller campaigns similar to an Iraq conflict....but they never once thought the simultaneous battlefields would centre on major conflicts involving Korea and Europe. This was not to say it couldn't be achieved but disturbing information from Europe had caused consternation and great concern to Maxwell and his Chiefs of Staff and, it now warranted a major rethink. The information causing the President and his staff to question America's role in the world, came to light 48hrs ago after the advancing Arab army had encountered its first military resistance against the Bulgaria army at Dimitrovgrad in the southeastern part of the country. As expected, the Bulgarian air force responded to the battle, but as soon as they appeared overhead to conduct air to ground operations, Russian fighter aircraft appeared and intercepted them....or so the report indicated. This was now a new and dangerous development and it became imperative to confirm the information. Confirmation came in the form of a video from Bulgarian military intelligence who had taken footage of a shot down Mig 29 Fulcrum with a body of a Russian pilot and a fuselage showing Russian markings. This was the information that had sent the President, his Joint Chiefs of Staff and NATO into a spin.

The President had come to the conclusion with his advisors that there was now something more sinister than mere terrorism pulling the strings of the United States and its allies in Europe. Al Qaeda was certainly the first strike ...but who supplied them with the devices. Rumours have long circulated of stolen Russia made suitcase nuclear devices but these would have degraded and be useless by now...and who masterminded the training and logistics for what seemed like thousands of Mujihadeen to undertake guerrilla warfare to the whole European continent, Russia?- Iran?- North Korea? The Russians hated the Mujihadeen fighters and could never bring themselves to train such a force...yet all the indicators screamed out that they were clearly involved and had revealed their intention to fight alongside the Arab armies. There was also information coming out of Korea that Russian Advanced Fighter-Bombers were in North Korean hands. Nothing made sense yet, other than for the United States military to take adequate precautions and be in a position of strength when the full plan revealed itself. The CIA didn't think Iran had the technology to produce a low yield covert nuclear device, yet 6-years ago the CIA didn't think that Iran had an advanced nuclear reactor programme. Could Iran have also hidden this from the world and activated a bomb on American soil? The North Koreans had nuclear technology but were quickly discounted on the premise that a suitcase device was way above their capability and their lack of resources would surely not have allowed it to occur. That left China and, the suggestion that China was somehow involved in all this, was treated with skepticism by the President and his closest advisors.

'Will'...said the president to his chief military adviser, 'I need your thoughts and advice more than ever on this one. I don't need to tell you that good men are dying in Korea and, by God, I feel them all Will.... and the support in place to bail them out lies at the bottom of the Indian Ocean according to our latest satellite imagery. Our one contact on Diego Garcia claims there are North Korean Commandos on the Island and after the transmission 4-days ago, I'm inclined to believe him. You know the Marine/SEAL task force will be in place to assault the island within 36-48hrs and only then will we have a clear picture of the real damage'

The task force President Maxwell alluded to was on an earlier mission and tasked to observe the large but controversial joint Chinese/Indonesian Naval exercise that was taking place around the southern Indonesian Islands over the next 3-weeks. The call to abort and alter course to Diego Garcia had come within hours of the communication from Diego Garcia that possibly North Korean commandos had invaded the Island. Included in the task force were 60 US Navy SEALs and 2,000 US Marines from the 31st Marine Expeditionary Force Unit/31 MEU. These were a unit normally located in Okinawa and part of a complete Marine Air Ground Task Force and who were now sat on their amphibious assault ships the USS Harpers Ferry, USS Essex and USS Juneau. Escorting them were elements from Destroyer Squadron 15 (DESRON 15). Not all the DESRON 15 ships were present but those that were consisted of 2 DD-963 SPRUANCE-class Anti-Submarine Destroyers, 2 OLIVER HAZARD PERRY-class Frigates designed to protect and escort amphibious landing groups and one ARLEIGH BURKE-class Guided Missile Frigate. The final vessel was a TICONDEROGA-class Guided Missile Cruiser and it was on this ship that the Commander of Battle Force Seventh Fleet in the Pacific and Indian Ocean hatched his plans with the Marine and Navy SEAL commanders to re-take Diego Garcia. Little did he know that if their course had taken the task force 300km further to the north they would have been in the same vicinity as the departing Sung submarine force.

The initial communication informing them of the North Korean commando attack on Diego Garcia had come from the base COMCEN (communications centre) but this went off line after the first hour. Since then, an air force Captain, (Captain Eustace Danvers), had been using a Thuraya satellite phone to send periodic updates. He had initially called his wife in San Diego who then passed the information via the Department of Defence. A number had been arranged for Captain Danvers to call if the information was critical and to conserve battery power as much as possible. Outside of that he had a pre-arranged time to switch on for a 2-minute window in case a message needed to be relayed to him. Danvers had informed his contact that he was only able to sustain limited observation of the airfield area but from his communications the assault force had been able to ascertain some of the commando's strong points in this location. 24hrs before the planned invasion the phone battery gave up and communication to Captain Danvers and the island was cut.

'Mr President' said General Bracken, *my thoughts as you know, were initially to pour everything we had into Korea and leave the Arabs to our European allies and the US forces in Germany. It's clear from the fuel status reports that we can't risk transporting our NATO contingent of tanks over 1,000's of miles without adequate fuel supplies and, as you know Sir, we have kept this knowledge from the public. Fuel stocks are already becoming scarce and it is the Arabs who have the resources to fight a mobile war. I also believed that NATO air, although badly damaged, had enough firepower to degrade the Arabs sufficiently for them to back down.... That was until 48 hours ago. The Russian intervention in Bulgaria has put a completely different spin on it and my concern is that we are being sucked into committing our strategic reserves and therefore, leaving ourselves open to something much larger. What that is Sir, I just don't know yet... but there is more than Al Qaeda and Arab Nationalism at work here'*

'What are you saying, Will.... That we don't reinforce Korea? We have to be seen to be doing something'

'If we go into Korea, Mr President, we will not have the means to deal with what could, in effect, be an Arab/Russian Alliance. Russia has almost a million men in its newly formed professional army with more than 26,000 Main Battle Tanks at the last count. Without adequate fuel supplies we have no choice other than to remain where we are and use our airpower to degrade the advancing Arab Army as much as we can. With the terrorist attacks in Europe continuing I think there is no doubt that the Arabs' game plan is to transit as fast as possible through the Eastern Bloc countries in order to engage the heart of Europe's military elite....by Europe's military elite I mean the forces from Britain, Spain, Italy, Germany, France and, of course, ourselves.

By committing large forces to Korea and fighting on both continents we run the risk of being drawn into a no win situation and if we do that... What I'm trying to say Sir is that we have no way of knowing what the next move is. Right now we are at war with North Korea, most of the Arab World and possibly Russia. No wonder the Russian President has refused to answer your calls. My advice Mr President...and you wont like this...is to pull all our troops out of Korea now - before we become embroiled and bogged down. Cut our losses now Sir and regroup for the battles that undoubtedly lie ahead. Yes, it will be a battle lost but we have to realise this is no quick 6-week campaign and it will be vital in maintaining our strength in Europe and at home. Our priorities are changing, Mr President, and we have to be prepared to change with them'

The President, head in hands and rubbing his temples, had not anticipated this from his chief military advisor, but what he had said made sense. Maxwell was still mulling over the consequences when there was a knock at the door. Ross Cochrane entered carrying an A4 sized brown envelope; he reached inside and pulled out a handful of glossy photographs and handed them to the President...

'Mr President...I think you should take a look at these.... they've just come in ...they were taken from a U2 spy plane over the North Korea/Chinese border earlier today'. Studying the photographs President Maxwell could clearly see column upon column of vehicles, tanks and men on the roads below. Maxwell looked up at Cochrane with a quizzical look...'

'They're Chinese Sir; Intelligence estimates the number to be something in the region of 150,000 to 250,000 forming up on the North Korean-Chinese border'.

'Jesus'.....Maxwell handed the photographs over to General Bracken. 'Ross.... get me the whole team in here now...and arrange a television announcement for 1900hrs tonight...broadcast to the nation'. Cochrane turned to leave.

'Oh yeau...one more thing Ross, get me Combined Forces Command Korea on a secure line in 30-minutes'

As Cochrane left the room Maxwell looked at General Bracken. 'I don't like this Will... not one fucking bit...those images mean only one thing...that the Chinese are in support of their North Korean allies. My God. Within days of the events here and Europe both Russia and China have deployed forces and Russia has tipped her hand in Bulgaria. What the hell are we facing here Will?'

'I'm not sure Sir,' responded General Bracken, 'but I know one thing... we can't fight Russia and China combined. We have to seriously consider a pull out from the Korean peninsula in order to preserve our forces and strengthen our own position in the Pacific by reinforcing Japan, Taiwan and Guam not to mention rebuilding Diego Garcia as an operating base. What we can't afford here is to be pulled and stretched without knowing what these sons of bitches are completely up to'.

The President stared at General Bracken for what seemed like minutes but was in fact just a few seconds. Turning away, Maxwell, head down and massaging his forehead, walked slowly over to the electronic situation board. He stopped in front of it and looked up. 'As much as it pains me Will, I know what you say is right- and to make it work I think we need to move fast' At that point, the door opened and the rest of the administration, including the Chiefs of Staff, all walked in.

After a heated exchange of views the President had the decision he wanted- a tactical withdraw from South Korea. Maxwell, as President of the United States and Commander in Chief of the Armed Forces, then took the call from his Four Star General in theatre - General Conrad D Eddison. The General, as head of the Combined Forces Command (CFC) Korea, with a Korean Four Star equivalent alongside him, was responsible for integrating the entire American and South Korean Force for war. With over 600,000 South Korean regular troops, a potential 3.5million-reserve force and a combined air, ground and naval force from the United States, it was deemed a formidable foe. The situation was fully explained to the General and, although reluctant to disengage the North's forces, he could visualize the bigger picture developing and agreed there was more to this than just Korea at stake. This was rapidly generating into a world conflict on a massive scale but the decision reached would be of no consolation to the South Korean population. However, General Eddison did make one last request of the President before he signed off…that if the North were to succeed in defeating the South, he would be the General leading US Forces if and when they returned; Maxwell agreed.

A series of emergency communications were then placed to the Secretary General of the United Nations, its European allies, Australia, Japan and Taiwan. The first and most crucial call though had to be made to the President of South Korea. It was a difficult moment for Maxwell and one he did not relish at all but this was no normal situation. If this really was a world war, and the indications were that it was, then America had no choice other than to realign its forces and fight on its terms - not the enemy's.

After he made the call President Maxwell spoke to all the other leaders before sitting down to prepare his speech to the nation, with General Bracken and Ross Cochrane present throughout. At 1815hrs the speech was ready and by 1830hrs he had shaved, changed, and had the obligatory make up applied for the TV cameras. Maxwell was clearly feeling the strain of the last week and today's activities in particular. He now needed to summon up the strength, determination and calmness when speaking to the American people that had become his trademark since the events in Washington DC, and like all his other speeches, Maxwell knew this would be broadcast around the world. It was to be his most important and crucial speech to date and it had weighed heavily.

With President Maxwell staring at the red light on the top of the camera, a TV technician, with clipboard in hand standing to the right of the cameraman, started attracting his attention by waving. As the President caught the diversion, the technician started counting down on his hand….five …four ….three …two…one….before the light finally changed to green.

The President looked directly into the camera and began his speech. He began by reassuring the American people he was confident that the United States no longer contained foreign nuclear devices on its soil. This was followed by a statement detailing the rescue efforts that were still ongoing in Washington DC, before he praised and thanked FEMA, the fire department and medical and security agencies for their dedication to duty, reiterating the success of the continuing security operations throughout the country. He then paused and looked down at his notes…he looked up slowly and began to speak again.

'People of the United States and all free countries around the world; as of tonight the United Nations no longer exists. Countries that had abided by its ethos have over the last week, unconditionally broken their oath and commitment to this organization'

'The United States and NATO are left with no choice other than to declare war on North Korea, Russia and undisclosed Nations from the Middle East. Some of these countries are possibly Iran, Syria and Egypt'…. another pause - *'The world is now facing a crisis not seen since World War II and this new crisis has all the hallmarks of a major World War in the making…The United States administration and NATO also accuses Turkey of forming an alliance with the Arab nations and holds them responsible for allowing their armies to enter NATO territory'.*

The impact of that statement immediately reverberated around the world and on top of the events of the last few days caused immeasurable panic and dismay to governments and communities everywhere.

Maxwell spoke clearly and calmly of the attacks on Diego Garcia and South Korea, but omitted for security reasons to mention the naval task force en-route to Diego Garcia. He then covered the events in the Middle East and Europe before speaking of the Russia intervention against Bulgaria, a NATO ally.

'It is now clear from these events that there has been a well-orchestrated and concerted plan to drive Arabic forces into the heart of NATO and that the nuclear devices against America and our allies along with the subsequent terrorist attacks in Europe are all part of the same operation. We have no confirmed evidence… yet… who perpetrated this abomination against America and Europe other than we know that Al Qaeda claim to have carried it out… but the suspects are narrowing. It is no coincidence that the Arab nations and North Korea were fully prepared and able to launch

massive attacks against Europe, Diego Garcia and South Korea almost simultaneously.

Another disturbing development has arisen from fresh intelligence reports, which indicate that there are some 200,000 plus Chinese troops poised on the Korean/Chinese border. The United States views this as provocation of the highest order from China and, from this deployment we have to conclude that China may also be part of this concerted effort to destabilize the world's boundaries.

7-hours ago and, after great deliberation as Commander in Chief of our proud Armed Forces, I gave instructions to the US General Commanding US forces Korea to disengage with the North Korean military as of immediate effect. Due to undisclosed operational reasons the United States will not be reinforcing South Korea but instead will be conducting defensive troop alignments within the Pacific Basin in readiness for the battles that will undoubtedly have to be fought'

Troop alignments actually meant increasing the manpower and fire-power at the remaining strategic locations in the Pacific, such as Guam, Okinawa, mainland Japan and Taiwan, in order to combat any expansion outside of Korea's borders, especially now that China was poised and looking menacing. The President in his speech only mentioned disengagement in Korea and deliberately ensured there was no indications of a rapid troop withdraw from the Korean Peninsula to Japan, which was now in fact underway. The President continued.....

'Having ordered a disengagement, it is my solid belief that the well-prepared South Korean forces have the capability to hold and then defeat the North Korean invasion on their own merits'

'I would also like to express America's gratitude to those troops serving in Korea and to those across the sea in Europe...and to those families with relatives serving in Europe...I say this. They will not be a forgotten army. The situation over there is, and will continue to be, assessed daily with the right decisions made as and when we deem it correct to act...they will be fully supported for as long as it takes. The American people and the world need to realise that this will not be a 6 to 8-week conflict and that we may be at war for years until democracy, freedoms and recognised boundaries are rightfully restored'.

Maxwell stressed to the American public the need to limit travel and announced that a series of fuel economy measures and a rationing system would need to be implemented immediately due to the blockade of the Middle East. He touched briefly on the fuel agreements that had been signed with Canada, West Africa and Venezuela to increase oil production with immediate effect. Nigeria in particular was now producing 25 percent of US oil needs with a commitment to increase this to 35 percent within 6 months.

Information not mentioned in the speech to the American public, was that the US fuel reserves were available, but only for troop deployments, and that Canada in particular, with its enormous but expensive to extract sand oil fields, was to be granted huge resources to expand its operation fourfold within the next 18 months. Nigeria would also be receiving 25,000 American Marines, a Carrier Battle Fleet including Hunter Attack Submarines and, Patriot Missile Batteries over the next 2 to 6-weeks in order to safeguard its supplies. Canada had oil reserves second only to Saudi Arabia, with over 7.4 billion barrels of crude oil and 315 billion barrels of crude bitumen. With an annual capacity of 2.5 million barrels a day, the US and Canada had hastily agreed to attempt an unprecedented expansion to produce 10 million barrels a day by mid 2013 using massive American finances and engineering resources. This was seen as a strategic imperative and no cap on cost was placed on this operation. The oil issue was not going to go away and America like the rest of the world would soon feel the pinch from the Middle-Eastern oil taps being switched off. There were still full tankers at sea but after a few weeks their supply would be delivered and then the Arab decision to impound and confine a great many oil tankers to its ports would start to bite. Measures to conserve fuel would have to be drastic over the coming months but the measures would have to begin now. People were not going to like it…not one bit…. but drastic measures were called for and these needed to be implemented quickly.

For security reasons President Maxwell had omitted to inform the public of the acute shortages of fuel for the military in Europe and that 2 of America's 13 nuclear-powered Aircraft Carrier Battle Groups had already been ordered to Europe to bolster NATO's strike aircraft numbers in response to the losses suffered by Mujihadeen ground attacks. The President had elected not to send ground troops at present; however, an immediate requirement for Europe was ammunition re-supply as vast quantities were destroyed on the first night of terrorist attacks on

European soil. The American air transport heavy lift capability was already looking to begin the re-supply within days but the problem with this re-supply was a lack of readily available specialist munitions, which impacted on NATO's capability to sustain any effective offensive operations for more than 6 to 8-weeks at the level required. The reality was that NATO and America were just not prepared to fight this type of war and cranking the industry up would take weeks, if not months. This would be further curtailed and made problematic by the Arabs completely cutting off all oil supplies to the West.

Maxwell continued. *'History will show that this past week has been a dark period for America, Europe and NATO. In the days ahead we may suffer more dark times but we will also have our share of military successes....of that I'm sure. I am confident and proud in the dedication and professionalism of our armed forces and those of the free world...and that remarkable attribute will, in the end, allow the people of this world to prevail'.*

'To achieve this we need to expand our military capability; therefore, from tomorrow, all military draft centres will be open 24/7 for a massive intake of new recruits to all arms of the military. Your country needs young men and women like never before and I implore all of you of serving age and ability to volunteer to protect your rights and freedoms. People of America...THE WAR STARTS NOW...and when we strike back we will strike back hard with no warning.... and rest assured...whatever we do...it will be on our terms'...

'Finally, I ask you all to remain vigilant and report anything suspicious to the security services, no mater how trivial you may think it is'.

'God bless you all and God bless America...Goodnight'

It was noticeable that the President had not spoken of nuclear retaliation and this was not only due to *no recognisable or feasible target* but came from a concern that any tit for tat nuclear game of chess could result in an escalation detrimental to the United States. To attack Russia or China with nuclear devices was to invite nuclear Armageddon, with Russia possessing enough nuclear devices to target all American major cities. As for the Arab armies marching through Europe...America or NATO had no proof that Arab nations were involved in the detonation of a nuclear device on American or European soil. North Korea most likely had a crude version of the bomb in some form or other, but not the capability, to construct a small tactical nuclear device, therefore, attacking North Korea with nuclear devices was not even considered as an option at this stage. There would obviously be calls from the more right wing elements in society to *"nuke them all"* but there would be no desire for this solution from the remaining 12 elected US politicians. The American people had witnessed nuclear devastation close up and personal, in all its naked terror and the public had no desire to invite another more powerful nuclear attack on its cities. The people were clearly angry but they were also pragmatic and content for the moment not to follow the path of a baying mob. For the time being, they agreed with Maxwell's judgment and the measures he had announced. Maxwell hoped that the clear intent made in his speech to expand the American military would concern America's enemies, who at the moment appeared to be pulling the strings and calling the shots.

.....48hrs after the Presidents speech two momentous events were.....
..... about to throw the US administration and the rest of the world into further turmoil.....

12-days after the President's announcement the last American soldier departed South Korea for Japan including SOCKOR (Special Operations Command Korea). SOCKOR, as it is called, is the only theater SOC that is not a subordinate unified command and was primarily responsible for the integration and command of all Special Operations Forces (SOF) in the event of war in Korea. They would now reconstitute in Japan and plan potential operations from their new base location. Air and naval assets were moved complete and only a third of 2nd Infantry Division's A3 Bradley Fighting Vehicles, M1A2 Abrams Tanks and 155 MM Self-Propelled Artillery were shipped over the Korean Strait to Japan. The rest, including the Multi Launch Rocket Systems (MLRS), remained with the South Koreans for arming their reserve units that were hastily forming up. During this 12-day period the North's advance remained unchecked with Seoul falling 7-days after the invasion began.

Fighting in Korea was proving to be extremely difficult and with its rugged mountainous terrain covering more than 80 percent of the country, it was proving to be manpower intensive. The Taebaek and Sobaek Mountain ranges were the two most dominant topographical features in the country and with large rivers winding away from them; these inhospitable areas were witness to some of the bitterest fighting after the fall of the DMZ. The North Korean thrust into the south was not halted until they had advanced almost halfway through the country. The North Koreans, were eventually held on a tenuous line running from Kunsan on the west coast, over to Taejon in the centre of the country and across to Pohang on the east coast. The war appeared to be approaching a critical phase with the South Korean army at long last justifying President Maxwell's confidence in them and, with a further 2-days passing without any new North Korean gains, the hope now was that the corner had been turned.

.....Within 24hrs of this impasse, 220,000 Chinese troops crossed the.....
.....border and entered the war.....

PART 11

ESCALATION
(D+9)

Indonesia has a massive sea area of 7.9 million square km, which is 4-times greater than its landmass of 1.9 million square km. It contains the largest archipelago in the world with some 17,508 islands stretching for thousands of miles. Java, the largest island and home to the capital Jakarta, has 118 million people crammed into an area the size of New York with a population density of 2070 people per square mile. When you compare it against Britain's population density of 591 and America's at 66 people per square mile, it becomes apparent why from 2008 to 2012; Indonesia's need for space became top of the Indonesian government's agenda. Once the proposal by China was placed on the table, there was only one place that occupied their thinking.

The idea of expansion was not a new concept for the Indonesian authorities and expanding its borders to alleviate the strain on its huge population density has long been considered a viable option. China's Dragon's Claw strategists had long worked on possible scenarios for the expansion of Indonesia in order to use them as a trip wire for early warning in case of American aggression in the region. Indonesia was the perfect foil for this and after the Iranian bombings in 2006 the climate was right for an approach to its Muslim government, which had become anti-American.

For 4 long years now the Indonesians, who still retained massive amounts of US military equipment, had increased their land forces twofold and substantially increased their naval capability at China's request. After much controversy the Chinese/Indonesian naval defence agreement had been ratified... with China, to a certain extent, having allayed the fears of Australia by claiming it was in response to Indian and Japanese expansion and a need to patrol and protect the huge expanse of Chinese and Indonesian coastline. The whole world knew that China and India had real issues over the Kashmir and the prime fishing areas and oil shipping routes in the Straits of Malacca; therefore, China's insistence on defending its interests was clear. China had cleverly manipulated its feud with India and persuaded those in the region its motives were defensive and not offensive but, the US and Taiwan quietly believed it was part of a sustained build-up to eventually invade Taiwan. The US was slightly impotent to Chinese naval expansion so they continued to support Taiwan militarily while maintaining over-watch of that potential flashpoint. China argued the need for a powerful navy to counter Indian naval expansion but in reality the opposite was true and the world was about to witness first hand the real reason for China's naval aspirations. The world had long suspected China was building its amphibious forces in readiness for an invasion of Taiwan. What they didn't know, was that the force China was amassing, was for something far more important than invading a small island.

China had acquired, as part of the Dragon's Claw agreement, 2-Aircraft Carriers from Russia in 2009, with a displacement of 85,000 tons each and although the United States protested vehemently, these were now part of a larger 3-Carrier Battle Fleet. The much-publicised Chinese/Indonesian naval exercise consisting of 38 ships would be passing close to the southernmost Indonesian Islands and only 100km from East Timor. It was supposed to be observed by a US Navy Task Force, but as Chinese planners had predicted and hoped, that force was now steaming towards Diego Garcia. If the American observance fleet had not diverted to Diego Garcia, China would have had no choice other than to attack it.

China's Carrier Fleet consisted of a *Kuznetzo*-class Carrier that was originally bought only 70 percent complete from the Ukraine in the 1980s. They also had 2-newly acquired *Ulyanovsk* nuclear powered multi-role Aircraft Carriers capable of carrying 80 Su27 Flanker variants called Su-33's. The Flanker Su-33 - the equivalent of the American F14 Tomcat - had been adapted for operations from Aircraft Carriers and was renowned for its exceptional range, heavy armament and very high agility.

China was also close to commissioning a brand new indigenous Aircraft Carrier of its own, and with the 78,000 ton vessel having been under construction for almost 6-years; it was almost complete, with plans already well established to begin production on its sister vessel immediately. Kept very hush hush and officially denied in 2005, the Aircraft Carrier project had continued and, by March 2012, the Chinese would launch this, their 4th Aircraft Carrier, to add to their expanding fleet.

There had been an agreement not to refit the *Kuznetzo*-class Carrier for operational purposes but the Chinese had started refitting this vessel for combat fairly soon after purchasing it. The Varyag, as it was known, was limited in carrying capability and only able to transport 17 Sukhoi Su-33 variants plus 11 Kamov Ka-27PL helicopters. The Kamov Ka-27 was the vessel's anti-submarine warfare craft with surface search radar, sonobuoys, dipping sonar, and magnetic anomaly detectors. Five of the Kamov Ka-27 were armed with bombs and rockets but could also be fitted with mines and torpedoes. This *Kuznetzo*-class Carrier was earmarked for the East Timor phase of the operation and came equipped with the P-700 Granit, otherwise known as the SS-N-19 anti-ship missile. The *Kuznetzo*-class vessel contains 24 vertical launchers with a total of 192 missiles and has a further defence capability via its Air Defence Gun and Missile System, which provides defence against anti-ship, anti-radar missiles aircraft and small vessels at sea. The system uses a radar/optronic director missile system, which provides fire control for the main 30mm twin guns and missile launcher. The optronic directors laser beam gives the missile a range variance of 1.5 to 8km, while the range for the gun ranges from 0.5 to 1.5km firing 10,000 rounds per minute. Its anti-submarine defence comes courtesy of its anti-submarine rockets called the 60 udav-1, which can destroy incoming torpedoes and, the 111SG depth charge, which can be dropped to a depth of 600-metres against enemy submarines.

For 5-weeks now, China and Indonesia had been slowly putting ship after ship out to sea, before they could finally meet up, far from land, in small groups. For some vessels the journey to Darwin from their point of origin, the port of Guangzhou in China, was a long haul of 3,375 miles. Vessels were spread far and wide but the smaller groups of ships were easier to hide in the vast oceans. One of these groups contained part of the S-4 project, which were 4 massive container ships bound for Australia. China had embarked on a massive remodernisation project since 1990 with an emphasis on employing more carrying capacity and producing more landing craft. As early as 1999, China had given the go ahead to build 4 gigantic 90,000 ton civilian container ships; these huge vessels, initially portrayed as a requirement for the ever expanding Chinese markets, were in-fact military Trojans and now formed part of the invasion force, responsible for transporting massive amounts of equipment to Australia. Once Darwin was taken these ships would disgorge their tanks, helicopters, all terrain reconnaissance vehicles, logistical supplies and ammunition cargo at the Darwin deep-water port before heading back to China. There were now 3-Chinese Carrier Battle Groups at sea with the smallest of the three heading to the northern coast of East Timor with the remainder of the fleet heading to a point 150 nautical miles (nm) from the Australian coast of the Northern Territory and Darwin.

Once the ships converged, a total of 67 vessels with a single Carrier Battle Group would eventually take part in the invasion of East Timor while a further 294 vessels, including 2-Aircraft Carrier Battle Groups, were intent on establishing a foothold on Australian soil. China had insisted that Indonesian controlled West Timor could not be used as a staging post for any troop build up as it would have been noticed; therefore, it had to come in by sea and air. The only 2 concession's had been the insertion of 2,000 Kopassus Special Operations Troops and the even later arrival of 4 huge Zubr-class air cushioned landing craft on adapted barges after their long journey from China to the sheltered Kapang Bay area on West Timors west coast. The Zubr-class vessels contained a reserve of troops; Medium Battle Tanks (MBTs) and Armoured Vehicles, and with a range of 350 nautical miles would be able to transit the last part of the journey under their own power in order to deliver their combat power quickly. The East Timor assault force contained an initial 11,000 Indonesian troops with the majority of these crammed amongst the 67 vessels making their way to the coast. They were expected to reach land at the same time that an airborne assault was being conducted on the 2 airfields on the Island.

On mainland Australia, 37,000 combat troops would be inserted in the first phase of operations with another 70,000 deployed through air reinforcement missions by the end of week two and by the end of the first month a total close to 158,000 would be on Australian soil. China and Indonesian had assessed that the number of initial combat troops being deployed would be enough to aggressively engage and nullify the 51,000 strong Australian military, of which only 12,000 were considered combat troops. The force in and around Darwin was assessed as the most powerful force in the Australian military and destroying this was a strategic objective. Once its destruction was achieved, victory would ensue.

Key objectives on East Timor were the airfields at Baucau on the northeastern coast and Comoro, which was located to the west of the capital Dili. Comoro, was clearly the more strategic of the two due to its proximity to the capital and the coast, where the Marine Amphibious Landings were to take place. The area was flat, easily accessible and would already be defended by the airborne assault troops before the Marines arrived. Any follow-on forces would then be in a position to reach out to key objectives in Dili and beyond as soon as they were established. The airborne troops would provide defence in depth before the Zubr –class vessels and their medium tanks and light armour arrived. Once the airfields were captured and made secure, transport aircraft would quickly build the occupying force up to 21,000. To ensure this could occur without incident the largest threat to the invasion force had to be eliminated. This threat came from the 650 combat troops from the Australian First Battalion (1-RAR) Light Infantry that was split between Batugade on the northern coast and Suai on the southern coast, a distance of 40km apart. The Australian Infantry were deemed the most dangerous element of the UN contingent on the island, so were to be attacked by the 2,000 Indonesian Kopassus Special Forces troops. These troops had inserted covertly into West Timor almost a week ago and were now infiltrating through the jungle by foot after transiting to the border region in canvas-covered trucks at night. Having inserted in company-sized groups they had rendezvoused at 2 pre-arranged RV's and reformed as 2 large assault formations in order to engage the Australian contingent. Almost 9-years since Indonesia gave up control of East Timor it was almost back in their grasp and, with it, billions of dollars of untapped oil and gas reserves that Australia was looking to extract. One of their final objectives would be to neutralize the small UN force still remaining on the island, which consisted of less than 1,800 Fijian, Brazilian and Bangladeshi logistical and administrational troops.

PART 12

A CLASH OF TITANS
(D+9)

DTG: Thursday-February 2nd ....2012.....0030hrs

LOCATION: Indian...Pakistani Kashmir Border Region....

SITUATION: Just 30-minutes before the invasion of East Timor and Australia...and only 6hrs 30-minutes before the invasion of Indian.... the Pakistani military build up continues.

Across the sea, on the other side of the Indian Ocean, Pakistani forces were using their last few hours conducting final preparations. They had already publicly amassed 150,000 troops and 400 Al-Khalid Main Battle Tanks (MBTs) on the border in response to the increased tensions in the Kashmir. India had deployed just over 60,000 on her side of the border with 150 T90 MBTs as it regarded this over zealous build up as Pakistani posturing again and did not feel the need to deploy anything other than a strong deterrent force. Little did the Indians know that this time, the force deployed against them was there solely to smash its way through the first line of Indian defences across the border. Further south, near Lahore, another force of 210,000 Pakistani troops with 700 MBTs was in place and ready to strike deep into Indian Territory. Pakistan would be attacking across 3 separate parts of the border in order to secure its strategic and tactical objectives, with the remainder of the Pakistani ground forces, some 250,000 troops with 1,100 Al-Khalid MBTs held in reserve and committed as required. With the Pakistani President believing that Chinese intervention would occur within less than a week he thought this would not be the case.

The tension in the Kashmir had mounted considerably in intensity since early 2011 with Pakistan accusing India of supporting Indian separatists in the region. These tensions had erupted into actual conflict between the 2 volatile nations with artillery duels the main weapon of choice. China had constantly warned India of its aggressive stance towards Pakistan in the disputed region while continuing to supply Pakistan with missile technology and new weaponry. The tension between China and India increased still further when the Chinese ambassador was killed in Delhi by a remote controlled car bomb in November 2011. The Chinese government, furious that India could allow an ambassador to be murdered in this way indirectly held the Indian government responsible for his death and accused them of aiding and abetting criminals. The reality was that Chinese intelligence acting under the highest authority from Beijing had, in fact, murdered its own ambassador to inflame their strained relationship with India, a move designed to further suit China's stance on the India/Pakistani stand-off.

The potential flashpoint in the Kashmir had been top of many foreign government's agendas before January 24th 2012, but after the events of the past week in Washington DC, Europe and South Korean, it had fallen off the political radar. China's jigsaw was slowly coming together and the final pieces were about to be placed on the board with the invasion of 2 more continents.

The number of Pakistani troops assaulting into India from the far north of the country amounted to 10 Divisions of 15,000 men, each with their own Brigade of Artillery, Communications and Engineers. Two of the Divisions were armoured and equipped with their very own indigenously produced Main Battle Tank (MBT) 2000 - the Al-Khalid Tank, which is based on the Chinese Type 90 MBT. For the initial assault, 5 Divisions' worth of artillery, along with the reserve forces artillery, had been brought forward and this was now part of the overall fires plan designed to overwhelm Indian defences quickly. A further 14 Divisions were waiting in their start-line to the south near Lahore and, were responsible for storming the Indian Punjab region with Amristar, Ludhiana and Chandigarh their main objectives. The massive weight of firepower from the artillery along with aircraft from the Pakistani Air Force (PAF) intended to provide gaps, which mechanized units could then quickly exploit. Pakistan's doctrine of limited offensive-defence was about to be put into practice. The doctrine concept revolves around a large offensive action into enemy territory, thus throwing an enemy off-balance with Pakistani forces grabbing as much land as possible.

This allows Pakistan to fight a war on enemy territory and not on its own land. By taking land of strategic importance it can later be traded or used as a bargaining chip as the conflict unwinds. Pakistan had learnt the hard way the need for efficient lines of communication from previous wars and had ensured now that its forces had the correct logistical resources in place with a 120 day reserve of ammunition and fuel already prepared and prepositioned for the war ahead, with another 90 in reserve as required. Pakistan, acutely aware of having too many resources in too few locations, had adopted a policy of mass logistical dissemination and deception. The intent was to construct multiple Forward Operating Bases (FOB) at the less recognisable Pakistani air bases while building false fuel bladders and dummy aircraft at the more recognised airbases. They also planned to utilise the captured Indian airfields and one of these key bases was Srinagar. This was to be one of the first captured airfields turned into a FOB and re-supply depot for Pakistani and Chinese forces. These airfields would also provide Chinese aircraft with a base from which to attack Indian forces later.

General Rafee Asif Ahmed had been given the honour by the Chief of Army Staff -President Rahman Gul Mahomed, to command the combined armed forces on this historic day. President Mahomed, realising that the battlefield was a soldier's domain, had allowed his General the freedom to make key decisions without reference to himself during and after the invasion began. He had only requested that he be informed of Ahmed's every move via his aides. This was seen by the military commanders as an inspired decision on the President's part and, by allowing his military commanders to achieve their objectives with no outside political interference, ensured critical decisions could be acted on at speed. This was all out war and President Mahomed knew it could not be side tracked by political manoeuvering. General Ahmed and his hand-picked staff officers had worked for months on the invasion plan and it was about to be put into practice. The last of the artillery units had finally moved into position over the last 72hrs and were now waiting for H-Hour at 0700hrs. They had prepared thoroughly and were ready to unleash their frightening but remarkable power on to the unsuspecting Indian Line of Control (LOC). The LOC was the 740km disputed ceasefire line, which was formalised in 1972. It culminated in India building a fenced line called the Indian

Kashmir barrier which consists of 550km of 12-foot high double row fencing topped with barbed wire. It is electrified in places and some areas are mined but both sides still dispute the areas that each claim is theirs. The fence line was completed in 2005 with Pakistan at the time complaining to the UN Security Council, as they see the area between Jammu and Kashmir as un-demarcated and, therefore, the fence should not have been built. Another less known cease fire line over to the east is the Line of Actual Control (LAC), which is the ceasefire line between the People's Republic of China and India.

The Pakistani plan was predicated by an air force attack on key Indian airfields and military locations near Srinagar, Jummu, Amristar and Ludhiana, followed by huge artillery strikes across a vast area. One of Pakistan's main thrusts was centred against the Indian LOC near the Kashmir region with the line of axis via Abbottabad and on through the Pakistan controlled Haji Pir Pass in the northernmost quarter before driving hard to Srinagar. The Haji Pir Pass is dominated on both sides by high ridges and viewed as a strategic point and one the Pakistanis were keen to keep open within the first few hours. This would allow the Pakistani Division's access to the main Srinagar-Jummu highway and ultimately the airport at Srinagar, which was viewed as a major strategic location and important to any defence of the Jummu region. Already a Battalion from the Special Service Group, or SSG, Independent Commando unit of the Pakistan army had infiltrated over rugged terrain some 12km beyond the heavily defended area into Indian Territory and was now in position to provide delaying ambushes on the roads leading to the Haji Pir Pass.

If India had any aspirations to block the Pass by reinforcing its troops near to this location, the SSG would be in a position to react to any Indian aggression in order to ensure it remained open. On call were strike aircraft and artillery and, armed with their standard G3 Hecklar & Koch (H&K) 7.62 Assault Rifles, MG3 7.62mm NATO German General Purpose Machine Guns, 81mm Mortars and the Chinese-copied Eryx Short Range Anti-Armour Portable Weapon System, they had the capacity to inflict severe damage on any Indian force approaching them. With the Mirabel thermal imager site, the copied Eryx provided the SSG with an improved capability in accuracy and penetration. Fired from the shoulder or using the tripod, it was capable of defeating all modern static or moving tanks equipped with explosive reactive armour (ERA), with its tandem, high explosive warhead, also effective against bunkers and earthworks. The SSG mission was to hold the ground for 4 to 6hrs before relief from heavier ground forces arrived. Another main axis of attack would emanate from the Islamabad/Rawalpindi area directly east towards Jummu airport, which lay south of Srinagar. These forces would then swing north to link up with those moving south before taking the strategic airfield at Srinagar in a pincer movement.

Further south, the third and final assault by 216,000 troops would see them advance from Lahore towards Amristar, taking the airport there, before moving east to take Ludhiana and Chandigarh in anticipation of cutting off any Indian reinforcement for those encircled Indian troops in the north. Once the Kashmir region and the northern part of the Punjab region were under Pakistani control they would turn their attention to Delhi, New Delhi and the Indian army who would no doubt be forming up and approaching from the south.

25-minutes before H-Hour, large numbers of multi-role fighter aircraft from numerous airfields in Pakistan were launched. The first wave of 250 aircraft from the Pakistan Air force (PAF) were roaring skywards to attack Indian forces on the other side of the border, before taking part in attacking depth military airfields at the edge of their endurance in India. A further 44 aircraft on a completely separate but secret mission were heading north for Tajikistan to attack the small but strategic Indian-controlled airfield at Farkhor, which contained 23 Su30K MK1's and 18 indigenously-built light combat fighter aircraft - the HAL Tejas. The base, which is located 80km (50 miles) south of the Tajikistan capital Dushanbe near the Afghanistan border, was considered too close to Pakistan to allow it to remain untouched and could pose a significant threat to Pakistani forces. Pakistan had earmarked 18 F16 Fighting Falcons and 26 of its latest upgraded JF-17 4th generation highly manoeuvrable fighter aircraft for this mission.

Pakistan had also deployed 2 Saab-2000 Erieye Airborne Early Warning & Control Systems (AEW&C) from Sweden and these were now providing 360 degree protection and tracking of air targets over the horizon near Afghanistan and India. The high performance AWE&C system comprises an active phased array pulse doppler radar, including integrated secondary surveillance radar and an identification friend or foe capability and brings to the battlefield a comprehensive modular command and control system, electronic support measures and communications, including data links. Although instrumented to a range of 450km a typical detection range against a fighter aircraft size target would have been in excess of 350km. The turboprop SAAB 2000 with a crew of 15 operates from its standard operational altitude of 6,000-metres (19,685 feet) and combines near jet speeds and climb rate. Unlike the rotodome antenna seen on other western AWACs, the SAAB 2000 has a fixed dual-sided and electronically scanned antenna mounted on top of the fuselage, which places less demand on a small aircraft.

At 0658hrs the first wave of aircraft crossed the border towards the Indian bases. 2-minutes later the Pakistani artillery launched a massive and coordinated artillery barrage, courtesy of more than 4,500 pieces of artillery at the well dug in Indian Army. Included in this firestorm was the 122mm T-83 Azar and the 107mm T-81 Multiple Launch Rocket Systems (MLRS), plus a mixed batch of 155mm, 203mm, 120mm, 122mm and 105 mm with large quantities of High Explosive shells.

Held in reserve and ready to move with the forward advancing elements were Pakistani artillery units who possessed American towed artillery, such as the 203mm M-110A-2, the 155mm M-109A-2 and the 105mm M-7. Also available to the front line troops were large numbers of the Chinese made 155mm PLZ45 Self-Propelled Gun-Howitzer, which China had been supplying for the last 3-years.

Squadron Leader Mostafa Hassan was an experienced pilot with the Pakistani Air Force and after 4-years' flying on the F16 Flying Falcons; Hassan had retrained on the JF-17 and flown this aircraft for the last 3. Squadron Leader Hassan had been given command of a special task force, which was now flying at Mach 1.1 towards the Pakistan/Afghanistan/Tajikistan triangle in the northwestern corner of Pakistan, the maximum speed of Mach 1.6 being somewhat curtailed with the heavy ordnance load beneath his wings. Although designed to carry both Air-to-Air and Air-to-Ground weaponry on its 7-store stations and a maximum weapons load of 3,800kg, Hassan's JF-17 carried only 2 SD-10 Beyond Visual Range Air to Air Missiles (BVRAAMs), 2 Medium Range Anti Air Missiles (AAM) and 2 Cluster Bombs. The majority of the other JF-17s carried similar loads with 8 aircraft carrying the HAFR-1 Airfield Denial Weapon in place of cluster bombs.

The task force mission was to destroy the Indian aircraft in situ at Farkhor and prevent further use of the runway before they had time to react to the events on the border with India. Hassan enjoyed flying the JF-17 with its many advanced technologies such as the BVRAAMs and multi-role day or night all weather capability. Similar to the Russian Mig-29, this aircraft was a joint venture with China and was fitted with Forward Looking Infrared (FLIR) Night Vision and Advanced Avionics from the Italian Grifo S-7 Fire Control Radar, which gave the aircraft a look-down, shoot-down as well as ground strike capability. The latest avionics update was 2-years behind schedule but it mattered not. The system was adequate and well proven and the pilots in Hassan's Squadron trusted the technology. With the JF-17s carrying their heavier loads the PAF F16 Fighting Falcons came only equipped for Air-to-Air Combat. Their mission - to protect the JF-17s during their bombing runs on to Farkhor airbase. They were equipped with 2, all-aspect Short Range Air-to-Air Missiles AIM-9Ls on the wing tips and a pair of AIM-9Ps on the outermost wing tip. The AIM-9 Sidewinder Missile, in its day, was one of the world's most successful Short Range Air-to-Air Missiles and was the export model from the United States. It came with a reduced smoke motor, a new insensitive munitions warhead and an improved guidance and control section. The F16s were also armed with the General Electric M61A1 Vulcan 6 Barrel 20mm Cannon, which fired M50 ammunition at 6,000 rounds per minute.

Hassan and the remainder of the task force had taken off in the dark from the PAF Base Sarghoda and 3 other locations, rendezvoused at their air RV point and headed north at 8,000-feet towards the North West Frontier Province. They then turned on a heading for the Hindu Kush, which lies near to the Afghanistan/ Pakistan/Tajikistan border. Here they would have to climb a lot higher to transit over the mountains rearing up in front of them but close enough to them to be evasive to radar. The remainder of their route involved cutting across Afghanistan airspace between the Tirich Tir (mountain) at 25,230-feet and, the Dorah Pass at 22,448-feet before descending once again towards the towns of Chakaran, Feyzabad and Rostag before the final swing north-west to the Tajikistan border and Farkhor. Once over the Hindu Kush the flight time would be relatively short and surprise against Farkhor would be complete.

As the artillery began smashing into the Indian lines of defence, mechanised infantry units started advancing across their start lines in their indigenously produced, upgraded version, of the M113 Armoured Personnel Carrier (APC) - the Al-Talha, along with thousands of BTR-70s and M113 APCs, with the heavier Al-Zarar MBT and Al Khalid MBT 2000s following on, closely behind.

Pakistani troops found the initial resistance light in comparison to the force numbers they were facing - that was until they came in range of the Indian Armoured Division and 2 Infantry Mechanised Divisions near to Srinagar airport. The Indians knew the importance of this location and had well-established defences with the city and airport well screened to the north and west. They were the first to be targeted by aircraft from the PAF and as a result suffered many casualties. There were also reports coming in from other hard pressed Indian units near the border stating that huge Pakistani forces were pushing in from Abbottabad. An Indian Brigade in that area had attempted to push forces into the Haji Pir Pass but had ran into well sited ambushes at great cost to their Mechanised Infantry's Reconnaissance Vehicles, APCs and T90 MBTs. The Indians attempted to push through twice but to no effect and, had to resort to limited artillery strikes against their attackers before being forced to withdraw as the PAF launched cluster bomb attacks against them followed by large numbers of Pakistani forces surging into and beyond the pass under cover of immense firepower. There was nothing for the Indians to do other than fight a delaying action as they were forced back towards Srinagar. The Indian Divisions and Brigades in this region were, in effect, being cut off and surrounded in a pincer movement as the large Pakistani force from Rawalpindi came within range of Jammu airport. Unaware of their fate the Indians continued to fight and defend Srinagar but, with the third Pakistan assault force pouring across from Lahore to Amristar, with a mission to block any Indian reinforcement to the north, the complete destruction of the 60,000 Indian troops defending the Kashmir region was imminent. Outnumbered and outgunned, it was only a matter of time before the Pakistan plan succeeded.

Pakistani forces were swarming into India on 3 separate fronts now, with the spread out Indian forces bending and breaking under the relentless pressure from air and artillery strikes. Indian air force assets were now involved in the battle and had achieved some success against the PAF and, against Pakistani ground troops, but the surprise and scale of the attack was proving overwhelming. More than 350,000 Pakistani troops were attacking across a huge front and the Indian army was unprepared for an assault on this scale. This was no longer a Kashmir incursion….this was a full blown invasion.

Teams from the Pakistani Special Services Group (SSG) were 14km inside Indian Territory having infiltrated into the area during the hours of darkness. One of these groups had set up a 4-man trigger OP (observation post) on the forward slope of a large feature with excellent views to their east and the road below them. They were the eyes and ears of their SSG Battalion who were in position 2km to their west. A short time after the PAF aircraft had swept down the valley they had heard the distinctive sound of vehicles approaching from down the valley. These were an element of vehicles from the Reserve Mechanised Indian Brigade and who were tasked with strengthening the Indian troops position further west. The first vehicle that came in to view was a BRDM-2 followed by 8 more before the configuration of vehicles changed to BMP-1 and BMP-2s, while at the rear were 12 T90 MBTs. Altogether 48 vehicles were passing their location. Corporal Iqbal, commanding the OP, was amazed that aircraft passing overhead had not picked the column up but it mattered not now; what was important was that his Battalion was going to get their first taste of combat against an enemy they had long desired to fight. After the third vehicle had passed, Corporal Iqbal thumbed the radio and passed the standby to his commander 2km away. His commander was situated in the centre of the killer group, which was spread out over 600-metres. The word was passed that an enemy column was approaching their position. The Pakistani's had laid out a typical linear ambush with 2 cut-off groups and a main killing group in the middle. Each cut-off was approximately 200-metres away from the killing group, and consisted of 2 Platoons each, while the killing group consisted of 2 Company strength numbering 240 men. In depth and out of site was a backstop of 2 further Platoons who were giving the ambush site protection from the rear. This location also contained the mortars and these were on call for the Mortar Fire Controller (MFC) who was collocated with the Battalion Commander in the killing group. There was a further team of 12 troops equipped with 4 of the copied Eryx anti tank weapon systems and 6 German MG 7.62 GPMGs with 2,000 rounds per gun. These were positioned 400-metres west of the right hand or most western cut-off position and from their location had a view down the entire road. Their mission was to take on the first few vehicles in the convoy once they reached the right hand cut-off. That would be the signal for the cut-offs and killing group to open fire on those vehicles in the ambush site. 11-minutes after the trigger OP had called standby, the first vehicles started approaching the left hand cut-off locations. All the Pakistani forces had thumbed off their safety catches and were now just waiting in cover for the signal to open fire. The ambush was set and the Indian troops were driving right in to the trap due to their eagerness to get to the Haji Pir Pass area. Their aim was to bottle up any Pakistani units attempting to enter India through this way but their haste in getting there was proving to be their downfall. The Indian Battalion located further up the pass had radioed in that they were under attack and elements from the Reserve Mechanised Indian Brigade was expected to bring much needed firepower.

Vehicles had been slowly passing the left cut-off now for 4-minutes and a large portion were already past the centre of the killing group. From left cut-off to right cut-off the distance was 1,000-metres and there were already 27 vehicles in the killing area. As the first vehicle reached the right hand cut-off the Eryx operator looked into his Mirabel thermal imaging site and picked out his target. The wire guided missile being ready to fire in less than 5-seconds was soft launched from its tube due to the enclosed firing point and as it sped towards its target, it was optically tracked by the operator using the system's semi-automatic command to line-of-sight guidance and, from 400-metres, with a head on shot, no real course corrections were required. It left the tube at 18-metres per second before it accelerated away to 245- metres per second towards its intended victim, its 137mm tandem shaped charge HE warhead hungrily anticipating impact. Seconds after launch the warhead struck the second vehicle dead centre of mass and the shaped charge penetrated the metal with ease. This was enough to kill those inside but the Eryx system releases a second charge inside after penetration and it was this charge that exploded inside the vehicle, causing it to disintegrate. 2-seconds later the first vehicle in the column received the same attention from a second Eryx operator. The ambush had been well and truly sprung.

The Eryx operators were reloading and firing their allocation of 2 missiles each and a total of 8 missiles were fired in less than 2-minutes. 7 missiles had destroyed 7 vehicles with the last missile slamming into the road near the 8th vehicle, possibly just out of the 600-metre maximum range that the Eryx operates under. Close on 600 men now fired everything they had into the stacked up vehicles from ranges of 200 to 300-metres. Indian troops began pouring out of the burning vehicles but ran straight into the 6 GPMG firers' sights and those of the cut-offs and killer groups massed weapons. The 6 GPMG firers had a clear line of site down the road and were able to use their weapons to the most effect by sweeping their devastating firepower up and down the rows of burning vehicles and running men. An alert Indian BRDM-2 gunner, seeing the carnage to his front had spotted the Eryx firing position. He quickly locked on his quadruple AT-2 Swagger ATGM System with its Semi-Active Infrared/Guidance and at a range of 700-metres launched the first of 4 missiles towards the Eryx firing point. The first missile slammed into the rocky area where the 12 man team was deployed followed by a second, third and fourth missile. The blast and shrapnel from rock and metal missile casing ripped into the Pakistani team and wiped out all but 3 of them. Indian troops were now in some form of cover on the side of the road attempting to return fire on to the Pakistani positions above them but to no avail. In 15-murderous minutes all those unfortunate to be caught in the ambush were dead or dying, with more than 31 vehicles destroyed. The left hand cut-off, however, was having a difficult time after they had come under direct tank fire from Indian T90 MBTs. The Pakistani patrol had had to resort to bringing in artillery strikes to push them back and, 30-minutes after the artillery strikes the area was clear with Indian forces pulling back, leaving their dead and injured where they lay. The injured would lie there for the remainder of the day until Pakistani relief forces reached the SSG location. One hour later the Indian army would attempt another probe on foot with 300 troops and tank support against the SSG left cut-off position but the SSG commander had already anticipated this and strengthened this position with 2 more Platoons from the killer group. The Indians this time were more prepared and aggressive in their attempt to destroy the SSG location but a culmination of small arms fire and a hastily called for air strike by 4 JF-17s using cluster bombs, ensured this second attack was repulsed.

After passing through their Initial Point (IP) the Pakistani aircraft were now just 4-minutes from their target- Farkhor. Squadron Leader Hassan and the remainder of his task force received a final update from the Saab-2000 Erieye Airborne Early Warning aircraft that 6 contacts had taken off from the Farkhor airbase. Hassan had a quick pang of anxiety but surely they couldn't know what was about to occur. Unknown to Hassan and his flight, the Indian pilots regularly took off at this time to practice take-off and landing drills before breakfast. Unfortunately for the Indians their aircraft were also unarmed…..

Dropping to 600ft, Hassan and the remainder of the JF-17s took up formation in 13 groups of 2 aircraft and began sweeping into the air base. Circling above the JF-17s, were the F16s and it was these aircraft that now hunted the 6 Su30K MK1's that had just taken off. Strung out on the airfield in 6 neat rows were the remaining 36 Su30K's and HAL Tejas Fighter Aircraft. There were also 4 large hangers that probably contained aircraft under maintenance. The unarmed Su30K's were no match for the Pakistani F16s and their AIM-9 Sidewinder Missiles, which were used with devastating effect. Outnumbered, 2 of the remaining Su30K pilots tried to go low and fly over Afghanistan but were eventually caught and shot down 20km inside Afghanistan airspace.

Back at Farkhor, Hassan, almost on target and flying in at 600kts, selected the cluster bomb dispenser under the wing and dropped it over the first row of fighters. As the dispenser dropped away from the aircraft it was stabilised in flight by the small fin assemblies and at the predetermined height of 400 feet above the target the proximity fuse on the dispenser opened up and discharged its payload of sub munitions over the aircraft below. They were a mixture of anti-material (AT), incendiary and anti-personnel (AP) bomblets. The mass of sub munitions released from inside their container covered an impact area 600-metres long and 100-metres wide, with the first rows of aircraft receiving multiple strikes before exploding. Two maintenance personnel standing next to one of the aircraft were wide eyed and open mouthed as Hassan's aircraft released its load. Trying to run from the sub munitions spreading over a huge area was impossible and both were obliterated in seconds after managing to run no more than a few metres from the aircraft. Over the following 10-minutes wave upon wave of JF-17 thunder aircraft released their rain of destruction onto the unprepared and undefended airfield. With the main mission accomplished, the JF-17s with the HAFR-1 Airfield Denial Weapon were ordered in to release their munitions. Once released, the HAFR-1's small deceleration parachute slowed the bomb before the main parachute deployed. The device then decelerated to 0.45-metres a second, under control and, to a height of 76-metres above the airfield runway before automatically detaching its parachute. At this point, the warhead became armed and a booster motor fired, which accelerated the bomb to more than 280-metres a second before it slammed into the ground. The bomb, on a short time delay penetrated through the runway surface before the warhead exploded. The pressure from the underground explosion headed upwards and broke the surface causing a large crater on the runway with large slabs and cracks radiating out from the crater beyond the initial impact area. After the JF-17s had dropped their final HAFR-1s, the airfield runway was inoperable to aircraft and would never be used again without extensive repair work. The tower along with the 4 hangers was destroyed by cluster bombs and cannon fire. The destruction of the second hanger was indeed spectacular as 2 fully laden aviation fuel tankers exploded, resulting in a huge 200-metre high fireball, which was observed for miles around.

It had taken 25-minutes to destroy Farkhor and Squadron Leader Hassan and his task force were now looping to the northeast before swinging south towards the Hindu Kush. Upon crossing the border with Pakistan they broke into three groups and headed for the airfields Chilas, Gilgit and Peshawar. Hassan's group of 12 aircraft were down to go to Gilgit, which was just a small limited facilities airbase, but fuel and munitions had been pre-positioned by Pakistan in anticipation of a quick turnaround so that all the aircraft could be used against the Indian army and enemy airfields to the east. Hassan and his flight were on the ground for less than one hour before taking to the sky once more. During the flight into Indian airspace Hassan had received a call from SSG ground troops near the Haji Pir Pass who were under direct attack from T90 Russian-made MBTs and Indian Infantry. He then ordered 3 aircraft to follow him to launch cluster bomb strikes against the tanks and troops in the valleys below before heading deep into Indian Territory to attack 3 major Indian Air Force airfields. Hassan lost 3 aircraft on that last mission and, from the 44 who attacked and returned from Farkhor, a total of 8 aircraft would not return after entering India.

Within hours Indian forces were on the back foot in the Kashmir and starting to move south to the Srinagar stronghold. Pakistani artillery had achieved the desired effect and broke the Indian lines, which was now being exploited by Pakistani ground forces. Srinagar was facing huge bombardments from aircraft and artillery but so far holding its own. The 45,000-strong Indian forces in that area were intent on holding their ground for as long as possible.

Two days into the war, Pakistani troops from the north had closed to within 3km of Srinagar and the southern Pakistani forces, having first taken Jammu airfield had approached to within 8km from the south. The Indian Divisions in Srinagar were now surrounded, running low on ammunition and facing annihilation if relief was not forthcoming. The Indian army was almost a million strong but they did not have the resources in place yet to mount a relief operation. After a week of fierce fighting the Indian garrison led by Major General Varindar Chaudhary surrendered, having suffered massive casualties and loss of equipment. 60,000 Indian troops had been defeated with Pakistan now in control of a third of the country from the Kashmir region south to Amristar and Ludhiana. The gains achieved by the speed of the invasion even surprised the Pakistan government and military commanders and, flushed with success, the Pakistani President decided to press the advantage further by committing part of his reserve to the forces in India to take the number of troops above 500,000 with the intention of taking the battle south to New Delhi and Delhi.

Huge numbers of Air Defence (AD) assets were now in operation over Pakistani airfields and cities as the Indian Air Force attempted to hit back but the Pakistanis' well-prepared AD systems exacted a heavy price on the 750-strong Indian Air Force (IAF) for any successes it achieved. The Pakistani Air Force, which had increased significantly in size over the last 4-years, was intent on not allowing India air superiority or supremacy over the battlefield. In anticipation of the potential tank battles on the plains of the Punjab and beyond, Pakistan forward deployed some of its 20 AH-1 Cobra Helicopter Gunships to Amristar and began deploying 150 of its M11 Short Range Ballistic Missiles (SRBM) and 54 M11 Launchers. The M11 Missile was one of the systems provided by China, with China even allowing a facility to be constructed in Pakistan with the sole intention of building the M11 in-country. With a range of 300km and a 500kg HE payload it was a formidable threat to Indian military forces, government establishments and cities. The M11 also had a nuclear carrying capability but Pakistan had reiterated strongly on world television that they had NO FIRST USE INTENTION of using their nuclear weapons and that the nuclear option was a deterrent only.

With just over a week gone since the invasion began, Pakistan continued to make huge gains into Indian Territory. India were faced with a well-trained and well-equipped Pakistani invasion force but with the third largest army in the world it would only be a matter of time before the full wrath of the 1.2 million Indian army could be unleashed. This was what China had been waiting for and had already rejected Pakistani calls to enter the war. China, in response to the ongoing crisis between Pakistan and India, had informed the world's press that it had deployed 55,000 troops to the Chinese controlled northeastern Kashmir region but in reality this figure was close to 350,000. They were also secretly moving troops and armour into Burma. The military junta in Burma, an ally of China and one that had benefited greatly from the relationship, had imposed marshal law due to the fighting on its border and placed the country under strict military curfew. This was all at China's request so that huge numbers of its forces could move unhindered through the country. Like China, Burma controlled the internet service providers and like China, had ensured the system was no longer in operation. China, clear in its objective and with more than 2 million ground troops to call upon, was mobilising its forces with pace. By the time its troops intervened in Pakistan it would have more than 900,000 ready to commence the mother of all battles against its biggest Asian rival, with more to follow if needed.

Two more weeks passed and Pakistan, still making huge strides through India, had taken Delhi and New Delhi and swept down the west side of the Ganges in the east of the country as far as Patna before continuing onto Agra and the Chota Nagpur Plateau near the Tropic of Cancer. They were now 800-miles into Indian Territory, with their forces spread out from Ahmadabad in the far west of the country, through to Bopal in the centre and as far to the east as Calcutta - a distance of some 1,600-miles. This was their first mistake in the whole campaign and India would look to capitalise on Pakistani's over extension. It was mid-March and 5-weeks into the war when Pakistani forces were held for the first time 350-miles south of New Delhi in a huge tank battle on the Chota Nagpur Plateau, a battle, reminiscent of those fought in World War 2.

The Battle of the Chota Nagpur Plateau proved to be India's Stalingrad. More than 1,700 tanks were involved - 712 from Pakistan and 1,200 from India - plus thousands of APCs, massed artillery and more than 273,000 infantry from both sides. The Pakistani MBT 2000 has an enemy engagement system that is one of the best in Asia but, outnumbered almost two to one it eventually succumbed. The battle, predominately mechanised, lasted for almost 4-days and losses were great on both sides but the end result was that Indian repulsed the Pakistani army after bringing in a reserve force of 90,000 at a crucial moment and it was this that succeeded in pushing the Pakistani forces back 10-miles. Not a significant distance but, after 6-weeks of almost non-stop fighting, defeat after defeat and continually conceding ground, this victory was most welcome. There followed a war of attrition along the line for the next 2-weeks with no side really dominating the other and India for the first time felt the tide may be turning their way. It was during the Chota Nagpur Plateau campaign that conventional Short-Range and Medium-Range Ballistic Missiles (SRBM – MRBM) were fired for the first time at each other's major military and civilian industrial areas, primarily because aircraft were unable to breach each others Air Defences effectively. The civilian loss of life was felt on both sides but the carnage continued.

Behind the scenes, Pakistan was now imploring China to step in as planned but China yet again stated its troops were not yet fully prepared and the glorious Pakistani military would need to fight alone for the time being. Pakistan was furious with China and made it clear this was a betrayal of their agreement but they also knew they had no real choice other than to continue fighting a war it now knew it could not win without China's much needed intervention.

The decisive swing in the war occurred 2-weeks after the massive tank battle at Chota Nagpur when a huge Indian counter attack on 2 fronts broke through on the eastern side, 80-miles north of Calcutta. Once breakthrough was achieved, Indian troops swung west and started to roll up the Pakistani lines that were under immense pressure from 640,000 Indian troops. The attack on the 420,000 strong Pakistani forces turned into something of a rout and they lost almost 170,000, either killed or captured, in the following 5-days. India was now on the ascendancy and pushing hard but it had not been without cost. Since the war started almost 2-months ago they had suffered nigh on 312,000 dead, injured or captured, lost vast amounts of tanks, APCs, aircraft and artillery. A massive amount had been lost and yet, the drive to push Pakistani troops out of India was just beginning.

The war was now taking on a savagery not witnessed in this part of the world for years and no quarter was given or asked for from either side. Pakistan had committed most of its reserves to the drive south and even brought in thousands of its border guards to act as infantry but to no avail. The Indian army, much larger and with more resources, was able to absorb the attrition rate better than the Pakistani army could. Pakistan still possessed a huge amount of artillery and without this support the result could have been much worse. Pakistan had already seen some of its major military industries destroyed by Indian missiles such as the Heavy Industries Taxila, which produced the MBT 2000 amongst other weapon systems. It was all having an effect on the outcome of the war but there was no option other than to continue until China intervened. President Rahman Gul Mahomed was raging at his Chinese counterpart but, was again assured that China was almost ready and only late heavy snow was making the movement of troops difficult and they had to hold a while longer. India also suffered important military industrial losses and none were felt more than the loss of their Su-30Mk1 factory at Ozhar near Nasik where they had made the Russian designed aircraft under licence since 2002.

Over the next 8-days India made huge gains in much the same way that Pakistan had done in the early days of the war and, succeeded in forcing Pakistani forces back beyond Delhi and New Delhi, through Ludhiana and into the outskirts of Amristar, where the Pakistani lines eventually held. This was more to do with the Indian military regrouping and conducting extensive resupplies of its forward units in anticipation of the next phase, which was to drive Pakistan from all Indian land and the Kashmir once and for all. Pakistan was down to 210,000 fighting troops now, with India still able to project 580,000 into battle. Pakistan knew full well that the last defence would be in the Indian Punjab region; if they were defeated here India would be free to invade the Kashmir and Pakistan at will.

With the war entering its third month the battle intensified around Amristar, and with the beleaguered Pakistani forces unable to give anymore, surrender was imminent. The time had arrived for China to intervene, and with Pakistan militarily impotent, 350,000 Chinese troops made their long awaited advance over the Line of Actual Control (LAC) from northeast Kashmir. They were to reinforce the Pakistani troops near Amristar and repel the Indian attackers, while lead elements from a second army of 580,000 entered India via Burma soon after and, began heading for the right flank of the Indian forces making for Amristar. China would, if necessary commit 1.5 million men into this war to ensure India was destroyed as an economic and military power. The Chinese plan was simple - with the timing of China's attack critical in ensuring that the Pakistan military was almost destroyed. This would ensure that any Islamic threat to the region from Pakistan was curtailed; the Indian army would be drained of its huge resources leaving it weak enough for China to complete what Pakistan couldn't.

The actions on the ground had indicated both scenarios had now occurred, with China content that the time was right to take on the Indian military machine by hitting it from 2 directions - head on and from their exposed right flank before bringing in, if necessary, reserves of 600,000 to destroy India completely as a military and economic power. Their manufacturing and heavy industries would be destroyed in the process and after that....China did not care. Their plan was not to occupy land, but solely to destroy their great Asian rival.

....The Clash of Titans had begun ....
....China officially declared war on India 2-hours after crossing the LAC....

PART 13

THE GATEWAY TO ASIA
(D+9)

DTG: Thursday-February 2nd ....2012......0300hrs and 0330hrs (time difference between locations)

LOCATION: Off the coast of East Timor and Darwin

SITUATION: Chinese & Indonesian amphibious assault forces are rapidly approaching their objectives and the beginning of a simultaneous assault on East Timor and Darwin Australia draws near...

Indonesian troops, aided by formidable Chinese naval assets, were about to begin their long awaited invasion of East Timor and Australia, with a huge armada of 361 ships containing 3 Aircraft Carrier Battle Groups, landing ships of various sizes, destroyers, frigates, submarines, merchant ships, resupply vessels, minesweepers and converted container ships forming up in the Timor Sea.

China had always known this would be a difficult operation to pull off and convincing the Indonesians had not been easy. Knowing the Indonesians had the manpower but not the amphibious capability meant China had to build her naval forces considerably to even consider such an assault and, covering 3,300 miles was never going to be easy. Dragon's Claw planning committees had long ago identified action points from their initial estimates and one of these was the modernisation and expansion of the People's Liberation Army Navy (PLAN). Initial changes occurred in the 1990s, but the real push had begun in earnest from 2000 with a massive jump in capability and new ships by 2005. By 2010 the pace of expansion had more than trebled, with a new generation of ships in place with advanced combat intelligence systems, better real time information capabilities and improved long-range surveillance. Other additions were Enhanced Anti-Submarine and Electronic Counter Measure Capabilities. It was one of the most ambitious build ups in the world and, with the economy growing at such rapid speed, money became no object.

Since 1990, 10 of China's largest ship builders had acquired western computer-aided design and manufacture software and in 2010 the China State Shipbuilding Corporation alone claimed more than 50 percent of global ship construction orders. A deal worth in excess of $4 billion annually was also concluded with Russia in 2004 for Zubr-class Air Cushion Landing Craft. The deal, initially for 22, was later increased to 40 of these high speed amphibious vessels. Crewed by a 27 man crew and capable of carrying 3 Medium Battle Tanks - the T-80B Tank, 10 APC's or 300 Assault Troops, the Zubr-class Landing Craft could also deliver 130 tons of cargo. It came fitted with its own integral defensive capability - the Strela-3 Air Defence Missile System and the 30mm AK-630 Air Defence Gun with 6,000 rounds, capable of taking on manned or unmanned air attack or sea skimming missiles. A limitation was its range of 300 miles but transporting 24 vessels over to Australia was seen as vital to the invasion.....so, to overcome this problem, a secret project was initiated.

China, not just intent on developing its own indigenous military shipping or purchasing Russian military amphibious vessels, worked extensively on merchant shipping at the same time. Part of the merchant shipping construction incorporated the secret project, called project S4. This was the construction of civilian vessels including 4 float on float off dry dock vessels similar to the merchant ships, Super Servant 3 and 4 and, the much larger Blue Marlin piggy back ships. By drawing in sea water these vessels sink and allow ships to straddle them before expelling the water to rise up again, leaving these piggy backed vessels on a dry deck before transporting their loads to a designated location to reverse the process.

The vessels China commissioned were nicknamed Sea Dragon's by the Chinese navy and were 229.5m long and 67m wide, with a maximum sailing weight of 81,000 tons. With more than 11,000 square metres of space, each of these dry dock ships were capable of carrying 6 Zubr-class Landing Craft with the full load of Medium Battle Tanks (MBT's), Armoured Personnel Carriers (APCs) or hundreds of combat troops in each craft. With their 60-knot speed the 24 Zubr-class vessels would be able to disgorge their combined combat force of 40 APCs, 33 MBTs and 2,700 troops faster than any other means available to the PLAN. It was a force multiplier in the true sense of the word and gave the Chinese military a decisive edge in building up combat power quickly.

The backbone of the Chinese amphibious assault force consisted of 28 Type 072-II Yuting–class Large Landing Ships, 23 of the newer Type 072-III Large Landing Ships, which could take 10 MBTs and 250 Marines on each vessel, and 17 of the double hulled Type 073IV-YunShu-class landing ship. The 68 vessels with a force projection capability of 612 Medium Battle Tanks and 17,000 men would carry a mix of vehicle and troop configurations to the carefully chosen landing areas that were being continuously monitored by Chinese agents in Darwin.

Their actual force delivery on land would consist of 17,000 troops plus a mix of 180 x T-80B Medium Battle Tanks and the PTL02 Assault Tank Destroyers, plus - 400 Type 89/YW Amphibious APCs, 100 Tiema C2200 6x6 7.5t High-Mobility Heavy Truck Vehicles capable of towing the Type 85 122mm Towed Howitzer, of which 36 were to be initially delivered, and more than 6,500 tons of ammunition/stores. Included in the manifest were 64 of the latest EQ2050 High-Mobility Multi-Purpose Wheeled Vehicles, which are a Chinese copy of the American HMMWV.

Operational for the first time were 4 of the brand new 20,000 ton LHD–class Amphibious Ships that transported the latest troop-carrying Type 722-III Dagu class Air Cushion Landing Craft in a concealed dock. With space for 1,400 Marines on board, this vessel can project all its forces onto land in 2-lifts, using the 4 landing craft and its 3 Super Frelon Heavy Lift Helicopters on the rear flight deck.

Following on from the main assault force were 18 of the older Yuhai–class Medium Landing Ships with 250 troops in each. In total the PLAN were looking to project a force of almost 25,000 Chinese Marines, with its own integral supporting arms including armour and artillery within the first few hours, followed by another 12,000 Indonesian troops within 12hrs. The Indonesian troops deployed throughout the myriad of civilian and military shipping would be inserted by the remaining 8 Yuhai–class Medium Landing Ships with 250 troops in each and with their own integral APCs. The remainder to be collected by returning Super Frelon Helicopters and Air Cushion

Landing Craft after the Chinese had conducted their 2 Divisional Amphibious Assaults. China was watching this invasion with keen eyes as the lessons learnt from this operation would expose key requirements for the eventual invasion of Taiwan.

The 2 Aircraft Carriers earmarked for the invasion of Australia were crucial to the assault and these were protected by their own Carrier Battle Fleet. The combined force was split into 2 Battle Groups with each Battle Group consisting of 3 Russian made Sovremenny-class Destroyers, equipped with what western defence analysts are calling an Aircraft Carrier Killer - the SS-N-22 Missile; with each destroyer carrying 8 of these missiles. In addition to the SS-N-22s, the vessel carried 48 Air Defence Missiles, Torpedoes, a Long Range Gun and a Mine Laying Capability and posed a serious threat capability to the Australian Navy. With a displacement of 8,480 tons these were the largest class of destroyer in the fleet and came armed with an Anti-Submarine Helicopter and Sophisticated Electronic Warfare Systems. The SS-N-22 Sunburn (NATO designation) is a sea skimming missile, which can be launched from 10-120km with a 300kg high explosive warhead before reaching a velocity of mach 2.5, or greater than 1,700 mph. A key defence for the Sovremenny-class Destroyer is made possible by utilising the vessels three dimensional circular scan radar. This performs target tracking for its 48 Surface-to-Air Shtil Missiles, which can engage targets with speeds up to 830m/s out to 25km.

There were also 2 type 052C Lanzhou-class Destroyers in each Battle Group. These were Air Defence Missile Destroyers and featured the Aegis style Phased Array Radar System and Vertically Launched HQ-9 Long Range Air Defence Missile System. The Aegis style system was a massive leap in technology for the Chinese, with the multi function 3 dimensional phased array radar allowing for advanced, automatic detection and tracking of 200 targets while performing missile guidance functions simultaneously over 200 miles. In the past a separate radar and fire control system was required for firing missiles and was limited in its operation but the Lanzhou-class now represented China's first true fleet air defence capability.

Eight (4 to each battle group) of the 3,400 ton Ma'anshan-class Missile Frigates were also deployed to provide protection for the Carriers with their YJ-83 Sea-Skimming Anti-Ship Cruise Missiles.

Each Ma'anshan-class Frigate incorporates 4 launchers for this system and an additional 8 cell launcher for its HQ-7 Surface-to-Air Missile (SAM). The vessel incorporates some stealth features and modifications such as the sloped hull design and radar absorbent materials. The rear is fitted for a helicopter fight deck with an Anti-Submarine Helicopter Capability provided by the Kamov Ka-27 using its surface search radar, sonobuoys, dipping sonar and magnetic anomaly detectors.

The final combat surface vessels attached to each of the Australian bound battle groups were 2 of the Russian-made Slava-class Cruisers. The Slava-class Cruiser was built to compete with the US TICONDEROGO-class Cruiser and was the largest and most powerful missile carrier in the Chinese navy. They were equipped with 16 P-500/SS-N-12 Anti-Ship Sandbox Missiles with a range of 550km (330 miles). Launched from the side of the ship from prepared launch systems, these could target surface vessels and land targets. For air defence the Slava had available 8 B-303A Long Range Missiles, which were fired from the Vertical Launch Systems (VLS) via the underdeck drum launcher at the front and rear of the vessel. This system, containing 64 missiles can be used against air, land and surface targets. Closer in defence is achieved from the AK-630 30mm Gatling Gun, which can discharge 100 - 30 round bursts out to a range of 2,960m, while the Radar Directed Twin Barrel Automated Shipboard Artillery System, can fire 65 rounds/per/min against land, surface and air targets. The Slava also has its own Torpedo Anti-Ship Capability, using 2 Type 53 Torpedo Launchers with 5 tubes on each side of the ship and a complement of 20 torpedoes. Situated at the front of the ship is the vessel's final weapon system - the RPK-8 Zapad/RBU 600 Anti Submarine Warfare (ASW) Rail Launcher with its 12 Tube Anti-Submarine Rocket Mortar System. These are in-effect depth charges with multiple warheads and can be used against hostile torpedoes and submarines.

Subsurface lurked 2 Type 091 Han-class and 2 Type 093Han-class SSN Nuclear-Powered Submarines. This gave each Chinese Carrier Battle Group a total of 14 combat vessels with the Timor Carrier Group containing just 6, exclusive of their Naval Support Vessels.

Allocated to the East Timor Carrier were 3 Type 051C missile Destroyers fitted with its 48 Russian made Altair RIF SA-N-6 Medium-Range Air Defence Missiles and 8 Anti-Ship Missiles. Guided by its

30N6E Phased Array Radar, this vessel was able to direct 12 missiles at 6 targets simultaneously and was working in tandem with 1- Slava-class Cruiser and 2-Yuan-class Diesel Electric Submarines. The Yuan-class Submarine was fitted with the YJ-8X 165kg Anti-Ship Missile with its time-delayed semi armour piercing high explosive warhead with a maximum range of 80-120km. It was the first Chinese submarine fitted with the operational Air Independent Propulsion (AIP) system, which allowed a diesel-powered vessel to remain under water for weeks instead of days. With this new system the Yuan-class Submarine was considered stealthy, flexible and a dangerous threat to submariners accustomed to conventional diesel or nuclear powered adversaries.

Close to the port of Darwin and patiently lying in wait were a further 2 Kilo-class Submarines fitted with the latest Air Independent Propulsion (AIP) system and a deadly cargo of VA-111 Shkval Torpedoes. The Shkval, when fired from its 533mm tube, reaches a speed in excess of 200 knots through supercavitating - a process where the water around the torpedo is literally vapourised and forms small bubbles of gas around the body of the projectile resulting in reduced drag and extremely high speeds. With Darwin the home port of a mixture of Fremantle and Armidale class fast patrol boats the Shkval, with its high speed torpedoes, would prove crucial. The Fremantle and Armidale-class patrol boats are used provisionally as fisheries and custom protection vessels but are also central to Australia's national surveillance effort using, their high definition navigational radar in the South West Pacific region. Armaments on the Armidale are provided by the Rafael Typhoon 25mm Naval Stabilised Deck Gun and 2 - 12.7mm Machine Guns, and on the Fremantle, one General Purpose 40/60mm Bofors Gun and 2 - ·50 cal Browning Machine Guns.

The Kilos were particularly interested in the 2 Adelaide-class Frigates that had been in port for the last 6-days. Normally split between the 2 main naval bases in Fleet Base East in Sydney and Fleet Base West in Perth, these 2 Frigates, based on the US OLIVER PERRY-class design were a major threat, especially with their ability to counter multiple simultaneous threats from the air, sea and sub surface. Once notice is given they can be underway within 30-minutes from cold. Armed with Harpoon Anti-Ship Missiles, Standard Surface-to-Air Missiles, 2 Triple Torpedo Tubes for their Mk32 torpedoes and their Phalanx Close in

Weapons System, these ships could not be allowed to leave port. The Chinese had been completely taken by surprise when these had turned up and agents on shore had passed the information immediately to Beijing. Unknown to the Chinese, the Frigates were only visiting and were intending to set sail back to Perth, 24hrs after the planned invasion date. Normally equipped with 2 MH-60 Sea Hawk Helicopters, the Frigates were carrying just one each.

It was imperative that the simultaneous assault onto East Timor and Darwin occurred at the same time. Any deviation from the planned landing hour would result in early warning and place troops on standby quicker. The assaults onto the 2 beach areas to the east of Darwin and the airfields on East Timor had to be synchronised to ensure complete surprise. The only real resistance on East Timor was the United Nations elements stationed there and once this threat was removed, it was imperative that Timor was turned into a Forward Operating Base (FOB) for supporting the invasion of mainland Australia some 659km away.

The 16 Indonesian Air Force C130K Mk1 Transport Planes, having mounted from Jakarta and subsequently flown 2,139km non stop, at low level and at 350 knots over the Savu Sea to West Timor, were now turning northeast along the Timorean coastline before reducing their speed for their final approach into their 2 objectives. 30-minutes behind the 16 airborne assault aircraft were 8 more C130K's, each containing a parachute resupply of twelve 1,000lbs pallet loads of ammunition and stores. Flying as low as possible they followed the same route as the assaulting troop's aircraft, which took them directly over the 2 airfield objectives on the northern aspect of East Timor to drop their precious cargo and depart for home to collect yet more supplies.

10-minutes out the 1,024 paratroopers who were crammed into the aircraft began final preparations. They had already fitted their heavy equipment packs to their parachute harness D-rings using their quick release snap hooks and attached the leg harness to stop the load moving too much in the airflow, their M16 5.56mm rifles slung over the shoulder down the left or right side of their body and held in place by the reserve parachute strapped to their front. The practice jumps had gone well but the 2hr low level rehearsals had not prepared them for the 6hrs and 10-minutes it had taken on this day. It had been an horrendous low level journey for the 64 paratroopers crammed like sardines in each aircraft and a bouncy flight, tight confined space, coupled with oppressive heat, body-odour and aviation fumes were all proven vomit inducers for airborne soldiers around the world. True to form this ride had proven to be no different and men had thrown up in sick-bags, over the floor and on each other and the stench and heat was now the driving force to exit the aircraft. All the paratroopers were checked off and hooked up and with the 2-minute sign given by the C130 load master, the side doors were opened, with the cold blast of air that ran down the length of the aircraft a welcome relief from the past 6hrs. It was still dark outside but would be dawn in one hour's time. The parachute jump master, staring at the two lights next to the door, saw the red light come on…..gave the thumbs up and guided the first man to the door…..GREEN ON…..GO…..out went the first…then a second and so on until 32-men from each side of the aircraft had departed including the jump master who was last. There were 2 airfields being assaulted simultaneously with 8 aircraft allocated to each. In waves of 2, and 200-meters apart, the C130s disgorged their heavily laden paratroopers from 600-feet. As each man exited the aircraft he was subconsciously counting 1,000…2,000….3,000… look up and check canopy; this was the paratrooper's way of knowing if he needed to pull the reserve parachute slung across his front. Buffeted and slung around in the slipstream like a leaf in a gale…. calm eventually returned, and after ensuring one was not about to collide with a fellow parachutist, the quick release snap hooks were flicked simultaneously and the heavy pack fell away some 12-feet below the paratrooper, suspended by a rope attached to the harness. After this the descent was relatively quick and men began landing heavily on both airfields. To the untrained eye on the drop zone, seeing these soldiers land as they did would have elicited thoughts of broken legs and backs but, to a man, they jumped up quickly, discarded their harnesses and released their weapons for potential conflict.

During the night the 67 ship assault force approaching East Timor had inserted Special Forces to confirm the landing sites for the assaulting Marines. This was achieved by 0300hrs and at 0400hrs the embarkation of the first wave of 2,000 plus Marines began. Approaching from the Banda Sea were 34 Small Landing Craft, each containing 62 Indonesian Marines followed by the 8 Yuhai–class Medium Landing Ships with 250 troops in each, complete with Light Armoured Vehicles (LAVs) equipped with 25mm Rapid Firing Cannon. The small landing craft deployments were the first wave of 3 identical small landing craft landings over the next 7hrs, with each wave bringing 2,108 men ashore at a time. 4 Zubr-class Air Cushioned Landing Craft, having been shipped covertly from China and pre-positioned closer to East Timor weeks before, had made the final 430km under their own steam and, would deploy 6 T-80B Medium Battle Tanks and 20 LAVs ashore that the Marines required in order to move around the Island quickly once security was established.

The landing, when it occurred, was unopposed and the first contingent of Marines arrived without incident and began to fan out to establish a defensive perimeter in order to allow the force to be built up. They remained in their defensive perimeter until the second wave arrived before pushing further inland. By 1130hrs that morning, the third and final wave arrived, along with the Zubr–class hovercraft vessels and, their remaining Indonesians Marines, who soon began securing their objectives after linking up with the parachute assault forces controlling the airfields. 25-nautical miles off the coast the commander aboard the Chinese carrier was content with operations on East Timor and, apart from a few Air-to-Ground fighter requests from Kopassus Special Forces against determined Australian resistance, nothing had troubled the amphibious part of the invasion.

Inland, things were playing out somewhat differently near the West Timor-East Timor border region. Kopassus Special Forces, who had inserted overland and attempted to surround the Australian Light Infantry troops, were now being aggressively engaged as the Australians recovered from their initial surprise. This would be the only battle on the Island as Indonesian troops gained complete control of all its objectives with relative ease. Although initially caught unawares, the Australian Infantry had recovered quickly and took the battle to the Kopassus forces. Outnumbered almost 3 to 1 and with their Battalion split, the Australians resorted to shoot and scoot tactics and laid snap ambushes as they were pursued. Equipped with limited supplies and ammunition, they managed to inflict more than 300 casualties on the

Kopassus Special Forces before Chinese fighter aircraft intervened and 1,800 Marine reinforcements approaching from the east eventually cut them off. The Australian troops, almost out of ammunition and looking at annihilation, had no choice other than to surrender after 5-days of intense jungle fighting. They had lost 42 men and had another 18 wounded. Having received HF encrypted radio transmissions after the first 24hrs they knew that reinforcements would not be arriving in East Timor as the Northern Territories were under attack and foreign forces had landed near Darwin.

Within 12hrs of the airborne assaults onto the 2 airfields, the first troop reinforcements started to arrive by C130 and civilian aircraft and, within 48hrs of the invasion, more than 16,000 Indonesian soldiers were on the Island. By the end of the first week that number would swell to 21,000.

659km away...... across the Timor Sea, lay the ultimate prize, Australia's most strategically positioned natural deep water harbour - Darwin. With Indonesian paratroopers flying in to descend onto East Timor's airfields, the battle for Darwin was about to begin. It was the culmination of years of planning by the Dragon's Claw strategists in Beijing and the sequences for an amphibious assault were now unraveling. First on the agenda had been the actual planning of the operation, which was only presented in detail to the Indonesian President and key military Generals 18 months ago. Planning had continued unabated in China for 4-years and only, with 12 months to go, were small scale rehearsals by Indonesian Marines allowed. Actual target details were not revealed to the sailors, soldiers or pilots until later. The main assaulting force of 25,000 out of the full 37,000 was to be almost entirely Chinese Marines using their tactics and their equipment. This was more for operational security than anything else and the first the Indonesian sailors, Marines and paratroopers knew of their actual mission was 2 months ago when they were placed into isolation and kept there or moved by ship out to sea to join with the growing armada now converging off the coasts of Timor and Australia. The larger movement of ships, logistics and defence of the armada had been entirely China's undertaking and the vast oceans had allowed the small groups of 15 and 20 ships to remain elusive. Orders and briefings had been conducted daily for almost 5-weeks now and all knew their missions. Embarkation and disembarkation drills for the Marines were practiced as and when the seas were calm enough and test-firing of some weapons achieved against towed targets. Rehearsals would never be perfect, especially with the way the armada had come together, but the Chinese and Indonesian commanders were pleased with the results achieved.

With the movement to the objective sequence complete, the remaining part of the plan was the assault and capture. A pre-assault reconnaissance would be deployed before midnight, and with agents in Australia already having confirmed the landing areas were free of underwater obstacles for the landing ships, the reconnaissance group would meet with Chinese agents on the beaches. It was anticipated the landing would be unopposed from the land but the Indonesian and Chinese forces were taking no chances, especially with the landing being the most crucial moment for the invading force. Once the offensive began it was imperative the momentum was maintained and any enemy action overcome without any interruption to the landing. Air superiority would be vital and, with the force projected by the Chinese far in excess of that ranged against them; they believed the sums added up. With no organic supporting arms other than infantry weapons, such as mortars, shoulder-fired anti-tank and small arms, it was important to build up the combat power as soon as possible. This is where the Zubr–class Air Cushioned Landing Craft would prove crucial. External fire support would be initially provided by naval airpower until the towed artillery and heavy armour could come ashore.

A big concern for the armada was the intervention of the Australian Navy and Air Force but they were content they had the forces in place to deal with such an eventuality, knowing that the Australian forces were deployed over such a vast continent. The problem with such a large continent, as China knew, was that it makes life very difficult for such a small defensive force like the Australian one in trying to maintain surveillance over such a vast coastline and there were, without doubt, huge gaps in Australia's Early Warning (EW) capability countrywide. The northwestern approaches, however, were a different matter and this had been taken into consideration. China also assessed that Australia, with its current troop dispositions and geography, would be unable to project enough force quickly enough to disrupt the landing. Chinese

Air Ops was acutely aware of the capability of the Australian pilots and their American made F111 Fighter Bombers and the AF/A/A-18/B Hornets with their laser guided bombs and harpoon anti-ship missiles. To counter that threat, Air Ops had dedicated a large number of aircraft to the destruction of located enemy airfields and installations, interdiction missions against approaching aircraft before reaching the task force and Electronic Warfare missions to jam communications. They were also providing land commanders with imagery of the landing area and subsequent campaign area, while also aiding the Carrier Fleet to enhance its radar coverage and protective screen beyond normal parameters.

Another problem for the Australian forces was not just their disposition of forces but their preparedness or lack of preparedness for total war. It's not as easy as observing the enemy attacking and then jumping in a tank or aircraft to counter attack. A response first requires an intelligence assessment to assess what is occurring before a response of some sort can be mounted, with any military action based on some sort of plan. A military unit, unless under direct fire, will want to know what it is up against before going into action, therefore, preparation of its vehicles, troops and supporting arms for combat was crucial. Combat vehicles, aircraft, men and all the logistical requirements have to be identified, administered and orders given before committing forces into action with the correct balance of firepower and support in place to maintain an offensive. To do otherwise is committing military suicide and possible annihilation. A limited amount of training ammunition will possibly be available to peacetime units but operational loadings will not be available in the quantity and calibre that the military needs as this type of ammunition will be stored in special ammunition depots that may be many miles from the force that requires it. During peace-time, tanks and armoured vehicles could be undergoing maintenance, troops may be on leave or on exercise and even if they are all sat in barracks, it will take days to prepare a force of any great number and potency. Any force build up that may be in range of enemy air is then open to targeting from an enemy who has been preparing for this very day for years. If Australia had a Battalion on 24hr notice to move, even it would be pushed to meet this timeline.

Air Ops had 140 of the very latest Su-33 Flanker for combat with a further 20 Su-33 aircraft dedicated to early warning (EW), and imagery tasking. Of the 140 Combat Aircraft available, 4 would always be airborne above each Carrier Battle Group with a further 2 on immediate launch status. In total 18 aircraft were rotating through this process. China's main concern was still the vulnerability of its Carriers as they were vulnerable from many different angles… hence the need to deploy the Carrier Battle Group Destroyers, Frigates and Submarines to protect the Carriers and place a protective 250 mile exclusion zone around the fleet. The entire Australian Air Force amounted to almost 100 Combat Aircraft, a maximum of 7 Airborne Early Warning Aircraft and a couple of modified 707 tankers, and even though most were 1,000's of kilometres away or on the far side of the Australian continent, they would still pose a serious threat once roused.

In the first 2hrs of the campaign Air Ops priorities were to destroy those key facilities on its target list. These were Darwin Naval Base, which is an element of the Larrakeyah Barracks complex with only 4 Army Landing Craft and 4 Heavy Landing Craft, plus the patrol boats and 2 Adelaide-class Frigates in port. Home to Northern Command (NORCOM) and near to the centre of Darwin, this was initially deemed a priority-2 tactical target only until the appearance of the 2 Frigates and, due to their presence it was upgraded to a priority-1 strategic target.

Darwin International Airfield, which is shared by the Royal Australian Air Force (RAAF) Base Darwin and located some 13km northeast from the business central district, was identified as a potential target but there had been no indication from Chinese agents in Darwin that combat fighter aircraft were at this location. It did, however, contain 10 covered open-ended hangers in 2 hexagonal pans on the south side of the runway along with one C130 transport aircraft. These would all be targeted and any military aircraft destroyed if found on site. Air Ops assessed that all these hangers would be hit with 100 percent certainty during the first wave of attacks. The civilian airport with small private aircraft to the north, along with the commercial part, would remain untouched as much as possible.

Robertson Barracks near the town of Palmerston was deemed the most potent threat to the invasion and was, therefore, a top priority target. Located only a few miles southeast of Darwin it contains the largest enemy elements that could potentially face the invasion force - 41 M1A1 Abrams MBTs and 17 Tiger Attack Helicopters. The units at this location are 1st Brigade (Brigade) and 1st Aviation Regt, 2nd Cavalry Regt, 5th and 7th Battalion Royal Australian Regiment (RAR), 8th and 12th Medium Regt, 1st Combat Engineer Support, 1st Command Support Regt and 1st Combat Service Support Battalion.

1st Brigade are part of 1st Division's Deployable Joint Force HQ and 1st Armoured Regiment (part of 1st Brigade) with their M1A1 MBTs form one of the main battle groups along with 5th and 7th RAR Infantry Heavy, complete with their M113 APCs and Bushmaster Infantry Mobility Vehicles.

Tindall Air Base (AB), which was only 310km to the southeast of Darwin was another critical target and was located 13km southeast of a town called Katherine. This base contained the same hanger configuration of 2 hexagonal-shaped groups as Darwin did, which provided a huge reference point from the air. The airbase is home to No75 Squadron Air Combat Group with their F/A-18s and, No2 Squadron with their 2 early warning AWACS. Their readiness for combat, in relation to weapon status and availability, was not known but, intelligence assessments suggested it would not be immediate and, if surprised, destruction of their aircraft could be achieved quickly. Tindall also contained the HQ element for the F111 Squadrons.

On board the command carrier, and 150nm from shore, Admiral Yimou, the PLAN Amphibious Task Force Commander was situated in the operations centre with the Commander Land Forces, General Li. They were discussing the landing areas for the assault force and reassessing yet again their actions should anything go wrong.

'Admiral'...said Li *'I am content everything has been done to the highest order for the assault and I have the utmost confidence in your subordinate commanders in getting my men ashore'*

Li and Admiral Yimou were looking at the electronic bird table that showed the carrier exclusion zone, the 2 amphibious landing areas - YELLOW and BLUE, the key military objectives, known enemy dispositions and possible enemy incursion routes.

The 2 landing areas YELLOW and BLUE were 9-miles apart and stood out on the electronic map board due to their size, with each landing zone marked by Latitude and Longitude degrees, minutes and seconds South and East coordinates.

Landing area YELLOW was in Shoal Bay and ran along the beach from north to south only 18.86 miles northeast of Darwin.

It's left northern boundary denoted by:
Latitude 12° 13' 27.44 - South....Longitude 131° 01' 3607 - East... elevation 27-feet

It's right southern boundary denoted by:
Latitude 12° 17' 02.00 - S.... Longitude 131° 01' 13.53 - E...elevation 22-feet.

Landing area BLUE was just 9.43 miles due east of Darwin and stretched along the beach from east to west.

It's left eastern boundary denoted by:
Latitude 12° 20' 08.58 - S... Longitude 130° 54' 41.54 - E.....elevation 4-feet

It's right western boundary denoted by:
Latitude 12° 20' 52.50 - S... Longitude 130° 52' 20.59 - E....elevation 16-feet.

There was an additional set of coordinates on the board and these were denoting low rock obstacles in the centre of landing area BLUE.

A major consideration for the Chinese had been Australia's land-based coastal surveillance radar, which was provided by the impressive Jindalee Operational Radar Network, or JORN as it was known. Depending on atmospheric conditions this system could detect air and surface vessels from 1,000 to 3,000km away and covered the strategically important northern approaches. JORN was operated from 2 main antenna array sites at Longreach, Queensland and near Laverton in Western Australia using their 3 to 4km long antennas. No.1 Radar Surveillance Unit jointly operates these from the JORN Coordination Centre (JOC) at RAAF Base Edinburgh in Southern Australia while Alice Springs contained a spare active operational system in the Northern Territory. JORN works by bouncing HF radio waves off the ionosphere and has the capability to detect even stealth aircraft.

China knew that any unusually large aircraft and ship activity would be observed, hence the movement of ships in small groups spread over a massive area. China had assessed that any increase in shipping and aircraft activity near the Timor coastline would be interrupted as normal due to the on-going well publicised Chinese –Indo naval exercises, which added to the already busy radar picture but the plethora of ships approaching Darwin would not. China clearly needed time to get its vessels near to the Australian coast without compromise and it became apparent the JORN radar facilities had to be taken off line.

China had long invested in attacking Command, Control, Communications, Computers, and Intelligence (C4I) systems and saw civilian and military information technology and communication infrastructure as critical for gaining information superiority. 3-days before the invasion fleet started to meet up out to sea, Chinese sleeper agents were about to play their part in the invasion. These agents had been part of the large Chinese community in Australia for years, and had gradually worked themselves into critical infrastructure companies such as the power grids and vulnerable collocated military and civilian telecommunication facilities. One such sleeper was George Tong. Tong, born Zhang Ziyi Sung in Beijing in 1966, had worked as a radar analyst for Chinese Military Intelligence for 4-years. After the 1989 Tiananmen Square Massacre, and at the age of 23, Zhang Ziyi Sung was offered an opportunity to begin a new life masquerading as a political refugee from China. As China had done so many times in so many countries previously, it planted such individuals with skills that eventually would not go unnoticed and then it was a matter of luck and ability as to how far that person could go in his adopted country.

George had a particular affinity with electronics and radar-associated technology and after initial Australian government screening confirmed his cover story he soon became involved in radar affiliated companies, with China adding to his reliability by demanding he be returned as a dissident. Clearly this was a request that Australian could not comply with, bearing in mind the persecution and murder of Chinese dissidents at the time. 10-years later, Tong took out Australian citizenship and, was accepted into the community as one of their own. George had been a long-term plant with the intention of acquiring radar and communications technology and fortunately for China, he was considered as one of the leading specialists in his field at the Australian Academy of Science where he worked. He studied Radar Ionosphere Theories and Advanced Tracking and Detection Techniques for Radar Systems. Noticed at an early age, he quickly acquired a reputation for his quite brilliant theories and design work and, after gaining citizenship was quickly approached by the military asking for him to be on their team for the implementation of JORN, working directly for the JORN Coordination Centre (JOC) at RAAF Base Edinburgh under Colonel Samuel Voyce, the project director. Now almost 46 years old and close to 23 years of that spent in Australia, Tong had risen to Chief Civilian Technical Director on the project and, had been given access to every part of the facility. He was now considered China's most valuable and strategic agent and although George knew his time in Australia as a free man was nearing an end, he felt no guilt for what he was about to do. China was his home country and the choice to live in Australia with the intention of passing back technology had been his. He could never have imagined that after almost 23-years the impact of his final act would allow for the invasion of Australia to go largely unobserved. George had no idea China had mustered an invasion force off the coast but had received orders to sabotage and destabilize the system for 72hrs with his handlers stating that this was the most important, and possibly last, request he would be asked to carry out. The JOC controlled both outstations and he was in the perfect position to carry out the request. The biggest challenge to George was covering his tracks so the fault was not discovered quickly and sabotage suspected. As Chief Technical Director he would be able to ensure most of this could be achieved but the military would be keen to get the system back on line and, would probably bring in their own technicians after a protracted period.

72hrs before the invasion was to begin, the 2 JORN radar systems at Longreach and Laverton unexpectedly lost their picture and failed to respond to control from the Edinburgh JOC. China was taking no chances with this system failure and needed to ensure the system remained shut down, so 68hrs and 40-minutes after the JORN facilities went off air, two 10-man teams who had driven to the remote facilities in 4x4 vehicles, made entry into the lightly manned desolate sites, took the staff there hostage and, at the predetermined landing hour began destroying the facilities with explosives. The technicians at the sites were left tied up even after the Chinese agents had departed, in order for the agents to get as far from the sites as possible before they were discovered. Even if the problem at the JOC was located, China was making sure the sites would never work again. At 0445hrs with the invasion imminent, the city of Darwin suffered huge power losses followed by communication blackouts as Chinese long-term sleepers began to systematically close down those electrical sub stations and communications hubs in which they now worked.

4hrs earlier the dedicated weather watch radar station in Berrimah near Darwin was taken over by 8-armed men and the employees held inside. They, unlike those at the JORN sites, would be tied and then released after the invasion had got under way.

With JORN no longer operational, the invasion fleet, consisting of 117 combat vessels was now within striking range of Australia. It included large and medium sized landing ships, the 24 Zubr-class Hovercraft, 4 Super Container Ships, 2 Container Ships converted to helicopter platforms, 4 Float on Float off Specialised Ships, 42 Indonesian Troop Carrying Vessels and an assortment of 129 stores and replenishment ships. They had gathered out to sea and approached closer and closer over the last 48hrs, with lines of ships now steaming as fast as possible to their respective objectives. The 2 Carrier Battle Groups were moving as 2 separate entities, but were in support of each other. They would remain out to sea at the 150 nautical mile launch point where aircraft could be released, while the large and medium landing ships made for shore. The Sea Dragon's transporting the 24 Zubr-class Air Cushioned Landing Craft had taken 2hrs to sink and jettison their load. Moving at 60knots per hour these impressive air cushioned vessels would soon overtake the other ships and be the first to project Chinese troops onto Australian soil. Even a modest moving vessel can cover 200 nautical miles in a day and time was now of the essence, especially as the JORN facilities were no longer operating. The huge invasion fleet having earlier passed the Australian 200 nautical mile Australian Fishing Zone (AFZ), converged 2hrs before last light, formed into their final assault groupings and, by 0210hrs were within 25 nautical miles of the coast. They were making good progress and set to hit their landing time of 0500hrs.

After being released from the confines of their submerged submarines near the mouth of Darwin Harbour, Chinese Special Forces had rendezvoused with Chinese agents on the 2 proposed landing beaches. Their mission, with the agents' help was to mark out the 2 beaches with a series of lights that would be shielded and only visible from the sea for the assaulting forces; this would ensure uniformity along the line of assault. As the initial landings were to be conducted in the dark and without guidance there was a tendency to centrally bunch and it was imperative that the whole beach was utilised for the quick build up of troops and combat equipment coming ashore.

With the Carriers' Air Armada 5-minutes from launch point, a launch sequence of a different kind was being plotted into the onboard computer of 12 Russian-made but Chinese adapted Novator 3M14E Land Attack Cruise Missiles (LACM). It was ironic that the system now being prepared to fire came about after China had received Israeli back door US technology from the 1990s. This technology was adapted by China and, by working extensively with Russia, had succeeded in producing their own cruise missiles that were capable of hitting land-based targets with accuracy. The new system was capable of reaching 600km, which was double its normal 300km range. With this technology and Russian cooperation they had achieved 100 percent hits on the 2 test firings in Russia during the summer of 2011. In 2009, in anticipation of Dragon's Claw, China had also launched her own Russian designed high resolution electro-optical and radar satellites to provide real time imagery of selected targets and, although China was in partnership and had access to the European Galileo Global Positioning System (GPS), this mission was going to fly courtesy of the Russian GLONASS GPS.

0430hrs and at a depth of 40m and 50km northwest of Darwin the crew of the Type 093 Nuclear Submarine made their final preparations, 5-weeks after departing from their base in Zhoushan, Zhejiang China. The crew, all hand picked submariners were on the threshold of making history. They had only performed 2-live firing sequences in Russia before today... but now they were to fire 12 missiles in total before sailing back to base. Once the target/mission data had been placed into the onboard computer the firing sequence was initiated and the first of 12 missiles fired from its 533mm torpedo tube under the power of a tandem solid-propellant rocket booster with the submarine shaking from the effort of expelling its load. One by one the missiles made for the surface and, having broken the waterline, accelerated away at speed - driven on by their small turbojet engines. After a low and short pre-programmed flight 20m above the sea the mid-course navigation system took over using a terrain following flight path whilst still receiving course corrections fed to it by the GLONASS GPS and real time imagery from the Chinese satellites. The Novator Land-Attack Cruise Missile was a redesign, with wings of a smaller span and, a stronger structure. This was done to combat the serious strains on the wings that heights of 50m and 100m above ground terrain place on the missile.

Travelling at 865km/h, the 6,200mm long projectiles with their 450kg warheads were closing rapidly on their targets, with information updates constantly being received into the on board navigator to ensure pinpoint accuracy. At missile launch the system weighed 1,770kg and, although now considerably lighter, the kinetic energy from the missile's velocity and the 1,000lb warhead meant there could only be one outcome.... complete destruction of whatever it struck. Of the 12 missiles fired only 10 would hit their intended targets with one falling short and one going completely haywire after crossing land and crashing into a caravan park killing 27 people. After years of meticulous planning and detailed targeting of military objectives, the first to die in the invasion of Australia were children, with their mothers and fathers fast asleep in their beds. Unlike the Western mindset in relation to collateral damage, concern for this was not on the Chinese agenda and did not even make a mention in the situation report to Beijing later in the day.

30-minutes after launching and 360km later, the first 5 LACMs struck their targets. At precisely 0510hrs and to within 1.1-metre of their programmed coordinates, the first target, Tindall Air Base near Katherine was hit, with 2 missiles striking the main tower building complex and another 3 causing massive damage to the headquarters buildings of the F111 Squadrons and those of No75 Air Combat Group.

Having taken a longer route out at sea to their target, to coincide with the 0510hrs timing, 6 more LACMs were slamming into their nominated targets, these being the main HQ building and infrastructures of Robertson Barracks. One missed its intended target building completely by 60-metres but landed close enough to inflict severe structural damage to surrounding buildings and destroyed numerous military vehicles in the vicinity. As the LACMs struck home and rocked Darwin and its environs to the core, simultaneous military actions were occurring all across the Northern Territories.

3-minutes behind schedule and roaring in at a reduced 40 knots were the 24 Zubr-class Landing Craft. Having already passed the conventional landing flotilla they split into 2 separate groups approximately 2-nautical miles from shore before proceeding to their respective beaches with the Captains navigating by GPS until they could pick out their marked landing zone. At 10-nautical miles out they had witnessed the street and building lights of Darwin go out and felt for the first time the anticipation and excitement of being involved in a real-time operation and the part they were playing in making history. Their route took them across the Beagle Gulf towards Clarence Strait before finally reaching their predetermined landing area. As the 12 Zubr-class vessels earmarked for YELLOW beach and 12 for BLUE beach raced ashore, the noise of low-flying helicopters passing overhead was drowned out by the huge wall of noise these massive vessels generated. Within seconds of coming ashore the huge craft had halted and opened their large doors. The decibels increased still further as their cargo's of T-80B Medium Battle Tanks, PTL02 Assault Tank Destroyers and numerous APCs started their engines and spewed forth onto the beaches and, at 0506hrs in the morning people were already beginning to step outside their homes wondering what the noise was. After disgorging their combat force as fast as possible the Zubr-class vessels backed out to sea and departed back to their mother craft to collect more troops from the Indonesian troop ships that were now within 25-nautical miles of the coast and just over the horizon. On their way back out and only 6-nautical miles from shore they could just make out the massive fleet of landing ships approaching Darwin.

At 0512hrs the first of 48 Russian-made Su33 aircraft that had launched from the 2 *Ulyanovsk* -class Carriers 20-minutes previously were commencing their aerial attacks using the latest KAB-500 S-E bombs. This was one of China's most accurate weapons using satellite navigation guidance and, unaffected by weather it gave added reliability. The KAB 500/560kg bomb, with its deep penetrating warhead, only requires a precise location coordinate and uses satellite navigation for the bomb to behave with similar characteristics as the American Joint Direct Attack Munitions (JDAM). 16 of the Su33 were equipped with a mix of Satellite and Laser Guided Munitions and these were then split into 2 groups. One group of 8 with KAB-500 on board headed directly for Tindall AB closely followed by another 12 Su33s who would provide the air defence screen while the bombers released on their targets. The second group of 8 headed towards Darwin International with 8 Su33s as air defence. 4 of the 8 bomb-laden Su33s heading for Darwin International were earmarked for a first priority strike against the 2 Adelaide-class Frigates and the moored-up Fast Patrol Boats in the bay. These 4 aircraft were not carrying Satellite Guided Munitions but using the KAB-1,500 TV and Laser-Guided Aerial Bombs, which were designed to hit ships up to 5,000 tons. Using the TV guided missile the target's picture is beamed to the pilot for flight corrections to be used before the target is struck.

The remaining 12 Su33 aircraft in the 48 aircraft configuration were to concentrate on Robertson Barracks, targeting specifically MIA1 Abrams MBTs, Light Armoured Vehicles and Tiger Attack Helicopters with their allocation of LGB-250 - 300kg/660lb Laser Guided Bombs.

Chinese Air Ops had a further 48 Su33 aircraft on the Carriers ready to go as soon as the first wave began dropping ordnance and these would ensure a constant number of 40-plus aircraft over Darwin for the next 6hrs and the foreseeable future. The rotation of airframes was crucial to maintaining air superiority and eventually air supremacy and, with 180 aircraft in the fleet; this was very much achievable against the RAAF. The Chinese knew there would clearly be a response at some stage and the high number of aircraft available to Chinese Air Ops was seen as critical in the battles ahead.

The Su33s with a combat range of 930 miles were fitted with a 30mm Cannon and a mix of Satellite and Laser Guided Bombs (LGBs). They carried a variation of R-734 or R-73A -AA-11 Archer Air Defence Missiles and the Vympel R-37 Beyond Visual Range Air-to-Air Missiles (BVRAAMs) - NATO codename, AA-X-13 Arrow, which had a range in excess of 300 km (185 miles). The Arrow was designed to shoot down AWAC aircraft from well outside the range of any aircraft guarding it.

With a ramp in-place of a catapult on the Carriers, the Su33s with a normal all up combat weight of 8,819lbs had to take-off with a reduced weight of 6,819lbs due to the decrease in take off speed. With that restriction in mind, those Su33s conducting Combat Air Patrol (CAP) profiles carried only air defence missiles, including the Vympel R-37 on their 12 weapon rails. A second ground attack wave was already armed and standing ready to depart from the Carriers with a mixed loading of guided munitions and air to air/air to surface missile systems. A large proportion of the second wave was predominantly fitted with the LGB-250 - 300kg/660lb Laser Guided Bomb. The LGB-250 had been developed primarily for export by the Russians with China being the first to purchase. The Chinese had worked extensively on producing a laser designator for such a capability and had succeeded in developing what they called a *Blue Sky* Laser Targeting Pod. Extensive trials between China and Russia in 2007 and 2008 saw the first fully integrated system used on a Su27 before it was eventually fitted on the Su33 in 2009.

Circling over their target areas the air defence Su33s with their comprehensive sensor suites would be able to track some targets while scanning others out to a range of 103 km. Equipped with the coherent pulse Doppler Radar called the Phazatron N001 Zhuk, information was slaved to the pilot's helmet-mounted sight and displayed in wide angle to the head up display (HUD). With these aircraft now providing top cover and actively searching for any Australian air threat, the first wave of dedicated bombers, 8,000 feet above ground level (AGL), began to release their Satellite-Guided Munitions onto the targets below. The hangers at Tindall AB were hit in the first 45- minutes by the KAB 500 deep penetrating 560kg warhead and whatever was inside was incinerated. Unbelievably, 4 RAAF F/A-18s somehow managed to depart the airfield between the LACM strikes and first Su33 attacks and were now flying in a southerly direction. It turned out that these aircraft were being prepared for a training sortie at 0730hrs and the pilots were already on site at the time. Once the missiles had struck the base buildings the pilots realising what the consequences of such an attack could be removed their aircraft from danger as soon as possible so that they could return to fight another day. The remaining F/A-18s and the 2 AWAC aircraft at this location were all destroyed and 121 airmen killed.

A small guard force manned Robertson Barracks, near Palmerston, Darwin, and the barrack block rooms contained some, but not all, of the unit's soldiers stationed there. A lot of the married soldiers were living in purpose-built married quarter accommodation some distance from the base area. The unit's vehicles were un-crewed, un-armed and therefore, vulnerable. In peace time the tanks and light armoured vehicles were kept in static rows around the camp and made a perfect target for those Chinese pilots circling overhead. Serving soldiers living in Darwin were woken by the noise like everyone else, and although not quite believing it, quickly realized what was occurring. The roar of fighter aircraft above the city and increased helicopter activity signaled Australia's worst nightmare scenario - an Indonesian invasion. Those who lived through the day would be even more surprised when they realised the invasion was conducted by 2 Divisions of Chinese Marines with Indonesian troops playing a much lesser role in the main invasion. But for now the requirement was to save as much equipment as possible before it was all destroyed by attacks from the air, however, the number of explosions in and around the base area indicated this would be more difficult than it first appeared.

At Darwin international airport the hexagon configurations where the hangers were situated were paid the most attention with all 10 locations hit by at least one LGB in the space of 35-minutes before the attacking aircraft switched across to Robertson Barracks to continue the blitz there.

Passing overhead of the Zubr-class Landing Craft were the first of 2 waves of 24 Super Frelon Naval Helicopters carrying 27 heavily armed Indonesian Marines in each airframe. These had lifted off from the 2 converted container ships and, having synchronized their approach to complement the amphibious landing timings, were now heading for their objectives. Their mission was to provide blocking positions on high ground to the south of Darwin and seize a key bridge. The furthermost point was the blocking position 37.72 miles southeast of Darwin. The high ground dominates the Arnhem highway to its north and the Stuart Highway to its west, with both these roads leading into Darwin.

The Mount Bunday feature at Latitude 12° 53' 38.82 – South …Longitude 131° 15' 54.83 – East elevation 178-feet, would allow occupying troops to dominate and deny ground in order to delay any advance of an advancing hostile force. Sandwiched neatly between Darwin and Mt Bunday was the key location of Robertson Barracks and a consideration for the Indonesian blocking forces was ambushing retreating forces that may be heading south. The main threat to the blocking force, however, was assessed as coming from the south where the second Australian Battle Group, 3 RAR from Adelaide, were stationed, but with the Indonesian troops expecting to marry up with Chinese Marines and their heavy armour before the day was out, 3 RAR were considered a medium threat. Formed in 2011, 4-years earlier than anticipated, 3 RAR was a 1,200 strong mechanised group plus supporting elements equipped with M113 APCs and the Bushmaster Infantry Mobility Vehicles, with the Bushmaster in particular ideally suited to the rigors of rough terrain found in the northern territories.

The other key objective and blocking position located at Latitude 12° 32' 28.67 - South, Longitude 130° 58' 34.79 - East…elevation 26-feet and, only 10.7 miles from Darwin, was a bridge running northeast to southwest and considered essential for the movement of Chinese troops from YELLOW landing area to Darwin by road.

In total, the Chinese were projecting 1,296 Indonesian Helicopter Borne Marines ahead of the amphibious landing force with on call Su33 assistance from the Chinese Air Force Forward Air Controllers attached to the Indonesians. 16 helicopters from the force of 24 were earmarked for the Mt Bunday objective, thus placing 432 troops on target in the first wave. The remaining 8 helicopters were then responsible for dropping their 216 troops at the bridge. The second wave of 24 helicopters would project exactly the same numbers, leaving 864 heavily laden troops on the high feature and 432 at the bridge.

Darwin was now in a complete state of panic. There was almost no power, no TV and only limited communications, with some cell phone networks only working intermittently. It was by this method that the rest of Australia came to realise that their country had been invaded. For those caught in the middle, many began leaving as soon as the bombs started falling and the roads were now beginning to stack up with departing vehicles. The explosions in and around the city were constant and lit up the early morning sky with huge flashes of light, followed by the loud roar of military supersonic aircraft overhead.

Rumours were spreading rapidly of foreign soldiers landing on the beaches to the east but it could not be confirmed; for those near the beaches it was no rumour and they witnessed a spectacle rarely seen or acted out since 1944.

The 12 Zubr-class Landing Craft that beached on YELLOW released their load as quickly as possible and extracted from the landing area as soon as the last APC was ashore. The force consisted of 20 Type 89/YW Amphibious APCs, 18 Medium Battle Tanks and 1,200 Chinese Marines.

The force onto BLUE consisted of 20 Type 89/YW Amphibious APCs, 15 Medium Battle Tanks and 1,500 Chinese Marines. Their mission was to initially secure the landing areas and provide protection for the incoming main assault forces. They came ashore with the sound of large explosions echoing in the distance, which indicated to the Marines that Chinese airpower was doing its job well. Pushing inland to form a protective shield, the tanks and APCs took up blocking and fire support positions, with the Marines digging into the soft ground prior to waiting for the main force to arrive. They didn't have long to wait and, 30-minutes later, the first of the large grey landing ships loomed menacingly out of the darkness and slammed onto the beach. The invasion was so far going to plan and the build up of 25,000 troops well under way. The first reconnaissance probes were sent out almost immediately to scout the ground that the 2 main landing forces would have to cross. Those on YELLOW were going the long way round to Darwin by heading east initially before swinging south towards Howard Springs and then southwest to Palmerston and finally to their main objective - Robertson Barracks. Those coming ashore at BLUE were to head straight for the heart of Darwin taking the port and international airport before pushing south to link with the force from YELLOW and hopefully catching any remaining armour or military assets in a pincer movement. Anything heading south would be the responsibility of the blocking force and naval airpower. The light blocking force would then be relived by heavy armour, air defence assets and supported by artillery and air power in anticipation of a reaction from troops stationed in Adelaide.

For the Australian nation this was turning into a disaster on an unprecedented scale and on a par with the surprise attack on Pearl

Harbour. 1st Armoured Regiments Abrams M1A1 MBTs and 2nd Cavalry Regiments Australian Light Armoured Vehicles (ASLAVs) were suffering enormous losses at Robertson Barracks and those troops in the vicinity who had tried to save some of their unit's hardware had paid with their lives as 1,000lb and 500lb HE munitions targeted them constantly. There was no way to get to the vehicles without becoming a casualty, as those brave enough to try had found out. The 1st Aviation Regiment had fared no better and in the first 45-minutes had lost all of its 16 Tiger Attack Eurocopters along with 3 Chinook Heavy Lift and 4 Blackhawk Troop Carrying Helicopters. Robertson Barracks was a peace time location and with no pilots on base it had proven to be catastrophic for the Australian military in the same way that Europe had suffered just over a week ago when the conventional attacks on airbases Europe-wide caught them all by surprise and resulted in a large proportion of NATO aircraft been destroyed or damaged.

In Darwin port the 2 Adelaide-class Frigates had each taken 3 direct hits from KAB-1,500 TV-guided bombs, the Su33 pilots making just slight adjustments as they observed their bombs all the way to the target before losing the picture on impact but, with the huge flash they observed from 8,000 feet reaffirming that it was a confirmed hit. The pilot's would later swap war stories on board the carrier's and comment on their first taste of combat, with many recounting the visual over pressure ring emanating from the centre of impact. Both Adelaide-class Frigates stood no chance and were never in a position to use their sophisticated weapons, but instead, were lying half submerged next to their mooring location - broken in two. The Fremantle and Armidale Patrol Boats had also taken a pounding from the accurate and deadly bombing before 2 vessels had somehow escaped undamaged in the confusion. Some crewmembers had returned and managed to board the vessels and get underway but, as they emerged from the mouth of the port, both were struck amidships by the ultra fast Shkval VA-111 Torpedoes that had reached a speed of 120 knots before impact. Although a long way short of their potential speed, the Shkval's with their 210kg warheads slammed into the small attack craft and, even without a high explosive impact, would have sunk the vessels. At the speed the Shkval's were travelling and with its large explosive warhead detonating internally, each vessel was lifted out of the ocean as if picked up by a huge hand and before hitting the water both had disintegrated into numerous pieces with no survivors. The Kilo-class Submarine, having made a covert approach to the mouth of the port in anticipation of taking on the Adelaide-class Frigates, had to be satisfied with the smaller and less potent Fremantle-class craft that had emerged. The Captain of the submarine, having already chosen his killing ground carefully, had targeted the vessels in deep water….thus making sure the sunken wreckage would not pose a problem to the invasion fleet.

Now that the large landing craft were coming ashore, the initial forces on the 2 landing beaches could begin probing aggressively inland and, 3hrs after the first Chinese combatant had set foot on Australian soil, the first reconnaissance vehicles from the Chinese Marine 1st Brigade entered the northern outskirts of Darwin City.

Word of the invasion quickly spread and the sounds of battle drove thousands of people out of the city. The Indonesians controlling the bridge to the southwest were allowing the migration of civilian vehicles to cross from Darwin but no vehicles were allowed the other way. Indonesia was intent on expelling all Australian citizens from Darwin anyway and the natural exodus aided this process. With limited telecommunication systems working, people had managed to pass the message to the rest of Australia and the world that an invasion of some sort was taking place in the Darwin area. The rest of the country went onto full military war alert, with all leave cancelled and a full mobilisation of the military, including the reserve, ordered immediately. Airports and ports were closed for the immediate future and contingency security measures were activated for all government and military buildings, facilities and personnel.

Flying out of RAAF Base Amberley, Ipswich (west of Brisbane) and without fighter cover, the 8 F111s were hugging the northern coastline for protection. Having taken off within 3hrs of the events in Darwin they were now heading due west towards the port city. The pilots and navigators, all from No 1 Squadron, knew of the devastation in Tindall and assumed, correctly, that they had lost many a friend and colleague today and for those reasons and the fact that their country had been attacked they were now focused entirely on striking back. The F111 day or night air combat strike platform, using its terrain-following radar until it was close enough to instigate an attack option, was the perfect machine to achieve such a strike. With its ability to maintain supersonic flight and stay close to the ground it was hoped it might remain undetected long enough to release its deadly munitions before heading back to base. The Australian government, constantly under pressure over defence plans, had decided to upgrade the F111 so that it was now capable of using the AGM-142 Missile as an anti-ship system using the range bearing launch mode. In this mode the victim was denied any early warning of an impending attack so today was the day when that investment strategy was to be examined and put to the test. The F111s had closed to within 125-nautical miles of the port of Darwin, and although uncertain of the threat ranged against them, had yet to elicit a reaction from enemy aircraft. 95-nautical miles from Darwin, the 8 F111s, keen to launch their missiles from height, pulled up sharply from their ground hugging height of 160-feet and climbed to 8,000-feet within 2-minutes.

They were now just 48-nautical miles out and with their firing solutions confirmed, the 8 F111s launched their entire complement of 16 AGM-142 Missiles, before pulling a sharp left across the coast to head back in the direction they had come from. As soon as they left the deck the Chinese Early Warning Systems went into hyper-drive, ships went on full alert and Air Ops immediately vectored 6 Su33 Air Defence Aircraft from Darwin to the contact area with a further 2 aircraft launched by each Carrier. From 53-nautical miles the Su33 Flankers over Darwin were already firing their R-37 supersonic Beyond Visual Range Air to Air Missiles (BVRAAMs) at the departing F111s. The R-37s with a range of 185-miles were capable of travelling at 2,960 mph and it would require all the F111's supersonic speed to get beyond their 185 mile range before the missiles, travelling at mach 4-velocity homed in.

Guided by their thermal imaging seekers the lethal salvo of AGM-142s raced towards their intended targets in Shoal Bay with the pilots of the F111s able to view the data-link picture from the missile in their cockpits. The 48-nautical miles distance was covered in no time by the missiles and the F111 operators, fearful of the incoming BVRAAMs indicated by their aircraft missile warning system, were now fine tuning and choosing targets in the crowded bay. As the missiles arrived the third wave of landing craft was coming ashore brimming with troops and equipment. The first vessel hit was a Yuhai-class Medium Landing Ship containing 250 troops, and was still 1,000-metres from shore in deep water. The 800lb penetrator warhead, guided to its optimum point, struck the vessel in the centre of mass just above the waterline, ripped through the single hull and exploded amongst the tightly packed troops inside. More than 70 were killed from the initial blast and many more horrifically wounded. The water, pouring in via two gaping holes, was pinning men to the side of the ship by its ferocity with those still alive trying to scramble over the dead and severely injured to escape the hell that was now enveloping them - but it was too late. The Yuhai–class ship listed to port within seconds, rolled on its side throwing dismembered and burnt men against its creaking metallic hull. With seawater pouring in, its human cargo was held down in the dark confines of the ship by the weight of water with the screams of drowning men heard by no one. The ships bow then rose up out of the sea before it was pulled back by some invisible hand under the surface and sank slowly beneath the waves. As it disappeared, it expelled its last remnant of trapped air and hissed its final breath before plunging 190 metres to the ocean floor.

The remaining 15 missiles were striking a variety of landing ships on land and at sea and causing maximum destruction. 3 more Yuhai-class vessels were hit, along with 3 of the larger Type 072-II Yuting –class. 4 of the newer Type 072-III class Landing Ships were also sunk or damaged from this attack, with some ships taking 2 strikes each. The invasion force had lost 11 landing ships in total and with 7 of these sinking with full loss of life, this was indeed a blow; the Chinese coldly assessing it later as an unfortunate but acceptable loss of life and assets, whereas the loss of a Carrier would not have been. The remaining landing ships making for land did so without further incident but the Australians had shown an unexpected speed of reaction and ingenuity in attempting a high risk attack and it had paid off, but not without a price. 5 of the 8 F111s had succeeded in evading the R-37 Arrows but 3 had been unable to out-run or evade the R-37 and they had taken direct hits before crashing into the sea or on land during their attempted escape back to Brisbane.

Having made their mark and given the invading force something to think about, No1 Sqn knew they would be called upon again some time in the not too distant future, knowing the enemy would be more alert next time and no doubt prepared. But for now, No1 Squadron could reflect on today's action knowing they had gone some way to avenging their comrades in Tindall who had fallen earlier, even though it had resulted in the loss of 6 more of their own. The Australians had not detected the Chinese Carrier Battle Groups locations but this had been a valuable lesson to the Chinese and it was evident their Su33 Early Warning (EW) capability was somewhat lacking and, not what it should be. The sooner Darwin was taken and the airport secured, the sooner EW aircraft from China could deploy and provide an enhanced EW capability.

Admiral Yimou, the PLAN Amphibious Task Force Commander (TFC), did not take kindly to the loss of 11 ships and thousands of lives and had vented his considerable fury at the Air Ops watch keeper, the Air Ops planners and then the Air Ops Commander. His anger was short-lived as he was now concerned that the carrier fleet and its 250-nautical mile exclusion zone was potentially compromised by being too close to the shore at 150-nautical miles out. More worrying for him was the fact that the F111s had used the coast to mask their infiltration to within 90-nautical miles before the alert was sounded. The Air Ops Commander had assured the Admiral that the EW bubble around the carrier fleets had now been strengthened and extended along the coastlines, including 150-miles inland and that as soon as Darwin airport was secure, Early Warning aviation units on standby in China would be flying in to give strategic coverage for the joint and combined air, amphibious and land forces over a greater area. The Admiral - still not convinced - took the decision to move the fleets out to 190-nautical miles. Commander Land Forces (CLF), General Li, angry and saddened by the loss of his men and equipment, was professional enough to know that tragic events occur in war and it was important now to concentrate on the task at hand rather than dwell on something that was beyond his control and, now a part of history. Understanding why it occurred was important but getting the reminder of his men ashore without further loss was now his and, Admiral Yimou's priority.

'We made a strategic and costly mistake Admiral'... said Gen Li, *'by not striking at the Australian bases in the neighboring territories we have put the battle groups at risk.. We should have deployed our strategic*

submarines closer and targeted their bases with our LACMs. Leaving them untouched has caused us embarrassment and loss of life and equipment that could have been avoided'...

'General'...said Admiral Yimou.... 'I agree totally with your comments about the submarines but do not feel shame or embarrassment over this unfortunate incident as the embarrassment is not ours ....it is the Dragon's Claw planners who determined the threat as low from the neighbouring territories and it is they who must take the blame for the loss of those 1,250 brave men, ships and equipment. Rest assured General...I will be placing this in my report tonight.'

'You are right Admiral...but it matters not ....we each have a duty to ensure the rest of the landings remain unmolested by enemy forces. The beachhead is strong now and we must begin moving the troops to their next objectives. The deep water port, the international airport and Robertson Barracks all need to be taken before 2200hrs tonight for us to remain on schedule.'

By 0930hrs - almost 4hrs and 30-minutes after the invasion began - the Chinese had projected more than 23,750 troops ashore from their estimated 25,000, with a further 10,700 Indonesians expected on shore by 1100hrs. By mid afternoon on the first day, 5hrs ahead of schedule, Robertson Barracks was assaulted and occupied by 2,000 Chinese troops approaching from Yellow Beach with Darwin airport and the port area having been secured by those approaching from Blue Beach to the north. At 1900hrs on the first day, the first of the 4 massive 90,000-ton container ships came into the deep-water port and began unloading its precious cargo of all-terrain vehicles, tanks, artillery, munitions, attack helicopters, air defence assets and logistical supplies. Once all 4 of these mammoth ships were unloaded, the equipment they brought would provide a large percentage of stores to sustain an army of 158,000 for 8 months.

The International Airport was secured, cleared and operational by 1830hrs with the first aircraft landing from 2100hrs onwards. Three Russian leased Beriev A-50 Mainstay AEW aircraft with a maximum flight endurance of almost 8hrs came in first, followed by Chinese and Indonesian military transport and commercial airliners packed with troops from Indonesian. The troop build-up needed to be implemented quickly as it was a vulnerable time and the A-50 would be able to provide the EW coverage far in excess of the Su33 options. By first light the next day more than 33 aircraft had landed and departed again after depositing 5,472 troops. After 7-days 38,304 troops had landed with this number increasing to 76,608 after 2-weeks and 153,216 within a month.

With war on the Australian continent just beginning and Chinese and Indonesian forces increasing rapidly, the Australian military and intelligence community were still scrambling around for answers and attempting to ascertain what the invasion force consisted of. It was this uncertainty; along with the other world events and the transition from a peace time existence to a war footing, that would allow the invading force to increase in number relatively unscathed. The first troops to move towards the area would be Special Forces troops from the Australian Special Air Service (SAS) who were able to move in smaller groups and therefore took less time to prepare. Their mission would be solely reconnaissance-based with an emphasis on enemy troop dispositions, types and numbers, and identification of potential weak points and assault locations.

Less than 24hrs after the invasion, Chinese and Indonesian troops were expanding their reach inland and by first light on the second day, a force of 1,200 Chinese Marines complete with 18 PTL02 100mm Wheeled Assault Tank Destroyers, 32 Type 63A Amphibious Medium Battle Tanks, 14 High Mobility Vehicles (the HMMWV equivalent) and 14 Tiema C2200 6x6 - 7.5t High-Mobility Heavy Truck Vehicles, reached the Indonesian helicopter borne troops holding the high ground to the south of Darwin. The Type 63A, although not the best armoured tank, came equipped with a 105mm gun and laser-guided anti-tank armour piercing missile capable of hitting targets out to 5.2km and penetrating 500mm of steel at 2,000-metres. The 7.5t heavily laden trucks arrived with ammunition and defence stores, allowing the troops to enhance their defences. Included in the re-supply were rations, 32 anti-tank mines, 40 Surface-to-Air Missile (SAM) launchers, 10 M-252 81mm Medium Extended Range Mortar with an operating range of 4,500 to 5,650-meters and 18 Type 98 120mm Anti-Tank Recoilless Rocket Launchers. With a range of 800-metres for day and 500-metres for night operations the Type 98 Anti-Tank Weapons were capable of defeating reactive armour, with its armour piercing capability able to penetrate 800mm of armour. Once unloaded the Tiema vehicles returned to Darwin with 2 of the HMMWV type vehicles and 5 Marines in each truck for escort to collect further stocks of ammunition, fuel, food and water. The Chinese troops would only supplement the Indonesian force at this location until Indonesian force numbers had grown significantly for relief to take place. The bridge to the south of Darwin was also strengthened when it received a further 800 reinforcements from Blue Beach at 2145hrs on the first night.

That same night only 12hrs after the invasion began, 6 Chinese TU-22 Backfire Bombers having taken off from their base at Zhangzhou/Chang-Chou in China, landed on the Indonesia military airfield of Iswahjudi Madiun on the Island of Java for a refuel, before taking off again towards the Australian coastline. Even this huge aircrafts range of 4,000 miles plus was not enough to get the aircraft from China to Australia and back in one go. The TU-22s, part of a 5-year agreement between Russian and China to provide 24 TU-22 aircraft, were from the first batch purchased from Russia in 2008 and, were the first aircraft to be fitted operationally with the latest Chinese missile development under their wings. Each aircraft carried 3 of the redeveloped Kh-55 Cruise Missiles called the Kh-55M...M standing for modified. China had adapted the technology after receiving 12 Kh-55 Granet Cruise Missiles from the Ukraine in 2001 and the purchase of the backfire bomber was a necessary addition in attaining a long-range supersonic aircraft capable of taking on targets in Australia. The 6 backfires were flying a specific mission profile and for reasons out of their control, were 24hrs behind schedule. They were now travelling low and at high speed as they crossed the coast 180-miles southwest of Darwin. After a leg of 1,696 miles from Java to the Australian coast another 500-miles needed to be covered before the missiles were launched.

At 0430hrs and 302 miles from their predetermined target each backfire fired its allocation of three missiles and as they released their deadly projectiles, a huge flash from each missile lit up the airframes and surrounding sky. With the missiles accelerating to their maximum speed of 3,600km per hour it would only be minutes before impact. Some of the 1,000 people working at the first site would only know what was happening when the missiles struck.... but for those caught in the immediate blast they would know nothing but a quick death. The first target was the highly secret US communications base at Pine Gap, which was located only 12 miles from Alice Springs in the Northern Territory. With the site belonging to the American National Security Agency (NSA), the Chinese viewed it as a controversial choice of target as they knew it would be viewed as the first direct attack against America. China believed it had no other choice though, as the site was a CIA SIGINT (signals intelligence) downlink in the region and, a direct intelligence feed to the Australian military, so the decision to destroy the site had been taken at the highest level in Beijing.

11-minutes after launch, 16 missiles with their 1,000lbs HE warheads slammed into the Pine Gap facility with devastating effect. The site contained 20 buildings and 12 radomes, which were all destroyed or severely damaged from direct hits or secondary blast damage. The first missile struck at 0441hrs and the last at 0444hrs. 3-minutes of utter destruction and death in the Australian outback resulted in the Pine Gap facility ceasing to operate. The remaining 2 missiles continued on and struck the spare and soon to be active JORN facility operations buildings at the Alice Springs complex, thus ensuring the whole system was out of action indefinitely.

A major concern to China was the American naval reaction to this invasion… so, to counter this potential threat, China had deployed a large fleet of 16 diesel and nuclear powered submarines into the region. The 12 Kilo class vessels returning from Diego Garcia would be turned around in less than a week and, with new crews already on standby, these vessels would supplement and relieve those already in the region. In addition to this contingency, the islands to the north of Darwin - Bathurst and Melville Islands - plus the protruding coastal areas on the mainland provided ideal locations from where to site and deploy the 3M-80 (NATO name SS-22) Moskit Sunburn Missile System. These anti-ship missiles with their 250km range and mach 3-velocity speed were designed to give ships little or no time to deploy counter-measures and were one of China's prime weapons against Carrier Battle Groups. Fired by any naval vessel or from land and travelling 20-metres above the sea, this system was designed specifically to defeat the Aegis Air-Defence System employed by US naval ships, with the sole intention of destroying US Amphibious Forces in the Pacific. By firing enough missiles, China hoped to overwhelm any US protective screen around the Aircraft Carriers with multiple strikes, in order to force the US navy into a tactical withdrawal from the region. This effective missile system was the first item to be unloaded at the deep-sea port after the first 90,000 ton container ship had docked.

Europe, the United States and the rest of the world now had to come to terms with a truly global conflict on a scale never before seen. War had come to Europe, Korea, India and now Australia with the United States and Europe, having been attacked by nuclear weapons. Russia and China had both tipped their hands in this conflict and it appeared both were involved in some sort of alliance with the Muslim countries against the Western World. The lack of oil supplies was having a profound and drastic effect in many parts of the world and, although the law and order issues had been resolved in most of the European countries, it had come with a cost to military manpower at the front. With the Arab armies advancing west, the problems associated with mass migration were now adding to the list of concerns with power cuts, lack of fuel and no gas throughout the continent.

The speed of advance by the Arab armies had surprised NATO commanders more than they cared to admit and, the use of modern motorway road networks throughout Europe, coupled with the Arabs policy of only taking on the defending armies ensured a rapid transit through some of the lesser-defended nations on their way to NATO's military heartland.

Russian airpower was also causing NATO problems in that dedicated NATO bombing of the Arab ground forces was often disrupted and sometimes impossible due to the amount of Russian aircraft conducting interdiction missions. Even a 31 cruise missile strike at the bridges spanning the Bosporus Strait in Turkey had failed, with all but one missile destroyed by the huge weight of Air Defence firepower in that region. The one surviving missile had struck the most southern bridge causing only damage detrimental to heavy tank traffic but not enough to prevent lighter vehicles crossing.

In mainland Europe, Mujihadeen ambushes had initially caught NATO convoys unawares but these terrorist groups were mainly on the defensive now as NATO troops hunted them down throughout the continent. By being hunted, however, the Mujihadeen were achieving their mission objectives by forcing large numbers of troops to be deployed by NATO on search and destroy missions and the guarding of key locations.

The Arabs next move was a major push west with an intention to take them to the edge of Germany and NATO's main defensive lines where the great battles would be fought. These were the Arab nations' main objectives - break these and Europe and NATO would be crushed.

In Korea, the introduction of 220,000 Chinese troops had tipped the balance in favour of the North once more and, with thousands dying every day, the South Korean government was close to surrendering. Unless the United States or the United Nations invaded and drove the North Koreans and Chinese out, Korea would be lost.

The South Korean government, knowing this was not going to happen, were suddenly resigned to their fate and the only decision now, was deciding how many more should die before surrender came. Further sacrifice seemed futile and surely it was better to fight another day than not to be in a position to fight at all. If all were wiped out attempting to halt the inevitable then their sacrifice would have been in vain

PART 14

A BATTLE LOST
(D+38)

DTG: Friday-March 3rd ….2012…..

LOCATION: Slovakia…Eastern Europe

SITUATION: Arab Forces having advanced into Slovakia were amassing huge formations of troops on the borders of Poland and the Czech Republic.

The Arab armies, with their overwhelming forces and firepower, had continued their advance northward and westward encountering only slight resistance. The Hungarian army, with only 35,000 troops, had proven to be no match for the 260,000 troops from the Syrian 6th Army Group and the still under-strength Egyptian 4th Army Group. Such was their superiority, that the US Airbase at Taszar and the Nordic Support Group Logistic Base at Pecs were both seized within days. This powerful combined force along with Russian airpower in attendance had swarmed through the plains of Hungary, the tight valleys and rugged hills of Romania and Slovakia, destroyed each of their armed forces' fighting capability in turn and advanced rapidly towards the Slovakian/Polish border, hoping to do the same to Poland's armed forces before pushing west towards Germany. The Egyptians, with 180,000 troops, remained split from the rest of their force, which consisted of another 170,000 men, but these were just one week away and following on fast.

The Syrian army had split in Slovakia and now provided an equal amount of troops to the Egyptians and the 3 Brigades of Mujihadeen heading north, with a second force containing the remaining Syrians attaching themselves to the Iranian army heading west with 2 Brigades of Mujihadeen. The Iranian and Syrian forces had passed via Kosice (pronounced Kosheetsay) in the east of the country and continued on towards Roznava, Rimavska and then Lucenec. They then continued towards Zvolen and eventually the capital Bratislava, which is situated on the western border with the Czech Republic. To the north of Zvolen lay a town called Banska/Bystrica and between the 2 towns there was a large airfield that would be designated as one of the four Russian controlled supply points for troops transiting through Slovakia. The other supply hubs were to be located at Kosice, Poprad and Bratislava. In 48hrs time, this airfield, along with all the others, would be accepting huge Antonov An-124 Ruslan transport planes with Russian logistic troops supplying and stockpiling massive quantities of stores, equipment and munitions. After a brief halt in and around Bratislava large numbers of the Iranian/Syrian force moved north past Trnava to their 3 predetermined jump off locations at Trencin, Dubnica and Zilini.

The Egyptian and Syrian forces heading north towards Poland were more limited in their crossing of the border and to a degree were channelled by the difficult terrain. Moving north from Kosice they had advanced towards Presov, where they encountered their heaviest fighting in what was typical tank ambush terrain before overcoming the resistance with massive firepower. They continued on through Presov, advanced west to Poprad and then formed into three separate assault groups. One group continued north-east to Kezmarok and then onto Stara Lubovna before attempting to cross the border at Piwniczna, a route, which eventually would see them advance on to the town of Nowy Sacz in Poland. The second group followed the first group past Kezmarok to Spisska Bela then swung northwest and eventually north to cross near to, or west of, the town of Spisska Stara Ves. The motorway tunnel dug under the mountain between Presov and Poprad having already been secured by helicopter borne troops who were inserted over 2hrs, at night, by 36 Russian Mi-17 Multi Purpose Helicopters mounting from Hungary. With 30 troops in each helicopter they were able to land 540 troops at each end of the tunnel to prevent the Slovakian army from blowing it up. The final group continued west beyond Poprad as far as the town of Dolny Kubin. From here they moved northeast to Trstena before the final advance to the Polish border. The second and third groups were to push in to Poland as far as Rabka, where they would join again with the first group over towards Nowy Sacz, before advancing to Krakow. The Arabs had been warned to avoid the town of Svidnik near the border as this would force them into what was known as the Ducla Pass. Russia had explained to China that this area may best be avoided because it is the obvious route into Poland and, during World War 2; it was the scene of a huge battle, which resulted in 100,000 Russians and 22,000 German and Czechoslovakian soldiers dying in massed tank and infantry battles for the valleys and ridges that dominate the region. If history was to repeat itself, China was determined that it would not occur here near Ducla simply because they failed to heed the lessons learnt from the past. If the Russians knew of its significance then so did the Polish army, therefore, they informed the Arabs to bypass the area. If the Polish army were there in force they would soon have to pull back once they realised the Arabs were advancing via the more difficult route. The Chinese had stressed to the Arabs that war was difficult enough without ignoring the lessons of the past, so Ducla was left untouched, leaving the Arab forces to focus their attention further west.

With Poland and the Czech Republic about to be invaded, the Polish army had indeed set large ambushes in the Ducla area, but upon word that the main thrust was further west, they had to quickly redeploy their troops. Arab commanders suspected that the Polish forces in particular were not going to be such a pushover as those they had encountered so far, especially with the tight roads in the hilly-forested border areas making it ideal terrain for ambushes and delaying tactics. This was what the Arabs had to overcome before they could make their huge numbers count. The rate of advance had been relatively kind to the Arabs up to now as they had managed in the region of 40-160km a day. The next week, however, would turn out to be hard on men, machines and timelines. Delays meant NATO troops in Germany had more time to prepare extensive defensive positions from which to fight; however, NATO was not having it all its own way in preparing for combat as those forces on the move in Western Europe had encountered Mujihadeen forces lying in wait. The delays resulting from the ambushes in Germany, France, UK and Spain would soon be mirrored in Poland but this time the tables would be turned with the Arabs been the ones to suffer delays as Polish troops initiated the same tactic that the Mujihadeen were conducting further west.

The Iranian 11th Army Group of 550,000 men and remaining 200,000 troops from the Syrian 6th Army Group including its Missile

Command, were on a different axis from their Egyptian brethren heading towards Poland. Their route was to take them west through the Czech Republic, missing out countries such as Croatia, Serbia, Bosnia and Herzegovina, Austria and Slovenia, before finally entering the southern part of Germany. The waiting was now over and the order to advance into the Czech Republic was given with troops deployed over a vast area. The main thrust was advancing from Bratislava towards Breclav on the Czech side of the border and then onwards to Jihlava. With the terrain more akin to tank warfare than Slovakia's rugged, hilly terrain, their speed of advance was nothing short of astonishing with the small but professional army of the Czech Republic quickly outflanked. The one and only major battle for the country took place near the town of Kolin, southeast of the capital Prague. At Kolin, 15,000 Czech troops became surrounded and trapped after a massive pincer movement by Iranian troops. Rather than surrender, the Czech army decided to fight on for the defence of their country but it was futile. They managed to hold off the inevitable for only 9hrs before they were overrun and slaughtered to a man by the overwhelming numbers attacking them, their bodies, mutilated by the Mujihadeen Arabs were spread over a large area and left in the open fields to rot, and there they would have remained if not for the local people who eventually buried them once the Arabs had moved on.

The killing fields at Kolin witnessed some of the worst atrocities of the war so far and with Prague defenceless there was nothing to stop the Arabs entering the city. Fortunately for Prague, the Russians intervened at the last minute and requested that the city be bypassed rather than entered, as long as the Czech government surrendered and ensured that no military were active in the capital. The government had no choice other than to agree to the terms, and with the surrender of the Czech Republic, the Arabs pushed beyond the city boundaries before going firm 30-miles to the west and north. 3-days after the battle of Kolin, 20,000 Russian troops flew into Prague claiming to be there to help stabilise the country and ensure safety for its people.

3-weeks behind and just crossing the Bosporus Strait was the Saudi 10th Army Group with its 415,000 strong force and the Iranian reserve numbering a further 350,000. 10th Army Group were earmarked to follow the route through Poland and on into Germany, with the Iranian contingent heading through the Czech Republic to reinforce those entering southern Germany. As these troops moved closer to the front, the one thing sure to greet their arrival would be the overwhelming smell of decaying and rotting flesh. With winter slowly subsiding, the temperatures would soon rise and the receding snow would reveal the frozen bodies of dead soldiers, civilians, cattle and sheep. Slowly thawing out, the rotting corpses would create a stench that would seep into buildings, passing vehicles and even ones clothing.

A further force of some 580,000 from Egypt and Syria was still in the Middle East as a strategic reserve with the larger Egyptian contingent of 365,000 men just beginning the long laborious move of its equipment over the sea to Saudi Arabia and Turkey. The Egyptians, hemmed in by Israel and the sea, had to move to a land locked country in case they were called forward into Europe. It would take at least 3-4 months to move such a force with its mix of 800 T72/T80s and 559 dated, but still capable, M60A3 MBTs over to Saudi Arabia or Turkey before they could even consider deploying.

Since the first intervention by Russian aircraft in Bulgaria, the air war had intensified significantly throughout the last few weeks with huge NATO air operations seeking to blunt the advancing Arab army's thrust but the interdiction response from Russia had curtailed this somewhat and the success was rather more limited than NATO had hoped for. Russian had been preparing for this war for 4-years, and had accumulated massive quantities of air-munitions, aircraft and trained pilots to sustain them for such a campaign. NATO was not prepared in the same way and was using stocks that were intended for what the politicians called limited campaigns. It was still a very powerful inventory but with the forces ranged against them becoming apparent, the rate at which their ammunition stocks were being used was worrying.

Near the Slovakian city of Kosice, in the east of the country, the Syrian Missile Command began a launch sequence for the first launching of its enormous arsenal of conventional warhead missiles at targets in the Czech Republic, Poland and Italy. They had deployed over a wide area in and around the small airfield of Letisko, which lies on flat terrain to the south of the city. The Syrians, over the following 48hrs, prepared and fired 125 Scud C and Scud D missiles, while Iran prepared and fired her own terrifying arsenal of missiles. A total of 43 of the longer-range Scud D missiles from the Syrian inventory were fired at Italy, where the east coast and central regions were just within range, with the remainder of Scud C missiles fired at targets in Poland and the Czech Republic. With a range of 700km the Syrians were able to deliver accurate HE payloads of 500kgs onto Italian civil and military airbases and ports.

To increase the terror and vulnerability even further, Iran fired 15 of its Ghader missiles at France, 12 at Germany and 6 at Italy. A further 16 were fired at the UK and with a range of 3,000km; these countries were easily within reach, with the Iranians, somewhat indiscriminate with their targeting. Main airfields and ports were targeted in general but the Iranian Missile Command could not resist firing 3 missiles into the centre of Paris, killing 318 people, and 2 at Rome, which exploded in the suburbs close to the Vatican, killing 170 people. The targeting of populated areas in France and Italy was condemned everywhere with Russia and China privately calling on Iran to suspend such action. The Iranians grudgingly agreed to concentrate their remaining missiles onto military and strategic targets smug in the knowledge that they had sown the seed of fear in those 2-countries populations.

For those people in Kosice, the firing of the Scud and Ghader missiles resulted in a light show far more spectacular than any New Year fireworks extravaganza. The white and brown high rise flats, stacked like dominoes on the hills on the outskirts of the city, were continually illuminated as the deafening missiles streaked overhead with their bright burning tails lighting up the area for miles around, with smoke trails, the only evidence remaining as they made their way westward and northward. For those watching, it was a frightening and apocalyptic spectacular and a sign that the war was real and a living nightmare…

More than 400,000 Egyptian and Syrian Arabs were now pushing into Poland, with a further 170,000 Egyptians a few days behind and another 415,000 Saudi Arabians from the 10th Army Group following up a few weeks behind them, but here in Poland, for the first time, they faced a large enemy with a proud tradition of warfare. During the Cold War the Polish Armed Forces were one of the largest in the Soviet Bloc but since then had joined NATO and undergone restructuring in order to prepare for tomorrow's battlefield. They had altered their posture and their infrastructure and looked at improving the mobility, deployability and interoperability of their military for combined operations with other NATO forces. Poland was spending $3.2 billion annually on its military and slowly transgressing away from conscription. By 2012, 75 percent of their military was professionally recruited and on a volunteer basis. With a military machine much reduced from its Cold War levels it now had 267 combat aircraft, a 132,000-strong army with 920 armoured vehicles including 40 T72M1 MBTs, 128 used Leopard 2A4s, 690 BMP1s and the 122mm 2S1, Self Propelled Howitzer. It would soon be time for the British-equipped Egyptian 19 Corp to live up to its reputation but until they could ascertain what it was they were up against, the first elements into the line were the Syrians. Poland was seen as a formidable foe and one that had to be neutralised as a military threat. An army as strong as the Polish one could not be left sitting in the rear during the invasion of Germany and the units lying in wait for the Arabs were some of Poland's most elite troops. These well-trained and well-motivated soldiers came from the Polish 6th Airborne (AB) Assault Brigade, the 1st Warsaw Mechanised Brigade of the Legions, the 21st Brigade of the Podhalan Riflemen Mountain Infantry Unit and Combat Engineers from the 1st Warsaw Mechanised Division. Choosing their ambush killing grounds in the Carpathian Mountains was relatively easy for the Polish troops, with the rugged countryside ensuring the Arabs would be unable to make their numerical armoured superiority count.

Further north, secondary positions, manned by the 10th Armoured Cavalry Brigade, had been set up, with this unit the only one to be equipped with German Leopard MBTs and American M113 APCs. Along side were the 1st Warsaw Mechanised Armoured Brigade and 4 of the 6 Territorial Defence Brigades. Within hours of crossing the border the Arab troops knew they were faced with a difficult battle when lead units from the Syrian contingent were savagely cut down and repulsed by well-sited ambush positions. The aim of the Polish military commanders was simple - to keep the Arabs bottled up on the tight-forested roads near the border region to prevent breakout into flatter ground where their large formations would have numerical advantages. The aim was to delay them as long as possible so NATO could improve its defences in Germany. The Polish commander's had known for weeks that NATO was not coming to Poland's aid as agreed in the defence agreement but, they did at least understand why. Without access to a full supply of fuel, the force would come to a standstill after 500km.

For 5-days the battle raged on the border with thousands of young soldiers killed on both sides from artillery strikes, ambushes and close-quarter fighting in the surrounding woods. The Polish troops, although running short of ammunition, had maintained a hold on their ground to the frustration of the Arab Generals but in anticipation of a breakthrough by the Arabs, secondary defensive positions had already been prepared. The pressure on the Polish lines was intense and continued unabated, especially after the Russian air force had completely destroyed Poland's air capability as a credible threat within the first 48hrs. The intervention by Russia made the Polish authorities and people very nervous. Poland, occupied by the Soviets until the 1980's was very concerned about Russia's alliance with the Arabs and although no Russian ground forces had yet crossed into Poland, their full intentions were yet unclear.

In Moscow, President Vladislav Sidorov was growing impatient with the progress of the Arab nations and, although he had agreed with China not to intervene with ground troops before NATO and the Arabs had fought each other to destruction, he felt compelled to push the assault on. He was sitting with his deputy Nikolai Demidovsky, Vasilii Svialoslavich - **Marshal** of the Russian Federation Armed Forces, General Oleg Mikhailovich- General of the Army and Marshal Iaroslav Ivanova - Chief Marshal of the Air force of Russia.

'Gentlemen…comrades' said Sidorov…*'after speaking with Marshal Svialoslavich and Chief Marshal Ivanova I have decided to alter the plan of action somewhat. As you all know, the Arabs have encountered some difficulty in smashing through in Poland and this impasse needs to be broken. I am not going to commit Russian forces to all out war but I feel it prudent and in our interest to fill the void left by the departing Arabs as they move west. This way we achieve two objectives; securing theirs, and eventually our, lines of communication, and secondly, we maintain a stabilizing force in each country.*

I have ordered Marshal Ivanova to use our air force to begin attacking Polish ground units for the first time in the border region and not just carry out air interdiction operations. The longer we wait the more prepared the Americans and the rest of NATO will be. General Mikhailovich, I want you to bring forward Operation Hammer immediately and push your forces into and up to the eastern edge of Polish Terroritory' Turning to his deputy.... 'Nikolai, you are to inform the governments of Slovakia, Bulgaria, Hungary and Romania that any attempt to interfere with the Arab advance will result in huge numbers of Russian forces entering their countries to quell any insurrection. Inform them that we will be ruthless in our pursuit of any rogue elements in their country. Tell them that at the moment only their army is destroyed... do not let it be their entire country..... and, although their industries have ground to a halt, they are still intact and will soon be running again. I have agreed with the Arab nations that from tomorrow 20,000 Russian troops will be sent to each of the defeated countries capitals to ensure their governments remain intact. This will hopefully prevent the Arab armies from ransacking their countries. When we eventually take Europe I want most of it intact...not destroyed, looted and needing massive rebuilding'

'And what of the Ukraine?,' said General Mikhailovich

'They have our ultimatum,' said Sidorov. 'Either join the Russian Federation or face defeat. I am confident that in a few days, General, you will see your forces swelled by 4,000 or so armoured vehicles and a large number of combat troops. At the end of the day it is about survival and the Ukrainian government has its people's interests to think about. I have also promised not to deploy Russian troops on Ukrainian soil if they join the Federation. They also know that NATO has not come to the aid of Bulgaria and the other NATO states in this war in any great capacity and will no doubt feel isolated and betrayed by the NATO promise that an attack against one is an attack against all. How hollow those words must seem now and how hollow they were in 2006 when the United States bombed Turkey...an ally and member of NATO.

Once on board we will use the Ukrainians to quell any dissention in the conquered countries while we march victorious to the French coast and complete our long awaited victory over the whole of Europe. After two World Wars...the end of the Cold War.... and millions of dead... Europe will eventually have one master...Russia'. They all smiled at the irony of Sidorov's last remark.

'One more thing comrades, our submarine forces that departed 2-weeks ago for the Atlantic have been in position for some days now and once our satellites confirm the location of the 2-American Carriers and their Battle Groups off the coast of Ireland, we will activate Operation Sabre to intercept them'

Sidorov was clearly referring to the 2-fleets that President Maxwell had sent to supplement NATO's airpower. Russian intelligence had received word as soon as the 2-Carrier Battle Fleet set sail from America and, knowing its firepower, had taken measures to prevent its use.

And so it began.... with Russia's massed armour, mechanized infantry and tracked artillery invading Estonia, Latvia and Lithuania. This in itself was an act of war but there was nothing these countries could do other than accept the inevitable. Belarus on the other hand, a long-term ally of Russian, gladly invited Russian forces in and allowed them to transit through its land in order to pressure Poland. The message to Poland was unmistakably clear - surrender or be crushed. The Russians, knowing the Poles' proud fighting traditions, suspected the army would refuse to surrender and that they would fight for their homeland and their people to the last. If this was going to be their stance, then so be it.

Private Aleksander (Alexander) Kaminski, 19-years old and having recently passed his infantry training had only been with the Polish 6th Airborne Assault Brigade for 6-weeks. He would be celebrating his 20th birthday next week and would have been looking forward to going home for the weekend to celebrate it with his family and girlfriend. That was until the horrific events in America and Europe, followed by the Arabs' invasion into Europe through Turkey. Aleksander's world as he knew it had changed completely and in such a short space of time. Upon joining his unit, he was interviewed by Lt Fryderyk (Frederick) Lewandowski, the Platoon leader who was killed, along with his runner, by an artillery strike on the first day of combat on a snow-covered hill on the border with Slovakia. As part of 7 Platoon- B Company-2nd Battalion, Pte Kaminski and the rest of his Platoon were now under the command of Sergeant Brunon (Bruno) Mazur southwest of the small town of Kokuszka, a few miles over the border in Poland and inside the Popradski Park. B Company was responsible for the 2nd Battalion's right flank and had been allocated a position on the west side of the main road in the forested areas with C Company located on B Company's right flank further west. Together, they were able to provide each other with mutual support in the event of an attack and had done so on numerous occasions. A and D Company were on the east side of the road covering the left flank with Support Company and their allocation of anti-tank weapons conducting the anti armour ambushes on the main road. Attached to the 2nd Battalion as reserves, were a further 2 Platoons from 1st Battalion - D Company and these were held in close proximity to where Support Company was located.

Aleksander had been literally frightened to death for the first few days especially when the artillery strikes began, but the calmness and confidence shown by Sergeant Mazur under fire had inspired him and others in the Platoon to think they could possibly survive this war with Mazur at the helm. Their tactics had been spot on and their response to the large numbers of Arabs coming at them through the woods had been violent, aggressive and deadly. Sergeant Mazur had taken Aleksander into Platoon HQ after the death of Lt Lewandowski and this allowed Aleksander the chance to observe a soldier he respected, trusted and aspired to be. The Polish Airborne Battalion had repulsed 5 separate mechanized attacks on the road and numerous infantry assaults on the flanks through the forests over the last 6-days. The probes in the woods were growing in intensity and Sergeant Mazur had noticed that the dress of the attackers had altered as well as their appearance. The first troops sent against them had been Arabs in typical snow camouflaged uniforms and a lot were clean-shaven or had moustaches. The latest Arabs appeared more resilient, had large beards, a mix of snow and wood camouflage dress and were so intent on breaking the lines that they could almost have been accused of committing suicide attacks. So far they had failed but with artillery strikes sapping morale and ammunition running low their attacks appeared to be growing stronger.

Arabic troops were now beginning to infiltrate past the hard pressed Polish troops in the surrounding hills. After the first 3-days of Syrian probes had proven unsuccessful, the Mujihadeen brigades had been brought in and tasked with breaking through the Polish flanks. By breaking the flanks, the Polish ambush sites would have no choice other than to pull back from the border roads, which would then allow Arabic armour to push through the bottleneck. With this achieved the road to Krakow and Warsaw would be open. The Mujihadeen units, trained in Iran, were saturated with Chechnyan and Iraqi veterans, how ironic that Russian jets were now helping them achieve their ultimate victory over the West. The Syrians and Egyptians regarded the Mujihadeen as nothing more than aggressive shock troops and, because they appeared to have no fear of death, considered them ideal for attacking well-defended positions. More than 8,500 Mujihadeen, along with 17,000 Syrian and Egyptian Infantry, were leading the line in an attempt to break the Polish flanks and these sustainable troop numbers, day after day, combined with the Polish troops' lack of ammunition, eventually took their toll.

Unbeknown to B Company and through a serious breakdown in communications, the Battalion had pulled back 1hr before the next attack on its position. The attack, when it came, was one that could not be held by B Company alone and, with the position lost, the Officer Commanding (OC), Major Konrad (Conrad) Kaczmarek surrendered to the Mujihadeen with 107-men. The captured soldiers were savagely beaten almost immediately and, without the intervention of what appeared to be their Mujihadeen commander, Sergeant Mazur was convinced they were about to be killed. Luckily, the beatings stopped as quickly as they had begun and men were, instead, bound and taken to a large barn near a small village called Czerc. At the barn they were crammed inside, less the OC, the Sergeant Major, 3 of the Platoon Commanders, 2 Sergeants and 3 Corporals. 10-men in total were blindfolded and marched away. 3hrs later, 10 distant shots were heard in the woods and those not asleep began to fear the worst. Sergeant Mazur was one of those listening and although not completely sure, was convinced that the shots he had heard signalled the death of his friends. 300-metres away in the woods the Mujihadeen had acquired the information they sought. Keen to know where the Polish depth defensive positions were they had savagely tortured the 10 Polish soldiers until they felt they had gleaned enough information from them before shooting them all in the head from behind. For those with fingers and eyes missing a bullet to the back of the head came as a welcome relief.

The rest of the men in the barn, all blindfolded and bound, were sleeping or squirming around in different states of discomfort. Sergeant

Mazur, sitting next to one of the barn's brick and wood walls, was able to rub his head against the coarse wooden slats so that one eye was partially free from the confines of the cloth blindfold. After adjusting his eyes he was able to make out the remaining 97-men of B Company in the darkened barn. They had only been prisoners for 3hrs and 30-minutes but it felt like so much more. Two paces away was Private Kaminski, sitting and shivering on the damp cold floor looking totally uncomfortable with both hands bound behind his back. Kaminski was suffering from the lack of movement and for him and many others in the barn the tight binding was restricting the blood flow to the hands, causing an almost unbearable numbing pain.

'Kaminski…are you ok?' whispered Sergeant Mazur

Kaminski…unable to see, stopped fidgeting and turned his head in the direction of his Sergeant's voice …*'is that you, Sergeant Mazur? What's happening to us? I'm cold and scared and I can't feel my hands properly…they're so numb yet painful at the same time…and'*

Sergeant Mazur jumped in…

'Calm yourself Kaminski…. I'm sure we will soon be moved from here to somewhere more comfortable and given food and drink'

'Do you think so, Sergeant'…said Aleksander with hope in his voice..

'Why not'…Said Sergeant Mazur…. *'After all, we are POWs aren't we? What else can they do with POWs? If they had wanted to harm us they would have done so by now…. don't you think?*

*'I suppose…*said Kaminski…still unsure…

10-feet from Sergeant Mazur a Corporal from 6 Platoon had also managed to push up his blindfold and was staring intently at Mazur as he spoke to Kaminski. The expression from the young corporal said it all and Sergeant Mazur, deep down, knew it too…it was a resignation that death awaited them all once the Arabs had decided what to do with them. The corporal knew that Sergeant Mazur was attempting to calm the younger inexperienced soldiers and as Sergeant Mazur caught his gaze Mazur slowly shook his head before the corporal lowered his gaze and closed his eyes. Sergeant Mazur wondered if the same fate awaited them that had befallen the Company OC and his friends…. probably a bullet to the head, he thought…. but whatever it was…please God let it be quick and not let these brave young soldiers suffer. He had noticed the difference in those who had captured them to those they had fought the first few days and Sergeant Mazur was fearful for his men, knowing the atrocities committed against captured Russian troops by Jihadists, or Mujihadeen as they preferred to be known, during their time in Chechnya… but for now he had no choice other than to push such thoughts from his mind.

All of a sudden from the crowd of cramped soldiers a voice from the corner asked a question…*'Why is this happening, Sergeant…the war, I mean…. and why now?'* …

Sergeant Mazur could not make out whom it was but he knew that those awake in the barn were listening and waiting for his reply.

'Who knows why man goes to war'…he said…. *'in the past… now…or even in the future…there are many reasons for war – Religion, power….. war has even been fought over a woman of all things'*

'Some fucking woman Sergeant' came a reply from the corner followed by sniggers elsewhere……….

Sergeant Mazur continued…*'exactly, or maybe it is just nature's way of ensuring we don't destroy ourselves…. I mean, technology allows us to keep alive those that once would have died and if mankind eradicated wars altogether, we would reproduce like fucking rabbits wouldn't we…until there were billions upon billions of people…who becomes the plague then, hey…too many people would not be able to sustain themselves on this planet's limited resources… so there would be a fucking war yet again…. I don't know why we are at war…maybe it is natures way to safeguard the planet and we are destined to fight each other for all time …*

…On the other hand, though… maybe it is because we all believe in different things and we always wants what another has…. because by nature…. humans are greedy…and wars are not just fought over the earlier reasons but because of the worlds precious resources such as oil or even water…how long before water becomes more powerful than oil.'

'Anyway you wankers…. the sermon is over for today and you men should not worry about such matters. You have all fought well these last few days and you should know I am proud to serve with you all…you are Poland's new heroes now and your families will be proud of your contribution in defending our country…. we are professional soldiers and we did not join the Polish army to go to war and die… but to a man we

all hoped to test ourselves in combat one day and live through it… and like anything in life …we must always be prepared for what lies ahead…so remember…. if the opportunity to escape comes, you fucking well take it…. do you hear me boys…you fucking take it'.

It had just turned 1305hrs and before anything else could be said raised voices could be heard outside. Seconds later the barn doors were flung open and Sergeant Mazur pushed his head against the wood to reset the blindfold. A blast of cold air poured into the barn signaling the chill outside and the change in light was even noticeable from under the blindfold. Arabs were shouting loudly at the men in the barn and strong hands started hauling the Polish prisoners roughly to their feet. Those prisoners slow to react were kicked and punched for their troubles and others close to them could hear their stifled cries. The Arabic voices sounded excited and there was lots of shouting as the prisoners were dragged forcibly outside. Sergeant Mazur was eventually pulled to his feet and with both hands bound behind his back and arms tightly held, he was marched quickly from the confines of the barn. Feeling completely helpless his instincts screamed at him that this rounding up was not in the prisoners' best interests but he could do nothing about it. Sergeant Mazur had every reason to be concerned but even he could not have foreseen the horrific events that were about to unfold over the next 8-minutes.

On exiting the barn Sergeant Mazur and the rest of the prisoners were moved quickly to wherever they were going… the only noise recognizable above the shouting was the sound of icy snow crunching beneath hundreds of boots. Sergeant Mazur's blindfold had not been fully pulled down and he could just see his feet and the snow through the bottom of his blindfold along with the boots of his captives and the lower half of their combat fatigues as he was literally dragged to wherever he was going. It looked and felt like they were being moved down a gentle slope and the journey took no more than 3 to 4-minutes. The 97-men of B Company were now lined up, 2-metres apart, along a snow-covered grass verge on the small road, 3km north of the town of Czerc. …. each prisoner held by 2 Mujihadeen with a third standing behind him. Other Mujihadeen were standing to the front, sides and rear of the bound men with their AK47 assault rifles pointing in the general direction of their captives.

Standing on the road was the Mujihadeen commander who demanded silence and who was now talking in Arabic to the hushed crowd. None of the Polish soldiers could understand the words but the tone sounded threatening and angry and some of the captives, not knowing their fate were now recalling Sergeant Mazur's words of escape. The Mujihadeen commander was actually telling his men that these bound infidels were responsible for the deaths of their Muslim brothers. These non-believers, as he described them, were, in his eyes, lower in status than a dog and their only punishment, as decreed by Allah, was death, with their bodies left on show for others to see, so that all who view them know that the Mujihadeen's method of administrating justice was one to be feared.

A raise of the hand by the Mujihadeen commander resulted in all the Polish soldiers receiving a stinging kick to the back of the knee, which forced them to drop onto their knees. Sergeant Mazur immediately felt the cold ground penetrate his clothing into his joints. As soon as he was on his knees he felt a sharp blow to the middle of his back and this forced him to hit the ground face first…forcing snow into his mouth and nostrils….

Breathing heavily…unable to move and still held firmly by strong hands, he felt what appeared to be a boot on the back of his neck, forcing his head flat onto the snow covered ground. Mazur's mind was now racing and in an instant he had realised they were not going to die with a bullet to the back of the head. Were they going to be tortured first? Were they just going to be beaten…or….dear God …please not that…please God not that…. he thought…

It was at that moment he felt something sharp penetrate the left side of his neck…a hand grabbed his hair and yanked his head off the ground and he felt the blade cutting deeper into his throat as the blade moved from left to right, leaving the spinal cord to last. Sergeant Mazur, kicking and struggling frantically once the realization of what was happening became clear, could not get up and in his mind Mazur was loudly screaming NOOOOOOOOOO…..but the only audible sound was a loud gurgling noise as the blood from his own severed carotid arteries flooded his throat and lungs. One man knelt on his back and continued to slice into his throat while the two others held him firmly. Before he passed out Sergeant Mazur's last sight as a living being was seeing the snow turning red from his own blood from under his blindfold. The pain now gone… Sergeant Mazur's final act before he died was to urinate and defecate himself as his head was severed from his body. With the cries of Allah Ackbar emanating down the valley, 97 heads were now held aloft then placed in the middle of the backs of the dead Polish soldiers. Along the line Private Aleksander Kaminski, 19 years and 360 days old died the same way as his Platoon Sergeant and the rest of his Company. 31-seconds after been forced to the ground B Company ceased to exist and the Mujihadeen, proud of their abhorrent murders, walked away singing songs of Jihad and victory.

2hrs later the first elements of the Egyptian army came down the road and stared in shock and disbelief at the sight that greeted them. Standing in silence at the scene before them…some of the Egyptian soldiers turned away in disgust, shaking their heads and a few even vomited into the snow. Word spread quickly along the line that the Mujihadeen were beheading captured prisoners so the Egyptian commander, Major General Jibade Youssef, made his way to the scene, as it was getting dark. Disgusted by what he found he immediately ordered a burial party to remove the dead soldiers and bury them as best they could in the woods, then ordered his lead elements to locate the Mujihadeen unit responsible for this and for their commander to return to Czerc to explain the actions of his men.

In Czerc, at the force HQ, the Mujihadeen commander, Commander Arash Muhammad Kermani, was angry at being called to answer for his men's actions. With him was his second in command, Colonel Farzam Kashani; both were Iranians. Kermani, having answered the call in early 2000 to conduct Jihad in Chechnya and Afghanistan, was a seasoned veteran in the art of terror and the beheading of prisoners had been eagerly learnt from the Chechens during his time there. During his ride in the back of a BMP-2 to the force HQ Kermani took out a letter from his inside right pocket and, on removing it from its waterproof case, read it once more. After reading the letter he placed it back from whence it came, closed his eyes, tapped his pocket and smiled. As he entered the makeshift HQ at the local school Kermani was surprised to see so many officers in the briefing room.

Major General Jibade Youssef, commander of the Egyptian ground forces, spoke first....

'Commander Kermani...I will come straight to the point...what do you know of the beheading of 97 Polish prisoners of war (POW) on the outskirts of this village?'...

'General'...said Kermani...'my men succeeded in breaking through the Polish lines and, in doing so we lost many of our Muslim brothers. The justice we meted out was in accordance with our belief'.

'So you admit it was your men that carried out this atrocity?.....not only did you murder them but you left their bodies on show like trophies'

'CAREFUL WITH YOUR WORDS GENERAL'...Kermani retorted loudly.....'My men are proven loyal soldiers of Allah and the only atrocity in our eyes is that we allow too many of the infidel prisoners to live'

'MAY I REMIND YOU COMMANDER'... said an angry General Youssef...'THAT THE MEN WE HAVE CAPTURED ARE PRISONERS OF WAR AND SHOULD BE TREATED AS SUCH'.....lowering his voice General Youssef continued.... 'Arabs soldiers do not kill prisoners, especially in the manner that you and your men have done..'

'For your soldiers, General, this may be so, but for the Mujihadeen those rules do not apply. Our Brigades are the swords of justice in this alliance and we will continue to strike down our enemies in a way that we deem suitable...if you do not like our methods then take it up with our superiors in Tehran...who I am sure will explain the situation to you'

'Your way Commander, and your superiors... as you put it, will ensure that NATO forces fight to the death, which will result in more Muslim soldiers killed than is necessary'

'Then this is Allah's will General...would you not agree?'

Commander Kermani knew that the General would not openly contradict Allah's will in front of the others. Kermani was using it now to justify the events carried out by his men. The belief by Muslims that everything was the will of God meant that whatever happens should not be questioned. To do so would be denouncing or questioning God's will.

General Youssef knew that, no matter what was said today, the Mujihadeen units were intent on exporting their methods of warfare, terror and their type of justice against what they saw as the Christian infidels.

'*Commander Kermani....you and you men will do well to remember that Allah is also merciful and that sometimes the deaths of your enemies can be avoided or spared....this too is Islam's message...is it not?*'

Kermani studied the General intently and without answering the question, asked.... '*will that be all General?*'

'*Yes...you are dismissed*' said General Youssef, knowing the Iranian was going to take no notice of his request.

Kermani turned on his heels and left the room with his second in command following behind. He was inwardly fuming and would ensure he and his men did not adopt the policy of what he considered the weak Egyptian army.

As soon as Kermani was out of sight General Youssef thumped his fist onto the table in anger....and then turned to his commanders present in the room...

'IDIOT'....he raged...'*the actions of a fanatical few will galvanise the will of NATO and any notion of surrendering will no longer apply if word of the Mujihadeen's justice, as he calls it, reaches them. The Mujihadeen in their blind hatred and desire to kill cannot see it....*

Gentlemen, from now on I want their involvement limited on the ground and they will only be committed as a last resort...do I make myself clear?'...All the officers nodded in agreement before being dismissed except for the second in command, Lt General Shakir Nkrumah...

'*Your thoughts, Shakir,*' said General Youssef..

'*The Mujihadeen are a liability General...that we know...but they are also good fighters. I do not see what else can be done. This war will be long and costly and the Mujihadeen will play their part as sure as night follows day...and I am afraid they will continue to fight the war in their own way*'

'*Then there is nothing else we can do, my friend, other than maintain some sort of control over them. I do have to question the wisdom of our alliance with such people...we are all Muslims, Shakir, but I do not see how Allah allows such men to kill in his name in the manner that they do..*

we kill as soldiers, Shakir,..... but they....they slaughter a man as you would a goat and it goes against everything I understand about Islam and warfare....I am a soldier, Shakir, as you are......and as soldiers we do what we must in order to achieve our mission and to achieve our ultimate victory....but killing prisoners... no matter what their religion does not sit easily with me or my men. Mark my words my friend…no good will come of this slaughtering other than to strengthen the will of the enemy. . I wonder what Kermani will say then when his men are faced with soldiers that are prepared to die as he is. I am unable to call that Allah's will, Shakir, instead I call it stupidity…and worst of all I can't do anything to prevent it…can I?

With Poland providing the sternest test to date, it took a further 2-days of intense aerial and artillery bombardments against the Polish lines before they broke completely with the bottleneck opening to allow hundreds of thousands of frustrated and resentful Arab soldiers into Poland. The advance to Krakow and then Warsaw could now begin in earnest. The price in young Arab lives to break the Polish lines was in excess of 23,800 dead and more than 6,000 wounded. Poland had suffered far greater casualties with Russian Air Power extracting a heavy toll even after the Polish troops had broken contact and attempted to withdrawal back to Krakow.

There was now a bubbling resentment festering amongst the Arab troops though, with some soldiers taking revenge on the small village populations. On their march from Turkey the Arab forces had been surprisingly disciplined but Poland saw the first instances of rape and reports of civilians being executed. The incidents were still fairly isolated yet serious enough for General Youssef to execute by firing squad two of his own men in order to maintain order and discipline for the murder of a family of ten at a remote farm. General Youssef did not know how long he could keep an army, whose human compassion was evaporating daily in check. Every battle they participated in resulted in the deaths of their brothers in arms and these losses continued to eat away a little more self restraint each time, they were beginning to hate the enemy they fought and, worst of all, they were beginning to turn that hate against the people of this land.

The fighting through the remainder of Poland, although violent and bloody, was never as concentrated or intense as the battles that had raged on the border and, with the Egyptian 19 Corp bringing its immense firepower to bear against the defending armoured and mechanised brigades, Polish units were now fighting a fierce rearguard action back to Warsaw. The deciding factors in the eventual defeat of the Polish military as a viable fighting force would be overwhelming numbers of men, equipment and the Russian air force. Krakow fell within 3-days of the border collapsing and Warsaw within 2-weeks. With Russian troops massing on Poland's eastern border, mass panic gripped the population, which resulted in thousands upon thousands of refugees and displaced persons moving west where they joined with those already fleeing. Even the destruction or partial destruction of key bridges, the first time such a tactic had been used had failed to halt the advance. This was partly due to partial detonation of explosives, the large enveloping moves by the Arabs or in most cases, the bridges had just not been prepared.

The gates to Warsaw had been well and truly smashed open, which meant there was now no credible military force between the advancing Arab armies and Germany. After Warsaw fell a tactical pause was ordered by the Arab Army Command HQ in order for reserves and logistics to catch up and for the next part of the plan to be briefed. During this break in combat a strong reconnaissance and holding force of 35,000 troops was detached to the German border area with the intention of destroying any remaining pockets of Polish military before seizing and holding key crossing points for the main armies. Throughout Eastern Europe large heavy goods vehicles and large haulage trucks confiscated in their thousands were now being driven to Slovakia by Russian and Arab troops. The logistic hubs in Slovakia were stockpiling huge amounts of stores from Russia and the Middle East prior to its eventual move to the frontline. Russia was providing the heavy lift aircraft to move such vast amounts of re-supply to the hubs and the Arabs were bringing in even greater amounts in massive convoys along the motorways that were now basically 4-lane resupply highways. The advancing armies would be short of nothing....not for a long time anyway. The confiscated heavy goods and haulage trucks were crucial in helping to move the much needed munitions, fuel, food and other essentials to the troops that required it in Poland and the Czech Republic.

After Warsaw fell, it was clear to the Polish authorities that the battle was lost and any attempt to take on the Arab forces was foolish, especially as the core of the Polish army had been defeated. The amount of traffic heading west was also a hindrance to any movement east.... so with great regret....and with what remained of the Polish armed forces, the Polish government retreated into Germany and redeployed its forces to line up alongside German, Belgium, Italian, American and British troops.

With both NATO HQ in Brussels and Supreme HQ Allied Powers Europe (SHAPE) near Mons having been destroyed in the first hours of Dragon's Claw, the new HQ relocated to Ramstein Air Base in Western Germany near the Rhein River in the state of Rheinland Pfalz. The airbase was again operational after suffering 1,238 dead in addition to a large portion of their heavy-lift capability being destroyed or damaged when Mujihadeen suicide groups made entry on the night that nuclear devices exploded across Europe. The gigantic base, near to Luxemburg and France, was chosen as the new nerve centre for all NATO operations as it housed the Allied Air Component Command Headquarters. The Command Centre, having sustained no damage during those first few hours, was able to function fully with land and air component planners now in situ.

In anticipation of the greatest challenge ever faced by NATO and Europe, the command centre and its surrounding buildings, which were initially designed for 800 people, now had close to 2,100 military planners working 24/7. Not all were in the main HQ building, though, with the most important elements working in underground operations rooms in the event of air or missile attack. The base was now the most fortified in Europe, with the Combined Air Operations Centre (CAOC) responsible for the air campaign in Europe and the protection of the HQ. NATO had deployed massive Air Defence screens, early warning systems to warn of air or missile attack and large numbers of aircraft, which were ring-fenced and dedicated to protecting its airspace out to 300-miles.

Of the remaining 25 countries in NATO, Romania, Bulgaria, Slovakia, the Czech Republic and now Poland had all suffered defeat at the hands of the mightiest Arab army ever to be raised and there had been no word from the Ukraine for some time. NATO's policy that an attack on one was an attack on all would normally have resulted in a response from the powerful NATO air armada and from the ground by NATO's Rapid Reaction Forces (RRF), however, the loss of a third of NATO's aircraft within hours of the start of the war, the damage to Europe's oil reserves and the Middle East's oil blockade, had resulted in a military that now found it no longer had the fuel to quench the thirst of its huge numbers of vehicles required to take on the armies advancing towards them. Some Western European countries still had to endure power cuts up to 6-times a day and the gas embargo by Russian had seriously affected industry output and left millions without heating for their homes. All this, combined with the Mujihadeen ambushes, had seriously undermined the capability of NATO to deploy strategically across Europe.

Huge amounts of manpower had been siphoned away from front line duties to hunt down and kill the Mujihadeen fighters as well as protect vital supply routes and key facilities, with other troops continuing to guard important government and military installations in case of new suicide missions. With all these factors taken into account the decision had been made early to let the Arabs advance at their own pace and allow the old East European states military to inflict casualties with NATO air power seeking to degrade them enough for NATO land forces to halt and finally defeat them in Germany. The plan, however, had not quite worked, as the only country to make any impact – Poland - had been quickly defeated with the Arab military machine remaining relatively unscathed. Massive Russian air power was making sure that many of the huge bombing missions planned against the Arab ground units were not having much effect and, to make matters worse, large Arab reinforcements were continuing to make good speed to the front line.

In preparation for the impending battle, Egypt had forward deployed its contingent of 240 F16 aircraft to bases in Slovakia and Poland under control of the Russian Federation, with Saudi Arabia providing 35 of its F15 Strike Eagles, .100 of its Tornado Fighter Bombers from a force of 182, plus 62 Euro Fighters…a combined force of 431 aircraft. Egypt had long courted the West for technology and the West always willing to oblige for a price had aided countries such as Egypt to make the leap to the next level militarily. Egypt had long ago identified weaknesses in its command and control and attack and support techniques, so during its modernisation programme, it not only sought equipment upgrades but also ensured the command and control issues were addressed. The Egyptian and Saudi aircraft were a welcome addition to the Russian air campaign and would initially be used in diversionary missions or Combat Air Patrols in the rear echelons rather than full on combat missions against NATO ground troops and aircraft.

Either side of the Polish/German and Czech/German border…2 opposing ideologies…2 very different worlds … were witnessing the formation of some of the most powerful military hardware ever assembled. NATO troops, never expecting to fight a war from a defensive perspective had under considerable pressures from insurgents and massed columns of refugees, prepared their defences as best they could and, although the forces in Germany were formidable, they should have been so much more. There were only 286,000 NATO combat troops on the frontline in Germany made up of 167,000 Germans with 40,000 other regulars helping the reserves to conduct counter insurgency search and destroy missions against Mujihadeen still operating in Germany. This, and key facility security, took soldiers from the front line. In addition there were 19,000 British, with the remainder still in the UK doing what the German forces were doing - hunting Mujihadeen fighters, 44,000 Polish troops, having withdrawal from Poland, 32,000 Americans with no more reinforcements sanctioned by the US administration, 18,000 Italian troops serving with the ARRC, and 6,000 soldiers from Belgium. Preparation had been ongoing for nearly 3 months now but they were still short of the numbers that they wanted to combat the massed Arab armies now forming up west of Warsaw. Britain, with a history of defence cuts in the last 20-years, had a standing army of just 85,000 and was no longer able to provide anything other than a strong Armoured Division along with 2 Brigades. The remaining troops were needed to maintain law and order and protect key facilities while, at the same time, ensure the Mujihadeen cells in the UK were hunted down and wiped out. The British contingent contained the 1st UK Armoured Division, 16 Air Assault Brigade, 3 Commando Brigade and 3- Sabre Squadrons of Special Forces Soldiers from the Special Air Service (SAS), along with their supporting troops - the UK Special Forces Support Group (SFSG). The SFSG contained elements from the Parachute Regiment, Royal Marines and the RAF Regiment and was formed to provide direct support to the SAS on operations. A 4th SAS Squadron remained in the UK together with the Special Boat Service to deal with any further potential terrorist incidents.

In Australia the Indonesian build-up had continued but not without incident. Two weeks previously, 2 Australian SSK Collins-class Attack Submarines, HMAS RANKIN and HMAS SHEEAN, had infiltrated the Chinese Carrier Battle Fleets protective screen and succeeded in sinking a Sovremenny-class Cruiser, while the Australian Air Force had managed to intercept and shoot down 3 - C130 transport aircraft on their way back to East Timor to collect more troops. On the ground Australian Special Forces had had some success in the Northern Territories before 3 patrols had been ambushed and were now missing, presumed dead. 3 RAR, with its 1,200-strong Mechanised Group, had attempted probes north of Pine Creek near to where Tindall Air Base was situated and, on approaching the Mt Bunday area had been subjected to a sustained and deadly cross-fire from well prepared and, well dug-in forces. With Chinese fighter aircraft also part of the operation, 3 RAR were eventually forced to withdrawal.

The war in India was indiscriminate and unbelievably vicious with heavy casualties taken on both sides and large numbers of civilians caught in the heavy artillery duels. India was predominantly on the back-foot and quickly attempting to mobilise its huge army in order to stabilise the situation before counter-attacking the forces that had invaded its homeland.

In the Ukraine, the Ukrainian government, realising they were not going to get NATO help, reluctantly accepted the terms of President Sidorov's Russian Federation and placed at his disposal the Armed Forces of the Ukraine. 11 Tank Divisions and 150,000 men were now part of the Russian order of battle and a major blow to NATO, especially after its boasts of enlargement and protection of its members. It wouldn't be long before Russia called upon them to commit forces to those nations already defeated in order to keep the lid on any disunion or dissension from the populations once the shock of invasion and occupation had worn off.

PART 15

END OF AN ERA

NATO troops had been allowed 80-days to prepare its forces for this war but they would have expressed shock to know what they were facing. After all, these were just Arabs and their armies had neither the expertise, weaponry nor the logistic know how to carry out such a mission, yet, here they were…on NATO's doorstep and ready to smash their way in with NATO commanders asking how this could be so. Although the Arabs lacked the very best of Western technology they did have a massive amount of Western weaponry at their disposal and they made up for any disadvantages with their huge amount of manpower and modern Russian equipment. An important factor was how they had used the last 4-years and, with Chinese and Russian aid they had been able to prepare and stockpile phenomenal amounts of munitions, fuel, water, rations and combat fighting vehicles. Chinese insistence on massive and detailed logistical requirements had angered the Arabs at first but it now was proving to be a force multiplier by allowing the momentum to be maintained. Massive resources had been channelled into this force build-up as there had been no real requirement to form or maintain a capable air force.

The build up was in stark contrast to the NATO members, who along with their politicians seemed to have a fixation with smaller mobile forces, capable of fighting the low intensity conflicts of today. This belief that asymmetric warfare was the in-thing had resulted in NATO's combat manpower being cut drastically over the last few years. The drop in manpower saw a slight rise in combat aircraft and other technological areas but air power was only useful if you had enough of it, and history had shown that bombing alone never really works if you want to win a war. Aircraft win battles but the man on the ground wins the war. The early Mujihadeen attacks across Europe had proven this and they had weakened NATO's capability to the point, where if they so wanted, the Russians, could exert air supremacy within weeks. The Russia air force was well prepared for war in Europe but for the time been was keeping the majority of its vast air armada away from the front-line for a very good reason.

The first of the 2 massive Arab armies now moving towards Germany on 2 fronts consisted of 986,000 in Poland, with the Egyptians now at full strength, and the Saudi 10th Army Group finally in place, with a further 365,000 Egyptians earmarked for Poland some 4 to 6 months out. The second force consisted of a further 706,000 in the Czech Republic with a 350,000 Iranian reserve on its way to bolster this number. Almost 1.7 million Arabs were advancing towards a NATO force of just 286,000 with another 715,000 Arabs yet to join the battle. In countries such as the UK, they were still looking at sending more troops to Germany as soon as the insurgent elements were mopped up and they were sure the reserves and police could control the situation.

6-weeks earlier, the United States had been on the receiving end of a massive anti-ship missile attack on its 2-Carrier Battle Fleets in the Atlantic. The fall-out from this was that America had confirmed it would no longer send troops to bolster the alliance, nor would it deploy more Carrier Battle Fleets to the region to provide extra air cover. They attempted to placate Europe by continuing the ammunition resupply by air and by allowing 70 percent of the 2-Carrier Battle Fleets aircraft to remain on the UK mainland to become part of the air force order of battle.

...............6 weeks ago...............

The incident in the Atlantic to the west of Ireland in early March resulted in a maritime disaster for the American Carrier Fleets with numerous ships sunk or damaged after been surprised by Russian Oniks/Yakhont Missiles, (a 4th Generation Anti-Ship Missile designed for hitting complex targets such as Carrier Battle Groups) and, large numbers of SS-22 Sunburn Anti-Ship Missiles. The Russians had positioned their 8 attack submarines in 3 separate groups with their focus aimed at catching the Carrier Battle Fleets in a supersonic missile crossfire. Two of Russia's newest Lada-class Submarines, fitted with an improved version of the ultra quiet Air Independent Propulsion System and their complement of longer range VA-111 Shkval Supercavitating Torpedoes, were positioned to the west and almost motionless. To the south of the fleet, 350km away, were 2 Severodvinsk-class Nuclear Powered Submarines equipped with the latest version of the 4th Generation Oniks/Yakhont Supersonic 400km Anti-Ship Cruise Missile. To the north of the fleet and lying just below the thermocline were the final 4 attack boats - the Oscar II-class Nuclear Powered Submarines with 18 SS-22 Sunburn Anti-Ship Missiles per vessel.

The Carriers and support vessels were 250km off the coast of Ireland and more than 100km apart. Between them the Carriers carried in the region of 160 fixed wing fighters with the distance to mainland Europe no real issue to these aircraft. The aircraft also had the option to remain on task for longer periods by using the air-to-air tanker refuel aircraft flying out of RAF Mildenhall in the east of England. However, in light of the lack of supply, aviation fuel was becoming a valuable commodity for the military planners. On current usage, NATO had enough to sustain operations at their current level for 2 months. An added problem for NATO was that Russian fighter aircraft were proving to be an equal adversary over Europe with the air war seemingly in the balance, with no side able to claim air superiority. For Russia, it was important it remained this way.

Within days of the Carrier Battle Group leaving America, Operation Sabre was put into operation. The first phase of Operation Sabre had been the insertion of the 8 attack submarines, knowing they had to transit the GIUK Gap. The GIUK gap was crucial during the Cold War and refers to the sea gap between Greenland, Iceland and the UK. During the Cold War a Sound Surveillance System (SOSUS) was placed on the seabed to listen to passing Soviet submarines entering the Atlantic. With the end of the Cold War in the 1980s and cuts in defence spending there had been less demand for the system and from 2008 the only people really listening to it were scientists monitoring whales. The submarines had passed through the gap almost a week before the American ships entered UK waters and although their presence had been noted the scientists wrongly assumed it to be American or British activity in light of what had occurred in the UK. With nobody the wiser, the Russian submarines simply disappeared into the vast ocean.

At 1830hrs on a clear night over France and Belgium, 2 of NATOs AWAC early warning aircraft flying at 30,000-feet were unaware that Russian aircraft were specifically targeting them. Critical time sensitive information had been received in Moscow on the whereabouts of the US Carrier Battle Fleets and with this information, phase 2 of Operation Sabre could begin. Within minutes of receiving the news, orders were issued and phase 2 was given the green light. AWACs were the air surveillance and command and control for all NATO commands and, in effect, were the eye in the sky with their long-range surveillance capability out to 300km. The attack on the AWACs started with a large diversionary raid deep behind NATO lines, which was intended to drag away the majority of the NATO Combat Air Patrol guarding the AWACs. The AWACs, far from the front line, were assessed as safe and even out of range of Russia's long distance Surface-to-Air Missile, the S-400 Triumph with its range of 400km. With the diversionary raid still ongoing, 4 of Russia's 5th Generation Aircraft, the S-37, were taking off from their base in Smolensk, Russia. The S-37 was Russia's stealthiest aircraft and had a Radar Cross Section (RCS) similar to the US F-117 stealth fighter. Climbing to 49,000ft they turned and moved slowly west. The S-37s were fitted with stealth technology using radar-absorbent material (RAM), a treated cockpit, which reflects radar waves and a plasma generator. The plasma generator produces a cloak of ionized gas known as plasma, which pushes out a plasma screen in front of the aircraft that dissipates incoming radar energy at low speed. By using a low speed, the S-37s were able to close to within 450km of the AWACs without being detected. At 450km from the AWACs the S-37s, as briefed, suddenly altered tactics and accelerated to a speed of 2450km or 1520mph utilising their high thrust to weight ratio and, with their presence no longer a secret, closed the distance to within 350km rapidly. Firing solutions had already been sent via the onboard computer and at 349km from their targets, both pairs fired their new anti-AWAC, air-to-air missiles, the Novator KS-172. The Novator was a fire and forget system so there was no need to watch the missiles onto target. Breaking north before looping east, the S-37s, pursued by a combination of Euro-Typhoons and F-18s were already heading back to Russian airspace on full after-burner and were too far away for the NATO aircraft to catch them.

The KS-172s, meanwhile, had acquired their targets and were now homing in on their prey. Realising too late, the AWACs attempted to turn off all their emitting radar but the KS-172s had switched to infrared homing and 2 missiles struck the first aircraft over France on the port wing and at the rear. With its wing and tail almost gone, the first AWAC became impossible to control and it plummeted in a downward spiral to the ground, killing all on board. The second AWAC over Belgium was struck directly behind the cockpit by one missile, with the final missile hitting the port wing but, for some reason, failed to explode. With a large segment of wing missing and the front of the aircraft disintegrating, all power to the engines was lost. With such a large aircraft losing all forward momentum, it appeared to hang in the air for just a moment, then slowly fell out of the sky backwards before breaking up from the huge G-forces placed on it during its awkward descent to the ground.

The diversion had worked and with NATO attempting to work out what had transpired, it meant the remaining NATO fighter aircraft had to search and fight using just their own aircrafts integral radar. The AWACs were the strategic eyes of NATO but had to be taken off air until a defence could be worked out against the latest Russian tactic employed against them. With the AWACs falling from the sky, the Russians instigated phase 3 of Operation Sabre. 16 Su32s, which had been circling close to the northern coastal area near the Barents Sea, were now able to conduct their low level insertion into the enemy's back yard and bypass the mass of aircraft over Europe. On receiving the phase 3 codeword they descended to sea level and headed west. The all weather capable Su32s, flying at 20 to 30-metres above the sea, raced along the coastlines of Russia and Finland, passed the north of Scotland, approximately 41km from shore and, then swung round onto a southwesterly bearing. The southwesterly bearing was now taking them away from Scotland and the Irish coast into the vast Atlantic Ocean. Satellite imagery had located the Carrier Battle Groups 2hrs earlier and time sensitive targeting was crucial if Operation Sabre was to work. Each Su32 was armed with just 2, R-73 Archer Short Range Air-to-Air Missiles and 2, R-77 Long Range Fire and Forget Air-to-Air-Missiles for their own protection, with the remainder of the aircraft weapons load containing the deadly Oniks/Yakont Anti-Ship Missile. Each aircraft carried 2 of these 4th generation ship killers and needed to get within 190km to unleash them. Flight Commander, Anatoli Lebedev, flying the lead Su32 was convinced the glorious past of the

American Carrier Battle Groups was almost at an end with Operation Sabre proving once and for all that such a force couldn't defend itself against a massed attack from supersonic missiles. All the Su32 pilots were operating at the limits of their flying capability and, the dark sea just 20-metres below, looked an uninviting way to die. As the aircraft closed to within 200km of the Carriers last known satellite co-ordinates, the Su32 aircraft turned due west, came off the deck and climbed rapidly to 2,000ft above sea level (ASL). *'FUCK!... where are those fucking Carriers?'* thought Lebedev.....there was nothing at all on the screen and Flight Commander Lebedev cursed his luck at their misfortune because he knew the American Early Warning Systems would now be going crazy having spotted his aircraft within their protective bubble. Suddenly, at 180km, the radar screen lit up and showed multiple contacts. Having located the armada of ships slightly southwest of their last known position, the onboard computer began sending the missiles the data they required and within less than 30-seconds the Su32s initiated their launch sequence. The missiles, having received the data, were released from the aircraft and in a flash raced off into the dark. Having fired their missiles the Su32s were beating a hasty retreat northwards at low level, using their after burners from their upgraded AL-35 engines, which enabled the aircraft to reach mach 1.15 at sea level. Equipped with a rear facing warning and fire control radar for the R-37 Air-to-Air Missile, the Su32 was a match for anything the US Carrier Fleet could throw at it. Near Scotland, 14 RAF Tornadoes, having been informed by the Carrier Fleet of the Su32s last known course, intercepted the highly manoeuverable Su32s on their way home and, in the ensuing aerial combat duel, 2 Su32s were destroyed with the less manoeuverable Tornado F3s suffering 7 losses before the remainder pulled off.

    The 3-ton Yakont Anti-Ship Missile was designed specifically to defeat a Carrier Force and as it departed from the Su32 launch container the solid fuel booster device switched on and accelerated the missile to 750-metres per second. Deaf to jamming, it was designed to perform complex tactical manoeuvers during flight on its way to its target. The American ships in the Battle Group had been given close to a minute and a half warning before the Su32s released their missiles but they now had less than 30-seconds to react to the incoming Yakonts. Only the

TICONDEROGA- class Cruisers and the ARLEIGH BURKE-class Destroyers had the Aegis 360 degree, Planer Phased Array Radar fitted and, working in conjunction with the fire control computers, these systems had already completed their calculations and were now firing their Sea-Sparrow Missiles from their M41 Vertical Launch System on board the ships.

With the US fleets located, Commander Lebedev immediately transmitted an encrypted message via a satellite link with updated coordinates back to his base in Russia. These were quickly passed to the submarine transmission site located on the Kola Peninsula near Murmansk. The site operates in the Extremely Low Frequency (ELF) band using a system called ZEVS, transmitting on 82 hertz. It is a one-way transmission that travels through the sea to submerged submarines and in the Atlantic, 8 Russian vessels were waiting for the updated information. 350km from the Carrier Battle Fleet, the 2 Severodvinsk-class Nuclear Submarines received the encrypted message from Murmansk giving the US fleet's coordinates and, clearance to initiate phase 4 by releasing their Yakont Anti-Ship Missiles.

The Severodvinsk-class Submarines quickly completed their launch sequence and fired their allocation of 32 Yakont Missiles, with these only 7-minutes behind those fired by the Su32s. All the other submarines had received the same information, including the 4 Oscar-class Submarines deep under the thermocline layer. The thermocline in water is the transition layer between the mixed layer at the surface and the deep-water layer. In the thermocline, the temperature decreases rapidly from the mixed layer temperature to the much colder deep-water temperature and sonar finds it more difficult to detect vessels below it, unless a towed sonar hydrophone is dropped beneath it. Even at 90km distance the commotion below and above surface had permeated into the depths and into the submarines' passive listening devices. The communication confirming the order to open fire and the noise generated by the Severodvinsk-class Submarines firing their missiles was the signal for the Oscars to come up to missile firing depth.

The 32 missiles fired by the Su32 aircraft were the first to draw the fire of the Aegis Defence System, which succeeded in destroying 28 of the 32 Yakont Missiles fired. 4 missiles did, however, get through, with 2 missiles exploding on one ARLEIGH BURKE-class Destroyer, which then sunk, with another missile striking an OLIVER HAZARD PERRY-class Guided Missile Frigate, which resulted in a crippled vessel and significant loss of life. The final missile would have been considered the most successful as it struck the Carrier - USS Eisenhower, amidships, causing extensive damage within the vessel, resulting in the loss of 26 men and 5 aircraft.

Before the crews had time to catch their breath the ships radar detected yet more hostiles coming towards them. 32 more missiles were heading in their direction and this time the effect would be more destructive than the first wave. First to be hit were 3 of the older SPRUANCE-class Anti Submarine Destroyers shielding the fleet from the direction the missiles came. Struck by a total of 11 missiles, all 3 vessels sunk quickly and, without any survivors. Next to be hit were 2 of the SACRAMENTO-class Fast Combat Support Ships, which were hit by 5 missiles, with one vessel sinking and the other catching fire before seriously listing to starboard. The Sea Sparrow Missiles took out a further 14 of the deadly projectiles, before the final 2, unexpectedly crashed into the sea.

This second waves of missiles had slammed into the Battle Groups from an entirely different direction and with the fleet defence dwindling, it was clear more missiles would reach their targets, causing greater devastation. The only visible light on deck was that provided by the firing of the ships Sea Sparrow Missiles, the computer-operated Phalanx Close-in Weapons Systems and the impacts from the Russian ship killers. Huge explosions could be heard over the alarms as the missiles impacted with ships nearby and for those suffering direct hits the shock and damage was immense. The crews on those ships that were struck and stayed afloat would later reflect and, consider themselves fortunate, especially after so many vessels had been sunk with all hands on board, and only a handful of survivors found the next day.

The 4 Oscar-class Submarines were the last to come up to missile firing depth and, in between the second wave being fired and impacting, they launched 12 missiles each, from their full complement of 18 per vessel. 48 SS-22 Sunburn Anti-Ship Missiles broke surface and then sped towards the mass of ships - that were already under attack from 64 other anti-ship missiles - at Mach 2.5. The Sea Sparrow Missiles had achieved great success overall but it was impossible to have a 100 percent success rate against the amount of anti-ship missiles coming in. In the end, the 112 Russian missiles were just too many and too fast for the ships defences to handle and, the missiles were now slamming into the unprotected ships with alarming regularity and with dire consequences for the crews.

The alarms sounded yet again in the ships combat information centres as 48 SS-22 Sunburn Missiles with their 300kg warhead roared in at supersonic speed. The Sea Sparrows continued to fire but their numbers were much lower than before due to the sinking and damage caused to the defensive screen. The Phalanx Guns were also firing at close in targets but in the main made little impression on the majority of huge missiles heading their way. The final wave of super fast projectiles homed in first on the TICONDEROGA-class Cruiser, which suffered 3 hits in total, one on the bridge and 2 just above the water line, but amazingly it stayed afloat. This was followed by impacts on one more SPRUANCE-class Destroyer and 2 ARLEIGH BURKE-class Destroyers that were hit and sunk. One of the ARLEIGH BURKE-class Destroyers was initially engulfed in flames before it eventually exploded and sank 4hrs later with all aboard being rescued less those caught in the initial blast. For the thousands of sailors aboard the mass of ships it was a truly terrifying moment in their lives, especially in the black of night, far out to sea, with sailors never knowing if one of the anti-ship missiles had chosen their vessel as a target. Incoming missile alarms had sounded incessantly and it seemed like hours rather than the 40-minutes of mayhem that it eventually was.

The massive carrier, USS Eisenhower, suffered 2 further hits from the final wave of Sunburn missiles and, although in distress, and with 20 aircraft destroyed, it miraculously remained afloat but non-operational. The last vessels to be hit were 2 OLIVER HAZARD PERRY-class Guided Missile Frigates guarding the USS George H W Bush and, who had sacrificed their ships and crew to protect this main flagship. Placing their vessels between the missiles and the Aircraft Carrier, the 2 Frigates had hoped to intercept the 3 missiles with their onboard defence systems. They only managed to take down one incoming missile before the remaining 2 impacted on the Frigates. Although severely damaged and with a significant loss of life on both vessels, neither sunk, and the Flagship Carrier remained unscathed.

Even with missiles approaching the fleets, the anti-submarine effort was still, in operation, with some of the multi mission MH-60R (Romeo) Sea Hawk Helicopters utilising their passive dipping sonar whilst others dropped active sonar buoys into the sea. The first contact came via one of the MH-60R Sea Hawks using its Airborne Low Frequency Dipping Sonar, or ALFS as it was known. This was passive sonar that listens without transmitting, unlike the active sonar buoys. By listening for sound travelling through the water it has the capability to listen for propellers, engine noises, vibration from internal power systems and the dropping of any equipment on board a submerged vessel.

The MH-60R had been conducting its sweep for the past 35-minutes and having been alerted to something within 3km of its last dip, lifted the sonar once more and moved 500-metres closer to the Lada, which was lying almost motionless. With the helicopter coming closer, the captain of one of the Lada-class Submarines thought it only a matter of time before he was detected. The 2 Lada's had been positioned 15km apart, lying in wait for a prime target where their supercavitating torpedoes could do the most damage.

Panicking, the captain ordered a firing sequence on the helicopter and, within minutes of the Sea Hawk pulling in its sonar 3km away, 2 Strela-3 Surface-to-Air Missiles broke the surface 2.5km away and headed directly for the helicopter. With its cooled infrared seeker homing in on the helicopter's heat signature the pilot had no option other than to take evasive actions from a missile that had a maximum range of 6km. The Sea Hawk pilot knew it would be close and luckily the first missile followed the countermeasures. It was the second missile with its 2kg warhead that smashed into the aircraft near the tail and with no rear end the Sea Hawk spiraled into the ocean 150ft below. The impact was hard with the turning rotor blades cutting sharply into the water before they snapped… but thankfully all were alive. With all lights extinguished the pilots struggled to release themselves from the confines of their seat restraints with the rear crewman already jumping into the water. Within 20-seconds the helicopter with the heaviest weight uppermost, rolled, and rotated 180 degrees before finally floating upside down on the surface. With water engulfing the interior the pilot and his co-pilot, both upside down, started groping for a way out in the darkness before the helicopter sank. Running out of breath, the pilot pulled free his Short Term Air Supply System (STASS) bottle from his vest pocket and pushed it into his mouth, exhaled what remaining breath he had before he drew breath from the small air bottle. He now had 2-minutes of air to escape his watery tomb. 30-seconds later he was free and after swimming to the surface, inflated his life vest. 40-metres away he could see his crewman's flashing rescue light and he made his way across to him. They were both distraught to find the co-pilot was still not out and their anxiety became worse as the aircraft sank beneath the surface and plummeted down into the depths. Punching the water the pilot screamed abuse at an invisible enemy in the sky to vent his anger; then suddenly, no more than 10-feet away, the co-pilot surfaced in front of them both with his STASS bottle still in his mouth and, upon removing it, smiled as if nothing had happened.

The Strela-3 Missile attack had drawn in a further 2 MH-60s who immediately dropped 2 Mk-50 Air Launched Torpedoes over the launch site. Straightaway the crew onboard the Lada-class vessel was informed of torpedoes in the water with the captain attempting evasive manoeuvers. The Lada-class Submarine was now attempting to escape to deeper water and as far from the area as possible, but dropped active sonar buoys were now emitting a pulse that pinged outwards and, upon hitting the submarine, reflected the wave back to the buoy. Transmitting the information back to the circling helicopter, it was able to collate the submarine's exact location, speed and direction of travel. Using the ALFS from another MH-60, onboard computers began processing all the information from the noises generated by the escaping submarine. Searching their databases the Americans soon identified what class of vessel it was they were up against. The 2 lightweight, high-speed Mk-50 Barracuda Torpedoes hit the water and immediately started their search for their target. The fire and forget weapon weighed 500lbs and with a top speed of 55-knots and a range of 8-miles could easily outrun the Lada, which only had a top speed of 20-knots. Its only defence now was the supercavitating VA-111 Shkval torpedo. The M-50s acquired their target quickly and were closing the distance fast. A firing solution was put into the first Shkval as the closest Mk-50 homed in. The order to fire the Shkval was given and the first torpedo exited the Lada's tube. The supercavitating system kicked in and allowed the torpedo to reach a speed of 140-knots before impacting the first Mk-50 at only 1,500-

yards away. The second firing sequence had been placed into the second Shkval but, before it could be initiated, the Executive Officer turned to the Captain and informed him it was too late as the Mk-50 had closed to within 350-yards.

As a last resort countermeasures were launched to decoy the incoming torpedo but the Mk-50, with its advanced Central Processing Unit (CPU), was able to determine the difference between a decoy and a submarine. If the Lada had been constructed with a double hull similar to the nuclear submarines the impact from the torpedo may have only severely damaged the vessel but as the Lada was a single steel hulled submarine, the impact had disastrous consequences for the ship and all on board. With the crew braced for impact the 100lb HE warhead struck the 2,700 ton submarine behind the tower with the shaped charge warhead easily penetrating the skin and, with a hole more than 7-feet in diameter, tons of seawater now began to enter the ship. Within seconds, buoyancy was compromised and the boat, with 37-men on board, began its final 12,000ft descent into the abyss. On board the sinking vessel, the sounds of the explosion and of men screaming could be heard by the sonar operators of the remaining Lada and Los Angeles- class Submarines and the Sea Hawks Helicopters. It was a sombre but fleeting moment for all the submariners as they listened to the final death throws of a vessel that just minutes before was hoping to send American sailors and aircrew to where they were now destined. Success and failure in war walks a fine line and, for those who failed, it had meant certain death.

The USS Albany out of Norfolk, Virginia, was one of 4 Los Angeles-class SSN Submarines attached to the 2-Carrier Fleets and its sensors had lit up like beacons as the Oscar-class submarines fired their missiles. Situated only 32km from the Oscars the USS Albany, along with 2 other Los Angeles-class vessels, the USS Hartford and USS Pittsburg were travelling towards the area at their maximum speed of 35-knots when they heard the launching of 2 Strela-3 missiles and the subsequent response from the US ASW Helicopters. The demise of the Lada-class Submarine was a poignant reminder how life can be suddenly extinguished here under the waves but the captain of the USS Albany quickly cast this aside to concentrate on the task at hand. The Oscar-class Submarines were important now and he wanted to exact some form of revenge for what he could only imagine had gone on above surface. Without warning, one of the other Los Angeles-class Submarines, the USS Hartford, suddenly fired one of its Mk48 Advanced Capabilities (ADCAP) Torpedoes in the wire guided mode at the fleeing Oscars. With the torpedo speed set to 40-knots and a range of 50km this was on the limit for the Mk48 but it was a chance shot that just might work. The captain had considered the faster speed of 55-knots but the distance would have been cut to 38km and the Mk48 would have run out of propulsion before impact.

12km to the west of the Los Angeles-class Submarines the remaining Lada-class Submarine captain on hearing the Mk48 Torpedo being fired, decided his new mission was to protect the Oscar-class vessels. After ordering a firing solution to be placed into 2 VA-111 Shkval Torpedoes he gave the order to intercept the Mk48 and the submarine that had fired it. 100-feet below the water the first of 2 supercavitating torpedoes were launched from the Lada's 533mm tube at 93kph. The rocket ignited and the VA-111 Shkval torpedo was on its way to the Mk48. The second Shkval launched 7-seconds later. Accelerating to 100-metres per second the supercavitating torpedo hit the Mk48 only 2-minutes after launch. The second Shkval was already in the water and the USS Hartford had no way of avoiding it.

As soon as the Lada-class Submarine made its presence known by firing its VA-111 Shkval's the USS Pittsburg and USS Albany had already plotted firing solutions and fired a total of 8 homing Mk 48 Torpedoes, with a mixture of passive and active homing configurations, at the Lada-class vessel before taking evasive measures themselves. However, the captain of the Lada-class Submarine, with 8 Mk48s inbound, had more to contend with than the 2 remaining Los Angeles-class vessels. Firing solutions were quickly selected and a further 6 VA-111 Shkval Torpedoes were dispatched, with the distance closing all the time between the MK48s and the Lada-class submarine. The first Shkval fired struck the Mk48 Torpedo chasing the Oscar submarines dead centre and, from the speed it generated, almost broke the Mk48 in half. The wire guiding it was snapped and the Mk48 fell away, out of sight. The Lada-class Submarine's second launch of 6 Shkval Torpedoes succeeded in a 100 percent kill against a further 6 Mk48s but the crew was unable to plot a solution for the remaining 2. As per the M-50, the Mk48 had the same capability to determine the difference between decoy and submarine and today was no different. Both the 19-feet (5.79-metre) long Mk48s impacted the Lada-class Submarine almost simultaneously, with their 295kg warheads instantaneously causing the vessel to disintegrate into 3 large pieces. Death was instant for most on board, with the rest drowning within seconds.

The Lada-class Submarine captain had sacrificed his vessel to save the Oscars and, although he had failed in his mission to destroy a carrier, he died believing he had succeeded in distracting the Americans long enough for the Oscar-class Submarines to escape the American hunter killers. His belief was correct and the Oscars had evaded the American submarines but not the US ASW helicopters or the 2 OLIVER HAZARD PERRY-class ASW Frigates now descending on their positions. Between them they launched 4 M-50 and 3 M-46 Torpedoes and, with 2 Oscars isolated from the group of 4; it was hoped that these could be destroyed as well.

The Oscar-class vessels were one of the largest hunter killer submarines in the world and regarded as unsinkable due to their double-skinned hull, with the outer hull alone being 8.5mm thick. The submarines were attempting to go deep and as far away from the torpedoes as possible but the M-50s had a maximum speed of 55-knots and it was clear the Oscar-class Submarines, with their maximum speed of 32-knots, could not outrun them. Another problem for the Oscars was that the M-50s had a maximum dive depth of 1,973-feet so the Oscars had to get below their official dive depth of 600-metres (1860-feet) to escape impact - anything less and the Oscars would still be in range of the M-50s. The lightweight M-46, with its slower speed of 28-knots failed to reach the escaping Oscar-class Submarines but before one of the submarines could get below the M-50 dive depth it was caught by 2 of the M-50s and these exploded on the port side of the vessel at a depth of 1,780-feet.

The submarine shook violently as the outer hull took the full impact from the combined force of 200kg of high explosive. Miraculously, the inner hull remained intact and the relief on the faces of all aboard was clear to see. Unknown to the crew aboard the Oscar, the M-50s shaped charge had penetrated the hull in 2 places and water was now pouring in. Still diving deeper, the wounded submarine pushed on beyond its maximum dive depth, hoping to escape any more torpedoes that may be fired. The second Oscar, having already passed the book specification of 1,860-feet was suffering no ill effects, levelled out at 2,300-feet and very soon after, lost contact with the circling force on the surface

It appeared to the Americans on the surface that all 4 had escaped and indeed, 3 had, but when the damaged submarine with 2 gaping holes attempted to level off at 2,336-feet found, it was unable to do so. Panic now gripped the entire crew but there was nothing they could do as the Oscar continued its descent into the depths of the dark Atlantic until it was finally crushed.

On the surface the USS Hartford was surfacing after suffering superficial damage after the VA-111 Shkval Torpedo had initiated with a proximity fuse rather than a contact fuse. She had been one of the lucky ones this night and would go on to fight another day after repairs but, the loss to the American Navy had been unimaginable and horrendous. Between the 2-Carrier Battle Fleets, 8 ships had been sunk, another 7, including the submarine, were considered non-operational and needed extensive repairs but, worst of all, was the thousands of American sailors that were now dead, horrifically burned or suffering loss of limbs. It was the last thing the American people and the world wanted to hear after the events in Washington DC, Diego Garcia, Europe and Korea.

The voyage home to Norfolk for the remaining fleet was sombre to say the least and although they thought they could keep the badly damaged TICONDEROGA-class Cruiser afloat, it was not the case. The damage sustained had taken its toll and the ship could not be saved. Having taken 3 direct hits from the anti-ship missiles, she had to be abandoned and scuttled 300-nautical miles from the US coastline before she succumbed to the depths of her own accord. The sinking of the TICONDEROGA-class Cruiser took the number of ships sunk to 9.

....................It was, the end of an era......................

PART 16

WAR OF WARS
(D+80)

*If I were an American, as I am an Englishman, while
a foreign troop was landed in my country I never
would lay down my arms, never! Never! Never!*
William Pitt, 1708-1778

DTG: Friday 14th April….2012…..

LOCATION: German Border with Poland

SITUATION: A massive Arabic Army of 1.7 million men is finally beginning its advance into the heartland of NATO and the West.

The battle for Europe was about to begin. This was what the Arabs' alliance had worked towards for the last 4-years, although China had unilaterally worked towards it for a lot longer. The destruction of Western democracy and its ideology was no longer a dream but a reality. Worryingly for the population of Europe, the Iranian contingent was attracting large numbers of Islamic militants from across Europe and the Middle East, with these being used to swell the numbers in the Mujihadeen Brigades as suicide shock troops. The Syrian and Iranian soldiers were aware of the capacity of these men to commit atrocities but they themselves, used to the brutalities of life, were content to allow this to occur. The sucking in, if you like, of Islamic militants was what China had hoped for….and China's boasts to Russia that the annihilation of Democracy and Islam was about to be decided on the battlegrounds of Western Europe was proving to be true. Literally thousands upon thousands of militants had joined the battle in anticipation of a Jihad against the West and they were arriving from all over the Middle East, Africa, Chechnya and Bosnia. In their eyes, this was the final stage of a war they had been fighting for decades and the lure was proving too great to resist. The Czech Republic was one country that had suffered more than most from this influx of radicalism, with looting, rape, isolated beheadings and now the burning of churches allowed to go unchecked by the Iranian and Syrian regular forces.

In those countries already defeated, the Russian and Arab troops had quickly targeted the country's communication facilities, especially Internet networks. China and Russia had already blocked their public's access to the net and, even though this had been instigated in other countries, footage was still been smuggled out through Poland into Germany and from Slovakia and the Czech Republic into Austria. Footage of huge massed columns of mechanised vehicles and tanks moving through Slovakia and Poland were captured on film. The firing of Syrian and Iranian Ballistic Missiles from Slovakia at mainland Europe was also shown, along with the massive devastation inflicted on towns and cities close to the conflict. The burning of churches in some isolated villages was a major concern and shown on American, European and world networks. The effect these images portrayed, especially throughout Europe, left many despairing at the possibilities and the newly-installed governments in Germany and France ordered the news agencies to refrain from showing such images again as it was destroying the populations morale and resulting in mass panic. If people had doubted the severity of what was happening around the world they had now seen it close up, and in colour and, it was very different to the small conflicts they had become accustomed to over the last 60 years or so. To the Europeans especially, it was hitting home hard that war was approaching them yet again and, for many, it already had.

The threat of chemical and biological weapons being used since the war began appeared to have passed but troops still had to be prepared for their worst war-fighting scenario. NATO had assessed that both sides had come to the conclusion that Mutually Assured Destruction (MAD) was best avoided but with tactical nuclear devices of sorts, having already been detonated in Europe and the United States; it could not be ruled out. There had been some high level communiqués going back and forth to the nations involved warning of the severity if such devices or agents were used and, their answers had stipulated that they would not be the first to use such a weapon. Such a response indicated that they had the weapons available but would withhold their use. Bluff or counter-bluff…no one really knew, so the conventional status quo was maintained and death came by the more conventional means only.

France, Italy and Spain were now fully mobilised with France and Spain ready to deploy to Germany. France, with a standing army of 90,000 troops, had increased those numbers to 110,000 by including reserves, with Spain providing 65,000 regular frontline troops plus 20,000 reserves. Italy, with 80,000 regular troops, had already deployed its 3rd Mechanised Division with its complement of 18,000 men to Germany as part of its Allied Rapid Reaction Corps (ARRC) commitment. With Leopard MBTs, Centauro Armoured Vehicles with their 105mm guns, DARDO Armoured Infantry Fighting Vehicles equipped with 25mm Cannon, a large selection of APCs and Artillery Units plus Anti-Aircraft and Ground Attack Helicopters, this force packed a punch and helped make the ARRC one of the most, if not the most powerful, military formation in the world. The remainder of the Italian troops stayed in Italy as SACEUR's southern reserve.

The Nordic countries of Denmark, Sweden, Norway and Finland, for some reason, had been completely ignored by Chinese planners and Arab terrorists, probably because they were assessed as being able to muster no more than 20,000 troops between them and were not regarded as a key military threat. In 2008, an agreement had been reached that Norway, Finland and Estonia would form a Nordic Battle Group. Since the attack on America and Europe and the mobilisation and involvement of Russian forces, Finland had decided to keep her forces in Finland near her border with Russia. Estonia separated by the Baltic Sea with Sweden remained stuck in her own borders, passive and impotent, so if any Nordic Battle Group were to be formed it would have to come from the Viking countries of Sweden, Denmark and Norway.

Throughout Europe imports and exports had stopped almost overnight with countries having to feed their own populations until alternative supplies could be found. Luxuries were now non-existent unless bought on the black-market and the bare essentials were all that were sold in shops. Large supermarkets had been ransacked and looted in the early days and these were now closed, apart from the military-controlled ones, which were used as rationing facilities. Winter had made the situation worse with fresh produce a major problem, but the European Union's enormous food surplus generated in 2011 would prove crucial in feeding a large proportion of the population until summer arrived. Massive storage facilities across Europe were packed full of huge amounts of powdered milk, grain, frozen beef, cheese and even wine but with distribution becoming a problem, millions of people would be unable to benefit from this food mountain.

80-days on from 24th January daily power cuts were still the norm and those areas which had had no power for weeks and, in some cases months now, had finally had it restored to a degree. Power blackouts across the European Union were still a cause for concern with damaged facilities and reduced transportation resulting is shortfalls in coal supply. The complete lack of oil flowing from the Middle East and the halting of gas supplies from Russia was also having a dramatic effect on power supplies. The UK for instance uses a variation of power stations and its coal/oil and gas/oil fired power plants were particularly affected. Europe imports half its gas from Russia and the shortfall in gas supplies to Britain and the rest of Europe was a disaster for their industries, not to mention every-day life. Cars were rarely seen on the roads anymore and the only vehicles on the move in any number were military or large heavy goods vehicles. The bicycle was the main method of transport for many people and the horse and cart made a startling comeback in rural as well as urban areas. Thousands of jobs were lost overnight and unemployment rocketed across the continent. France, with its insistence on nuclear energy, was managing much better for power than most other European countries but it was dependent on Russian gas for some industry and heating houses. Half of Germany's power also came from nuclear facilities but again; they were feeling the effects of no gas and no oil supply. It had been nothing short of a miracle that no Nuclear Power Plant had been attacked and damaged but this had been more to do with requests from China and Russia rather than luck. Change had come overnight and it was frightening at the speed that it had occurred. The acute, civilization-changing energy crisis that experts had debated in 2006 was very much becoming a reality in 2012 but, not in the way they had envisaged.

Civilian flights were still not permitted over European airspace unless cleared by the military and, those that were allowed, were all heading west to the United States, Canada and South America, with civilians desperate to escape the approaching storm. Nowhere was deemed safe in Europe anymore and, with ballistic missiles exploding at military airfields or within a city every few days, people with the means and the money to escape were doing so. Others couldn't escape and surprisingly, many were determined to fight and protect their country, literally begging the military to train and equip them. The military was attempting to speed up basic military training for the masses of volunteers, with older ex-soldiers being utilised as home guard type personnel. The reserves were primarily earmarked for guarding key facilities, with specialist personnel such as doctors, medics and communications personnel deployed to Germany. It was important to try to get some of the regular experienced troops back to the front line and away from the mundane but, still important job of facility guard duty and, with Mujihadeen attacks almost non-existent, it was hoped this could soon be achieved.

In the North Sea, the British Navy was joined by French, Dutch, Danish and Norwegian naval vessels in protecting the North Sea oil facilities. This precious commodity was now, solely earmarked for the European market as they attempted to combat as much as possible, the lack of fuel throughout Europe. The combined navies were also aggressively looking for any Russian submarines, especially after the attack on the US Carrier Fleet, with the GIUK gap monitored as closely as it was in the Cold War Era.

Throughout Europe, military airfields were regular targets for ballistic missile strikes, which meant air forces, had to resort to using small and medium-sized civilian ones to try and hide their aircraft from these strikes. Chinese and Russian satellites constantly photographed the military airfields and some countries had resorted to placing blow-up replicas of military aircraft on the runways while placing their real aircraft in small quantities around the country. A lot of the ballistic missile strikes were wasted on dummy aircraft but their impacts had severely devastated some of the military facilities. Even military airfields in Luxemburg, Holland and Belgium had been subjected to these terrifying missile strikes with these taking the brunt of the onslaught for no other reason than their close proximity to Germany.

3-weeks after halting close to Warsaw, the Arab armies were ready to advance yet again. Large numbers of artillery units had already departed for the German border 5-days earlier in anticipation of this advance. The logistical quantities and its subsequent movement north into Poland had been mind-boggling but the support was now in place and capable of sustaining the vast Arab armies for 3 months, with more on the way. At 0300hrs a vast area resounded to the sounds of diesel engines kicking into life as the first elements of the Arab assaulting force prepared to move off. In their sights and only 350km away was their main objective - Germany and NATO. The weather was perfect for the movement of massed armour with the cloud base at 400-feet. It was this poor weather window that the Arabs had been waiting for before setting off. In the northern and central part of Poland the 35,000-strong Arab forces that had gone ahead 3-weeks earlier to secure bridges across the River Oder were in position near to the border, protecting the numerous crossings between Szezecin and Cryfino. Weeks earlier, these same bridges had carried retreating Polish forces over into Germany. If these bridges were crossed and a beachhead established, Berlin could be within their grasp.

At 0500hrs on 16th April….just over 48hrs since the massed armour and mechanised infantry had departed Warsaw; 2,800 guns, ranging from large numbers of D-20 152mm, M-46 130mm Towed Artillery, M109A1 155mm Self-Propelled Paladin Howitzers and an enormous number of the Russian 2S series of Self-Propelled Artillery were stretched out along a 179km frontage from Szezecin in the north to Zielona Gora in the south. Their target area was considerably less than that distance, with the massed artillery focusing on known NATO troop dispositions near the border, or west of the potential crossing points. 2 Infantry Divisions protected these forces with SA-16 and SA-18 MANPADS - Man Portable Air Defence Systems or shoulder launched SAM systems, as they are sometimes referred to, while dedicated air defense unit's deployed large numbers of the TOR-M1 Surface-to-Air Missile System. Some of the massed artillery units with less gunnery range had transited past numerous Polish towns at night and moved into positions closer to the border. Those guns with a longer range were positioned on the flanks but all were working to the same coordinated fire-plan. In Germany, 127,000 NATO troops were covering a lesser frontage with their main forces generally focusing on the bridge choke points on their side of the border. NATO had assessed that the firepower generated by this force was more than capable of fixing and then destroying any advancing Arab armoured columns before they were able to break into the North German Plains where their superior numbers could have a decisive edge. Those NATO troops in range of the Arab shelling were in for a rough ride but the majority of combat armour and troops were further west and out of effective range. One constraint for NATO was the issues concerning ammunition quantities and supply. Even with the US supplying as much as it could and munitions factories in Europe attempting to produce as much as possible when power cuts allowed, there was still a projected shortfall for a protracted war. With this in mind NATO commanders had decided they needed to make their firepower count so had planned to suck in and then smash the Arab forces in Poland on the German side of the border. Leaving the bridges intact was not without risk but NATO wanted the Arabs committed into the bottleneck rather than allowing them to go elsewhere, so instead of blowing the bridges they had decided to entice the Arab lead elements over before unleashing the full might of NATO firepower onto an enemy who would have no room for manoeuvre. The Arabs appeared to be taking the bait and preparing the ground where NATO commanders thought they would attempt to cross.

As the artillery barrage began, NATO, using Fire-Finder, was conducting counter-battery fire. Fire-Finder is the Artillery-Locating Radar capable of missile or artillery detection out to 300km. It had collated the target data on a vast amount of Arab artillery and those Arab units not maintaining their fire and movement discipline were soon to find out what counter-battery fire could achieve. The operators were looking for the units that remained static and dozens had been identified. This information was quickly relayed to the theatre artillery commander who ordered the firing of his all weather High Mobility Artillery Rocket System (HIMARS). HIMARS is designed to fire the complete inventory of MLRS and Army Tactical Missile System (ATACMS) munitions and was the ideal weapon system against time sensitive targets. For this mission, each HIMAR launcher carried one long-range ATACMS missile and these were now firing at targets 148km away.

The targets identified were in the main the towed D-20 152mm guns with their range of 17.4km and the M-46 130mm Towed Artillery Batteries with their longer range of 38km. Each Artillery Battery contained between 4 and 6 pieces of artillery per battery and in due course 950 anti-personnel/anti-material baseball sized cluster bomb submunitions were about to rain down on these static positions with devastating effect. There were 46 HIMARS conducting counter-battery fires that first day and the system's accuracy would ensure the Arabs resorted quickly to fire and movement again with their Towed Artillery Batteries. The ATACMS didn't take long in arriving and, once overhead, released their submunitions onto the dispersed gun lines. The submunitions exploded on contact and ripped unprotected men and machines to pieces, killing hundreds of soldiers operating the artillery or driving vehicles. Artillery optic sites were shattered and some artillery pieces pierced and rendered non-operational. The explosive submunitions also compromised the integrity of some of the lightly armoured BRDM-2 Amphibious Reconnaissance Vehicles and these burst into flames along with the 5-ton trucks containing spare ammunition and the units fuel trucks, which were only a few hundred metres from the artillery batteries. With vehicles in close proximity to each other, ammunition and fuel trucks suffered sympathetic detonations, with the clouds of black smoke evident for miles and large pieces of shrapnel blown over a wide area.

More than 200 separate Arab artillery guns had been destroyed or severely damaged by the HIMARS strikes with smoke trails from the burning vehicles drifting west towards the German border. It was an expensive lesson for the Arab commanders to learn as they felt for the first time NATOs technical capability. 4hrs later the Arabs retaliated by firing an unusually large amount of Scud C and Scud D into German military establishments from Slovakia in retaliation but, they possessed no capability to target the HIMARS. That same afternoon, 12 Shahab-3 Ballistic Missiles with conventional warheads were fired at cities throughout France with a further 14 fired at the United Kingdom.

The United Kingdom, with an interim military command structure acting as government under the newly installed Chief of the Defence Staff (CDS), General David Dennison, appeared to be recovering slowly from the effects of the nuclear decapitation of its leadership and the devastating attacks on its civil and military infrastructure. General Dennison had taken over the reins after the assassination by the Mujihadeen of his predecessor and all decisions relating to the United Kingdoms interests were now made through his Crisis Management Centre at the Permanent Joint Headquarters (PJHQ) in Northwood, London. Normally the Ministry of Defence would have provided policy and strategic direction to the PJHQ commanders but, as there was no longer any government, policy now emanated from the CDS and his staff directly.

The PJHQ Command Centre under its Chief of Joint Operations (CJO) Lieutenant General Jonathon C Brown had already deployed to a green field site in Germany some weeks before and was now responsible for the planning and execution of UK Joint and Multinational Operations in Germany and for exercising Operational Command of UK Forces assigned to multinational operations. The UK component commanders such as Land, Air, Logistics and Special Forces each had their own HQs and reported directly to the PJHQ who in turn passed the details to London and The Supreme Allied Commander Europe (SACEUR). SACEUR was the senior military commander for NATO Strategic Command (SC) Europe and a US Four Star General commanded this position. At the time of the crisis General Jefferson T Lynch of the US Marine Corps held this position.

Mulling over the scenarios with his deputy, Lieutenant General Nick Brewster, General Dennison was furious that nothing had been done about the continuing ballistic missile strikes in the UK but he knew that aviation fuel was at a premium and any attack at the point of origin in Slovakia was deemed too far into enemy territory without a massive protective screen. Austria, who had not been invaded, surprisingly wanted to maintain its neutrality and had denied NATO any airspace clearance, therefore, it was deemed unrealistic for an air strike, especially with the amount of NATO aircraft needed to combat the masses of Russian aircraft seen on a weekly basis over Western Europe. This lack of action and the reluctance of the American administration to commit anything other than the forces already in Europe made for uneasy times and Dennison was concerned that the United States President, President Maxwell, had responded to a request for high altitude bombers as *non-implemental at the present time…*

'Nick...do we have anything new on the weather lifting over the next few days?'... said General Dennison.

'Fraid not Sir. The front is in for at least 4-more days before it lifts.... once it does we can get the updated imagery of what they are up to'

'You have to hand it to them Nick,'.......a pause,........'they've played it well so far but it's crucial we stop them in Germany........what time are the Spanish moving north?'

'They'll be pushing into France later this evening, Sir....then linking up with the French near the French/German border within 3-days. They will have a joint force of almost 200,000 and, once we know for sure what the Arabs are up t,o they will be committed as SACEUR deems fit'

'Urrmm...ok.....How much faith do you place on the latest intelligence estimates of 500,000 Arabs in the Czech Republic and a similar amount in Poland.....bearing in mind of course that they didn't think the Arabs would get beyond the Carpathian Mountains on the Polish border?' Said Dennison

'Unless we have anything more definite, I think one has to go along with their estimate and plan accordingly, Sir. Do you have doubts on this assessment'?

'I'm not sure Nick, I find it hard to believe that only one million enemy troops are looking at taking on NATO even though we are severely weakened and restricted in mobility for protracted periods,.... They've bull-dozed their way through East Europe and, yes, I know they have the Russian air force in support of them, but there is still a nagging feeling for some reason. I do feel better now the French and Spanish can move into Germany as you know as well as me how stretched we are along that southern border. I saw the situation report from Jonathon (CJO PJHQ) this morning and there is not even anything in the report from the SAS lads in the Czech Republic or the German Special Forces on enemy numbers or movement.

The Arabs' radio discipline has been very good and apart from their continued shelling of the central and northern region for 2-days, we still have no sight of their armoured columns...I'd like to know what the fucks going on in their minds, Nick.......if only this fucking weather would clear. I know how the allied commanders must have felt during the Battle of the Bulge now'

'*Quite*' said Brewster laughing before a knock at the door stopped the conversation...'*come in*', said Dennison

'*Sorry to interrupt you Sir, but casualty figures are in for the latest ballistic missile attack*' said a home office civil servant….

'*Is it bad Charles?*' asked Dennison,

'*Most of the strikes were at military facilities again, Sir, and resulted in light casualties but one of the missiles hit a 14 storey block of flats in Birmingham and initial reports are stating 200 bodies recovered so far with more feared buried in the rubble….*'

'*Damm……ok Charles…thanks for that and keep me informed on the rescue efforts please*'….

'*There is one more thing Sir. The meeting that was planned for 1900hrs with the London Major over the lifting of the exclusion zone around the Nuclear blast site in Westminster has been moved back to 1930hrs….There will also be an update from the Food and Fuel Crisis Management Council with projections of shortfalls for the coming months across the country.*'.

'OK Charles …. I have no problem with that'…Charles nodded and closed the door, leaving the CDS and his deputy to discuss the issues in Germany, Korea, India and Australia.

The lead elements of 200,000 Arab troops were now approaching the German border and the artillery barrage that had been constant for 48hrs upped its rate of fire, focusing intently on the areas west of the crossing points; however, the counter-battery fire, which had been so devastating only 10hrs previous did not match its intensity.

SACEUR, in addition to his deployments on the Polish/German border, was wary of the Arabs in the Czech Republic so had deployed 110,000 troops on the German/Czech border. This left SACEUR a reserve of 31,000 who could support either force as the need arose. He also had the French/Spanish force of 200,000 forming up on the France/German border and these would be available to him within 3 to 5-days. This combined force was now fully mobilised, fully equipped and moving north.

In the Czech Republic the 706,000 strong Iranian/Syrian contingents had not yet made their intentions known but had pushed some elements to within striking distance of the border.

To their north in Poland, hundreds of thousands of Arab troops were moving through the country but not in the direction NATO commanders had predicted. The 200,000-strong force heading for the bridges west of Warsaw and backed up by the already deployed

35,000 Mechanised Infantry and a massive screen of artillery and air defence personnel was, in effect, a massive feint, but it had to appear strong enough to persuade NATO that this was deemed the major crossing area into Germany and that a major offensive was underway. Although this attack was planned as a feint the Arab Commanders had still decided that a 95,000-strong Egyptian force, inclusive of the 60,000 strong 19 Corp, would remain in Poland as an aggressive and fast response ready to exploit any weakness that may materialise during the offensive. Further attachments to the Egyptian reserve were 620 Abram M1A1 MBTs from the Saudi 10th Army Group, along with 11 Mechanised Infantry and Armoured Brigades from the Syrian army with 421 T-84 and 386 T-90 MBTs. This brought the total reserve force to 145,000 and contained some of the most technical and powerful land forces the Arabs possessed. NATO was not to know that, at this stage; the Arabs in Poland had switched their main axis and were now heading south to follow the route used by the armies in the Czech Republic. The additional troops heading into the Czech Republic would swell the numbers there to almost 1.3 million with the intention of overwhelming the NATO forces in southern Germany. The Arabs heading due west into the NATO bottleneck was still a very powerful and determined force and if they achieved nothing else, they would succeed in depleting NATOs ammunition stocks.

The battle for Germany opened on 2 separate fronts on 18th April with one on the eastern border with Poland and another on the southern border with the Czech Republic. In the east, 9 bridges were to be crossed simultaneously into the Province of Brandenburg under a massive artillery screen and by mid-afternoon, in the southern area of operations, the leading Division from 60,000 Mechanised and Armoured troops of the 11th Army Group would begin their advance north towards the Czech town of Liberec, which was just short of the German border, before continuing their advance into the German Province of Sachsen.

Moving off at 90-degrees to the Liberec force the remaining 646,000-strong Iranian and Syrian armies headed due west for Nuremburg in the Province of Bayern in what was to be a new front. Stretched out from the outskirts of Prague to the town of Plzen in the Czech Republic and all the way to the border, these troops were moving as fast as possible along the main 4-lane motorway that links Prague and Nuremberg in Germany. The assault through Liberec was yet another powerful feint designed to draw NATO troops from other areas along the massive southern border. The Arabs weren't to know it yet but the delay in mobilisation by the French and Spanish military had resulted in SACEUR having to spread his forces too thinly in places and this would be seen as crucial to events in the following days.

The 561,000 Egyptian, Saudi and Syrian forces heading south out of Poland to the Czech Republic had also sanctioned 48,000 troops in support of the Iranians at Liberec, with the remaining 513,000 travelling the same motorway axis to Nuremburg through the Bohemian Forest before eventually turning north into central Germany.

Lying in wait, close to and north of Liberec, were patrols from some of NATO's Special Operations Forces (SOF). On the southern front the British SAS provided these teams and they had inserted 10 patrols into both sides of the border and set up their covert observation posts (OPs). There were 4 patrols set up in the Czech Republic, with 6 in Germany. These OPs had been up and running for 9-days now and since occupying their sites they had not moved out of their locations once. Normal duration for a patrol was 10-days but these teams had enough supplies for 4-weeks, after helicopters had dropped extra supplies and other equipment onto night time landing sites 5km from the OP positions and it had taken a few journeys over 2-nights to get all the stores to the OP. Any ground sign left behind during the move into the OP had now been eradicated by the elements, with the locations chosen specifically for their dominant views over large areas of land and key choke points. Maintaining hygiene in such circumstances was paramount and these well-trained troops knew that defecating onto cling-film and urinating into large plastic containers ensured just that. The only movement was when personnel moved around to change position from sleeping, eating and observing. These troops were on hard routine, which meant no cooking and everything they ate or drank was cold. Anything not in use was packed away in their large bergans/ruck-sacks, including their own human waste. Set up with long-range cameras and telescopes, the Special Forces had been monitoring the area day by day with no results.

On Germany's eastern border, German Kommando Spezialkraefte, or KSK for short, were conducting a similar mission. Using their laser range finders incorporated into binoculars they were able to provide range data, which was then transmitted via the local area network to the Navipad before it was transmitted onto other units including the artillery. The German troops were also equipped with the NavlCom Command, Control, Communications, and Computers, Intelligence (C4I) system, which provided them with real time situational awareness including target coordinates. In conjunction with the laser range finder data, all the information on the enemy was passed via their data radio communication system, to the relevant units and aircraft.

The first layer of OPs were there to act as triggers and report enemy numbers, types of vehicles and weapon systems, direction of travel and recognition of any command locations or command vehicles. 5km north of the German/Czech border other SAS patrols were tasked with a very different mission. They were in position to relay target coordinates and spot for the artillery strikes while directing attack aircraft onto the enemy by passing information to the pilots using the Forward Air Controllers (FAC) in their teams.

It was 1500hrs when the teams in the Czech Republic first heard what sounded like a far-off continuous wave of noise that began to grow louder and louder. What they were hearing was the sound of thousands of vehicles' and their diesel-powered engines as they advanced northwards. Unlike the forces in the east, who had prepared the area for 48hrs using artillery as a screen, this force was conducting an advance to contact in that it was waiting for the enemy to make the first move before reacting.

The remaining members of the SAS patrol quickly jumped out of their sleeping bags and were awe struck at the site that greeted them. Although the weather was misty and murky in places, there were literally hundreds upon hundreds of vehicles that they could observe. These were spread over a massive area to the east and west of Liberec, with every single vehicle heading towards Germany. The patrol immediately relayed this information to their Tactical Group Headquarters (TGHQ) and, knowing they were in for a busy afternoon, began collating as much information as they could about the enemy forces. This was the trigger PJHQ and SACEUR had been waiting for and forces in the south were immediately placed on standby. BRDM-2 Armoured Reconnaissance Vehicles appeared to be the lead elements, with modernised BTR-70 and BTR-80 APCs following on behind, intermixed with T-84 and T90 MBTs. 20km southeast of Liberec and unsighted to the SAS patrols were the powerful Self-Propelled Artillery formations containing 2S1 122mm GVOZDIKA, 2S3 152mm, 2S19 152mm Msta and 2S5 152mm GIATSINT-S Batteries. The logistical tail containing the ammunition trucks and other stores were following on well to the rear, with logistic hubs in the Czech Republic already well stocked during the 3-week build up phase. 24hrs behind this tail were the Liberec reserve force of 48,000 from the Egyptian, Saudi and Syrian armies.

With only 17km separating Liberec and the German border, the lead Arab elements quickly crossed into German territory. Liberec, with a population of 95,000, was situated in a valley with high ridges northeast and west of the city about 1,000-feet higher than the valley floor. Most of the population had departed the city and escaped into northern Germany and west to France in order to escape the battle that appeared imminent.

The SAS patrols positioned on either side of the 2 high ridges on the forward slopes had excellent views into the lower ground. In daylight and in good weather the patrols were able to observe out to 10km from their positions and even on this day they could still observe a vast amount of land, stretching from the town of Tanvald in the east, through Liberec and, across to the town of Jablonne v Podjestedi in the west. It was a distance of 38km and the Arab advance easily covered this frontage. With the undulating ground and poor weather conditions some units became partially hidden by dead ground and poor visibility. One thing not in dispute from the SAS patrols was the size of the assaulting force, which was truly a visual spectacular. With sight reports and situation reports constantly flowing into PGHQ confirming the direction of travel, the numbers and types of vehicles, NATO commanders wrongly assumed this was the lead element of the main southern axis.

In the meantime, the lead Arab units who had raced beyond Liberec were passing the final town of Hradek n Nisou in the Czech Republic and were beginning to think the invasion of Germany was going to be unopposed. The border was now so close with the lead reconnaissance vehicles able to make out the small town of Zittau on the German side of the border. The Iranian vehicle commander, believing he was going to be the first Iranian into Germany scanned the ground furtively all about him before whispering quietly to himself, *'Allah Ackbar'*. Realising this was history in the making he quickly whipped out his digital camera and started taking photographs to freeze his moment for eternity. He could scarcely believe that an Arab army could do what it had done to NATO….but here they were….making history and entering Germany without a shot being fired…

PART 17

CROSSING THE LINE

From an historical perspective Germany was officially invaded via its southern border at 1710hrs on the 18th April after an Armoured Reconnaissance Patrol of the Iranian army crossed the German/Czech Republic border. They were soon followed across by much larger forces and with daylight now precious and with the light soon to fade, the second line of SAS patrols radioed in their fire missions. They were particularly interested in those vehicles that were massing or congregating in groups or, had halted for some reason. Some were caught at natural choke points and these were a prime target with their coordinates passed first.

The Arab commanders had made two serious mistakes today in their zest to cross the border into Germany and they would pay dearly before the day was over.

The first mistake was thinking the bad weather and low visibility would aid them in hiding from NATO aircraft, and although it would have been very difficult for aircraft to target the columns accurately, it was made so much easier by having eyes on the ground in the shape of Special Forces troops who were able to pass their locations. The Arabs had no forward observers on the ground to do the same and here, NATO had a massive advantage. Once the information had been passed, the firing solutions were passed to the artillery batteries and they stood ready, waiting for the order to fire and deliver their deadly salvos into the Arab lines. With the artillery batteries waiting to fire, scrambled NATO F16, F/A-18 and Euro Fighters were downloading target data provided by the Special Forces troops into their BLU-110 Mark 83 Joint Direct Attack Munitions (JDAM), JDAM being the tail-fin attachment that turns a normal freefall or unguided bomb into a 1,000lb inertial/GPS-guided all weather killer. At 22km away from the invading Arabs, the first wave of 8 aircraft pulled up sharply to 15,000-feet and, at 20km from their targets, tossed one JDAM each from their aircraft. 2-minutes behind were a further 8 aircraft and,

2-minutes behind that, another 8, followed by a 4th and final wave of 8 aircraft.

At 20km away the aircraft could not be seen or heard and the 32 JDAMs were silently gliding to their predetermined target locations. Minutes later the first wave of 8 JDAM, 1,000lb bombs slammed into the tightly packed armoured formations congregating near natural choke points with devastating consequences. Vehicles were too close and moving too slowly to escape the blast fragmentation and power of 1,000lbs of high explosive. The JDAM's kinetic energy also added to the carnage as the bombs completely disintegrated, shredded or lifted completely off the ground the lightly armoured vehicles. For those unfortunate to be near or inside these vehicles, it meant death or serious injury. Vehicles hit by a direct strike added to the shrapnel effect and the shock of been on the receiving end of one of these attacks was instant. No sooner had they recovered from the first strike than another arrived, and then another, and then another. Realising what was happening, vehicles were now attempting to distance themselves from each other and look for any kind of cover, while others continued with their advance, unaware of the devastation going on in other parts of the line. As the first JDAMs struck, the order to fire the artillery was given and this allowed the massed HIMARS, MLRS and 155mm NATO Artillery Batteries to pound the Arab forces across the whole width of their assault frontage prior to the final wave of JDAMs arriving. The SAS patrols were constantly radioing back instant corrections to the 155mm artillery lines, in order to make their fire more effective and, to relay new target coordinates as fast as they could. It took just 1hr and 35-minutes for the first assault to fail, with Arab units beating a hasty retreat across the border back into the Czech Republic. The light was fading now but, on the slightly undulating ground, dozens, if not hundreds of smashed APCs lay ruined, with a loss of more than 2,640 men killed and another 1,060 seriously injured. It had been something of a turkey shoot and an embarrassment for the Arabs. In retaliation, the Arabs resorted to firing artillery across into Germany, at no particular target.

Their second mistake of the day was to attack without waiting for Russian airpower to arrive overhead to perform their Combat Air Patrol/interdiction missions above the low cloud. The Russian Air

Force had been on standby waiting for the order to fly and provide cover during the invasion but it had not been forthcoming. The first indication of the invasion taking place was when Russian radar noted the ingress of NATO aircraft towards the Czech and Polish borders, but by then it was too late to react.

News of the failed first assault reached the Arab command centre in Warsaw but, they were unperturbed by the losses. They reiterated to the Iranian commanders that they were to continue their advance again and again as their role was important for the main invasion to succeed. With their orbat soon to receive a 48,000-strong reserve, they were ordered to concentrate their force on one main area, hoping to break the NATO line. Once the weather cleared, Russia, who had earmarked 2,500 combat aircraft for this phase of operations, would provide a protective screen above the invading formations as best they could and conduct dedicated bombing missions against NATO ground troops. The Arabs weren't to know but, the number of NATO combat troops directly facing the attack through Liberec into Germany was just 27,000, with another 52,000 spread thinly over a large area towards Bad Salzungen further to the west. A beefed up German Division of more than 30,000 troops was also in the south and had deployed as a blocking force east of Nuremburg.

It was now dark and the poor visibility was making it very difficult for the Special Forces troops to see any great distance. The only decent night vision optic was the Thermal Imaging (TI) sight, which succeeded in picking out heat sources all over the valley. They could hear the constant roar of engines all around them but so far no vehicle of foot patrol had wandered close to the OP site. It would probably be a quiet night for the patrols and they would have to wait for better weather or daylight to target the Arabs again effectively.

In the east of the country, German Special Forces had achieved a similar success to that of the British, with upwards of 20,000 Arab troops allowed over the bridges at 1430hrs before they were engaged by large numbers of NATO aircraft carrying JDAM and artillery strikes. Unlike the battle in the south, this one had continued for 5hrs with the Arabs refusing to pull back. They had persevered and pushed more soldiers across into Germany hoping to break NATO's grip but, It was a tactic doomed to failure and eventually they had no choice but to pull back over the bridges leaving just a few scattered remnants from their early assault Brigades on the German side.

By 19th April huge armoured columns were crossing into the Bayern Province in Southern Germany via the Czech Republic using the main highway and numerous tracks through the Bohemian Forest before passing the small town of Waidhaus on their northern most flank. With the main thrust continuing on the main Motorway/Autobahn axis, formations of Arab units now fanned out across the undulating ground and advanced across the German countryside through its patchwork of villages, valleys and ridges that dominated this part of Germany. The Iranian and Syrian columns snaked across the ground for hundreds of kilometers back to the Czech Republic, with follow-on forces of 513,000 from Poland joining the mix. There had been no contact with NATO forces until they reached the outskirts of Bruck in der Oberpflaz on the southern side of the main highway. It was here that the advancing Arab formations were first sighted by reconnaissance troops from the 13th Mechanised Division

The massive number of vehicles over such a large area was causing the NATO defenders huge problems and large flanking enveloping movements by the Arabs meant they could, if allowed, surround and isolate any small groups of NATO troops in this part of the country. The third front opened up by the Arabs was not unexpected but the numbers involved were, with the route though the Bohemian Forest always considered as the least favourable option. If the forces had been available, SACEUR would have positioned the French in this sector but their army had taken almost 3 months to mobilise completely, as had the Spanish, and the number of NATO troops in the region were nowhere near strong enough to counter such a large force. NATO had been caught out by the amount of troops pouring through at this point, with the Arab advance continuing deep into Germany before finally running into stiff resistance near the town of Pfreimd at the major highway choke point where the A6 Autobahn heading west joined with the A93 highway heading north and south. This was a well-defended position and holding this key ground was crucial in preventing and delaying the Arab armies from using the 4-lane transport networks in this region at will. Europe had built more than 60,000km of motorway and it was this network that had been instrumental in the speed at which this invasion had progressed.

The German troops at this junction were from the beefed up 13th Mechanised Division and they had been informed by SACEUR that reinforcements to their location would soon arrive from France and Spain, so, until they arrived they were to hold for as long as possible, even if surrounded. There were 31,000 German troops holding the junction and these were initially positioned in a half moon configuration covering 15km to the east, 12km to the north and 12km to the south of the huge intersection. Their PzH2000 155mm Self Propelled Howitzers were placed another 10km further to the west but as soon as the German forward and flank reconnaissance units reported massive enveloping pincer movements taking place the German defensive posture had to be altered fairly quickly. The amount of enemy approaching this position was a shock to the German commander so he had to rearrange his forces into a tighter triangular-shaped defensive pocket around the junction, with the eastern base of the triangle roughly 8km long…just over 4km either side of the junction with their PzH2000 155mm Self Propelled Artillery in the middle. It gave the defenders some room to manoeuvre within the pocket but, without air power, there was a good chance they could be breached or destroyed within days. The Arabs did not want to bypass this position as they saw this German force as a key NATO objective and their main aim, after all, was to destroy NATO militarily.

The 13th Mechanised Division contained the 37th and 41st Mechanised Brigades, which provided 2 Armoured Battalions, 4 Mechanised Infantry Battalions, 2 Reconnaissance Battalions, plus Signal, Logistic and Engineer Battalions. The 13th had been further strengthened by detachments from the 1st Armoured Division and the 14th Panzergrenadier Division. The 1st Armoured Division had provided 3 Artillery Battalions with 27 of their PzH2000 155mm Self Propelled Artillery, half an Artillery Rocket Battalion with 2 Artillery Rocket Batteries containing 20 MLRS and an Air Defence Battalion. The final troops attached to the 13th Mechanised Division were the 18th Panzerbrigade, detached from the 14th Panzergrenadier Division for this mission only. The remainder of the 14th Panzergrenadier Division having been directed only 24hrs earlier by SACEUR to move northeast to support the NATO troops and counter any Arab advance from Liberec.

With German reconnaissance units arriving back in their defensive lines the reports reaching the German Divisional Commander, Major General Eberhand Wilhelm Wenck, were disconcerting to say the least. Reconnaissance teams were reported hundreds of T-90 and T-84 Main Battle Tanks (MBTs) plus, what seemed like thousands of BTR-80 and 90, BRDM-3 and BMP-3 Armoured Personal Carriers (APCs) approaching from 3 different directions - the east, northeast and from the south. By 1022hrs 13th Panzergrenadier Division had their first sighting of this massive force approaching them. From initial sightings they appeared to be outnumbered at least 4 to 1 and, no sooner had the enemy lead elements come into view that high explosive shells from Arab artillery exploded on the German positions in great numbers. Little did they know that the troops attacking them were; in fact, only the lead elements of an enormous army containing 1.3 million men. The Arab tactic was quite simple in that it was just going to bulldoze its way through the German lines, using its massive weight of firepower and superior numbers but, Major General Wenck, although concerned, was also annoyed by the arrogance of the force attacking his position. He was a Divisional Commander in the German Army, practiced in the art of war and in no mood to roll over so easily to the Arabs. The Divisions 27 PzH2000 155mm SP howitzers opened fire almost immediately once the Forward Observation Officers (FOO) had identified the mass of targets advancing on their position with the FOO continuing to provide the gun lines with correction updates. Once the corrections and new target data had been placed into the computerised gun systems the next salvo of high explosive shells arched towards their targets. The incoming Arab artillery was also accurate, constant and a lot heavier than that which was outgoing, with explosions all across the German lines.

Within its increased orbat, 13th Panzergrenadier Division had 180 Leopard 2- A6 MBTs and almost 200 PUMA Fighting Vehicles equipped with 30mm Cannons. In addition to this, there were also 72 MILAN Anti-Tank Guided Missile Systems (ATGM) and 12 - 120mm Mortars to call upon.

The Divisions Infantry Battalions of Jaeger Light Infantry were equipped with the small 2.5t Wiesel 1 AFV carrying a mix of Mk1/

TOW ATGM, 20mm Cannons and 120mm Mortars. In addition to their personal weapon, the HK G36 5.56mm Assault Rifle, they were equipped with the 7.62mm MG3 and its replacement, the 5.56mm Light Machine Gun. They were well dug in and confident of seeing out the current bombardment; with their greatest concern coming from a direct hit on their positions.

Once the Arab AFVs and APCs closed the distance to within 5km of the German Division's eastern baseline, the 120mm Mortars began firing from the rear of the Wiesel 1 AFVs, while the Leopard 2 A6s gunners chose their targets and prepared to fire their 120mm Smoothbore L55 Rheinmetall guns. The A6 gun was 55cm longer than the A5 version and the extra length gave the gun a muzzle velocity of 1,750-metres per second. Once fired, the time to hitting a target 5km away took less than 3-seconds. Each Leopard 2 had arrived with its standard allocation of 42 rounds but with extra ammunition arriving on the position 24hrs earlier; their full allocation would be nearer 84 per tank. In the meantime their initial rounds were slamming into the advancing armoured formations. A large proportion of the Leopards were hulled down/dug in almost below ground level, their hatches closed due to the artillery fire landing on their position. This made it difficult for the Arab gunners to locate their target, even with their thermal site. The Leopard gunners though, had a perfect site picture using their thermal imaging and were able to pick off the Arab MBTs almost at will. Some of the T-90 and T-84 MBTs that had been hit full frontal continued advancing, which was testament to the advanced armour these tanks possessed. Their weakness, however, was from the side and lying in wait biding their time on the eastern baseline were 36 MILAN missile tubes and their 2-man teams, with each team equipped with 4-missiles. As the Arab MBT formations closed to within 2.5km MILAN operators were scanning for side-on profiles and, once presented, let loose their guided missile at their maximum range of 2km.

The MILAN, once fired, had to be directed onto the target by the operator and from 400-metres to 2km these missiles were highly accurate. The wire spieling out from the rear of the missile was carrying the corrections from the operator and at this maximum range the missile had time to react to his instructions. The MILAN High Explosive Anti-

Tank (HEAT) Tandem Warheads streaking out towards their targets started impacting on the tanks and APCs with devastating effects and no sooner had one struck home than the empty missile tube was ejected from the launcher and another tube with its rocket was rammed into place. The battlefield was now littered with burning and exploding vehicles on both sides with some resembling pressure cookers as the over-pressure within some of the burning vehicles reached a point where it had nowhere to go except through the weakest point - the turret - with those inside incinerated. The majority of destroyed vehicles were primarily in the open ground on all 3 sides of the German lines. Some of the MILAN firing positions had been compromised and destroyed emphatically by direct fire from the T-90/T-84s aided by BMP-3s with their 100mm Guns and the BTR-80s with their 30mm Cannons and 14.5mm Heavy Machine Guns.

Spandrell-3 and Spandrell-5 Anti-Tank Guided Missiles were also finding targets and the T-90 AT-11 Sniper Laser Guided Missile fired from the barrel was also achieving success. With a range of almost 5km this missile was impacting on the Leopards and PUMAs within 12-seconds of being fired, with its warhead ensuring penetration of any Explosive Reactive Armour (ERA). Even with momentum slowing the Arabs continued their suppressive fire and launched the next phase of their assault across the whole breadth of the German Divisions northern, central and southern defensive lines.

Racing in under cover of fire and smoke were 1,700 BTR-80s/90s and BMP-3s. Using the terrain as best they could they closed to within 300-metres before halting in as much cover as the ground allowed before disgorging their infantry. Once this manoeuvre was complete the vast majority of these vehicles moved back 1.7km to provide fire support with their 30mm Cannons and14.5mm and 7.62mm Machine Guns. Some of the hulled down and camouflaged German PUMA AFVs, with their 30mm Automatic Cannons, now revealed their positions by opening fire at the lightly-armoured Russian-made APCs and at this range the 30mm shells chewed them to pieces before they themselves came under fire from Russian equivalent calibre weaponry. The Wiesel 1 AFVs TOW ATGM was also enjoying some success and accounting for a lot of the Russian-made APCs and even some of the T84/T90 MBTs, but there were literally thousands of vehicles manoeuvering about the battlefield and the German gunners sometimes hesitated at which target to fire.

The Arab units were now concentrating their fire on all 3 sides of the German lines but the Arab AFV and APC formations attacking the southern side had been particularly savaged by the German defenders at this location and were being driven back by accurate and sustained fire before deploying their infantry. On the northern and central points of attack, the Arab APCs drove on and succeeded in deploying their infantry in huge numbers close to the German lines. Once out of the confines of the APCs, these assaulting troops swarmed across the undulating ground towards the German infantry who were dug in only a few hundred metres away. 11,000 Arab infantrymen were now assaulting on foot across a frontage of 10km into the German defensive lines and the Arabs were soon to learn that it was a mistake not to focus their main effort on one or two specific areas. The German Infantry equipped with their individual weapon, the Hecklar and Koch -5.56mm Assault Rifle and the H&K AG36, which was the 40mm Grenade Launcher under the G36, started firing almost immediately at the advancing troops. Also available to them were the 7.62mm MG3s and 5.56mm Machine Guns and it was these area weapons with their rapid firing rate that was causing the most hurt to the Arab Infantry at close quarters. With support from their 120mm Mortars, the advancing troops were cut down in droves. With infantryman killing infantryman, German Leopard MBTs continued firing at the Arab T84s/T90s and APCs with their 120mm main armament. The Arabs' return fire emanating mainly from the BMP-3s, BTR-80s, Ukrainian-made T-84 120mm Guns, aided by their French SAGEM Thermal Gunner's Sight and from their T-90s using their 125mm rounds. Both sides' accuracy was astonishing and, whether static or on the move, high explosive rounds were impacting on their selected targets with great consistency.

The Arab infantry had fought hard to get within 100-metres of the German lines but, after assaulting headfirst into a constant and deadly wall of fire, their decimated ranks had only one option left open. Unable to break into the German positions, the attack eventually faltered and broke. After 83-minutes of sacrifice and savagery the first Arab assault was finally repulsed, with the surviving infantry attempting to reach safe ground and their armoured protection. The first attack had resulted in 78 Arab MBTs, 296 APCs and almost 7,500 Arab troops killed in action. The German Division had suffered 21 MBTs, 5 Pzh 2000 155mm Self Propelled Howitzers and 18 PUMA AFVs destroyed and 1,021 men killed in action. The Arabs were in a position to take the losses, with 1.3 million men and their machines stacked up behind the initial assault, but the German losses could not be replaced. With artillery continuously targeting the German positions the casualty rate increased still further and, within the hour, Arab forces launched a second similar sized-attack, which also failed.

During the first assault, 154,000 Arabs had already started bypassing the junction to the south before continuing west towards Nuremburg and Stuttgart. Their orders were to cut off the German Division's westerly withdrawal route and seek out and destroy any more NATO troops that they might come across. Over the next 21hrs the assaults on the beleaguered German defenders would continue, with large numbers of Mujihadeen fighters thrown into the fray as assaulting shock troops for the first time. Time and time again the German troops would hold their lines, inflicting massive casualties on the determined Arab troops. On the 4th assault, just prior to last light, 8 Russian Su27 and 2 Su35 fighter bombers appeared overhead and using KAB-500S-E bombs/560kg satellite-guided munitions, were directed onto the German positions by the attached Russian Forward Air Controllers, who had lazed the German positions and identified their targets before relaying the latitudinal and longitudinal positions to the aircraft, who then dropped their ordnance from above the clouds. This action succeeded in destroying more than 18 Leopard MBTs, 9 of the MLRS launchers and 23 PUMA AFVs along with other associated vehicles. It was their one and only involvement during the whole battle and, for reasons unknown, they did not return.

The 5th and 6th assaults continued on into the night with the Arabs content to hammer away through the dark hours in their almost obsessive quest to destroy the ever diminishing German Division. The 6th assault took place at midnight and, failed as all he others had done previously. The next assault never materialised during the night with the Arabs content to use their artillery only. The Germans had stayed awake all night waiting for another attack on their position but the

Arabs had decided to rest. With artillery targeting the Germans all night the Arabs were planning a massive and sustained assault at first light on the morning of the 20th.

Time and ammunition was running out for the Germans in this location and Major General Wenck, slightly wounded, knew it. He sent radio orders to the Brigade commander in charge of the 18th Panzer Brigade to prepare what was left of his Brigade for a breakout to the north before it became light. There were just 44 Leopard MBTs left from a force of 180, and only 38 PUMA AFV from a force of 200, capable of making the journey. Others were dug in but non-manoeuverable due to track and other damage and these were used solely as gun-emplacements. 2hrs before first light the remaining 155mm Self Propelled Howitzers stood-to, along with the yet to be used, Artillery Rocket Battalions MLRS. The 155mm guns and the MLRS were going to use all their remaining ammunition to blast a way through the Arab lines to aid the escaping troops. Once the order came to move, all drivable vehicles headed to the vehicle assembly point in the northern sector. Those left behind were quietly resigned to their fate, yet adamant that if this force of 2,232 men escaped, they would consider it a victory.

30mins later the breakout began, starting with the remaining 11 MLRS firing their full quota of 12 rockets each. General Wenck was looking to shock the Arabs in the northern area of operations using the MLRS to lay down a carpet of metal rain across a vast area, with the first dual purpose anti-personnel/anti-material grenades landing 10km forward of the German position and out to 22km. The first 10km, therefore, were the responsibility of the 155mm guns, and between them, the Artillery and Rocket Batteries were looking at opening up a corridor 1km wide and 22km long.

With a mass of German artillery crashing to earth, the escaping battalions had to drive headfirst into the Arab lines. The speed at which they advanced and the pounding and shock effect from the artillery, especially the MLRS, had taken the Arabs completely by surprise and, by concentrating their entire force onto one single focused area, the commander of 18th Panzer Brigade succeeded in breaking the Arab line 38-minutes after departing the German pocket. They had lost 8 Leopard MBTs, 4 PUMA Armoured Fighting Vehicles and

103 men during the escape. After punching through they continued running north to safety but, although free, they knew their actions had condemned those remaining behind to their deaths. The 18th Panzer Brigade commander was aware of the sacrifice General Wenck and his men had made and, although he felt guilty, he also felt enormous pride in the actions of the German army.

As dawn started to break on 20th April the carnage across the battle ground could be assessed and it was mind numbing. Thousands of destroyed, burnt-out vehicles littered an area for miles around, with the ground strewn with the bodies of the dead and dying. Thousands of men had been wiped out and the encirclement and continuous assaults on the German troops meant they had to rearrange their lines once more to form a small box of just 3km by 3km square around the junction. The anticipated and massive dawn assault began at 0500hrs and the attacking force appeared to fill one's view from horizon to horizon in all directions.

Major General Wenck had long thought his position was somewhat untenable and, even with NATO air flying again, he was unfortunately proved correct. Wenck's Division had received no air support whatsoever in the battle and he knew from what had transpired that his defensive enclave would be breached within the first 24hrs. For 20hrs now the German Armoured, Mechanised and Infantry Battalions had stood their ground, resisting all attempts to expel them from their defensive position. They had killed literally thousands of Mujihadeen and regular troops storming their dug-in positions, and overall destroyed an immense amount of armoured vehicles, including more than 312 T84/T90 MBTs and 1,026 APCs.

The final early morning assault was overwhelming in its ferocity with every piece of ground fought over to the last man but, with the German defenders running short of ammunition the breakthrough came quickly on the southern aspect of the pocket and before long thousands of opposing infantrymen forced their way into the German defences, supported by tanks, APCs, ZSU-23-4 with their 4 - 23mm Cannon and the 2S6 Integrated Air Defence asset with its 30mm Cannon in the ground role.

In an even-numbered fight the Germans would have repulsed and defeated the Arab forces but the massive numerical advantage had worn them down and it now became a rout. With the tide now turning in the attackers' favour it became a slaughter of the remaining German defenders. From the 31,000 troops who had been defending this location, only 2,129 had managed to survive, by smashing their way north through the Arab lines.

Major General, Eberhand Wilhelm Wenck, died fighting for his country at 0637hrs on 20th April alongside the men he had commanded for 2-years.

After receiving the shocking news that 13th Panzergrenadier Division had been wiped out in less than 24hrs, SACEUR realised the situation in the south was far worse than he had expected. New satellite imagery and imagery collected by the Tornado GR4A Tactical Reconnaissance Aircraft, using their Sideways Looking Infra-Red and their Line-Scan Infra-Red Surveillance System's had verified the reports received from Major General Wenck that the situation on the ground was indeed different to how it had been perceived back in NATO HQ. The images and reports confirmed the majority of Arab forces were now streaming through the Czech Republic, into Germany at the least defended point. What NATO thought were the main points of attack had turned out to be distractions for the real thrust into Germany and, although powerful, these initial main points of attack were showing far less troop activity than first thought.

By 20th April, on the Polish eastern front, the low cloud had all but cleared and, with it, came a clear rise in air temperature. Wisps of thin cloud were still attempting to block out the blue sky but, after the lull in aircraft activity over the last few days, aircraft had earlier become noticeable again by their sound. The frontline had first resounded to explosions at 0300hrs, as NATO aircraft carried out continuous and sustained bombing missions against the Arab forces. Within 30-minutes of the first bombings, Russian aircraft were also overhead counteracting some of NATOs missions, as well as bombing NATO ground troops who were dug-in. High overhead a deadly game of aerial combat was taking place with many aircraft on both sides falling victim to both shorter range Air-to-Air Missiles and the longer range Beyond Visual Range Air-to-Air Missile Systems (BVRAAMS).

From the 20th onwards, the pressure across the NATO lines increased further, with waves of assaults continuing on both the eastern and southern fronts - only this time, Russian aircraft were in a position to target any NATO artillery once they began firing at the Arabs. Tens upon tens of thousands had so far died in the battle to invade Germany and there appeared to be no let-up in sight. For the Arabs this was the whole reason for being in Europe and the thought of defeating NATO and the West was clearly driving them forward.

After the decimation of the German Division near Pfreimd the massive Arab armies continued west to Nuremburg where they split into 2 groups once more. The Iranian and Syrian army with their ever growing Mujihadeen contingent, continued west, and 3-days later on 25th of April, they clashed for the first time with French and Spanish troops near Stuttgart, which resulted in Northern Germany, now effectively split from Southern Germany. The Egyptian and Saudi armies now swung north using the A9 autobahn as an axis to begin their advance into central Germany, but not before detaching their Syrian contingent back to the Syrian army aligned with the Iranians.

On receiving this information SACEUR believed that the force advancing north now had the potential to cut off the remainder of his forces protecting the southern most forward areas, so he was left with no choice other than to order a withdrawal. He issued orders for forces in the southwest to instigate hit and run delaying tactics while those troops furthest southeast and north of Liberec, were to withdraw north towards Bautzen, leaving the SAS patrols isolated and with no immediate support.

On the eastern front, on the German/Polish Border, the war was particularly brutal, with vast numbers of Arabs being killed in their attempts to cross the river Oder and gain a foothold; yet they continued attacking. The original force of 200,000 was now down to approximately 138,000 and gearing up yet again for another attack, with the appearance of the Russian Air Force proving a great motivator for the beleaguered Arabs.

With NATO troops pulling back northwards during the night, the defences on the southern border north of Liberec in the Czech Republic were now open to exploitation; therefore, on the morning of 22nd April a Heavy Armoured Division, supported by a Mechanised Infantry Division from the Egyptian army, advanced unopposed 18km into Germany and reached the town of Zittau, before moving on to the towns of Ebersbach, Grosshennersdorf and Herrnhut. Progress was cautious and slow near these towns as the heavily-wooded areas and tight tracks were ideal ambush territory but, unbeknown to the Arabs, NATO forces had now consolidated 24km further north in a new defensive posture covering from Zgorzelec on the Polish border to Bautzen over to the west.

SACEUR had pulled back his remaining troops in the south and ordered them to protect the western flank of those in Bautzen. Their position was considered fairly strong, with 43,000 NATO troops dominating a large proportion of the 79km long piece of high ground stretching from the towns of Bad Salzungen and Eisenach in the northwest to Meiningen and Suhl in the southeast. SACEUR knew that if NATO was forced from this key ground then the Fulda Gap over to the west would be exposed and the remainder of his troops to the east in Bautzen and Zgorzelec would be vulnerable and in a position to be rolled up. SACEUR was still holding onto his reserve of 31,000 just incase events spiraled out of control and had no intention of deploying these just yet. 12hrs later new imagery showed the huge columns of Arab forces advancing north were now heading for the large feature near Meiningen to engage with NATO troops deployed there.

NATO and Arab armies locked horns, near the spur like feature, late afternoon on 23rd April. What followed were 6-days of continuous and bitter fighting before NATO troops had to withdrawal from this dominating location. The Battle for the Meiningen feature was lost for 2 reasons – a shortage of ammunition and a large flanking movement by the Arab units. NATO did not have the forces on the ground to deal with the massive changes of direction that the Arabs were capable of and with the Arabs providing a target rich environment, ammunition quantities were being depleted quicker than predicted. Although ammunition was in abundant quantities in Germany, NATO was just not able to transport it to the front in time. By 29th/30th April, NATO troops over to the east and close to Bautzen, were having to move northwards once more, this time to the town of Cottbus, which was only 110km from Berlin. With NATO troops pulling back from Meiningen on the western flank and those in the east pulling back to Cottbus, it meant Dresden was going to be left unprotected and abandoned to its own fate.

In the early hours of 2nd May, the last NATO troops were eventually extracted from the Czech/German border region. The SAS troops, having received orders to extract on 29th April, were sent confirmatory grid references of their extraction point's Helicopter Landing Zones (HLS). Over the next 2-nights they patrolled to their nominated HLS and, having arrived early, observed the location all day on 2nd May before they were happy the area was secure and the final radio message could be sent confirming HLS clear. To cut down on losing too many patrols if a helicopter was taken down, 5 HLS were nominated for the extractions, with 2-patrols dedicated to each HLS. At 0130hrs on 2nd May, American UH-60K Blackhawk's lifted out all the patrols less one team. The UK SF helicopter capability having been destroyed in January meant their US Allies were now responsible for such operations. Chosen for their Full Defensive Aids Suite (DAS), Forward Looking Infrared (FLIR), Terrain Avoidance Radar and ability to withstand 23mm Air-Defence Fire the Blackhawk was considered capable of extracting the teams quickly and as safely as possible. On arrival back in Ramstein Air Base one helicopter had sustained superficial damage from small arms fire and there followed a de-brief on the whole mission and, to ascertain what had occurred to the missing patrol. Sadly, the missing patrol was never heard from again. They were presumed dead or captured and they soon became just another statistic in the never-ending loss of life.

The southern most regions were now unprotected, with only the French and Spanish military in a position to engage the advancing Iranian and Syrian armies. Their aim was to contain and defeat the 700,000-strong force and prevent it from reaching French soil. It had been 7-days now since French and Arab forces first engaged each other in battle and so far the French and Spanish armies were holding their ground against the overwhelming number of Arab troops near Stuttgart, but this was the only good news available to SACEUR. The Arabs in southern Germany, who were advancing north, had paid a heavy price in pushing NATO from the large feature near Meiningen but, even with huge losses to their manpower and armoured vehicles their progress had remained steady. More than 47,129 Arabs had lost their lives taking the feature, with NATO losing 11,756 killed in action. The Egyptian and Saudi armies who had advanced north from Nuremburg were still

379,000-strong, despite the losses at Meiningen, and still a major force to be reckoned with. They had previously split their forces between the eastern and Liberec fronts but it was now time to join up once more. Of the 108,000 soldiers who had advanced north from Liberec, only 69,500 were operationally effective and, from the force attacking over the River Oder in the east, 329,000 were assessed as available for combat operations; this included the Egyptian and Syrian Heavy Armoured and Mechanised Reserve Units, the Artillery Batteries and the Air Defence Units. Estimates had put the death toll in excess of 100,000 on this front alone, with the vast majority being Arabs soldiers.

With NATO forces being pushed back in the south, the Arabs were sensing a fundamental shift in NATOs centre of gravity; so, to maintain the pressure, Arab High Command, located close to Gorzow near the German/Polish border, ordered their reserve forces in Poland to join the battle on the eastern front in order to facilitate a major breakthrough. This was to be coordinated with a massive blitz by Russian air power that would be playing a pivotal role in the operation.

The blitz began in the early hours of 8th May. More than 1,300 Russian bombers and fighter aircraft were dedicated to smashing NATOs defences in conjunction with massive ground assaults from the newly committed Arab reserve. With coordinated attacks all over the 3 fronts, NATO airpower was stretched and unable to combat the attacks in the east to any great extent. The relentless attacks from air and ground forces soon forced back the NATO defenders and breakthrough was achieved at long last. With thousands of Arabs now pouring over the crossings to exploit the gap, .NATO attempted to destroy the bridges over the river. By mid-afternoon 3-bridges had been dropped at a cost to NATO of 14 aircraft destroyed but 6 other bridges remained shielded by a massive air-defence screen and large numbers of Russian fighter jets. With the net tightening around NATO forces in the north of Germany and a massive Arab army engaging the French and Spanish armies in the south, NATO Command HQ felt threatened enough to depart its HQ in Ramstein Air Force Base. This they did with haste and subsequently set up in the small provincial town of Brunssum, Holland at the NATO Joint Forces Command, Brunssum.

By 1800hrs that night more than 53,000 Arab troops - on the eastern front - had advanced 9km into German and were pushing the

NATO defenders hard. By first light the next day almost 100,000 had crossed the bridges and the race across the North German Plains had begun. After the collapse on the eastern border the NATO troops in and around the town of Cottbus were, in effect, sandwiched north and south by Arabic forces and within hours of the breakthrough, were given orders to extract northwest towards Berlin - 110km away. The remaining troops in the south were ordered to continue their hit and run tactics to Halle, Gottingen and Dortmund where new defences would be prepared. They were to be joined within a few days by those troops who had been ordered to withdrawal from Cottbus.

Berlin was only 72km away from the first Arab forces crossing the River Oder and the decision to pull back across the River Elbe west of Berlin was imminent. Berlin was almost a ghost city now with millions of people having already departed west to Holland and north to Denmark. Many more had stayed and so far, NATO had not deployed troops in the city, thus sparing its remaining inhabitants from the worst of the fighting. The Elbe would provide a natural barrier from the Arabs on the eastern front but the problem was the large force in the south heading north. The rivers run in a mainly south to north direction and the Arabs had literally straddled the main rivers and were, in effect, advancing north on the west side of the River Elbe and River Wesser. Any defensive lines set up by NATO to the north could now be open to exploitation by these rapidly advancing troops.

Fatigue was also taking its toll, with rest between battles limited, but the NATO forces had no choice other than to continue delaying and wearing the Arabs down as much as they could.

The rivers would normally prove to be a major obstacle for any invading army but, with the large feature near Meiningen and Eisenach now taken, the Fulda Gap was relatively open and undefended to the massed Arabic armour and, with the ground between Eisenach to the River Rhine relatively flat, they could if they so wished advance unhindered and unopposed. The route through the Fulda Gap was assessed as the quickest route to the River Rhine but for some inexplicable reason the Arabs seemed only concerned with engaging NATO forces head-on.

With the eastern front collapsing, SACEUR made the decision to withdrawal his units west over the River Elbe and concentrate his forces into a tighter pocket. Enticing the Arabs to once again come into prepared killing fields was predicated by the success of the tactics on the Oder. For the Arabs to advance further into Germany they would have no choice but to fight for the bridges that remained intact, therefore, some of the bridges over the Elbe were blown and dropped by NATO demolition charges, while a selected few remained intact. SACEUR was now forced to deploy his reserve of 31,000 to the southern front in order to block the Arabs approaching Gottingen and Halle, with a secondary fall back final defensive line spreading across from Osnabruck in the west, through Hamburg and onto Magdeburg in the east. These towns were all joined by a small tributary running east to west from the River Elbe across the country and it was here that the Arabs had to be held or Germany was lost. The troops returning to Berlin from Cottbus, and who were initially earmarked to head west to Gottingen, were now given new orders and redeployed to the eastern front on the west side of the River Elbe, only 129km from Berlin.

SACEURs reluctance in blowing all the bridges stemmed from his belief that the Arabs could never defeat NATO and, that the Islamic armies would eventually be defeated and NATO would then need those bridges to drive the Arab armies back east. With the Nordic Battle Group not yet committed and the Italian army still to be blooded, NATO was far from defeated. What did concern SACEUR and his planners, though, was the presence of hundreds of thousands of Russian troops on the Polish border, but so far they had remained static and passive. If the Russians and the Arabs were true allies why hadn't Russia aided the Arabs by committing ground troops? After all, they had committed aircraft and submarines, which managed to sink numerous ships from 2-US Carrier Battle Fleets. What NATO didn't know was that Russia had already sanctioned the use of its ground troops by providing 2 Brigades of Engineers with river crossing equipment, should it be required. These units were already on the Polish/German border and prepared to establish tank-crossing capability if called upon.

With the push to invade Germany from the east successful, there was no lull in the fighting and the Egyptian 19 Corps with its attachment of Saudi forces and their western-made tanks wasted no time in attempting to advance further west. A surprise to the Arabs was that NATO appeared not to want to commit its forces in large-scale tank battles on the German plains but instead was instigating a series of deadly ambushes that frustrated the Arabs and curtailed their movements considerably. The ambushes were large, well-sited and involved the use of Infantry Battalions conducting day and night anti-armour ambushes with MILAN ATGM Systems, supported by air and massed artillery strikes and, for the first time the use of the AH-64D Apache Helicopters. Flying only at night these aircraft inflicted serious damage on the Arabic armoured formations using their 16 Hellfire Air-to-Surface Missiles. The Apache weapon systems are fitted with a millimeter wave seeker that allows for fire and forget operation and, with a maximum range of 12km the tank and APC crews on the Arab formations peripheries never knew the attack was pending until their vehicles were struck. The radar dome on the Apache Longbow was plotting the speed and direction of 256 targets from one scan and this, coupled with the information supplied to the pilot via his Arrowhead targeting and night vision system, allowed for a fast engagement of the enemy. The use of this aircraft resulted in the Arab Air Defence systems having to push further out from the formations in order to combat their effectiveness in sneaking up and releasing their weapons unhindered, but this also left them vulnerable. The Apache's success on the battlefield ensured that Russian air planners were beginning to take an interest in its activities and, after a raid on 14th May, the Apaches were themselves ambushed by Su27 flankers, with short range air-to-air missiles. The Russians succeeded in destroying 7 Apaches from a force of 24 and after the third such ambush on the Apaches, their use was curtailed and they were only used sporadically.

 The gains made were slower than the Arabs had hoped for and, with NATOs tactics responsible for an unprecedented and unexpected drain on manpower and equipment, Arab commanders demanded their reserves from Iran and Egypt be moved to Europe as soon as possible.

PART 18

THE FORGOTTEN VIKINGS
(D+174)

DTG: 17th July....2012.....

LOCATION: Western Europe

SITUATION: A lack of progress in Europe has resulted in the Arab commanders demanding more reinforcements to join them in Poland and the Czech Republic, ready to be deployed to the frontline. With NATO reinforcements also arriving in theatre the defining moment appeared to be nearing.

After the initial success in breaking NATO lines the following 2 months had proven to be an anti-climax for the Arabs, with their forces becoming bogged down near Dortmund and Gottingen in central Germany and, to the east of the River Elbe in the north. In mid June, the 3rd UK Mechanised Division consisting of 17,641 troops and another recently formed British Infantry Brigade of 3,500 troops had at long last landed in Belgium and reinforced the German NATO contingent in the south.

Near the France/German border, Iranian and Syrian forces had achieved greater success in taking land and, had pushed the French and Spanish back from Stuttgart and then advanced through Gerlingen, Leonburg, Renningen and then towards Niefern-Osschelbronn before entering the patchwork of small towns such as Karlsbad and Ettlingen, Malsch, Bietigheim, Rastatt and eventually Seltz on the River Rhine. Crossing the River Rhine in numerous areas had forced the French and Spanish troops back into France, with the Arabs reaching the towns of Saarbrucken, Heidelberg and Karlsruhe. It had, however, come with a heavy price, with the Arabs suffering close to 212,000 dead and wounded, compared to the French and Spanish armies' casualties of 26,412 killed in action. The loss to the French and Spanish commanders was offset by the arrival of 25,000 troops from Portugal, who were immediately tasked with protecting the left flank of the Spanish army. They had been amazed at the speed and the very size of the forces descending upon them and this underestimation had been one of the reasons why the Arabs were allowed to cross over bridges that should have been blown up. A stalemate was now spreading over the front line and new defensive positions had been established across a vast area northwest and southeast of the city of Strasbourg in France. With NATO troops in the area, this city, along with others in the region, started receiving indirect fire from Arab artillery units, resulting in large numbers of civilian casualties and, what could best be described as virtually unlivable conditions in a short space of time. As many towns and cities had found out before …it takes decades if not centuries to build one into a modern metropolis but only hours or days to destroy it.

The Arab commanders in Poland were relishing the arrival of their long-awaited reserve forces and saw this as the final nail in NATO's coffin and hopefully bring about its complete destruction. 365,000 raw and untested Egyptians had made their way across Europe and were now in Poland ready to move to Germany and form part of what was to be 3 Main Army Groups in their relentless squeezing of NATO troops in Germany. The Iranian reserve of 350,000, plus another 20,000 Mujihadeen fighters from across the Middle East, had unexpectedly split in Hungary with 150,000 heading for the Czech Republic, Germany and France and the remaining 220,000 making their way into Slovenia.

The Russians had earlier informed the Slovenian government to accept Ukrainian troops on their land or face complete destruction. With no other choice they relented and 35,000 Ukrainian troops, along with 10,000 Russians entered Slovenia in late May, taking control of the major bridges over the 3 rivers that run north to south across the country. After crossing the River Mura in the east of the country the Iranian troops quickly reached the second, the River Drava, and eventually they crossed the final obstacle, the River Sava near the capital. Ukrainian and Russian troops manning the bridges and safeguarding the capital Ljubljana watched in amazement as the enormous columns of vehicles made their way to the western town of Nova Goria and on towards their ultimate destination...Italy. There was a feeling that the war had reaching a critical period and the next few weeks and months would prove crucial in determining defeat or victory for NATO.

The arrival of these large numbers of troops gave the Arab armies a lift and their momentum began again fairly quickly. With this influx of troops on the eastern front, the Arabs were able to form a Southern, Central and Northern Army Group with a combined strength of 670,000.

On the French border the 150,000 extra troops had pushed its combat force number up to 712,000, with another 220,000 descending on Italy through Slovenia.

It was not just the Arabs bringing in reinforcements, and those German troops that had been hunting and fighting Mujihadeen terrorist cells throughout parts of the country were now released from this duty to be sent to the front, along with ex-soldiers and reserve personnel who had been drafted in. Another 100,000 German troops were available for combat and these were boosted by Holland sending 10,000 troops to fight alongside them. The 3rd Mechanised Division and the extra Infantry Brigade provided by the UK were also strengthened when the Canadian Expeditionary Force Command (CEFCOM) sent 7 Battalions of Infantry, less their vehicles with Combat Engineers from their 1st and 2nd Canadian Mechanised Infantry Brigades, plus Support and Logistical troops. Poised and ready elsewhere, and unbeknown to the Arabs, were 35,000 troops from the newly-formed Nordic Battle Group and last but not least, a force that SACEUR had held back for the last few months. The time had now come to allow this force to do what it was trained to do and with reinforcements in position SACEUR decided it was time to be proactive instead of reactive and hit back.

The introduction of Arab reinforcements once again turned the tide in the Arabs favour and within 3-weeks the French and Spanish were having to withdrawal south once more. Extra French and Spanish reserves were being rushed to the front and these were needed to halt the Arab's march into central France. At first, the 48,000 reserves had no effect and the Arabs pushed on regardless. Paris was ignored altogether, with the Arabs concentrating solely on engaging and defeating the retreating troops heading south. The advance was eventually checked 280km inside French territory on a line running from the town of

Troyes, through Chatillon-Sur-Seine and southeast to Dijon. Having let the Arabs over extend their forward lines the French and Spanish armies launched, what was, a planned counter-attack. Backed by hundreds of combat planes the French, Spanish and Portuguese armies succeeded in driving the lead Arab units back, forcing their whole offensive to come to a grinding halt. The counter-attack was possible because Spanish and French aircraft were suddenly operating with relative immunity, with Russian air power inexplicably seeming to diminish considerably over the last few weeks. It had clearly had an effect on the battle, with the Arabs suffering substantially heavier casualties and equipment losses than their French, Spanish and Portuguese counterparts.

In the north the Arabs' invasion would have faltered without the introduction of fresh reinforcements, especially after NATO ambushes and Apache raids had accounted for a significant portion of the Arabs' heavier combat power. The hit and run tactics had been slowly draining the Arabs resources but the introduction of 365,000 fresh troops allowed the Arabs to once again continue their momentum into the heart of NATO. The NATO pocket was suddenly struggling to contain this increase in numbers and the pressure first became apparent in the far north when the River Elbe was crossed on 28th July and with it, the fall of Hamburg. With pressure also being exerted on the southern aspect of the pocket, SACEUR ordered all bridges over the River Rhine to be destroyed in Cologne and as far south as possible. If the Arabs were contemplating a large left flanking operation at some stage SACEUR sought to delay or prevent any Arab advance via Belgium or Holland into the Rhur valley, which was the industrial heartland of Germany and NATOs final defensive position.

The route through Slovenia by Arab forces had not been anticipated and, apart from 20,000 Italian troops on Italy's eastern border, the majority of Italy's army was deployed over to the west near to the French border. A few remained in the north of the country, observing the Austrian/Italian Alps, but the open plains on the eastern border were relatively open to exploitation by a large mobile army. The Italians had a standing army of 80,000 regulars with 18,000 of these already committed to the ARRC in Germany but, they were now faced with an invasion from the opposite direction. The Iranians quickly pushed into Italian territory with Udinese being the first city to feel the wrath of the Iranian gunners. This Iranian Army Group had been specially chosen for its task, with its real aim kept from the other Arab states, the Chinese and the Russians. The majority of these invading soldiers were the most militant and religious in the Iranian army and committed in their ferocity, their indifference to civilian casualties and their almost obsessive desire to kill anything non-Muslim. The elite Qods (Jerusalem) force were an ideologically loyal military formation dedicated to their cause and the main reason why they were chosen for this mission.

With the 20,000 Italian troops under immense pressure their line buckled between the cities of Treviso and Venice about 115km inside Italy. They were left with no choice other than to fall back allowing the Iranian forces to break through. With breakthrough achieved, the majority of the Iranian army made a direct line for the Italian army over to the west. After receiving orders that the Iranians had entered Italy through Slovenia the Italian force on the French border had about turned and were now on a collision course with the Arabs. 190,000 Arab troops were closing in on 55,000 Italians and the first combat engagement would take place north of Parma. Under cover of darkness and unsighted to the Italians a secret force of 10,000 Iranian army personnel and 20,000 Mujihadeen, on a mission all of their own, broke away and started heading due south as fast as they could.

As the battle commenced near Parma the Italians were surprised at the poor tactics and almost suicidal attacks the Arabs employed against a less numerical but more sophisticated army with modern weaponry at its disposal. The number of Iranian casualties per hour in the first 4hrs of the battle near Parma was greater than any suffered since the war started, with the Italian Air Force destroying large numbers of heavy armour and mechanised vehicles with relative ease.

Not all was as it seemed, however, and it was almost 9hrs before the Italian government and its Military Command received reports that a large Iranian force had bypassed the city of Perugia and was seen heading south towards Rome. This news shocked the government and immediate orders were sent to 15,000 Italian troops to redeploy south to Florence in order to engage, delay and destroy this force. The Italian government, assuming it was a surprise attempt to capture them, could not have been more wrong. Italy had been fortunate in placing 14,500 reserve troops in Rome in case of civil unrest and it was these lightly-armed troops who were tasked with putting in a blocking force on the roads leading into the city. It was only 384km from Venice to Rome and Perugia was just over halfway. With the Italian Air Force given priority to attack these troops, it was hoped they would never get to the city. Italy still had a large number of aircraft available to its forces and they too had noticed the lack of Russian aircraft from their previously high numbers. It was these aircraft that could prove critical in ensuring the Italian ground forces got the better of the Iranian troops in their country.

By the time the Iranians reached the reserve Italian units on the outskirts of Rome they had been depleted by 18,000, with the remaining 12,000 now having to deal with the Italian units catching up with their rear elements. It had been the Italian air power that had delayed the move south and the local Iranian commanders were cursing the Russian's for not providing enough air power to combat them. However, with 12,000 Arab troops still available for combat it was hoped their mission could still be achieved. The Italian reserve did particularly well at delaying the Arabs with their well sited ambushes depleting the invading force every time they advanced. It had taken the Arabs 24hrs to cover the 384km from Venice to Rome; they had known they would be pursued once their intentions were signaled but they had not anticipated such a fierce reaction so quickly. As night fell and the confusion on the battlefield increased 1,000 Mujihadeen fighters found a way through the city's defences and entered its outskirts at 2300hrs. What followed was a bitter house-to-house battle in the narrow streets of Rome in the north western segment of the city against 480 Italian reserves and, from their direction of travel, it was apparent what their target was - St Peters Basilica, Vatican City.

The 11,000 Iranian troops were now caught between the force from the north and the reserve units in the south, with the Italian Air Force bombing them into submission in the middle. The destruction of the trapped Iranian troops and their Mujihadeen combatants was now a key priority but 1,800 Italian infantry from the chasing force of 15,000 were ordered to move beyond the holed-up Iranians and continue the hunt for the 1,000 Mujihadeen who had managed to get beyond the defences into the city.

After some bitter street fighting, 300 Mujihadeen fighters eventually reached their objective at 0100hrs and smashed their way into the Vatican. As soon as the military realised the objective, Italian officials had liaised with the Vatican and insisted on the Pope and his staff to leave the building. If their mission was to kill the Pope then it had failed and they had missed him by 1hr and 30-minutes. Once inside the Vatican, shots could be heard and some of the buildings were set ablaze with the most wanton acts of destructive vandalism taking place. The militant Mujihadeen had longed for this day for years and their hatred and the destruction of anything not aligned to Islamic teachings or beliefs was considered a target but tomorrow, the repercussions of their actions would reverberate across Europe and the world.

Throughout the night a fierce battle ensued in St Peters Basilica, with Italian troops finally storming the sacred rooms the next day to prevent any more damage to what was, for some Italians, more important than life itself. The Mujihadeen had, for reasons known only to them committed the ultimate desecration and as soon as the news filtered out on pirate radios throughout the hugely religious Catholic countries of Eastern Europe, massive disorder ensued and demonstrations occurred across the conquered continent. In Poland, Hungary, the Czech Republic and Slovakia the disorder quickly exploded into violence and resulted in the deaths of Arabs and demonstrators alike. Russia, seeing the unrest this unsanctioned action had caused, ordered the Ukrainian government to deploy troops into those countries affected and to restore order and, more importantly prevent the Arabs from slaughtering demonstrators. The Arab high command in Poland was livid and so were the Chinese and Russians. The reaction in Italy was unparalleled anywhere else in the world and it seemed to the Arabs that the whole population had risen up to destroy them. Just 2-weeks after 220,000 troops had entered Italy; the last effective combat unit was effectively defeated by an Italian military and a population hell bent on revenge. Their method of victory no longer followed the rules of war and an angry Italian army committed many atrocities. Only 3,700 Iranians were taken prisoner but these had to be transported to France, as their safety could not be guaranteed in Italy.

The Iranian defeat in just 14-days was a huge turning point, as this was the first time the Arab armies had suffered a defeat of this magnitude and the first step backwards since January. After mopping up the last Iranian troops, 48,000 angry Italians advanced into France and joined forces with the French, Spanish and Portuguese to aid in the defence of France and NATO. They were literally a force possessed and the French General had to curtail their enthusiasm in wanting to unilaterally attack the huge Iranian forces facing them. Joining the battle were another much needed 440 Italian aircraft and these would be put under command of the French Air Force and used as they saw fit.

In the north of Germany, the increase in Arab manpower for the Northern Army Group pushed NATO to the edge and forced them to withdrawal from the River Elbe defence lines. With the bridges about to be compromised, the defensive pocket would shrink yet again and NATO would be under massive threat of defeat. The first Arabic troops over the River Elbe were always a trigger to the Nordic Battle Group and as soon as word reached them of the incursion, the Swedish, Norwegian and Danish armies launched their Armoured and Mechanised Brigades down the east side of the River Elbe near Hamburg, slicing into the Arab assaulting units on a 33km frontage. Sweden was not a NATO country but its troops, along with the NATO contingent from Norway and Denmark, had infiltrated across the German border 7-days ago after satellite imagery confirmed no Arab forces were that far north. They had crossed the 130-metre wide river near the town of Rendsburg before regrouping into their assault formations near Neumunster and Bargteheide. The river obstacle effectively runs southwest to northeast and cuts across the whole thin strip of land where Denmark and Germany join. With this obstacle out of the way 262 Leopard A4 MBTs, supported by Swedish Grippen Fighter Aircraft, Norwegian European Typhoon and Danish F16-AM/BM Fighter Aircraft began their long-awaited counter attack and participation in this war. The Viking soldier's sole aim was to take their fight right into the northern flank of the Arabs' Northern Army Group with the intention of throwing their assault forces off-balance and, in conjunction with the actions of other NATO units, force on the Arabs a change of mindset within their ranks. With the Nordic Brigades catching the Arabs unaware, SACEUR now allowed what remained of his most powerful unit - the Allied Rapid Reaction Corps (ARRC) - to conduct the type of warfare that it was trained to do.

The ARRC was the land component of the ACE Rapid Reaction Forces and normally consisted of 10 Integrated Multinational Divisions (IMD) capable of a rapid response, with the Commander ARRC (COMARRC) being a British Three Star General. The formations attached to the ARRC in July 2012 came from only 4 countries, with other countries' contributions unable to take part. Those unable to join the ARRC's ranks were the Greek Division, the Spanish Rapid Reaction Division, the 2nd French Armoured Division and the already deployed UK 3rd Mechanised Division. A joint Polish/Romanian Division had replaced the Turkish Division in 2008 but these had been somewhat decimated in combat during their battle against the Arabs earlier in the war. What remained was still a remarkable and powerful fighting force equipped with the most modern weaponry known to man. Capable of taking on forces far in excess of its own number this force was given a mission with 2 main objectives - destroy what remained of 19 Corps as an operational unit and exploit any weaknesses in the Arabs' area of operations. If all 10 of the ARRC's Integrated Multinational Divisions had formed up in Germany, its number would have been well over 120,000-strong but, even depleted; this unit could still project an estimated 67,000 troops and almost 1,150 MBTs into combat. SACEURs intention was to shape the battlefield how he wanted it, with his main aim being to split the Northern Battle Group from the Central Battle Group, and destroy it as a fighting entity.

Those units within the ARRC that were about to conduct aggressive armoured operations came from Germany, the UK, the US and Italy. The German army contingent was provided by the 7th GE Pz (Panzer) Division, containing 2 Armoured Brigades. Each Brigade contained 2 Panzer Battalions with their Leopard 2-A6 MBTs, a Mechanized Infantry Battalion and 2 Armoured Artillery Battalions. Supporting arms came via their own integral, Signal, Logistic, Reconnaissance and Engineer Battalions.

1 UK Armoured Division was comprised of 3 Armoured Brigades –the 4th, 7th and 20th...with each Brigade consisting of 2 Armoured Regiments, equipped with Challenger Main Battle Tanks (MBT), Scimitar Reconnaissance Vehicles and 2 Armoured Infantry Battalions equipped with Warrior Armoured Infantry Fighting Vehicles and MILAN Anti-Tank Missiles. Additional combat support came by way

of an Armoured Reconnaissance Regiment, 3 Artillery Regiments, an Air Defence Regiment, 4 Engineer Regiments – including amphibious bridging equipment – an Aviation Regiment and a Signals Regiment for communications. These were supported by 2 Transport and Supply Regiments, 3 Medical Battalions, 3 Repair and Recovery Regiments and 1 Military Police Regiment.

The US contribution came courtesy of the 1st US Armoured Division or Old Ironsides as they were known, with its 13,500 soldiers and 6,600 vehicles, including 230 Abrams M-1 and M-2 MBTs, 60 integral aircraft, including Apaches and Cobras and close to 200 Bradley Fighting Vehicles. These were supported by 72 M109A6 Paladin 155mm Field Artillery pieces and 18 MLRS.

The Italian contingent was provided by the 3rd IT (Italian) Mechanised Division with 18,000 troops and its complement of Leopard MBTs, DARDO Armoured Fighting Vehicles and its integral artillery capability using the M-109L and MRLS, supported by Mangusta Ground Attack and Multi-Role Helicopters. The M-109L was the Italian 155mm Self Propelled Medium Howitzer capable of sending a 98lb shell out to 23,500-metres.

Committing the ARRC was SACEURs main counter move and it had to succeed for the sake of NATO and Europe, especially with only a few months of the current ammunition levels remaining. One plus side on ammunition was the amount of freefall bombs available to NATO aircraft, which numbered thousands. The ARRC's main thrust covered a 56km corridor and concentrated on the southern flank of the Northern Battle Group so that the Arab army was hit from 2 flanks simultaneously. The 2 coordinated attacks by the ARRC, and the Vikings, caught the Arabs completely by surprise, which resulted in consternation within their ranks at both the strategic and tactical level. That NATO still possessed the capability to conduct such an attack had not even been considered and this now caused an element of self doubt in the minds of the Arab commanders.

Just prior to the counter attack by NATO, Arabs troops had been conducting their own aggressive assaults over the River Elbe bridges and the shock attack by the Nordic Brigades had completely thrown their plans into chaos. Crisis management was now taking precedence in the Arab HQ with commanders angry that they had received no warning from Russian intelligence of a force build-up on their northern flank. Russia tried to play this down by explaining that there was only limited satellite coverage and that daily reconnaissance flights were only monitoring the main areas of operations. If the Arabs had known the real reason for Russia's apparent incompetence and lack of aircraft they would most likely, have struck a deal with NATO.

The 2-pronged assault in the north of the country was seen as a pivotal phase, with implications for both sides should either be defeated. The Arab Generals were relaying orders for their forces to hold their ground at all costs and to repel the counter attack but the situation in the far north was confusing for the Arab units on the ground and this confusion allowed the Nordic forces with their relatively unchallenged air-power, to cut a huge swathe into the Arab lines; so much so, in fact, that the Arabs believed the force to be larger than it really was. The ARRC, attacking all over their 56km frontage, had made good progress and forced the Arab units back by 20km on the first day. After day 2 of the offensive, this had increased to 48km before it eventually succeeded in cutting the North and Central Battle Groups in half. With this manoeuvre completed, the ARRC now swung its axis north and advanced towards the centre of the Northern Battle Group's lines. Their intention, along with the Nordic forces, was to squeeze the Arab units from 2 flanks using a pincer movement. With an attack from 2 sides, SACEUR hoped to destroy their most powerful units before they had time to react and extract. The Arab commanders, seeing what was occurring, gave the order for a tactical withdrawal away from the central area before their whole Northern Battle Group was cut off. By extracting east with their stunned forces the Arabs hoped to regroup and launch their own counter attack.

197,000 soldiers from the Northern Battle Group were now on the back foot for the first time in the conflict and many were unsure how to react. Command and Control was breaking down and what should have been a controlled withdrawal turned into chaos and from the chaos, panic set in. Arab units on the flanks were under extreme pressure from attacking NATO forces and their panic was filtering through to the remainder of the army. With panic and rumours now spreading throughout the Arabs frontline troops, the destructive seed of self-doubt was well and truly blossoming.

The Nordic Battle Group and ARRC formations were pushing hard, and the speed of the assault had resulted in vast numbers of Arabic armour, men and complete units being destroyed or captured. With NATO on the offensive, the pursuit of the Northern Battle Group was relentless and continued for 3-days. Instead of a tactical withdrawal the pull out by the Arabs was turning into a panic stricken retreat and in the maelstrom, 19 Corps was caught and savaged by the ARRC, meaning it could no longer be considered a viable fighting force. 19 Corps Challenger 2 MBTs littered the battlefield, its masses of Warrior Fighting Vehicles were destroyed and its artillery capability was all but wiped out. Arab commanders had suddenly lost control of their army and, more importantly for NATO, their area of responsibility, with their remaining forces now having to retreat east and then south in an attempt to join with the Central Battle Group to form a new defensive line.

Demand for ammunition was outstripping supply and it was this that brought an end to the drive by NATO. After the destruction of 19 Corps, the ARRC had joined with the Nordic Brigades and together they advanced south before setting up a new defensive line. NATO had succeeded in retaking the ground around Hamburg and as far northeast as Schwerin. They had recaptured the ground south to Magdeburg and Wolfsburg with the front line then continuing its route west from Magdeburg, to Hanover and Osnabruck, before ending at the Dutch town of Enschede on the River Rhine. The reclaimed ground now gave the defensive bubble around the Ruhr Valley a very distinctive bulge on its eastern side and, with the line settling down, the Belgium army deployed its remaining 15,000 troops along with another 3,500 Dutch troops into Germany. Deployed on the west side of the River Rhine, near the destroyed bridges south of Cologne, their mission was to prevent the Arabs from gaining a foothold in the areas where river crossing operations may take place.

Even though the NATO counter attack had petered out due to logistical issues, it had, in effect, removed the Arabs' Northern Battle Group from much of the land it had occupied and, forced them east to Berlin and south to link up with the Central Battle Group. If the Central Battle Group had not swung its most northern troops round to the southeast to face the NATO advance, the attack may well have rolled up the Arabs in Germany causing the war in Germany to be lost. The Arabs wrongly believed it was their forces that eventually stopped the counter attack along with Russian air-power, but the Russians had cleverly increased their deception to the Arabs by bombing only open ground, old positions and not the attacking NATO forces.

The ARRC attempted another counter attack against the Central Army Group in late July but this was halted after just 5km by a determined and powerful enemy defence. By early August the fronts in Germany and France had settled down somewhat and, although the Arabs continued with their massed mechanised attacks, none had succeeded in breaking NATOs lines. The Arabs clearly had the ascendancy in manpower, equipment and, most definitely, in ammunition and fuel stocks with more on the way. This worried COMARRC and SACEUR immensely and they knew they could not out last the Arabs in a war of attrition. Something had to be done to break the deadlock…but what?

PART 19

BETRAYAL AND RETRIBUTION

DTG: 9th August....2012.....

LOCATION: Moscow......President Sidorov's office.

SITUATION: In Northern Germany, the Arabs' Northern Battle Group had been forced to withdrawal with hundreds of kilometres recaptured by the attacking NATO troops, while on the central and southern aspect of the defensive pocket and, in France; NATO was continuing to hold the Arab forces at bay. However, NATO planners had informed SACEUR that the current ammunition levels will last for only 6 to 8 more weeks and then they can expect the Arabs to advance in force once they realise there is a serious decrease in NATOs capability.

President Vladislav Sidorov was holding court with his Deputy Nikolai Demidovsky, his Prime Minister Grigory Petrova and Marshall Ivanova on the progress of the Arab armies and in particular, their setback since the introduction of the Nordic countries.

'*It went better than we could have imagined, Mr President; by allowing the Scandinavians to attack the exposed flank of the Arabs we prevented the possible collapse of NATO in that part of Germany,*' said Vasilii Svialoslavich, **Marshal** of the Russian Federation of all Forces Ranks.

'*And the air force?*' inquired Sidorov turning to Marshal Iaroslav Ivanova, Chief Marshal of the Air Force of Russia.

'*Our pilots have been conducting their deception missions with great accuracy, Mr President, and continue to do so....the Arabs have noticed a drop in the numbers of aircraft over the battlefield but they suspect nothing about our targeting process...or lack of.*'

'*Are we now in a position to instigate phase 2 of Operation Eclipse?*' said Sidorov..

'*Mr President....*began the Prime Minister, Grigory Petrova, '*I think the time is perfect. If the Arab armies are not bombed into submission they* will return to the Middle East a powerful force and, empowered by their success, they may well prove difficult to work with. By pulling back now we can expect NATO aircraft to have even greater success and if they possess enough bombs, as we suspect they do, they should be able to decimate the remaining Arab armies?'

'Excellent,'....said Sidorov....'we begin phase 2 from tomorrow morning, by slowly pulling the vast majority of our remaining aircraft from frontline combat missions.....claiming lack of ammunition...maintenance issues...too many NATO aircraft,...anything as long as our Arab allies have no reason to suspect what we are up to. If it should become difficult then we will conduct a quick show of strength again, claiming we are committing aircraft that are not fit to fly for their cause to make the Arabs think we are still involved. Is that clear?'

They all nodded before Marshal Iaroslav Ivanova then left the room leaving Deputy President Nikolai Demidovsky and Prime Minister Grigory Petrova alone with President Sidorov. With Ivanova gone, the former KGB colleagues reverted to first name terms.

'Eclipse is risky my friends and if the Arabs ever find out about our betrayal they will surely claim that we are the next great Satan and we can then expect Russian involvement in the Middle East to cease'....said Sidorov...

'There is no way that they will ever know, Vladislav, unless we have a traitor in the air force. From the force of 1,200 that took part in the last campaign only 212 pilots were used on the deception missions with the others conducting normal interdiction missions against NATO aircraft' said Grigory Petrova

'You and Nikolai know as well as I'.... said Sidorov... 'from our days in the KGB together, we proved that we cannot rely on those who may not share the same vision as we do'...

'but Vladislav.... these men have all been vetted and hand picked by Marshal Ivanova and sworn to secrecy about their missions.....even the other pilots think they are carrying out bombing missions against NATO ground troops and know nothing of the plan to deceive'...... said Nikolai Demidovsky

'uurrrmmmmm' said Sidorov stroking his chin...'.nevertheless.... people talk and we can't take the chance. After eclipse is over we need to safeguard what we have done and ensure this can never get out. I am not concerned about the other pilots but I feel we have no choice other than to make sure the silence of those pilots on the deception bombing missions is guaranteed….do I make myself clear, Grigory? We cannot afford to have that amount of loose ends and as much as I hate this decision…we must ensure we and Russia have no comebacks. The future of Russia is more important than any of us and I need to know if you are with me on this?' Sidorov's friends both nodded in agreement…

'Very well then….Inform the security services that they are to use their ingenuity for this one and that they have the authority to conduct a removal operation for up to 12 months. They don't need to know why. They should be able to make it look like natural deaths due to the war in Europe and then there are accidents of course. The official line will be they were lost in combat or suffered an unfortunate accident and, of course, we will generously look after their families for their sacrifice to Mother Russia. There must be no word of this to anyone, so, nothing to the others….this is between the three of us and the security services'

The Prime Minister bowed in submission to Sidorov's cold blooded request…..'Will that be all, Vladislav?'

'No Grigory, what are the latest estimates from the air force on numbers of aircraft we will have ready after NATO and the Arabs destroy each other?'

'The latest from Marshal Ivanova was that we should have a minimum of 5,850 available for combat by mid November now that the Ukrainians have seen the benefits of being an ally with Russia once more '

They all laughed at the joke and then Sidorov nodded and dismissed his Prime Minister. Grigory Petrova left and made his way directly to the secret intelligence building to speak to the director of secret services, while Sidorov and his deputy spoke briefly about their plans for Africa and its key resources.

On the frontline between Hanover and Magdeburg, 16 Air Assault Brigade had been continuously patrolling the vast woods in the area attempting to conduct ambushes against Mujihadeen and Arab army patrols who were probing NATO lines every few days. The Arabs had achieved some success with their patrols, surprising a few observation patrols from 16 Air Assault Brigade and taking some soldiers prisoner. The Arabs had only taken one prisoner at a time but horribly mutilated the other three men in these positions. It was the way their fellow soldiers and friends had been killed that caused the greatest anger amongst this elite British unit.

The Brigade had been running patrols with mixed success for weeks now and for the last 4-days 3 UK Special Forces (SF) patrols and a company from the British Parachute Regiment had split up and were actively searching the heavily foliaged woods hoping to locate the route that one particular Arab group was using to infiltrate NATO lines. After 72hrs of searching the woods a well used track was located; it was clearly used by a large number of people and the sign left by those using the route was relatively fresh. The Arabs had been conducting regular patrol patterns and yesterday, one of these patrols had been contacted near an OP in an unsuccessful attempt to snatch a prisoner, so intelligence suggested that tomorrow or the next day would be the next incursion into 16 Air Assault Brigades' area of responsibility. With a potential infiltration route now identified, a reconnaissance of the area was carried out to locate the best place to position the 53 men of D Company from the 2nd Battalion, the Parachute Regiment. With communications established the paratroopers and the SF patrols met at a rendezvous point away from the ambush area where they then carried out administration, preparation of equipment and issued orders, before moving to the ambush site. One of the SF teams stayed close to the track maintaining over watch incase the enemy turned up and passed by.

The SF patrol and the paratroopers had been conducting anti-armour and anti-personnel ambushes on and off for months now and were quite rehearsed in the tactics and movement required for what can sometimes be a complex mission. The familiarity of these troops allowed for faster orders but it was still important to cover some of the key headings. The scaled down orders covered the ground, the routes to the site and the order of march, the ambush site area in detail, group and individual tasking, actions on various scenarios and, for this ambush in particular, a detailed initiation and actions by the teams on the ground once initiation was instigated.

The patrols had learnt from some of their earlier ambushes that the enemy can sometimes slip away after the initial opening shots and were planning on using a slightly different tactic to that taught in the field manual.

The SF patrol who conducted the reconnaissance of the site had specifically chosen a piece of ground where there was only recognised cover on one side for an enemy to hide in once he was fired at and, knowing what the reaction is of troops caught in an ambush, it was an obvious piece of ground for an enemy to use before they either returned fire or used the cover to extract from the ambush site.

Normally on a linear ambush there would be a cut-off left and right but these were replaced by small OPs whose task was solely to indicate the presence of an approaching enemy. This task would be carried out by 2 of the SF patrols with the only other depth provided by a small Platoon Sergeant's group to the rear of the ambush site. The remaining 48 paratroopers and SF soldiers from the third SF team were all located in the killing area.

One member of the SF patrol was then detached with 3 of the paratrooper's snipers and given the task of locating a position on a raised piece of ground that was situated on a prominent bend overlooking the whole length of the killing area. The team, equipped with 2 Accuracy International L96/8.59mm sniper rifles and 1 UK Accuracy International AW-50/12.7mm (·50) sniper rifle had a perfect snipe location and with a range of only 70-metres, the snipers could have made the hit with a normal rifle. With their camouflaged ghille suits made from fabric constructed over netting, enhanced with natural foliage and with their weapons and sights camouflaged, this team was completely invisible from the track.

The remaining paratroopers and SF personnel were laid out 4 to 5 paces apart just 38-metres from the path. With the heavy foliage they had excellent cover from view but no real hard protection if fired upon. The frontage covered by the 49 British soldiers was almost 300-metres in length and every 5th soldier carried a MINIMI 5.56mm belt fed Light Machine Gun. With all the teams in position and having received radio communications from the trigger OPs that the ground was clear, nominated small 2-man teams made their way to the ditch on the other side of the track and began to bury their explosive devices, before attaching their detonating cord tail to the long length of detonating cord that ran the entire length of the ditch. The SF personnel were showing where to site the devices and these ranged from anti-tank mines, which were buried low down, to improvised explosive devices and anti-personnel claymore mines that were buried high up on the ditch's side and aimed up and down the gully. All the devices were buried or camouflaged and joined to a single piece of detonating cord. The long length of detonating cord was then buried so that nothing was visible. Once this was complete a final check of the camouflage was carried out by the SF troops before all returned to the ambush site, less the demolitions expert from the SF patrol. The charges, when they exploded, would be very close to the paratroopers and SF soldiers but with the explosives buried in a ditch and below ground level the risk was deemed acceptable and the closeness of the troops was key to this ambush's success.

Once the 2-man teams returned, all the troops in the ambush area knew that 'ambush set' was in 15-minutes and this ensured there was no need for a verbal or radio confirmation. The SF demolitionist was the only man in the ambush killing area and he knew he now had 15-minutes to get back to the rest of the soldiers 38-metres away. He carried out the final attachment of the detonator to the detonating cord before attaching a length of wire to the electric detonator's protruding wires, unrolled the length of electrical wire from where the detonator was attached and ensured it was buried under the foliage before he extended the wire across the track. Taking special care to ensure the wire was buried under the track he then took the wire all the way back to the centre of the troop's camouflaged area. He then attached the 2 ends of the wire into the firing device ready to initiate the explosives. He was back in position with 4-minutes to spare and as soon as the 15-minutes were up, all the soldiers with a MINIMI flicked their safety catch off. The SF trigger OPs had located excellent vantage points onto the track and had enhanced their security by placing out claymore anti-personnel mines. All they could do now was lie and wait for enemy patrols to use the track through the woods.

At the NATO Joint Forces Command, Brunssum, SACEUR was waiting for a decision from the President of the United States in response to a request he had made 24hrs earlier. SACEUR had explained to the President and General Bracken that NATO was sure to collapse within 6-weeks if something was not done to level the playing field. SACEUR had already won one argument a few months ago when the President informed him that he was contemplating pulling out all US troops from Europe. SACEUR had argued that point strongly and stressed that any such move would have been political suicide and damaged the US military's morale and credibility considerably if that decision had stood. President Maxwell had listened to the impassioned plea from his top General in Europe, and, after deliberation, had agreed, that to cut and run was not an option. However, SACEUR had accepted the Presidents decision not to send any more troops.

SACEUR had reiterated to the President that with the Arabs close to achieving the unthinkable, he was prepared to fight alongside their European allies to the last, even though some of Europe's politicians had ridiculed the United States and its policies for years. Unity was more critical than ever, especially with Russia and China operating as potential allies and with the war now on a global scale…friends would be needed around the world, especially in Europe.

Strategic bombers had been turned down once before after a request by the UK's Chief of Defence Staff/acting Prime Minister and the request from SACEUR, to the President, via General Bracken, Chairman of the Joint Chiefs of Staff, was causing heated debate in the US Administrations Emergency HQ in Edwards Air Force Base, especially with Operation Recompense about to start in 5-days' time..

'*But Sir,*' replied Ross Cochrane, National Security Advisor (NSA)…. '*Most, if not all of our strategic bombers are preparing for Operation Recompense and the submarines will be in position within days*'

'*I know all that, Ross, but General Lynch has a valid point and in this war we will need all the friends we can get. I think all present would agree we have a long way to go - maybe years - to undo what has been done around the world but if we are to overturn the events of the last 8 months we will need those nations in Europe on our side. The world has changed forever and God only knows how it will all pan out, gentlemen.…but what I do know is that we have to show the people of Europe we are still looking to help them in their hour of need, even though, we are not sending ground troops in addition to what we already have there. It will also send a message to the Arabs, Chinese and Russians that we are still a force to be reckoned with and capable of projecting force anywhere we wish. Coupled with Operation Recompense, I'm sure the message will be well and truly rammed home*'

'*What are you proposing then, Mr President*'…said General Bracken.

'That we delay Recompense by 7-days and release a mix of 48 B-52 H Stratofortress and B-2 Spirit Stealth Bombers for 8-days of round the clock carpet bombing of the Arab ground troops starting in 48hrs time. General Lynch has suggested 4-groups of 12 bombers working 24/7 over this 8- day period....General Lynch has also indicated that there are vastly lower numbers of Russian fighters over Germany and France and for some reason their bombs have been missing their targets on a regular basis....possibly a GPS targeting problem....but whatever it is, it has allowed for the right circumstances for bombing to take place with less risk to our crews.'

'I agree the circumstances for bombing are much improved Mr President,' said General Beasley, Chief of Staff of the US Air Force. *'but if we agree to this request it means that the Eighth Air Force will only have 48hrs to turn around and instigate Recompense, Sir'.*

President Maxwell looked over the top of his glasses at the General and nodded....*'then you'd better inform USSTRATCOM* (US Strategic Command), *our pilots and maintenance crews to prepare for the toughest 12 days of their lives General...the bombing begins in 48hrs,....make it happen, gentlemen'*

'And what about the hundreds of thousands of Russians on the Polish border Mr President?' inquired General Beasley.

'Having spoken with General Bracken and the Vice President, General, we are of the opinion that we don't know for sure what their intentions are.....we know they have deployed small contingents of troops to Bulgaria, Hungary, Romania, the Czech Republic, Slovakia and Poland and we know they have the Ukrainians helping them but their air force appears to be pulling back or....another reason is they are as fatigued as we are...but I doubt it somehow. The fact is General, we just don't know what they are going to do and at the minute we are concentrating on the Arab armies only......as long as they remain on the border they are not an immediate threat' said President Maxwell

'And if they do cross the border in force....what then?' asked Ross Cochrane

'Then we're in the shit'...said the President as he looked over at General Bracken

48hrs later the first wave of American B-52 heavy bombers left from Barksdale AFB Louisiana and from Minot AFB in North Dakota. At the same time B-2 Sprit Stealth Bombers stationed at Whiteman AFB in Missouri also took to the air on their way to Europe.

In the heavily forested areas near Magdeburg, Germany, UK soldiers, having lain in wait for 14hrs, suddenly received a standby on their radios from one of the trigger OPs. The SF patrol had first noticed movement through the trees and 40-seconds later the first of what were eventually 36 Arab troops had come into view and passed their location on the track, heading directly for the ambush location. Walking slowly and 5-metres apart, these Arabs were distinctive by their long beards and mixed dress…a sure sign that these were Mujihadeen combatants and not regular Arab troops. They were spread out over a distance of 200-metres as they made their way to the ambush location some 400-metres away.

In the main ambush location those soldiers with the MINIMIs, slowly and carefully raised them up off the ground, with fingers poised alongside the trigger. Any undue noise now and the ambush could fail. The riflemen - weapons in hand - remained with their heads low waiting for the signal that would initiate their part in this ambush.

In the sniper location, safety catches were eased off with the snipers waiting for their targets to come into view. Using their telescopic sights to scan through the trees towards the track, the first Mujihadeen soldier was spotted almost 200-metres away but the snipers had specific orders not to fire until they were within 70. Controlled by the Special Forces soldier, the 2-snipers using the L96 - 8.59mm sniper rifles were focused on the first 2 Mujihadeen at the head of the column, waiting for the command to fire. These were clearly the lead scouts and would be taken out on the first volley. The sniper with the AW-50 12.7mm (·50) sniper rifle was focused on the third man in the column and, having observed him for 130-metres, the sniper assessed him as possibly the leader of the group, as he appeared to be controlling the 2 lead scouts.

As the first Mujihadeen soldier approached the 70-metre mark the SF soldier, controlling the group and, lying between the snipers, whispered…… *'standby….standby…..fire'*.

The sound of the 3 sniper rifles firing simultaneously echoed through the woods and the first 3-men in the column dropped like stones as the bullets tore through their bodies, the third man in the group being almost decapitated as the kinetic energy from a ·50 bullet entered just below his right eye.

Almost instantaneously the MINIMI gunners opened up into the Mujihadeen troops with their predetermined 15-seconds of suppressive automatic fire, spraying their belt fed weapons left and right across the ambush frontage. As predicted, the Mujihadeen reacted as soon as the ambush was initiated and those not hit in the initial fire immediately jumped into the ditch on the opposite side of the path to escape the murderous fire.

The SF demolitionist in the ambush position was observing his watch and counting down the 15-seconds. As soon as the time was up he initiated the third phase of the ambush and detonated the buried explosive charges and claymores in the ditch. The huge explosion along the 300-metre frontage sent clods of earth, dust and human body parts high into the air before gravity took over and brought them crashing back through the trees near to the ambush party. The ditch was a perfect enclosed killing ground and the explosives hidden in the bottom had caught the Mujihadeen totally unawares. The impact from the explosion had also shocked the British soldier's 38-metres away but knowing it was coming ensured they recovered quickly.

With the debris still falling to earth and the dust filling the air, the riflemen and MINIMI gunners, with their ears still ringing, were already on their knees when the command MOVE boomed out from the SF commander. This shout was repeated by soldiers all along the line and was the signal for alternative men to advance forward 10-metres covered by the other soldiers who were firing single shots into the ambush killing zone. After covering the 10-metres they knelt down and began firing into the ambush killing area. As soon as these were firing the other soldiers came alongside and advanced 5-metres beyond them before they knelt down and began firing as well. This caterpillar effect continued beyond the track and up to the ditch where any remaining Mujihadeen still alive were shot dead.

From the first sniper volley to the assault up to the ditch, the whole ambush had taken 53-seconds and had resulted in 36 dead enemies. It was their most successful ambush to date. Over the next 5-minutes the trigger OPs, happy there was no follow up force quickly collected in their claymore mines and began making their way back to the ambush area. In the ambush site the troops were already searching the bodies for any information that may be of use to the intelligence agencies. As the third man in the column appeared to be the leader, he was a priority search and, luckily for the British soldiers he had not had time to jump into the ditch, otherwise he may never have been found. His head was almost severed from his body by the force of the bullet that had hit him but disappointingly, the only thing found on him was a letter written in Arabic, which was found in his inside pocket inside a waterproof packet. This was added to the haul of maps, note books and small wallets found on the dead Mujihadeen soldiers, however, it would be almost 48hrs before these were all translated.

The paratroopers and SF patrols were due to be on the ground for a further 36hrs before making their way back to their own lines and were looking at conducting a similar ambush in another area 10km further east but as they were making their way to the new location they received orders to return to base immediately. None of the patrols were informed why they were being recalled other than it was imperative all were back no later than 0300hrs tomorrow morning. Only when the patrols reached base at 0130hrs were they informed of the massive bombing campaign that was to begin later today. The information the ambush teams had collated from the dead Mujihadeen was handed over to the Intelligence Officer and the next morning the commander of the SF troops inquired if there was anything useful in the haul.

'There's not that much here apart from this letter you recovered and a map showing what appears to be the routes through the woods in the area'... said the Intelligence Officer

*'Shame...at least we can check out the marked routes and exploit later....What's the letter about then?'...*inquired the SF commander

'You're not going to believe this....but it appears to be a personal and private correspondence from the President of Iran ....and in it he praises the recipient of the letter on his past Jihad campaigns, etc......but the interesting part is here in the second paragraph where he wishes him luck in the long awaited European campaign and states that he has his full personal support in conducting his method of Jihad against Western institutions, including those practicing the Christian faith. It goes on to say Allah is their God and only he can judge their actions...etc etc ....there's a little more after that reference the Iranian President asking for the letter to be destroyed after it's

been read etc …... .it's then signed off with Allah Ackbar and a signature of the Iranian President with his Presidential stamp.…..Obviously the recipient couldn't bring himself to destroy the letter for whatever reason '

The SF commander whistled at the enormity of what this letter meant knowing the governments throughout Europe and in the United States would clearly be interested in its contents.

'*Who was the recipient Mike*' asked the SF Commander

'*errrrrmm…it's a guy called Arash Muhammad Kermani*'…said the IO.

'*Never heard of him*' said the SF Commander as he turned away and walked out of the operations room.

On the morning of 11th August 2012 Major General Jibade Youssef…the Egyptian ground forces commander emerged from his fortified Operations Centre 15km from the frontline. His forces had been halted by NATO but he knew it was only a matter of time before the Arab armies' greater number and vast stocks of munitions, fuel and stores forced the collapse of NATOs defences.

It was a warm summer's day with the sky visible through the thin wisps of cloud at 6,000-feet. Over to the north the sounds of battle could be heard as artillery rumbled in the distance. Looking up at the sky General Youssef thought he saw something shining high up… but then it was gone…. …intrigued… General Youssef continued scanning…there it was again…a quick flash as the sun caught what must be a metallic object. He rushed inside his underground home and emerged with a pair of binoculars, brought them up to his eyes and focused the rings; there it was again and this time he could make out what the sun was reflecting off. He lowered the binoculars hoping his eyes had betrayed him, but no, what he had seen was all too real. The huge shape was very distinctive even from this distance and as he moved the binoculars around the sky, he could see another and then another. He counted 6 B-52s in total but now other flashes were drawing his attention and he could make out the mass of smaller fighter aircraft escorting these giant bombers. The formations had been flying in an easterly direction but had slowly turned northwards directly over where his frontline troops were. Before General Youssef could utter the words '*B-52s*' the sound of aircraft became faintly audible followed by what sounded like a low rumble of thunder emanating from the front line.

He knew immediately what this noise was and, for 3 long minutes, the thunderous sound grew in intensity and reverberated across the front line ……the carpet bombing of Arabic forces in Germany and France had begun.

For 8-days and nights the bombings continued relentlessly and the massively reduced Russian Combat Air Patrols found themselves unable to get close to the heavily defended bomber formations. The Arab commanders were distraught and furious with the carnage these bombers were causing and secretly acknowledged that they were being bombed into oblivion.

The collateral damage was immense but the decision to carpet bomb massive areas of land was the final throw of the dice in preventing Western Europe falling into Arab hands. The dilemma whether to bomb or not had weighed heavily on the US President and his military staff and he had spoken to the heads of governments in Europe to confirm their thoughts. It had been a joint decision in the end and one that was not reached easily, but what choice did they have left. Knowing that the bombing could result in the deaths of thousands of civilians was not a palatable thought, but it was a necessity after SACEURs assessment of impending defeat. With war approaching, many people had left their towns and cities but, with the frontline being so vast, it was inevitable people would remain, as they had nowhere else to go.

On the 9th day the bombers failed to show but the effects of the bombing had left a lasting impression on the Arab soldiers and those who had survived it in Germany and France with, a numbing sense of shock at what they had just gone through very evident. The whole front was a scene of the utmost carnage and devastation. Whole forestry blocks had been flattened or trees snapped like twigs and stripped of their entire foliage. Small hamlets and villages on the bombing line were completely obliterated with not a single building left standing. Deep craters and smashed vehicles littered the areas where the bombs had fallen and there was an eerie quietness to the whole area with no sounds other than the odd vehicle as it meandered its way between the shattered Arab defences. The death toll from the bombing would never be known but it was indeed massive and on a scale greater than anything that had gone before it. Whole Arab Divisions had ceased to exist and apart from a few shell-shocked survivors, the enormous loss of manpower was mirrored by the enormous loss of equipment. The Arab soldiers suddenly realised it was a war they could not win but their masters in Iran, Syria and Egypt ordered them to press on and avenge the loss of their brothers. Shaking their heads at the stupidity of their leader's directive, the Arab commanders in Germany and France knew they had little choice other than to obey. In a climate of bewilderment the Arab commanders began to rally their remaining forces as best they could to continue the battle against NATO.

2-days after the last bomb from the B-52s fell in Europe; those airfields in the United States, which housed these huge craft, were watching them take to the skies once more. From America, to Guam and Diego Garcia, 101 B-52s were staggering their take-off times, in order for them all, to be in position to fire their 20 cruise missiles at H-hour.

In Guam 12 B-2 Stealth Bombers having landed there 3-days earlier were preparing for take-off with their mix of ordnance on board. 8 of the B-2 Stealth Bombers carried 12- 1,000lb JDAMs each, another 2 carried 80 GBU-39/250lbs, Small Diameter Bombs (SDB) each, which are GPS-Guided Weapons with the same penetration capabilities as 2,000lb bombs. The final 2 aircraft were carrying just one 5,000lb BLU-122 bunker buster each, which were designed to defeat deeply-buried Command Centres/Targets.

Off the coast of China in the East China Sea 6 US SSGN Cruise Missile Submarines had been in position for days, waiting for their moment to strike back at enemies who had caught them all so unawares months before. There was no proof that China or Russia were behind the nuclear devices going off in the United States or Europe but many suspected one, or both, had knowledge or involvement of some form. Nuclear retaliation had been considered but sensibly rejected and, for the sailors on board the submarines, this was the next best thing. With their Vertical Launch Systems jam packed with 154 Tomahawk Land Attack Cruise Missiles (TLAMs), China and its allies were going to find out first hand that the United States still possessed the capability to reach out to its enemies wherever they were. Off the Russian coast in the Barents Sea near Finland 6 more SSGN Cruise Missile Submarines were lying in wait, they too were primed…waiting patiently for the moment to release their deadly cargo.

With a total of 113 massive bombers in the air and 12 submarines coming to launch depth, Operation Recompense was about to be unleashed on those who had conspired to destroy the United States and the democratic free world.

Flying across the Atlantic and down the Spanish southern coast the huge formations of B-52s entered the Mediterranean Sea and, at their predetermined launch points released their cargo containing hundreds of cruise missiles. Their targets were Syria's capital Damascus, Saudi Arabia's capital Riyadh, Iran's capital Tehran, Egypt's capital Cairo, the bridges over the Turkish Bosporus Strait and almost all the Middle East's oil producing facilities and refineries. 80 B-52 Stratofortress released 1,600 cruise missiles in total, with 88 of these allocated for the bridges linking Turkey and mainland Europe. It had been decided not to attack Istanbul direct, other than the bridges, as there was some sympathy in the US administration for Turkey's involvement in this war, especially after the bombing of its troops and subsequent humiliation they suffered before withdrawing from NATO. The feeling from some in NATO and the United States was that Turkey could be persuaded to come back to the fold later on.

180-nautical miles off the Finnish/Russian coastline in the Barents Sea, American submarines began launching their missiles, while somewhere over the Pacific Ocean 21 B-52 bombers flying from Guam and Diego Garcia initiated the launch of their combined quota of 420 cruise missiles.

It was 11pm in China when the first wave of cruise missiles from the submarines struck Beijing and other cities. They were the first of 924 to be fired from the 6 submarines in the East China Sea that were designed to devastate the country's military, government and communication facilities, with another 220 missiles racing in after being fired from 11 B-52s.

The North Korea capital was also facing a blitz by 200 cruise missiles fired from 10 B-52s - with their forces in South Korea also attracting the attention of 10 of the B-2 Stealth Bombers who were dropping 120 of their GPS-Guided 1,000lb JDAMs and 160 of the GBU-39/250lbs Small Diameter Bombs on known missile and rocket batteries on their east coast.

With waves upon waves of cruise missiles hitting Beijing, the final pair of Stealth aircraft had managed to slip into Chinese airspace unnoticed and, after identifying their target released their 5,000lb BLU-122 bunker busters. Their target was the Chinese Intelligence Building in Beijing and US intelligence had long known this building contained an underground facility and was thought to be the nerve centre during any war. The BLU-122 bunker buster is a modified 8-inch/200mm artillery barrel capable of penetrating 30-metres below the ground and, although specified at 5,000lbs All Up Weight, the High Explosive content was considerably less. The targeting had been perfect and the 2 bombs slammed into the street at the base of the Intelligence Building just 3-seconds apart, penetrating more than 28-metres into the ground before detonating. The effect that these 2 bombs had, as they exploded deep underground, could never have been imagined by US military planners. The lifting effect from what was, in effect, a tamped explosive resulted in the foundations being ripped from one side of the building. This weakened the tall structure's strength on one side considerably and with the stress from thousands of tons of concrete and steel, it collapsed like a felled tree into an office complex across the street. Fortunately, the building was closed for the night and the only death was the security guard who was standing in the foyer watching in awe as Beijing was rocked by explosions. The explosions underground, followed by the weight of the collapsing structure, caused the Intelligence Operations Centre under the building to be breached, resulting in 73 people being crushed to death. General Dèng Shangkun, the architect of Dragon's Claw, had left the building only 2hrs before and escaped with his life but Chairman Zhou, working late on the 4th floor was not so lucky, and he died as the building disintegrated.

Russia was also about to feel America's wrath too and at 6pm she was subjected to a massive bombardment with 924 missiles now hitting key military facilities and government buildings countrywide. However, the large Russian oil and gas fields in Eastern Siberia, Western Siberia and the Volga-Urals Oilfields, which supply 20 percent of China's oil and gas needs, was spared for the time being. America was taking a chance here but had the capability to destroy it as and when. The thinking behind this decision was based on America's need for oil from Nigeria and the assessment was, that by sparing the fields in Russia, it was hoped Russia would reciprocate by leaving the Nigerian fields alone.

Russia and China had long expected a response from America but not of this magnitude and the attacks on the Middle Eastern oilfields were totally unexpected, as was the size of Operation Recompense. The fallout from this huge attack by America had rocked China, Russia and their Arab and Korean allies to the core. This attack had followed on from the massive bombing campaign in France and Germany and China's assessment that America would retreat to fortress USA was, according to President Sidorov in Russia *'looking like the largest, most incompetent intelligence assessment of the century'*. However, Sidorov was unrepentant and still determined to take Europe and fulfil a life long ambition and quench a thirst for power that had been burning inside of him for 4-years.

Huge oil fields and refineries in the Middle East were either burning or had been completely destroyed and no matter how optimistic they appeared, this was a massive and unexpected body blow for China and Russia in their quest for world domination. The playing field had been well and truly leveled and soon, the sudden lack of oil from the Middle East would have massive repercussions on their operations worldwide.

Over the Bosporus Strait in Turkey, many of the cruise missiles had failed to hit their targets, having had to run the huge air defence gauntlet, but one bridge had been struck enough for a 60-metre span to collapse into the sea below while a second bridge was damaged sufficiently for it to be considered unsafe for heavy vehicle traffic.

In one massive night of bombing, America had shown to the world that its reach was unlimited but, more importantly had gained some recompense for the tragic events that occurred on 24th January in Washington DC. With a lack of fuel now an issue for all those at war, it would not be long before the transportation of supplies to the Arab armies in Europe dried up.

PART 20

ATTRITION AND THE RED SWARM
(D+11 MONTHS)

The events in August had prompted the Arabs to push on for all out victory. Knowing their supplies were now going to be squeezed and probably no longer replaced, the Arab armies were finding that NATO aircraft were suddenly proving the most difficult obstacle to overcome. Arguments were now common between Russian and Arab leaders over Russia's lack of air protection with Russia claiming maintenance issues and lack of serviceable aircraft for the shortage with promises to help as much as they could. NATO aircraft had also diminished from their previous numbers, suffering from fatigue and maintenance problems of their own, and they were still 6 months from having the brand new F-35 Joint Strike Fighter enter service, after falling behind its initial service date of 2011. The dwindling stocks of aviation fuel throughout Europe further compounded the problems and it was now beginning to bite. Those still flying were aided by the lack of Russian fighters and this allowed them to conduct day/night bombing missions against the Arab positions using their copious amounts of freefall ordnance, which was wearing the Arab forces down considerably. The last big ground offensive by the Arabs, occurred in September but it failed to make any significant progress against the NATO lines and only resulted in thousands of deaths on both sides.

A war of attrition had now set in and this continued into late October, with neither side gaining any ground from the other. The only real winners in Europe and on the other battlefields around the world were death and destruction, with the casualty figures now in their millions. Civilians were intertwined with the devastation as they always are in war and, disease was once again rearing its head in those parts of Europe that had suffered as a result of the destruction, with millions of people also displaced and with nowhere to go. In Moscow, President Sidorov was growing impatient and he knew that the bombing of the Middle Eastern oil fields was a serious blow to Russia's quest for

European dominance but he knew Russia still possessed the reserves needed to fight in Europe for 2 months if required. The key now was waiting for the Arabs to be decimated enough so that Russia could fill the void and do what they had failed to do…destroy NATO.

By 12th November and with winter looming the Arabs were a spent force. More than 3.5 million men had made the journey from the Middle East since January, not counting the thousands and thousands of militant Mujihadeen who had swarmed to the battleground like flies round a dead carcass. 11 months later, less than 350,000 would be going home. Estimates put the Arab combat troops remaining alive in Germany at 212,000 and a further 131,000 in France. NATO was left with 59,000 combat troops in France and 118,000 in Germany. It would take years to rebuild both their forces to pre-war levels at a cost of billions of dollars.

For the third time in just under a hundred years, a generation of young men from both sides, along with millions of civilians, had been lost, with large parts of rural Germany and France destroyed. Both countries were strewn with the remnants of war and now the winter rains were turning the battlefields into scenes last witnessed on the Somme during World War 1.

The call for the Arabs to withdrawal came from Beijing, with the Chinese convincing the Arabs that they had done all they could and that NATO was no longer a viable military force. It was time to come home and rebuild their countries, free from Western influence. On 18th November the first Arab units in Germany disengaged with NATO troops and began the long move back to the Middle East. By 24th November both fronts in Germany and France were quiet for the first time in months. It appeared over and as soon as it was confirmed by reconnaissance flights that the Arabs were moving east the whole of Europe rejoiced, with thousands coming onto the streets to celebrate in relief more than victory.

The Arabs were returning, believing it was they who were victorious, having achieved what they set out to do. Even with their last remaining reservoirs of fuel, many tanks and armoured vehicles failed to make it home, so the Arabs resorted to using military trucks to transport their remaining men. It was during this move back to the Middle East that Arab soldiers committed some of their worst atrocities on the civilian populations, particularly in Poland. The Polish people, having already risen in anger after the attack on the Vatican, did so again as they witnessed the Arab soldiers transiting through Poland. During the last insurrection, Arab troops in the country had been beaten and killed before tanks took to the streets to restore order.

Ukrainian troops were trying to contain the animosity but the Polish people were unable to resist another attack on the soldiers as they moved back, with some Arab soldiers shot as they passed through the small towns and villages. It was these attacks on the Arabs that resulted in large numbers of Polish civilians been massacred throughout Poland with no regard to guilt or innocence. It took 3 more weeks before the last Arab soldier departed Poland, with the majority now trailing home through the Czech Republic, Slovakia, Hungary and Bulgaria before they crossed the last remaining bridge over the Bosporus Strait.

On their return home the Arab troop's first images of their homeland were black clouds trailing across the skies from some of the still burning oilfields, with their countrymen fighting to prevent the black gold from going up in flames 4 months after been bombed. With the acrid stench of burning oil permeating everywhere, the euphoria of victory and thoughts of a glorious homecoming suddenly seemed a distant memory as they realised that war had also visited their lands as they fought in Europe. The sacrifice of so many and the price paid in blood could never be measured and in the days and months that followed, many an Islamic veteran from the war in Europe would question in private that price, which had been paid.

At NATO HQ, General Lynch and his staff had other pressing matters to concern themselves with and, after assessing the latest intelligence reports on the increased military activity on the Belarus/Polish border, they were convinced the Russians were about to invade and, SACEUR knew he could do nothing about it. Exhausted, militarily unviable and with questionable ammunition stocks, NATO was no longer in a position to stop the Red Army. Blowing all the bridges would only postpone the inevitable and cause greater misery for the populations of Europe than it would for the Russian military and, even if 200,000 American troops landed tomorrow it would still not be enough.

Skidel is a small town in Belarus. It is located just 41km from the Polish border and only 737km from Berlin. The town was currently home to the Headquarters of the Russian Federation army who were preparing for the invasion of Western Europe. During the night, the Russian Marshall of the Russian Federation of all Forces Ranks, Vasilii Svialoslavich had flown in from Moscow on a surprise visit to see how the preparation was going. His visit was a precursor to the invasion of Poland and the rest of Western Europe and a morale boosting call to the troops. During the day he had spoken informally and, at great length with many of his officers, explaining the vision portrayed by their President, of a Europe controlled by Russia.

Later that evening, Svialoslavich was sat in more formal surroundings addressing the most senior of his Generals in the HQ briefing room and explaining that they were about to achieve something their ancestors had been unable to and, that their moment in Russian history was beckoning.

After the address, an old friend and former colleague of Marshall Svialoslavich asked for a private moment together. General Anatoliy Gurov had served in Afghanistan as a green 20-year old lieutenant and again in the early days of Chechnya with Marshall Svialoslavich who was and, always has been, his superior officer. Their time spent together in combat had cemented their friendship for almost 30-years but on meeting Marshall Svialoslavich, General Anatoliy Gurov looked troubled and immediately asked if the meeting could be an off the record conversation between friends.

Marshall Svialoslavich looked at his old friend with a quizzical look knowing that this request was most unusual from him…..*'You have never requested such a thing of me before Tolya'*….(Tolya was the nickname given to him by Marshall Svialoslavich)……*'but for you old friend I will grant whatever you want'*…. said Svialoslavich…. *'what is it that troubles you?'*

'There is only one way to say this so I will get to the point…. There are concerns amongst the officers and men over our President's decision to invade Western Europe. Has history taught us nothing, Vasilii? It is littered with examples showing that trying to conquer nations and whole continents does not work. In the short term… yes of course…but in the long term it always ends in disaster. The Roman and British Empires are but two examples and in more modern times Germany and Japan with

their crazy quests for world domination…they all failed, Vasilii. Even the attempts to dominate smaller countries like Vietnam, Afghanistan, Iraq and dare I say Chechnya have all failed…..and we know why more than most'

'Tolya,… Tolya' …countered Svialoslavich…holding his hands up as if in surrender…'I hear your words, my friend, but this is dangerous talk that you speak and I will not jeopardize my life or that of my family by speaking ill of the President's decision to go to war and neither should you'

'Vasilii,'…said Gurov, 'you know as well as I that I will not utter these words outside of this room and it is because of our friendship that I bring this subject up…..the murmurings are rife amongst the men and there are those who have their doubts about what we are about to do…we got through the Cold War without destroying each other, Vasilii, but now we are looking to do what our ancestors could not…and for what?…What will Russia gain from this war apart from an increase in security on our immediate borders and the ego of a maniac soothed. The perception that NATO expansion into former East European countries is a threat to Russia is ludicrous and you know it. I fear the real reason is power…and we know from past history that too much power corrupts even the best'

'GENERAL,'…shouted Svialoslavich, 'you presume too much and have gone way too far, my friend…be careful with your tone from hereon in…I have known you for 28-years and never once have you defied me or questioned my orders'

'And I do not question them now' said Gurov, 'just the reasoning behind the invasion. You know I will carry out your orders, as I have done so many times in the past, but I need to know if you agree with our Presidents vision….that's all'

'Listen to me, my friend, and listen well,' said Svialoslavich, 'It's irrelevant whether I agree or disagree with the President…he gives the orders and we follow and, take my advice Tolya, if there are men under your command doubting the directive you would be wise in taking measures to quiet them before Sidorov's spies bring their dissent to his attention. If this should reach his desk he may well think it is you that is fostering this doubt in your ranks and, as the Senior Officer…. need I go on?……As for my thoughts….I prefer to keep them to myself as should you. After this meeting Anatoliy I never want to hear of this conversation again….do I make myself clear?'

'*Yes…perfectly clear,*' said Gurov, grasping the severity of Svialoslavich's last remark.

'*I am serious, Tolya….There are many spies at work in Russia at the minute, especially in the military, and to forget this could result in the death of you and your dear family. Promise me old friend that this will be the last conversation on this matter*'

'*I promise, Vasilii…but…*'

Marshall Svialoslavich held up his hand and cut short General Gurov before he could continue…'*The matter is now closed, Anatoliy… just do your duty and let it rest….now let us drink to old times and forget this nonsense*'

One hour later General Anatoliy Gurov left the room despondent but acutely aware of the dangers that Marshall Svialoslavich spoke off. He knew that he had to quell the dissent in his ranks as he had long suspected Sidorov's spies were extending their influence within the military. Although it was hypocritical, General Gurov knew he had to be seen to be acting in order to safeguard his family and make sure his troops were focused on the job at hand.

The next day Gurov had 2 officers and 2 other ranks arrested on suspicion of treason and by that afternoon they were sent to Moscow under security police escort. Gurov hated himself for what he had just done but he knew this was the only way to prevent the rest from speaking out and, in Gurov's eyes, sacrificing a few of his men had probably saved the lives of many others. Those harbouring the same thoughts would now suppress them and concentrate on fighting NATO. President Sidorov would have his war with his army and Generals following his instructions to the letter. To do anything else was too great a price to pay……..

Later that day, Marshall Svialoslavich was about to board his helicopter prior to his flight to the military airfield where he was to catch a plane to Moscow, when General Gurov approached him to see him off.

'*It was nice seeing you again Tolya,*' said Marshall Svialoslavich, as they shook hands '*and I know the decision you made this morning must have been a hard one for you but I am sure it will be well received in Moscow and it will undoubtedly convince Sidorov of your loyalty….I beg of you to keep it that way*'

'I will, Vasilii,....I will....Goodbye'

As Gurov watched the aircraft depart his mind returned to his mission. The Russian military had restructured and retrained for the last 7-years now and the drive for a professional army was about to pay off. In 36hrs time the full might of the modern Russian military with 800,000 troops and thousands of aircraft would be sent into battle for the first time against a depleted and severely weakened NATO army.

36hrs later the invasion began and as the tanks rolled into Poland and the rest of Europe, the only resistance encountered by the Russians came from Finland with its army determined to stubbornly fight over every piece of ground. Finland had been targeted because the Russians wanted control of their coastal regions and complete access and control of the northern sea approaches. The Austria military, embarrassed by its leaders reluctance to aid NATO did finally offer some resistance against the Russians but soon realised there was no way to prevent the inevitable without assistance, so, to spare its own population from all-out war, it surrendered after 14-days of fighting. The euphoria in Europe was replaced by complete and utter despair for millions of people as they now realised what was about to unfold.

SACEUR had already been resigned to Europe's fate but had requested a final act of defiance from the United States President before the inevitable happened. While Marshall Vasilii Svialoslavich was visiting his troops in Belarus, SACEUR instigated Operation Retrieval. All over Western Europe every available jet liner was crammed with combat veterans from the European campaign with America flying countless military heavy-lift sorties to Europe to collect thousands more. The air move was huge and on a scale reminiscent of the amphibious extraction of troops from the beaches at Dunkirk in the Second World War. Before the first Russian soldier crossed the border 178,000 troops from Britain, France, Germany, Poland, Spain, Italy, Norway, Sweden, Denmark, Belgium and Holland had been transported to America. It wasn't only the army moving west, as a vast armada of NATO naval vessels including Aircraft Carriers, Destroyers, Frigates and Submarines had secretly set sail at the same time and were now well across the Atlantic and, out of reach of Russian aircraft by the time the invasion began. In addition to the troop and ship exodus, 1,800 NATO aircraft including the first batches of uncompleted F-35s were heading in the same direction, flying first to Greenland then continuing on into Canada before reaching the United States.

SACEUR and the other NATO commanders had known they could not fight Russia in their current state so they had no choice other than to concede land. A few thousand soldiers in each country, unwilling to part from their families, had remained in most European countries and these would form the basis for resistance forces over the coming months. Hundreds of ammunition caches were set up with large quantities of small arms weaponry, small arms ammunition, plastic explosives with detonators and anti-tank mines along with other caches containing weapons of various sorts, night vision equipment and satellite and HF communications. These locations were remote, well prepared and known only to a few key individuals, and all electronic and paper records of those serving or having served in the military were now being shredded, burnt and completely erased throughout Europe.

It took the Russian army just 2-weeks to reach the coast of France with most countries surrendering without a shot fired in anger. The Russians had expected at least some resistance but to encounter nothing except in Austria and Finland was bewildering and surreal. The devastated terrain and shattered towns and cities in Germany and northern France in particular did, however, bring home to the Russian troops the reality of what had occurred on the continent of Europe only weeks before.

On January 07th 2013, 25,000 Russian troops in Zubr-class Landing Craft crossed the English Channel and landed unopposed on the Norfolk coast. A further 8,000 came ashore in Dover after 400 Russian Special Forces had taken the port during the night. With Russian troops establishing a beachhead in Norfolk, reconnaissance forces pushed out and took over the evacuated US Air Force Bases at Lakenheath and Mildenhall and, over the next week built up their numbers considerably. With 61,000 Russian troops split between Dover and Norfolk and their preparations almost complete, their advance to London was imminent. Before the Russian forces set off for the Capital, the Chief of the Defence Staff, who was acting as the UK government representative on a caretaker basis and who had decided to remain in the UK, surrendered to the Russian authorities promising no resistance. The 6,000 soldiers who had remained in the UK, which included a large contingent of Special Forces soldiers, would observe their occupiers' actions, their routine and gather intelligence on potential targets, train others willing to fight and only when instructed would they begin to fight back. Ireland was spared an invasion as long as it agreed not to allow American troops onto its land. It had no choice other than to obey the request.

Europe was now under Russian Federation rule and there followed a period of relative calm throughout the whole continent. Food quantity and distribution were still major issues throughout Europe and rebuilding would be slower than anticipated with the lack of oil from the Middle East hampering any chance that the Russians had of convincing the population that their occupation would eventually be good for the continent. The areas worst affected by the war, were predominantly in Germany and Northern France, with the devastation there causing thousands more to perish from the cold or lack of food over the winter months, however, Sidorov's vision of a Russian super-state had been realised and his Red Army had swarmed across the borders of Europe as he had ordered. In the months that followed, Russia deployed 1,000,059 troops from its professional army of 1.2 million with thousands eventually stationed throughout Europe. There were 88,000 troops in the UK, 260,000 split between France, Spain and Portugal, 112,000 stationed in Italy, 200,000 in Germany, 47,000 in Holland and Belgium, 66,000 in Austria, a further 73,000 throughout the Scandinavian countries, 33,000 in Switzerland and 180,000 spread over Poland, Slovakia and the Czech Republic. Ukraine, Russia's reluctant partner had troops in Hungary, Romania, Slovenia and Bulgaria and although Sidorov had stated that the troops were there to protect the population and to maintain law and order, the covert rounding up of possible dissenting voices had already begun in all the controlled states.

..........Conquering land was the easy part....
keeping it would prove more difficult.........

PART 21

NEW LINES DRAWN
(APRIL 2013-FIFTEEN MONTHS AFTER D-DAY)

The war across the globe had left 9.8 million people dead in just over a year, with a further 11 million classified as displaced persons or refugees. 1.7 million people were believed to have perished when the five nuclear devices exploded in January 2012, with thousands more grotesquely disfigured.

On Diego Garcia all remnants of the assault by North Korean commandos was eradicated apart from a memorial statue in memory of those who had died during and after the invasion. It was now home to 11,000 US Marines and a large contingent of B-52 bombers but the war stock that had been sunk had not been replaced.

The amount of aircraft based on Guam had risen above pre-war numbers with B-52s and B-2 Stealth Bombers taking pride of place. The military force levels on Guam had also been raised with 29,000 troops now stationed there.

Off the coast of China, Taiwan had been subjected to Land Attack Cruise Missiles (LACM) attacks fired from Mainland China on at least seven occasions and Chinese air activity had increased significantly. During this spike in activity, a single Chinese Kilo-class Submarine had been detected in Taiwanese waters 12-miles off the coast where it was subsequently attacked and sunk with all hands lost. China had ludicrously called this an unprovoked attack, claiming the vessel was in international waters. Satellite imagery also showed large amounts of Chinese troop activity on the mainland, directly across from Taiwan, but so far there had been no sign of an amphibious force forming. As part of the US realignment policy there were now 32,000 troops on Taiwan, primarily there to counter any Chinese amphibious assault.

Japan had also been subjected to LACM attacks with these being fired from South Korea. This resulted in Japan declaring war on North Korea, however, these attacks halted after Operation Recompense. The US had steadily increased its manpower in Japan and now had 64,000 troops stationed there with 41,000 of these on the strategic Island of Okinawa where large US bases are situated.

North Korea had completely annexed the South and continued to receive direct military support from China but its amphibious invasion capability was deemed non-viable and any invasion of Japan would have to be achieved with Chinese help.

Pakistan was considered militarily impotent after losing most of its armed forces to India and no longer considered a destabilizing Islamic influence in the region. Pakistan needed to rebuild after the war with India so its reliance on China and Russia was now guaranteed. They would provide aid to Pakistan in its comprehensive rebuilding programme but only drip feed them with military hardware. This way it would allow them an element of control over the Muslim state and ensure they shaped the country to suit their needs.

Chinese participation in the war against India had started in April 2012 and after 11 hard months it eventually came to an end in March 2013. China's philosophy of war was based solely on a massive ground and air offensive with an end state resulting in the complete destruction of India's military and economic capability. With victory assured and all its objectives complete, Chinese forces throughout the country began to depart for home to begin preparations for future attacks on Japan, Taiwan and Africa. During the exodus, China removed dozens of amphibious vessels from what remained of the Indian navy along with hundreds of combat aircraft from the air force. India had been slowly drained of trained fighting men, equipment and modern weaponry with an estimated 3.5million soldiers and civilians killed as a direct result of the conflicts with Pakistan and then China. Some 2 months after the war ended, famine and death caused by disease and lack of food would strike some of India's larger populated areas, dwarfing anything seen in Europe during the previous World Wars. India was suddenly destitute, defenceless and struggling to feed its people effectively but this was of no concern to China. They had the satisfaction knowing they had pushed India back economically by 20 to 40 years.

The Middle East was attempting to rebuild after its oil infrastructure suffered catastrophic damage during Operation Recompense. Kuwait, who had not supplied troops to the invasion had been spared from the destruction for political and humanitarian reasons and was now having to supply its surrounding Arabic neighbours with petrol just to keep their economies working in some sort of capacity. Militarily, the Middle Eastern countries were extremely weak after their campaign in Europe and in no position to defend their homeland from outside attack. Israel was the most dominant force in the region now but they had received warning from China and Russia that to consider military action against its neighbours would be an attack against them also. Israel was, therefore, isolated and over the following months would grow weaker and weaker as a result of no fuel from its Arab neighbours or direct aid from America. Syria still had close to 100,000 plus troops in the region and Egypt a similar amount but these were only considered a light deterrent against any Israeli aggression and were no match for the well equipped Israeli Defence Force if it attacked.

Within the Middle East there was an undercurrent of civilian unrest surfacing with the Muslim populations openly criticising the decisions of their militant governments in going to war with the West…and for what? Oil output in the region had almost halted since the attack on its oil infrastructure, inflation was rocketing and thousands of jobs were being lost every week with the quality of life for its people rapidly deteriorating.

Turkey had no real allegiance anymore to anyone and, with its desire for revenge quenched, it now found its economy stagnating and suffering from a lack of market opportunities. It was strong militarily but the next few months, and maybe even years, would prove to be very difficult for its huge population as it attempted to establish some sort of trade with the newly-expanded Russian Federation, the Middle-East and China.

Indonesia was riding a wave of popular nationalism and looked to be in complete control of the region and its newly acquired state – East Timor. It had eventually leveled out its troop numbers to 168,000 in Australia and consolidated in the Northern Territories. 11,000 Chinese troops still remained in Australia but these were mainly air force technicians and a contingent of 2,800 Chinese Marines. Their were a further 24,000 Indonesian troops in East Timor and the invasion of Brunei in December 2012, had been a complete success giving Indonesia access to the Sultan of Brunei's oilfields.

Australia was still a country in shock and mourning the invasion of its homeland but had vowed to reclaim every last yard of territory, no matter how long it took. There was now a massive recruitment drive going on in Australia and large numbers of New Zealand regulars had arrived to bolster the Australian force numbers while Fijian recruits were also arriving in their thousands ready to undergo a rigorous training regime in the hope of forming a Fijian Light Infantry Division in the future.

Australian regular forces had attempted 3 large probes into the Northern Territories since the invasion and each time they had ran into well prepared defensive positions. With the Indonesians too great in number and firepower the Australian army units had been beaten back by overwhelming numbers of Chinese aircraft in support. It was during one of these attacks that the occupying force fired what appeared to be the first known launch of a Chinese WS-2 long range rocket weapon. Used in a defensive or offensive role the WS-2 has the capability to fire out to 350km. Faced with an ever expanding Indonesian army and new weaponry, the Australian Government soon realised that its forces were just too small to be effective in the short to medium term.

In May 2013, Russia and China finally decided to launch a Joint Expeditionary Force into North Africa. They mounted the operation from Italy using Russian amphibious ships complemented by the first ever Russian/Sino airborne drops into Tunisia. This was followed by a rapid airlift using giant Russian transport aircraft to build the force up quickly in order for it to break out and secure its objectives. The Russian and Chinese had made a big show of the assault on a country barely able to defend itself and it was thought the message was to highlight to the world the capabilities of the Russian and Chinese war machine. In total, Russia had earmarked 77,000 troops to the campaign with China supplying 55,000. The objective was to advance west into Algeria and east into Libya, secure their oil reserves then move south to Chad and the Central Africa Republic. Morocco, Mali, Niger and Mauritania all capitulated to Russian/Chinese rule soon after, giving the alliance control over a third of the huge continent. Once these countries were subdued, the heart of Africa beckoned. The Democratic Republic of Congo was the jewel in the crown as far as China and Russia were concerned as it contained vast reservoirs of untapped natural resources and mineral wealth such as copper, cobalt, diamonds, gold, petroleum and wood.

Nigeria, over on the west coast, for now, remained under US protection and, so far had received no direct or indirect threat from the Russian or Chinese expeditionary forces. By July, Chinese troop levels in Africa had risen even further when another 67,000 arrived to reinforce those already swallowed up in the vast expanses of the African continent.

To counter Russian/Sino aggression in Africa, a defence pact was agreed between Nigeria, Cameroon, Gabon, Angola, Zambia, Botswana, Namibia, Mozambique, South Africa and the United States with America increasing its military force in Nigeria to 29,000 initially, before another 22,000 deployed after the latest Chinese reinforcements arrived with follow on forces on standby in America incase the Nigerian oil reserve or any member of the defence pact was threatened

The worldwide shortage of oil was an issue for both sides now and the search for alternative resources of energy could be critical in determining the outcome of this war. The economic downturn across the globe was enormous, with many countries economies collapsing altogether. The war had shown that the world was indeed a world built on oil and, like any addict this period of cold turkey was going to prove extremely difficult until alternatives were found.

How long this war was to go on for, no one really knew, but as many had found out, a year is a long time in war and, in such a short space of time nations had already seen the world's boundaries altered dramatically. In some countries the lines on the map had been redrawn completely, with many others out there wondering who was next.

PART 22

THE NEW WORLD AND A STRUGGLE FOR FREEDOM

The autumn of 2013 saw the end of the honeymoon period for occupying troops across Europe with the first Russian soldiers killed as a result of resistance activity. It occurred in England, on the outskirts of a town called Brize Norton near Oxford, when a 3 vehicle convoy of BRDM-2s was ambushed resulting in one vehicle blown up and, completely destroyed by a French made anti-tank mine specifically designed for vehicle ambush. The 12kg mine with a thin electric breakwire placed across the road, ensured the mine was initiated as the first vehicle passed, with a shaped charge firing an explosive formed projectile into the side of the vehicle from 3-metres away. 4 soldiers died in the blast and, a further 3 were killed by snipers in London on the same day. In total, there were 14 incidents in the UK that day and many more across the continent of Europe in what appeared to be a coordinated attack. The message to resume hostilities against the Russian occupiers had been passed from America and, over the coming months, most of the occupied countries resistance elements were targeting the Russian invaders wherever they were with deadly effect.

Russia predictably responded by sending more troops to the countries involved in an attempt to quell what it considered to be, terrorist actions, but the attacks increased as the weeks and months passed. A violent and bloody crackdown on some communities ensued but this just alienated the population further and failed to stop the attacks increasing in intensity.

In America, President Maxwell and his Chiefs of Staff had met to discuss their options with other high ranking military Generals and their international force counterparts at a secret meeting. It was here that Maxwell and General Bracken, his Chairman of the Joint Chiefs of Staff, presented a 5-year plan designed to curtail Chinese and Russian expansion, restrict their ability to project force and eventually isolate and destroy them militarily, especially in the lands they had taken by force.

The President and General Bracken had explained the plan in full and informed the audience that America was already 18 months into a 36 month recruitment drive to produce a regular army of 3.5million men by the spring of 2015. Recruitment had begun in March 2012 and, the US army had already increased its combat manpower to 1.8 million men. There had been no shortage of manpower after the events in Washington in 2012 and with massive job losses in the United States after the Middle Eastern oil embargo, many were seeking employment too. The army had instigated a rigorous selection process and training regime for troops in this new army with particular emphasis on physical fitness, tactics training coupled with tactical awareness and expert weapon handling on numerous systems. This was an army designed for one thing, and one thing only – total war. It would not be supplemented by reservists or National Guard as those units were to be solely tasked with the defense of the US Mainland. The training regime had been more than realistic and was not without its casualties but in the circumstances this was an accepted part of life in today's new world. After basic training and unit integration, operational build-up training took precedence and by the time their extended training regime was over, the newly formed army would be a force ready for combat anywhere in the world. The American troops were to be joined by the combat experienced veterans of the international force made up of those NATO European forces that were airlifted out of Europe. These troops had fought for months on the European continent and were already used to the traumas that newly trained soldiers had yet to face. They would be further enhanced by Canadian soldiers, which would eventually push the international force number to 290,000 men. The second part of this international army would include the Australian, New Zealand and Fijian troops, meaning that the number would rise to half a million men.

With the recruiting and training ongoing, General Bracken had explained how the massive NATO ship armada and the US Navy would combine and look to dominate the North Sea, the Mediterranean Sea and the Barents Sea plus the Atlantic, Pacific and Indian Oceans. The aim would be to exert influence in those areas, thus restricting Russian and Chinese vessels to their coastal zones only, which would then allow the US and her allies' freedom of movement across the Seas and Oceans. Degrading and destroying Russia's naval influence in the Atlantic, Mediterranean, Barents and North Seas was crucial in containing Russian and Chinese expansion in Africa and had to be achieved before the Russian and Chinese military were destroyed as a viable fighting force in that part of the world. Another crucial objective of the plan was to deter or prevent China from invading Taiwan and Japan. In the short term, troop reinforcements were considered the best deterrent with the long term deterrence reliant on the navy taking control of the Pacific Ocean and Sea of Japan.

Some of the other issues outlined were - maintaining the pressure on the Middle Eastern oil infrastructure so that the Russians and Chinese continued to suffer similar problems as the US and its allies. The targeting of Russian and Chinese satellites and their ground stations to limit their Command, Control, Communications, and Computers, Intelligence, Surveillance and Reconnaissance (C4ISR) capabilities was now a priority and once complete would limit their satellite guided munitions.

A presentation was given explaining how the resistance across Europe had taken shape and the success it was having against the Russians everywhere. It was reiterated that the clandestine support to the resistance would continue especially as its activities were locking up thousands of Russia regular troops on the continent as they tried to counter the insurgent activities.

General Bracken stated that it was imperative the alliance reclaimed Australia, East Timor and Brunei from Indonesian occupation in order to isolate China to its own borders and, once the Oceans and shipping routes were considered safe, they would resurrect relations with India and look to rebuild its military in some capacity.

Liberating Korea had not been mentioned in the plan at all because invading Korea would allow the Chinese to maintain a war on the peninsula indefinitely. As unpalatable as it was, South Korea would be left in the hands of the North in the hope that the South's way of life may eventually spread northwards and influence that troubled part of the world for the better.

In the coming months, the US and international force navies started to implement the plan as specified by the US President and his Chief of Staff. It began when the enormous naval armada available to the US and international forces started squeezing Russian and Chinese naval vessels around the world. The hardest thing for the Americans and the international force navies was projecting enough airpower without having land based airfields from which to operate especially in the Atlantic and Barents Sea areas of operations. China and Russia had the luxury of pulling their ships back close to shore where they then came under the protection of their large air forces. This was acceptable to the US and its allies as it meant their surface vessels were being confined to their coastal areas, leaving the Oceans relatively free for transit, however, the Russian, Chinese and North Korean submarines would pose another problem and it was one that had to be addressed if the Oceans were to be completely free.

In private, China and Russia had secretly argued over the Dragon's Claw planner's assessment that the United States would react to the events of 2012 by retreating into a fortress America. Their assessment that the Americans siege mentality would result in unilateral isolation from the rest of the world, thus ensuring America's superpower status was shattered, was suddenly looking like a massive error of judgment. Although slow in coming forward, the stance taken by the United States and its allies was, in fact, the exact opposite, of that predicted by China. The determination of the Americans had been demonstrated by the carpet bombing of Arab troops in Germany and France and, Operation Recompense. The effects of which were still being felt in the Middle East, Russia, China and Korea.

2-years after the attack on Washington DC and Europe, and only 3 months after President Maxwell had briefed his Generals on the 5-year plan, 190,000 troops from the international army, 650 combat aircraft, including F-35 Joint Strike Aircraft and F-22 Raptors, along with 108,000 American troops, started a 4 month build-up of forces by landing on Australia's east coast by ship and military airlift.

Once established in Australia these forces were to join with the ever growing and newly-formed 160,000-strong Australian and New Zealand Army Corps (ANZAC) including the Fijian Division in what was to be the start of an 8 month campaign to reclaim Australia, East

Timor and Brunei from Indonesian and Chinese control. What some had started, others were now determined to finish and Australian's boast that every piece of land taken would be reclaimed back was soon to be put to the test.

............The Struggle for Freedom had Begun............

.......End......

We have to face the fact that either all of us are going to die together or we are going to learn to live together and if we are to live together we have to talk.

Eleanor Roosevelt

A big thank-you goes to John Pike of Globalsecurity.org
and the
Australian Ministry of Defence

THE AUTHOR,

Michael Jaden is 44 years old. He spent 22 years in the British Army before leaving in June 2004. In 1983 he joined the 2nd Battalion the Parachute Regiment before joining the British Army's Special Forces unit- 22 Special Air Service, where he served for 17 years.

He currently lives in England with his wife and children and is in his third and final year of studying for an MSc in Security Management.

Printed in the United Kingdom
by Lightning Source UK Ltd.
113272UKS00001B/247-255